The
BLANK WALL

The
BLANK WALL

A NOVEL OF SUSPENSE

by
Elisabeth Sanxay Holding
INTRODUCTION BY PETER SCHWED

Academy Chicago Publishers

To L. W.

Published in 1991 by
Academy Chicago Publishers
213 West Institute Place
Chicago, Illinois 60610

Printed and bound in the USA

Library of Congress Cataloging-in-Publication Data

Holding, Elisabeth Sanxay, 1889-1955
   The blank wall : a novel of suspense ; The innocent Mrs. Duff : a
novel of suspense / by Elisabeth Sanxay Holding ; introduction by
Peter Schwed.
      p.   cm.
   ISBN 0-89733-366-7
      1. Detective and mystery stories, American.   I. Holding
Elisabeth Sanxay, 1889-1955.   Innocent Mrs. Duff.   1991.
   II. Title. III. Title: Innocent Mrs. Duff.
   PS3515.03418A6   1991
   813′ .52--dc20
                                                    91-31464
                                                    CIP

Cover art by James "Ozzie" McMahon
Cover design by Julia Anderson Miller

Introduction

The financial crash of 1929 changed the lives of a great many people. In the case of Elisabeth Sanxay Holding, it stopped her from writing long, serious, critically acclaimed novels, and forced her into a new career, penning shorter, suspenseful mysteries. The reason was simple. An author back in those grim days had great difficulty in selling the sort of book that Mrs. Holding had written so brilliantly through the 1920's, either to a magazine for serialization or to a book publisher, but a regular market continued to exist in both areas for mysteries. And Mrs. Holding had two small daughters to support.

The half dozen books that she had written previously, starting in 1920 with *Invincible Minnie,* displayed a style that stood her in good stead the rest of her writing life. That went on for another 25 years, in the course of which she wrote just about a book a year. *The New York Times'* review of one of her early novels (*The Silk Purse*) said:

> She has managed to make every one of her characters, however unimportant, important. They are as real a collection of people as ever said yes when they wished to heaven they could say no. Like real people, they talk when they should be silent, are silent when they should say something, and, with the best intentions in the world, quietly wreck each other's lives.

This same unusual talent for depicting believable characters informed all of Mrs. Holding's subsequent work, and she was a forerunner — very possibly the forerunner — in the creation of the story of suspense, as opposed to the conventional mystery.

All of Elisabeth Sanxay Holding's suspense novels were first published in hardback form, and then reissued a year or so later in paperback. Most of them were chosen by mystery and detective book clubs, had foreign editions, and a few also were serialized in national magazines. But the fate that befalls practically every novel eventually befell Mrs. Holding's prodigious output. The books were allowed to go out of print, and stayed that way for some years.

They achieved a renaissance early in the 1960's when a collection of Raymond Chandler's letters (*Raymond Chandler Speaking*) was published both in the United States and in England; included in it was a letter that Chandler wrote to his British publisher, Hamish Hamilton:

> Does anybody in England publish Elisabeth Sanxay Holding? For my money she's the top suspense writer of them all. She doesn't pour it on and make you feel irritated. Her characters are wonderful; and she has a sort of inner calm which I find very attractive. I recommend for your attention, if you have not read them, *Net of Cobwebs, The Innocent Mrs. Duff, The Blank Wall.*

By this time, Mrs. Holding had died and I, then a book publisher myself and Mrs. Holding's literary executor, saw a chance to revive her books for the benefit of her two heirs, my sister-in-law and my wife. Accordingly, armed with the Chandler letter and a number of excellent reviews of all her books that I had collected, I interested a reprint house, Ace Books, in re-issuing more than a dozen of Mrs. Holding's novels, two in a volume, much like the present book you hold in your hand.

That was very satisfying, but after a while time once again took its toll, the books were allowed to go out of print, and Mrs. Holding's work has not been available in the bookstores for the past quarter of a century. So it is with real gratification that my sister-in-law, Skeffington Ardron, my wife, Antonia, and I see two of her best suspense novels being put out again now by Academy Chicago. You will note that both *The Blank Wall* and *The Innocent Mrs. Duff* were cited by Raymond Chandler as being among the author's best, and *The Blank Wall* was the prime selection chosen by Alfred Hitchcock for his classic anthology, *My Favorites in Suspense* in 1959, which included twenty short stories by other masters of the genre; but *The Blank Wall* was the only full-length novel. That fact elicited from James Sandoe, in his lead review in the *Herald-Tribune Book Review*, the statement that *The Blank Wall* was "by that astonishing artist, the late Elisabeth Sanxay Holding, whose evocation of nightmare was and still is unique, as reprint publishers might recall to their benefit."

Well, Academy Chicago has recalled it, and a major beneficiary will be you, the reader.

PETER SCHWED
NEW YORK CITY
1991

Chapter One

Lucia Holley wrote every night to her husband, who was somewhere in the Pacific. They were very dull letters, as she knew; they gave Commander Holley a picture of a life placid and sunny as a little mountain lake.

"Dear Tom," she wrote. "It is pouring rain tonight."

She crossed it out, and sat for a moment looking at the window where the rain slid down the glass in a silvery torrent. There's no use telling him that, she thought. It might sound rather dreary. "The crocuses are just up," she wrote, and stopped again. The crocuses are up again for the third spring without you to see them. And your daughter, your idolized little Bee, has grown up without you. Tom, I need you. Tom, I'm frightened.

It was one of her small deceptions to pretend that she had lost her taste for smoking. Cigarettes were very hard to get. It was difficult to keep her father supplied. She would sit by while he smoked, and refuse to join him. No, thanks, Father, I really don't seem to care for them any more.

Yet, hidden in her own room, she always kept a few cigarettes, for special moments. She got one out now and lit it, leaning back in her chair, a tall woman, slight, almost thin, very young looking for her thirty-eight years, with a

3

dark, serious face, and beautiful dark eyes. A pretty woman, if you thought about it, but she herself had almost forgotten that, had lost any coquetry she had ever had.

The house was very quiet this rainy night. Her son David had gone to bed early; old Mr. Harper, her father, was reading in the sitting room. Sibyl, the maid, had stopped creaking about in the room overhead.

Bee was shut in her own room, rebellious, furious; perhaps she was crying. I'm not handling this properly, Lucia Holley thought. If only I were one of those wise, humorous, tolerant mothers in plays and books. But I haven't been wise about this and I'm not tolerant about the man. I hate him.

If Tom were here, she thought, he'd get rid of that beast. If David were older . . . Or if Father were younger . . . But there's nobody. I've got to handle it alone. And I'm doing it badly.

She remembered, with a heart like lead, the visit to New York, to the dingy little midtown hotel where Ted Darby lived. She remembered how she had felt, and how she had looked standing at the desk, asking the pale and supercilious clerk to tell Mr. Darby there was a lady here to see him. Countrified, in her old tweed coat, gray cotton gloves, and round felt hat, she was already at a disadvantage. She did not even look like the wise, humorous, woman-of-the-world mother she so wished to be.

"Mr. Darby'll be right down," said the clerk.

She had sat down on a bench covered with green plush, and waited and waited, in the gloomy little lobby. Presently, as the doorman in uniform sat down beside her, she realized that the bench was for him and his colleagues. He was quite an elderly man, and she thought it might hurt his

4

feelings if she got up and went away too quickly, so that she was still sitting there beside him when Ted Darby came out of the other elevator.

He had come straight toward her, holding out his hand.

"You must be Bee's mother," he had said.

She had taken his hand and that was a mistake. Only, she had never yet refused an outstretched hand; she had acted before thinking.

"Suppose we go into the cocktail lounge?" he had suggested. "It's quiet in there, this time of day."

It was a very small room, dimly lit, smelling of beer and varnish. They had sat at a table in a corner, and after one quick and apprehensive look at him, she had been silent. He was so much worse than she had expected, blond, thin, with an amused smile. Puny, she had thought, and dressed with a sort of theatrical nonchalance, in a powder-blue coat, darker blue flannels, and suède moccasins.

She had refused a drink, and he had ordered a rye for himself, and this had given him another advantage over her. He had been easy and relaxed and she had been in misery.

"I don't want my daughter to see you again, Mr. Darby," she had said, at last.

"My dear lady, isn't that for Bee to decide?" he had asked.

"No," Lucia had said. "She's only a child. Only seventeen."

"She'll be eighteen next month, I believe."

"That doesn't matter, Mr. Darby. If you don't stop seeing Beatrice, I'll have to put this in my lawyer's hands."

"But put what, dear lady?"

"I understand that you're married," she had said.

5

"But, my dear lady," he said laughing, "what will your lawyer do about that? After all, it's not a crime."

"It's altogether wrong for you to see Beatrice."

"Well, really . . ." he protested. "The poor kid tells me her life is miserably dull. She likes to get around, meet interesting people, and I'm very happy to take her around. She knows I'm getting a divorce, but she doesn't think that's any reason for refusing to see me."

Her visit had been not only utterly useless, but harmful. Ted had told Bee about it and she had been bitterly angry.

"Ted's so good-natured that he only laughed," she had told her mother. "But it doesn't make me laugh. It's the most humiliating, horrible thing that ever happened to me."

"Bee," Lucia had said, "unless you promise not to see him again, you'll have to stop going to art school."

"I *won't* stop going, and I *won't* promise."

"Bee," Lucia said, "Bee, darling, why won't you trust me? I'm only thinking of what's best for you."

"Why don't *you* trust *me?*" Bee had cried. "Ted's the most interesting person I've ever met. He knows all sorts of people, artists, and actors, all sorts of people. I'm *not* having a nasty love affair with him."

"I know you're not," Lucia had said. "But, Bee, you must believe me. Bee—he's not the right sort of man for you to know."

"Well, I *don't* believe you," Bee had said. "You think you know, but you're just terribly old-fashioned. You couldn't possibly understand anyone like Ted."

Then Lucia Holley had used her last weapon, with heavy reluctance.

6

"Bee, if you don't promise me not to see him, I shan't give you any carfare, any allowance at all."

"You *couldn't* do that!" Bee had cried.

"There's nothing I wouldn't do, to stop this thing," Lucia replied.

She meant that. A week ago, her cousin Vera Ridgewood had telephoned her.

"Lucia, angel, I wonder if you know that your precious child is playing around with a *quite* sinister-looking character. I've seen them *twice* in Marino's bar together and today I saw them going into a place on Madison Avenue."

It doesn't mean anything, Lucia had thought, and she had spoken to Bee about it with very little anxiety.

"Bee, dear, is there someone in the art school you go to bars with?"

"That's Ted Darby," Bee had answered. "He doesn't go to art school. He's in the theatrical business."

"I'd rather you didn't go in bars with anyone, Bee."

"I never take anything but ginger ale."

"But I don't like you going to bars, dear. You could go to a drugstore with this boy."

"He isn't a boy," Bee had said. "He's thirty-five."

Lucia had been anxious now.

"Ask him out here, Bee," she had said.

"I wouldn't ask him under false pretenses," Bee had said. "He wouldn't come like that, either. We talked about it, and I told him that if you knew he was married, you'd never let him set foot in the house."

I didn't say the right things to her, Lucia thought, watching the rain against the window. I've made so many mistakes with Bee, even when she was a little girl. I've objected

7

to her friends. I've been upset when she changed her mind about things. I've done so much better with David. If Tom was here, he'd know just what to say to Bee. Here, now, Duckling . . . ! She did use to look like a little yellow duckling, all ruffled . . .

She got up, and went over to the window, restless and heavyhearted. The rain was streaming down the glass, glittering, with an oily look, the trees swayed a little. At the end of the path stood the queer long shape of the boathouse and beyond that lay the invisible water.

It's too lonely here, she thought. It was a mistake to come here. There aren't enough young people. David doesn't much care, but if Bee had met some nice boys, perhaps this wouldn't have happened. Perhaps.

There was someone in the boathouse. She saw a little flame spring out and slant sidewise and die. She saw another one that was steady for an instant. Someone was striking matches in there. A tramp? she thought. A drunken man, who'll set fire to the place? I'd better tell . . .

No, I'm not going to tell Father, or David, and let them take risks. I'm not going myself, either. If he does set fire to the place, the rain will put it out long before it could reach here. As long as nobody can get in here . . .

She wanted to make sure the doors were all locked, the safety catches on the windows. She went out of her room, moving swiftly, her feet in slippers, and along the hall to the stairs. And in the hall below, she saw Bee, cautiously sliding the chain off the door. She ran down to her.

"Bee," she said, very low. "Where are you going?"

"Out," Bee answered.

She was wearing a transparent, light blue raincoat, her pale blonde hair, parted on the side, hung loose to her shoulders, her blue eyes were narrowed, her mouth had a scornful twist. She looked beautiful and terrible, to Lucia.

"It's raining, Bee. I don't want you to go out."

"I'm sorry, but I'm going," said Bee.

It was plain enough now.

"No," Lucia said. "You can't."

Bee began to turn the doorknob, but Lucia caught her wrist.

"Bee, you want to meet that man."

"All right, I am going to meet Ted," Bee said. "You won't let me go in to New York any more, but I called him up and told him to come here. At least I'm going to explain to him."

"What's this! What's this!" cried old Mr. Harper from the doorway of the sitting room.

Nobody answered him. He stood there, lean and soldierly, with his neat white mustache and his clear blue eyes, an open book in one hand.

"What's this?" he asked again.

"Mother refuses to let me go out of this house," said Bee.

"Your mother's right, Beatrice. Too late, and it's pouring rain."

"Grandpa," Bee said. "I've got a special reason for going out and Mother knows it."

Lucia could see now what the child's tactics were to be. She was counting upon her grandfather's immense indulgence for her, hoping to use it against her mother.

"You take your mother's advice, Beatrice," he said. "Best thing."

"It's *not!* She doesn't understand anything about this. She hasn't any faith in me. She thinks I'm a sort of juvenile delinquent."

"Come, now!" said Mr. Harper.

"She does! Ted's come all the way out here to see me."

"A man?" asked Mr. Harper. "Where is he?"

"In the boathouse. I want to see him for a few moments."

"Your mother's perfectly right, Beatrice. If you want to see this fellow, have him come to the house."

"He couldn't. Not after the way Mother's treated him."

"Beatrice, if your mother doesn't approve of this fellow, she has some good reason, you can be sure of that."

"No!" cried Bee. "I asked him to come, and I'm going to see him, just for a few moments."

"Afraid not, m'dear."

Oh, Bee, darling! Don't look like that! Lucia cried in her heart. As if we were enemies . . . Under the light in the ceiling the child's pale hair glistened, the blue raincoat glittered, she looked so beautiful, so delicate, and so desperate.

"Do you mean," Bee said slowly, "that you and Mother would stop me by force from doing what I think is right?"

"It's not going to come to that, m'dear," he said. "You're going to be a sensible girl and not worry your mother. You know she's thinking only of——"

"Oh, *stop* it!" Bee cried, stamping her foot. "I *won't* . . . I won't . . ."

She began to cry, she tossed her head as if the tears stung her; she turned around and went running up the stairs. Her door slammed.

I hope she won't wake up David, Lucia thought. I shouldn't like him to know anything at all about this.

"Now . . ." her father said. He laid his hand on her shoulder, and a great sense of comfort came to her. "Have you a nice book to read, Lucia?"

"I'm writing to Tom, Father."

"Run along and finish your letter, m'dear," he said. "I'll be down here to see that everything's all right."

She understood what his words implied. He would stay in the sitting room, in a spot where he could watch the stairs, all night if he thought it was necessary. She trusted him as she trusted her own heart. She trusted even his thoughts. He would not misjudge that poor, reckless, furious child.

She kissed him on the cheek. "Good night, Father," she said, and went up the stairs to her own room.

DEAR TOM:
    David is sending you some snaps he took of this house, so that you'll have a better idea. It's really very nice. The victory garden isn't doing so very well, though. The soil is too sandy. But the tomatoes are coming along . . .

Her writing was neat and small. It took so very many words to fill a V-mail page. I'm so *slow*, she thought. I'm stupid. I've done so badly with Bee.

The wind had died down and the rain fell straight now, pattering on the roof. A door closed. That's the front door! she thought. Ted's got in!

She hurried out into the hall and from the head of the stairs she saw her father taking off his overcoat. She ran down.

"I went to the boathouse, m'dear," he said. "I had a few words with this fellow. Very unsavory character, I'd call him. Inclined to be troublesome. When I told him to leave the premises, he refused. But I dealt with him. To tell you the truth, I pushed him off into the water."

He was pleased with himself.

11

"Water's no more than four feet deep there," he said. "Wouldn't drown a child. Won't do the fellow any harm. Do him good. Cool him off."

He patted her shoulder.

"Yes . . ." he said. "I sent him off with a flea in his ear."

Chapter Two

To wake up extra early in the morning was always a delight to Lucia Holley. It gave her an exquisite sense of freedom and privacy. She could do whatever she pleased, while all the others were sleeping.

This morning she waked at five o'clock. For a moment she lay thinking with a heavy heart about Bee; but life and energy were strong in her, and she could not lie still. She got up and put on a black wool bathing suit and a white rubber helmet. She took her rope sandals in her hand and went down the stairs barefoot. David made such a fuss about her swimming alone.

"Anyone that's water-wise," he said, severely, "wouldn't do that."

"I *am* water-wise," Lucia said. "I've been swimming since I was a baby."

"Nobody ought to go swimming all alone," he said. "And anyway, the water's too cold the beginning of May. I wish you wouldn't *do* it."

She felt sorry to do anything that might worry David. But he never wakes up before half-past seven or eight, she thought, and by that time I'll be all dried and dressed. He'll never know, and this is such a wonderful time of day.

She unchained the front door and went out, and sitting on the steps, she put on her sandals. It was a gray morning, but fresh and somehow promising, not like the beginning of a rainy day. I'll row out a little way, she thought. And she thought that when she would be swimming in the gray water, under the soft sky, she would think of some new and better way to talk to Bee.

Something else to offer her, she thought. If I don't let the poor child go in to her art school, what *is* she going to do? I'll have to branch out. I'll have to meet some of the people here, on Bee's account. But I'm so poor at that. It's so hard without Tom.

She had married at eighteen, and she had never gone anywhere without Tom, never had thought of such a thing. And before her marriage, she lived with her mother and father, a tranquil, happy home life with very little going out. She was by nature friendly and uncritical, but she had very little to say for herself. She had no talent for social life and no desire for it.

And that's wrong, she thought. With a daughter Bee's age, it's my *duty* to do things. Maybe I could get Father to go around with me and call on people . . . Maybe Father and I could join the Yacht Club here.

The boathouse was a queer-looking structure, a long wooden tunnel over a cement basin where the boats were moored, and attached to it, on the landward end, a little two-storied cottage with a porch. Ideal for a chauffeur or a couple, the real-estate agent had said, only Lucia had no chauffeur or couple, only Sibyl, who did not care to live out here.

The wooden wall of the tunnel led to an opening with a ramp. She went down this, into the dimness where the rowboat, the canoe, and the motorboat were moored to iron staples. They had all swung out to the end of their
14

ropes, following the ebb tide, and she began to pull in the rowboat. It came as if reluctant, and as she stepped into it, she saw the body.

It was a man, face down in the motorboat, in a strange and dreadful position, his legs sprawled across the thwart, his head and shoulders raised by something. She could not see his face, but something about him, the shape of his head perhaps, made her almost sure it was Ted Darby. And she was almost sure he was dead.

Almost sure was not good enough. She stepped into the motorboat, and it was Ted Darby, and he was dead. He had fallen on a spare anchor, half upended on the seat, and it had pierced his throat.

Father did that, she thought.

She stood in the gently rocking boat, feet apart for balance, tall and long-legged in her white robe. Of course it means the police, she thought. Then Father will have to know that he did this. They'll find out why Ted came here, and Bee will be dragged into it. And I shan't be able to keep it from Tom. Not possibly. It'll be in the tabloids.

It will be so horrible, she thought. For poor little Bee. For Tom. For David. But worst of all for Father. He'll have to go to court. He'll be blamed. He'll be so shocked, so humiliated.

If I were able to get rid of Ted, she thought, I would do it. If I could think of any way to save us all . . .

I could do it, she thought, if I could get him off the anchor.

Standing there, swaying a little as the boat rocked, she knew that she could get him off. She had the resourcefulness of the mother, the domestic woman, accustomed to emergencies. Again and again she had had to deal with

15

accidents, sudden illnesses, breakdowns. For years she had been the person who was responsible in an emergency. She had enough physical strength for this job. What she lacked was the spirit for it. I *couldn't* touch him, she thought.

That's nonsense, she told herself. I thought I couldn't possibly kill old Tiger with gas. But I did. When that laundress had a fit and we were all alone, in the house, I did something about it. When David fell down the cellar stairs and just lay there with blood all over his eyes . . . No, I can do this.

It was very difficult, for the body had begun to stiffen. It was very dreadful. When she got Ted down in the bottom of the boat, her breathing was like sobbing. She got a tarpaulin out of a locker, and spread it over him; then she cast off and started the engine.

The noise was stupendous, terrifying in this enclosed space, in the early-morning quiet. She had trouble, too. The engine started and stopped and started again. Bang, *bang*, puttputtputt. *Bang.* They'll hear it at the house and somebody will come, she thought. Even when she was under way, the noise was atrociously loud.

She steered through the narrow inlet through the reeds and out into the open water of the Sound, in a world gray, soft, and quiet. There was no other craft in sight. She had already made up her mind to take Ted to Simm's Island. She had decided upon the best spot. On the side of the small island that faced the mainland there was a row of bleached little summer bungalows, all empty, as far as she knew. But I shan't go near them, she thought.

She and David and Bee had come here for a picnic lunch a week ago. They had been looking then for a nice place.

16

She was looking now for a half-remembered place, so far from nice that no one would be likely to go there. It would be dreadful if a child were to find him, she thought.

Here was the place, a narrow strip of sand, and behind it a stretch of marsh where the tall reeds stirred in the breeze. She stopped the engine, and dropped the anchor. She drew a long breath and set to work.

Ted was very slight, but even at that, it was hard enough to lift him out of the boat. Then she took him under the shoulders and dragged him to the marsh, well in among the tall reeds. He looked grotesque and horrible with his arms and legs sprawled out; she tried to straighten him and could not, and she began to cry. There he lay, staring at the sky.

I can't leave him like this, she thought. There was a big blue bandanna in the pocket of her terry robe. She took it out and dried her eyes with it, and spread it over his face. But the breeze lifted it at once. There were no stones here to anchor it down. She knelt beside him frowning, still crying. Then with her strong sharp teeth she tore two corners of the bandanna into strips, and tied it, cater-cornered over his face, to two reeds.

It's better than nothing, she thought, and went back to the boat. The engine started easily this time. When she was out in the open water she stopped it again and cleaned the bottom of the boat with an oily rag. There was very little blood. I hope it was quick, she thought. I hope he wasn't there a long time—alone . . .

She tied the robe tight around her waist and turned in the lapels across her chest, for the breeze seemed chilly now. She started the engine, headed for home. It's done, she told herself. I'm going to put it out of my mind. But

17

suddenly she thought of the bandanna. Well, nobody could identify it, she thought. It's just one I bought in the ten-cent store ages ago. There must be thousands and thousands exactly like it. Fingerprints? I don't think they get fingerprints from cloth of any kind. Anyhow I could say I'd left the bandanna on the island the day we had the picnic.

Anyhow, I can't help it now. It's done. And I'm not going to brood about it. I'm not going to think about it at all.

As she approached the boathouse, she felt a faint shock of dismay to see David standing there, thin and slouching, in blue trunks and a khaki windbreaker. But she recovered herself at once. It's just as well to have to start right in, she thought.

"Hello, David," she said, cheerfully.

"Hello," he said unsmiling.

As the boat glided into the tunnel, he moved along to the ramp, and was waiting to help her out.

"I couldn't believe my ears," he said, "when I heard the engine start. I thought someone was stealing the boat and I got down here as quick as I could, and I saw you scooting away."

"I like the early morning," she said.

"That's all right," said David. "But why didn't you take the rowboat, like you always do?"

"Well, I thought I'd like the motorboat for a change."

"Well, I ask you not to do it again," said David. "It's dangerous. You don't know one darn thing about that engine. If it stalled or even the least little thing went wrong, you'd be absolutely helpless."

"I didn't go far," said Lucia.

18

"Well, I ask you not to do it," said David. "It's darned eccentric, anyhow."

"There's nothing so terrible about being eccentric once in a while," said Lucia.

"Personally," said David, "I shouldn't like any of the fellows I know out here to see you scooting around in a motorboat at half-past five in the morning."

David's like Father, Lucia thought. But he looks like Tom with those furry ginger eyelashes and those nice green eyes. He's only fifteen. Only a child. But in three more years . . . if the war goes on for three more years . . .

Again and again and again that thought would come to her, piercing her heart. She put her arms around his thin shoulders.

"I'm quite sure none of your friends saw me, dear," she said. "But I won't do it again, if it worries you."

"Well, that's good," he said.

"Let's go along to the house and get some breakfast."

"Sibyl won't be down yet."

"I can manage," said Lucia.

She took her arm away from his shoulders and they walked in side by side.

"What's the matter with Bee?" he asked.

"What do you mean, David?"

"You certainly must have noticed it," he said. "Of course most of it's an act. She's always putting on an act. But something's been bothering her lately, all right."

"Doesn't she ever talk to you about things, David? You used to talk everything over together."

"I don't encourage that," said David.

"It does people good to talk over their troubles to——"

19

"Well, it doesn't do me good to listen to them," he said with unexpected vehemence. "I don't like anything that's sappy and emotional and all, and I don't want to get mixed up in things like that. Not now, or any other time."

He held open the screen door and she went past him into Sibyl's beautiful kitchen. The sun was breaking through the clouds; a shaft lay upon the green and white linoleum floor. It was a lovely thing to be getting breakfast for David.

Chapter Three

We could wait till tomorrow," said Sibyl. "Only this is the day for the chicken man."

"Then I'll get you a taxi," said Lucia.

"Better if you go, ma'am," said Sibyl, standing by the kitchen table, tall, portly, her dark face impassive.

"You're a much better marketer than I am," said Lucia.

"My business to be so," said Sibyl, quietly. "But the chicken man don't like colored people. Don't hesitate to say so."

"Has he ever said anything to you, Sibyl?"

"Yes, ma'am," said Sibyl.

"We won't deal with him any more," said Lucia.

"He's the only one got any chickens," said Sibyl.

"Then we'll do without chickens for the rest of the summer."

Sibyl smiled a smile, gentle, infinitely affectionate.

"No, ma'am," she said. "If you go, maybe you can get us two nice roasting chickens and I'll cook them Saturday and we'll have a chicken salad Sunday. I'll give you the list, ma'am."

They had been together, day in and day out, for eight years, in complete harmony. Sibyl knew that Lucia was not the wise, thrifty housewife the family believed her to be. Sibyl remembered the things Lucia forgot, found the things

21

that Lucia lost, covered up Lucia's absent-mindedness, advised her, warned her. She had lent Lucia money, to conceal a shockingly careless overdraft, and had herself gone to the police about the chauffeur Lucia could not bring herself to accuse.

She knew Lucia better than any one else did. But Lucia knew curiously little about Sibyl. She did not know Sibyl's age, or where she had been born, what family she had, or what friends. She had no idea where Sibyl went on her afternoons off, or what she did. Simply, she loved and trusted Sibyl without reservation.

"Well, maybe I can speak to the chicken man," she said.

"No, ma'am," said Sibyl. "Can't change this world."

From where she stood, Lucia could see her father at his breakfast in the dining room, the soft collar of his blue shirt revealing his lean old neck. He was wearing the black and white checked jacket he had bought in London years ago, and cherished so fondly, getting it relined and patched up again and again. Rather have a really decent jacket like this even if it was a bit shabby than a cheap flimsy new one, he often said.

He could very well have got himself a new one, not cheap and flimsy, but his daughter never pointed this out to him. He thinks it's more English to be shabby, she thought, and why shouldn't he if he wants?

I'm so glad I was able to get Ted away, she thought. Now no matter what happens, I don't see how Father could even find out what he did last night, or be connected with it in any way. Nobody will ever know.

She went in and kissed the top of his neat white head.

"Father," she said, "I think it would be better not to let Bee know that you saw that man last night."

"I didn't see him," said Mr. Harper.

"But, Father . . . !"

"Too dark," said he, pleased with the joke. "Don't worry, my dear. I shan't tell Beatrice. And I don't think we'll be troubled again by the young gentleman."

Bee was coming down the stairs. She came straight into the kitchen.

"Good morning, Mother," she said. "Good morning, Sibyl. Is my orange juice in the icebox?"

"Yes, Miss Bee."

Bee brought out the bowl that held the full pint of orange and lemon juice combined which was an essential part of her new Vitabelle diet and carried it into the dining room.

"Good morning, Grandpa," she said.

This, obviously, was to be her attitude, polite, cool, aloof; no smiles for her oppressors.

"Going in to your school today?" Harper asked, surprised by her appearance in blue overalls and white shirt.

"I'm not allowed to go any more," Bee answered, very clearly.

"Oh . . . I see!" he said. "Number of pretty scenes around here that you could paint, I should think."

She gave the smile Lucia, watching from the kitchen, hated to see. The child was so lovely, with her soft fair hair, her delicate skin, her fine little features, but she rouged her mouth into a sort of square, and when she smiled this way, with her lips scarcely parted, and her eyes narrowed, she looked almost ugly.

She couldn't really have cared so very much for a man like Ted, Lucia thought. Of course she'll be terribly upset when she hears that he's dead, but she'll get over it. She's so *very* young. Poor Bee . . . I must do something about

23

branching out, finding more friends for her. And there's no reason now why she shouldn't go back to the art school, only that I can't tell her. Can I just say I changed my mind? Or had I better wait until Ted gets into the papers?

She telephoned for a taxi and changed into a costume suitable for the village, a blue and white checked gingham dress, a blue belt, blue sandals, a wide black straw hat. Sibyl had the list ready for her and when the cab came, off she went, with the big green denim market bag.

I'll tell Bee this afternoon that I've changed my mind, she thought. Then she can go in to her school tomorrow. It may be quite a while before Ted gets into the papers, and there's no reason why she should stay home, poor child. Is she going to mind very much, when she finds out? It's so hard to understand how she could possibly have cared, even the least little bit, for a man like that. So cheap and sneering . . .

It was a morning of frustration. The chicken man would sell her only one chicken, and a smallish one at that. There was no margarine, no sugar. She could not get the brand of soap flakes Sibyl particularly wanted. The only potatoes she found were old and soft and sprouting. The only cigarettes were an unheard-of variety.

She could not get the tooth paste her father wanted. She could not get the magazines David had asked for. Bee's shoes, promised for last week by the shoemaker, still stood untouched, on a shelf. She went from one shop to another, the bag growing heavier and heavier. She was hot, flushed and tired, but still with her air of earnest politeness. She stood patiently in line at counters, she engaged in conversation with other housewives, she was zealous with her ration stamps.

24

When she had got what she could, she had a big paper bag in addition to the market bag. They'd hate me too much in the bus with all this, she thought, and crossed the main street of the village, pulled down by the bag, to the railway station, where three taxis stood.

"Got to wait for the train, lady," the first driver said.

He could put three or even four passengers in together; he was not interested in this single fare.

"If I drive you out to Plattsville," said the second, "I got to come all the way back empty. It don't pay me."

"Well, suppose I pay a little extra . . . ?" Lucia said, hot and tired.

"Well . . ." said the driver, "we're not supposed to do that. I'd have to charge you two dollars and a half."

That was outrageous. For a moment she contemplated trying the third, but he would realize that he was the last resort and he might take advantage of it. He might be worse.

"All right," she said, and got into the cab.

Just at that moment the train came in and her driver waited. A little crowd of people descended; the two other cabs pulled up to drive away, and a man came, leisurely and deliberately, toward Lucia's taxi. He was a stout man, in a gray suit with the jacket open. He walked with a sort of roll, bearing his portly stomach proudly.

"Know where some people named Holley live, son?" he asked the driver.

"Nope," said the driver. "You might ask the ticket office."

"You run along and do the asking, son," said the stout man.

Lucia sat back in a corner, looking at him in unreasoning dismay. His eyes . . . she said to herself. They were very

25

pale eyes, light-lashed, with a curious blankness, as if he were blind. He's a detective, she thought, and he's come about Ted.

"I got a fare," said the driver, "the other cabs'll be coming back."

"You go find out where the Holleys live, son," said the stout man, in the same even, indifferent voice, and it increased Lucia's dismay to see that the far from obliging young driver was prepared to do as he was told. Everyone would do what that man said.

"I'm going out there," she said.

The stout man gave her a glance, a thorough one from head to foot.

"You told me the Maxwell place," cried the driver, shocked and aggrieved.

"I know," Lucia said. "But we've rented it."

The stout man opened the door of the cab and got in. He sat down beside Lucia with his knees apart, taking up a good deal of room.

"Get going, son," he said.

He's one of those horrible detectives that you see in the movies, Lucia thought. He's . . . the word sprang up in her mind. He's merciless, she thought. He'd be merciless to Father.

"Your name Holley?" he asked.

"Yes."

"You got a sister or daughter name of Beatrice?"

"Yes," she answered again.

"She's the one I want to see," he said.

"Well . . . what about?"

"I'll take it up with her," he said.

"I'd rather you didn't," said Lucia. "I'm her mother. I can tell you anything she could tell you."

"She's the one I came out to see," he said. "Beatrice Holley."

"You might as well tell me what you want to see her about. She'll tell me herself, later on."

"Think so?"

"Yes, I know it. I wish you wouldn't talk to her. If you'd please talk to me instead . . . ?"

"It's Beatrice Holley I want," he said.

Something like panic assailed Lucia. He'll tell Bee that Ted's been found, she thought. It must be that. What else could bring him here? He'll ask her questions and questions, and she'll tell him things that'll get in the papers. I can't let her see this man, alone.

"My daughter's a minor," she said. "I'm sorry but I can't let you see her."

He turned his head and gave her another glance, his light lashes flickering up and down. Then he turned away again.

"That won't work," he said.

It was intolerable that Bee should have to endure this.

"I'm going to send for my lawyer," said Lucia.

He did not trouble to answer that; he sat with his double chin resting on his chest, looking straight before him, thinking his own thoughts. Lucia was of absolutely no interest to him.

They were in sight of the house now. David was strolling across the lawn of coarse grass; when he saw the cab he stopped and waited.

"What's the fare?" said the stout man.

"Dollar," said the driver, and the stout man gave him a dollar, no tip. He opened the door of the cab and got out without a glance at Lucia. He was speaking to David before she got her dollar out of her purse.

"Two-fifty was the rate," said the driver.

She gave him another fifty cents and got out, with her two big bags. The stout man was standing in front of the house.

"If you talk to my daughter, I'm going to be there, too," she said.

He didn't answer her. She stood there with the bags, utterly at a loss, but determined to protect Bee as best she could. The screen door opened and Bee came out. She looked with a frown of surprise at the two standing on the lawn, and ran down the steps.

"You wanted to see me?" she asked.

"You Beatrice Holley?"

"Bee—" Lucia began. "Don't."

"It's just something about the school, Mother," said Bee.

"It isn't!" said Lucia.

"It isn't," said the man. "I told the boy that. Makes it easier. No. I came to ask about my good friend Ted Darby."

"Well . . . Who are you?" Bee asked.

"The name's Nagle."

"Well . . . What do you want to ask?"

"Bee . . . !" said Lucia. "Don't!"

He's not a detective, she thought. He's—I don't know— a crook, a gangster, something horrible.

"Ted came out to see you last night," said Nagle.

"What if he did?" said Bee.

"He never came home again," said Nagle.

The statement was shocking to Lucia and frightening. But Bee was not alarmed.

"You mean he didn't go back to his hotel?" she said. "Then he probably went to visit someone. He has plenty of friends."

"Did he tell you he was going to visit somebody?"

"My daughter didn't see him last night," said Lucia.

"You saw him?"

"No. Nobody saw him."

"You're saying he didn't come here?"

"I don't know whether he came or not. I'm just saying that none of us saw him."

He turned to Bee.

"You called him up," he said. "You asked him to come out here last night. Well?"

"Well?" Bee replied. "I can't see what right you have to come here and ask me questions."

She was not in the least afraid of Nagle. She met his pale eyes steadily.

"Why didn't you see him?" asked Nagle.

"That's my own business," she said. "Come in, Mother, let's——"

"Wait!" said Nagle. "It's not that easy. I want everything you've got about my good friend Ted Darby. Names of any friends he's told you——"

"I'm not going to tell you anything at all," said Bee. "You can wait till he gets back and ask him."

"If you know where he is," said Nagle, "you'd better tell me."

"I'll take the bags in, ma'am," said Sibyl's voice behind Lucia.

She took the bags and walked away, erect and stately.

"I shan't tell you anything at all," said Bee.

"That's just too bad," said Nagle. "That's too bad for Ted."

"What do you mean?" Bee demanded. "Are you threatening him?"

"I ask questions," said Nagle. "I don't answer."

"That goes for me too," said Bee.

She's—tough, Lucia thought astonished. That slender girl in slacks, her light hair down to her shoulders, that child, who had lived all her life at home, protected and cherished, was talking now like a tough girl in a movie, looking like one, too, with her eyes narrowed and her fine mouth scornful.

"Okay! Okay!" said Nagle, and turned away.

Lucia stood looking after him, with dread and dismay in her heart. He'll come back, she thought. This is only the beginning. . . .

Chapter Four

"Dear Tom," Lucia wrote, "it was so very nice to get an air-mail from you this afternoon, especially a letter telling about the details of your life and your friends and your men. Things like that seem to bring you so much closer, Tom."

Only they didn't, really. I haven't much imagination, she thought, regretfully. I can't imagine Tom being a naval officer. I think of him as he was before he left, over two years ago, and probably he's not like that any more. No, he'll have changed, and I'll be just the same.

She went on with her dull, earnest, loving letter. Thank goodness Tom doesn't expect me to be wonderful, she thought. He knows what I'm like. When Tom had first met her she had been seventeen and still in school, a very earnest student but never excelling in anything, never a leader in anything. She liked everyone and was interested in no one. You're the hardest girl in the world to make love to, Tom had told her once. You're just so blamed friendly.

When she was eighteen they were married. When she was nineteen Bee had been born, and that was that. She had always been faintly disappointed in herself, disappointed in school because she had not been remarkable, disappointed when she married because she had not become the perfect housekeeper, most of all disap-

31

pointed in herself as a mother. Whenever she visited her children's school she felt singularly inept among the other mothers. Simply not *real,* she thought.

I don't cope with things. That Nagle . . . Bee wasn't at all afraid of him. But I was. I am now. Suppose he tells the police that Ted was coming here . . . ? Well, I'll say he didn't come. But if they start asking Father questions . . . I'm pretty sure he's never heard Ted's name. But he'd say, yes, there was a man, and I sent him away with a flea in his ear.

If Father knew he'd killed Ted, he'd tell the police at once. He's like that. I know just how he'd talk. My dear, I am always prepared to accept the consequences of my acts. The full consequences. And then, of course, Bee would be dragged into it. And Tom would have to know. Why can't I look after my own daughter?

Lying in bed in the dark, a desperate, almost panic compulsion *to do something* rose in her. But she mastered it at once. Don't be frantic, she told herself. Just one day at a time. Just take things as they come.

She got up and lit a cigarette; when it was finished, she stubbed it out carefully and closed her eyes. I'm going to wake up at five o'clock, she told herself.

So she did, but to a morning of wild wind and rain. I'd love a little swim in this weather, she thought, but I'd worry David too much. No . . . I'll take a little walk out of sight of the house.

The idea was strong in her mind that she must stand guard over the house, that she must protect the inmates. She dressed in an old blue flannel skirt, a black sweater and tennis shoes. She tied a white scarf over her hair and went stealthily down the stairs and out of the house.

And out in the rain and the rough wind, she forgot her fears and distress. She went down the drive to the highway and walked up and down, as if patrolling, her skirt flattened against her long legs, her dark face wet and glowing.

"You look like a gypsy," her father said, benevolently, when she came back to the house.

The morning routine went on. The newspaper came and there was nothing about Ted. Old Mr. Harper went out for his constitutional. David went off in the motorboat to visit some friends he had made; Bee was shut in her own room. And Lucia did the things appointed to be done on Thursday. She stripped all the beds, she made out the laundry list. She tidied and dusted the sitting room and the bathroom she shared with Bee. In a blue cotton pinafore, she had an air of serious efficiency; nobody would know that all this was arranged entirely by Sibyl.

Before lunch, she knocked on Bee's door.

"Come in!" said Bee.

She was sitting at a table by the window, drawing, in a candy-striped play suit, her silky hair pushed back from her forehead.

"Bee," said Lucia. "I've been thinking things over . . . I can't bear for you to stay away from your art school, Bee. Go back tomorrow, dear, and I'll simply trust to your . . ."

"If you think you'll stop me from seeing Ted by saying you 'trust' me," said Bee, "you're mistaken."

"Bee, you don't need to be so hostile. Not to me."

"Mother," said Bee, and was silent for a time. "I know you're terribly fond of me. I know you think you're doing what's best for me. But I don't agree with you about *anything*."

33

"Bee, you do!"

"No. I'm not a fool about Ted. I realize he isn't our kind of person. Daddy wouldn't like him any more than you do. But I want to know all kinds of people. I want to live out in the world. I'd just as soon be *dead*, as have a life like you."

"Bee!" said Lucia, startled, even shocked. "I've got all the things that are most worth having in the world."

"I think your life is *awful*," said Bee. "I'd rather——"

"Lunch!" called David from the hall, and Bee rose promptly.

"I'm sorry, Mother," Bee went on with a sort of stern regret. "But I'm not like you. I'm not going to have a life like yours. If you can call it a life. Getting married at eighteen, right from school. Never really seeing anything or doing anything. No adventure, no color. I suppose you like feeling safe. Well, *I* don't want to be safe."

"Come on, Mother!" called David.

He was always a little irritated by the private conversations that Lucia had with his sister. He himself never sought private conversations. He was willing to talk to anyone about anything. When the clergyman had come to call, he had shown a disposition to discuss religion with him which Lucia had had trouble in suppressing.

At the lunch table, he discussed the Pacific campaign with his grandfather while Bee sat silent, with a look of faintly amused boredom. I think he's very intelligent, Lucia said to herself. I like the way men talk.

As they were about to leave the table, Sibyl appeared in the doorway.

"The refrigerator is gone again, ma'am," she said, evenly.

34

"I don't know what you people *do* to that icebox," said Mr. Harper, frowning.

It was an unbreakable convention that whenever the refrigerator went out of order, nobody but Mr. Harper could turn off the gas properly. He now did this, and it was all he could do. He was not at all handy about the house. Neither was David, who was further disqualified by being candidly indifferent.

"Why worry?" he said. "People didn't use to have mechanical iceboxes, and they got on all right."

"Then they had cakes of ice," said Lucia.

"No," said David, reasonably. "Grandpa's told me, plenty of times, that when he was a boy in England, they *never* had any ice. If they specially needed it, if anyone was sick or anything, they had to send to the fishmonger's."

"Well, that's a different climate," said Lucia.

"The temperature's only sixty-six now," said David. "You couldn't call that so very hot."

He strolled away. Mr. Harper had already gone.

"I'll telephone the company," said Lucia.

"Yes, ma'am," said Sibyl, with the same doubt and heaviness.

This recurring trouble with the icebox was a catastrophe they both dreaded. Lucia went to the telephone and she got that girl.

"Holley?" said the girl. "All right. I'll put it down."

"When do you think the man will come?"

"I haven't any idea," said the girl. "He takes all the calls in order. You'll just have to wait for your turn."

"Naturally," said Lucia, coldly. "I simply wanted to know if you could give me any idea . . ."

35

"He'll come when it's your turn," said the girl. "This company doesn't play any favorites."

"Damn you," said Lucia, but not aloud, and returned to the kitchen. "They won't say when he's coming," she told Sibyl. "I suppose we'd better have the fish tonight . . . ?"

"Better had," said Sibyl. "They won't like fish two nights running, but if the man doesn't come this afternoon . . ."

They both knew he would not come this afternoon.

"Well, as long as he comes before the week end . . ." said Lucia, and was silent for a moment, thinking about it. "I think I'll take a little nap," she said, apologetically. "But call me if anything turns up."

"Yes, ma'am," said Sibyl, with indulgence. She approved of Lucia's taking naps.

But Lucia was longer than usual in falling asleep today. If the Nagle man comes back, she thought, I don't want Bee to see him alone. I don't want Father to see him at all. Ever. Maybe I ought to stay awake, in case something happens . . .

In the end, drowsiness overwhelmed her. She lay stretched out, long and lean in a shrunken gray flannel dressing gown, her hands clasped over her head.

"Mrs. Holley, ma'am . . . !" Sibyl's voice said, insistently.

"Yes?" said Lucia, sitting up.

Sibyl stood beside her, grave and impassive.

"There's a man here wants to see you," she said.

"What man, Sibyl?"

"Wouldn't give his name," said Sibyl. "Just said he wanted to see you about something personal."

Their eyes met in a long look.

"Sibyl . . . What's he like?"

36

They were still looking straight at each other, and into Sibyl's amber-flecked dark eyes came a troubled shadow. She was a reticent woman. It was hard for her to find words for her thoughts.

"He don't look like a man you'd know," she said.

It's Nagle, Lucia thought. I knew he'd come back.

"He's on the veranda," Sibyl went on. "I can send him away."

"I'd better see him," said Lucia and got up, standing tall and straight on her narrow bare feet.

"You don't have to, ma'am," said Sibyl. "Told him I didn't know if you were in."

"No. I'd better see him," Lucia repeated. "Tell him I'll be down in a moment, please."

"Let him in?" Sibyl asked, and again their eyes met.

"Yes. Yes, please," said Lucia.

She had to let him into her house, for she dared not keep him out. She stood motionless until she heard the front door close, and then she began to dress quickly and carelessly, in the checked gingham dress that was limp now. He's in, she said to herself. He's in the house.

She went down the stairs and into the sitting room. But the man who stood there was not Nagle.

"Mrs. Holley?" he asked.

He was a big man, broad shouldered and narrow flanked, very well dressed, in a dark suit, a sober and expensive necktie. He was a handsome man, or could be, or had been. But there was something curiously blurred about him, like a fine drawing partly erased. His strong-boned face looked tired. His dark blue eyes looked somehow dim.

"My name is Donnelly," he said and his voice was muffled.

"Yes?" said Lucia evenly.

Maybe it's nothing, she told herself. Maybe it's just about the insurance. Or selling War Bonds. Or, something just ordinary.

But she could not believe it. He came from some other world, the world of Ted Darby and Nagle, strange and unknown to her as the banks of Lethe.

"I'd like a few words with you," he said, and jerked his dark head toward the open door behind her.

"Well . . . what about?" she asked, with an attempt at defiance.

He moved light on his feet, he reached past her and closed the door.

"You'll be wanting these letters," he said.

"What letters?"

They were standing close to each other, facing each other; she looked up at him, still attempting that defiance, and he looked at her absently.

"The letters your daughter wrote to Ted Darby," he said. "The price is five thousand dollars. Cash."

Chapter Five

She was aware that she was not really thinking at all. Not yet.

"Well . . . Sit down, please," she said.

He waited until she was seated, and then he drew up a chair, facing her, and sat down, carefully hitching up his trousers. He was remarkably neat, his dark hair neat on his narrow skull, his big hands well kept, his shoes gleaming. He was so strangely, so dreadfully indifferent, simply waiting. A blackmailer, she thought. This is blackmail.

"My daughter . . ." she said. "There's nothing in her letters . . ."

"Would you like to see one?" he asked.

He took a handsome pigskin wallet out of an inside pocket, drew out a sheaf of folded papers, and looked through them. He selected one and handed it to her.

TED:

I just wasn't alive until I met you. But you came like a fresh wind blowing through a stuffy room. I don't know, Ted, if I can make up my mind to do what you asked yesterday. But just the fact that you *did* ask, and that you thought I had the courage to take such a chance makes me feel proud.

Ted, I'm thinking about it. I'm not sentimental; you know that. But just the same it is hard to break entirely with the past, and go against everyone and everything you were taught.

See you Friday, Ted, and maybe by that time I'll have made up my mind.

BEATRICE

The clear beautiful printing Bee used made the words so stark . . .

"That doesn't mean anything," said Lucia. "She's only a child. That doesn't mean—anything."

"It looks like something," he said, and held out his hand for the letter.

"No!" she said, putting it behind her. "I shan't give it to you. I—the police will make you give me those letters."

He didn't bother to answer that. He sat leaning forward a little, holding the handsome wallet open on his knee. Simply waiting.

"I'm going to put this in my lawyer's hands," Lucia said. And she had a vision of Albert Hendry, Tom's lawyer, ineffably distinguished, listening to the story of Bee's disastrous folly.

"Why do you not pay the money and forget all about it?" asked Donnelly. "There's nothing else you can do at all."

"No!" said Lucia. "I wouldn't pay blackmail. Never!"

"There's someone else will," he said.

"Who?"

"Your father, maybe."

"No!" she cried. "No! You can't . . . No!"

She checked herself. She tried to breathe evenly. She tried to think.

"How did *you* get hold of these letters?" she asked.

"Darby wanted to borrow a bit," said Donnelly, "and he left me the letters till he'd pay me back."

40

"Do you mean that *he*——?"

"Oh, he had it in mind to make the girl pay for them," said Donnelly.

His tone was not at all threatening. There was no hint of violence in him. But his matter-of-fact acceptance of this incredible treachery, this criminal demand, seemed to her infinitely more alarming than violence and infinitely more difficult to meet. The word "blackmail" disturbed him not at all.

"Darby's run out on me now," he said, as if explaining a business affair. "He went off without a word. And I cannot afford to lose what I lent him."

He doesn't know what happened to Ted, she thought. When he finds out, will that change things? Make this better? Or worse? If I could only, *only* think this out.

The rain rattled against the window, the room seemed close, filled with a gray light. Here she sat with this man, this criminal, so well dressed, so unclamorous . . .

"I'll have to have time to think this over," she said coldly.

"I'm going to Montreal," he said, again with that reasonable air of explaining matters to her. "I'll need the money before I go."

"I haven't got five thousand dollars," she said.

"You'll think of a way to lay hands on it," he said.

"No . . . No. When you get that, you'll ask for more."

"I would not," he said, simply.

"No! There's nothing in those letters. Nothing at all wrong."

"They would look wrong," he said.

"Don't you realize," she began, when the door opened and old Mr. Harper entered.

41

"Oh," he said, "sorry, m'dear. I didn't know . . . Getting near teatime, I thought . . ."

Donnelly had risen; he stood there, like any polite stranger, waiting to be introduced.

"Father . . ." she said, "this is Mr. Donnelly."

"How d'you do, sir?" said Mr. Harper.

But he was not satisfied with this. He wanted, naturally, to know who Mr. Donnelly was and why he was here.

"From Tom's office," she said, in her desperation.

"Ha! From Tom's office," said Mr. Harper, and held out his hand. "Glad to see you, sir. Sit down! Sit down!"

No! No! No! Lucia cried to herself.

"Mr. Donnelly's just leaving, Father," she said.

"You can wait for a cup of tea, eh, Donnelly? Or a highball?"

"Thank you, sir," said Donnelly, and sat down again.

"How is everything in the office?" asked Mr. Harper.

"I couldn't tell you," Donnelly answered, "for I left there three years ago. Government work."

"I see!" said Mr. Harper. "Lucia, m'dear, d'you think you could ask Sibyl to bring along the tea? Or if you'd prefer a whisky and soda, Donnelly?"

"Tea, if you please," said Donnelly.

There were no bells in the house to summon Sibyl. Lucia rose and went out to the kitchen. As she pushed open the swing door, she saw Sibyl standing at a table under the window, cutting raw carrots into little flowers, her dark face in profile was proud and melancholy. She turned at the sound of Lucia's step.

"Sibyl . . ." Lucia said, and could get no further. She was crushed and overwhelmed by this catastrophe.

42

"What's wrong, ma'am?" asked Sibyl with compassion in her eyes.

"He's staying . . ." Lucia answered.

"That man?"

"Yes. Father's asked him to tea."

Sibyl, too, was silent for a moment.

"We must just do the best we can," said Sibyl. "Don't fret, ma'am."

"But he's——"

"Yes, ma'am," said Sibyl. "I know."

She turned and put the carrots into a bowl of cold water.

"You go back now, ma'am. I'll bring in the tea. Don't fret, ma'am. Sometimes there's good luck in this life. No harm to hope for it."

That was language Lucia could understand. Her father and her husband never spoke like that. In the blackest days of the war, old Mr. Harper had never had the slightest doubt of England's victory; he considered doubt to be a form of treason. And Tom, when he went away, had had the same resolute optimism.

"I'll come through all right," he had said, looking at her pale, averted face. "It's half the battle, Lucia," he had said, "to feel hopeful. Sure that you're lucky."

She did not believe that. She believed that a shell or a bullet could strike a brave and hopeful man as readily as a miserable one. She did not believe that the guilty were always punished; or the innocent always spared. She believed, like Sibyl, that life was incalculable, and that the only shield against injustice was courage.

She had courage.

"All right, Sibyl," she said and turned away.

43

Old Mr. Harper was having a good time. He was talking about the First World War to Donnelly who, it seemed, had been in it. In France and Belgium he had seen some of the English regiments whose names were glorious and almost sacred to the old man. Donnelly was far from eloquent, but his few words entirely satisfied Mr. Harper.

"Have you ever been in England, Donnelly?"

"I was in and out of Liverpool for nearly a year, sir."

"Oh, Liverpool . . ." said Mr. Harper, politely dismissing that city. "Never been there myself. But London . . . Ever been in London, Donnelly?"

"I have, sir. It is a fine city."

"I imagine it very changed now, Donnelly."

"It has a right to be," said Donnelly, gravely.

Lucia sat on the sofa with the tea table drawn up before her. She poured tea; when her father remembered to include her in the conversation, she responded quickly, with a bright smile. If I could only go out and take a walk, she thought, I'd be able to think. I've got to think. I've got to find a way out of this. I've got to stop being so stupid and dazed.

And then, to complete the nightmare, Bee came downstairs.

"Oh . . . !" she said from the doorway, as if surprised to see a stranger here.

But Lucia noticed that she was much more carefully got up than was natural for an ordinary afternoon at home. She was wearing a lemon-colored organdy blouse and a black skirt; she had blue mascara on her lashes and fresh make-up on her mouth.

Go away! Lucia cried in her heart. Don't you come in here . . .

44

Mr. Harper waited, but his daughter was drinking tea, her eyes lowered.

"This is Mr. Donnelly, Beatrice," he said. "From your father's office. My granddaughter, Donnelly."

Donnelly rose.

"Oh . . . How do you do?" said Bee, and he gave a slight bow.

She sat down on the sofa beside her mother, and lit a cigarette.

"No tea, thank you, Mother. Is there any grape juice?"

"It's too many points," said Lucia.

"Then could I have some iced tea, Mother?"

"I'm sorry, but there's no ice. The refrigerator's out of order."

"What a life!" said Bee laughing.

She wanted to get the attention of this stranger. It would have irritated David, but to Lucia it was heartbreaking. She saw Donnelly glance at her lovely child, an unreadable glance, and then turn to listen to old Mr. Harper, and a fierce, desperate rebellion rose in her.

I let him get in, she thought. There he is, with Bee's letters in his pocket. Trying to blackmail me. I'll get those letters somehow. I'll do something.

Donnelly rose.

"I'll have to be going," he said, "but I'll be in the neighborhood for a while."

"Oh, stopping out here?"

"It is business," said Donnelly. "Mrs. Holley, could I stop by in my car tomorrow around eleven, maybe, and drive you to see the old house we were speaking about?"

His effrontery was beyond belief. Here, under her own roof, in the presence of her father and her daughter, he

45

dared propose this rendezvous. But she had let him get in, and her home was no longer safe.

All right! she thought. All right! She raised her dark eyes and looked straight at him, a hot color in her cheeks, a defiance in her heart.

"Thanks. That would be very nice," she said.

I'll settle with you, all right, she thought. I'll think of something. Just wait and see.

Chapter Six

All right! All right! she thought. Let him take the letters to Father, and see what happens. Just let him try to blackmail Father.

It will be hard for Bee. But Father'll know that there's really nothing to those letters. No matter how they sound. She went to sleep with that in her mind, defiant and resolute.

But when she waked in the early morning, all that was gone. I simply can't trust Father, she thought. He's so upright. He'd probably want to go to the police. We must see this through, my dear. And then the police would connect Bee with Ted, and when they found Ted . . .

No. I'll put Donnelly off. I'll pretend I'm getting the money for him. That'll give me a little more time.

And what was she going to do with this time? Think of something. Do something.

It was a soft, mild morning of pale sunshine. With a regretful thought for David, she put on her bathing suit and went quietly out of the house, and down to the boathouse. She took the rowboat this time; she went out through the tunnel at the narrow inlet through the reeds into the open water. Oh, this is the best thing! she thought and laying the oars in the bottom of the boat, she made a shallow dive into the water.

"Hey!" she cried aloud, because it was so cold. But, in a moment, as she swam, the water no longer felt cold, only exquisitely refreshing. There were gulls flying overhead, and she turned on her back and floated, to watch them, one swooped so low that she could see its fierce face.

She lay floating in the sparkling water, looking with half-closed eyes at the gulls and the little clouds in the soft blue sky. She turned over and swam around the boat twice, happy in the smooth rhythm of her muscles. Just for practice she swam under the boat, in cold shadow for a moment, and came up with the sun again.

A motorboat had started somewhere. David, coming after me? she thought and climbed hastily into the row-boat. But the motorboat was now behind her. It was coming from the island. As she took up the oars she saw it. There was a policeman in uniform behind the wheel and in the stern sat another policeman, and a young man in a gray suit, a big young man with big, outstanding ears and a big bony nose. Motionless, she sat watching them, and the young man turned his head, looking at her; as they passed, she met his eyes, dark, gentle and a little sad.

Then they were gone. The rowboat rocked violently in the swell. They'd found Ted, she thought. *Now* what's going to happen?

She began to row homeward. All right. All right. I'll take things as they come. One at a time. I'm not going to worry. I'm not going to borrow trouble. I'll manage, all right. She took off her rubber cap and let her dark hair blow loose in the wind. She rowed slowly, and let the sun dry her woolen suit.

And if the police come asking questions about Ted, I'll

say he never came near us. Father doesn't know who it was he spoke to. I'd better tell him something this morning.

She got back to her room, unheard by David. She dressed and sat down by the open window. Now, if anybody comes, I'm ready, she thought. I don't care what I say. I don't care how many lies I tell.

She heard Sibyl go creaking down the stairs and a few moments later she followed.

"Certainly hope that laundry man comes today," said Sibyl. "I don't know how Mr. Harper's going to hold out, with only one clean shirt to last him a whole week."

It was like gears meshing. This was the day beginning. This was life.

"I'd better go into New York and try again to get him some more shirts," she said. "And David, too. But they're so scarce and so expensive."

"We could manage," said Sibyl, "if the laundry man'll do what he said he'd do. But it's nearly two weeks since he came. Doesn't bring back what he's got. Doesn't pick up what we got ready for him."

"If he doesn't come today, I suppose I'd better telephone . . . ?" said Lucia.

"Better had, ma'am," said Sibyl.

She drank a cup of coffee in the kitchen, waiting, very restless, for old Mr. Harper to come down. She was waiting for him in the hall.

"Father," she said, "you know that man who came to the boathouse night before last . . . ? I thought I'd better tell you something about him."

"No need to, m'dear. Not unless he comes again, and I don't think that's likely. No, I don't think he'll be back in a hurry. I sent him——"

"Yes, I know you did, Father. His name is Stanley Schmidt."

"Schmidt, eh! German name."

"He is a German. He's a very queer, shady sort of man, Father, and I shouldn't like it ever to get known that Bee had had anything to do with him."

"What d'you mean, Lucia? How is he—shady?"

"I think he's a Nazi agent," said Lucia, readily.

"What! What! Then he ought to be reported."

"I did. I sent an anonymous letter to the F.B.I.," said Lucia. "Only you can see that we can't possibly let Bee get involved in this."

"No. No, of course not. Have you told her your opinion of the fellow, Lucia?"

"I thought it was better not to," said Lucia in a special tone, quiet, very significant.

It was a tone she had used on Tom, too. It implied that she and she alone could understand the mystery of a young girl's heart. It had always made Tom uneasy and it had the same effect now upon old Mr. Harper.

"Well . . . I dare say you know best," he said.

David came down now, followed a few minutes later by his sister. They all sat at the table together; a steady breeze blew in at the open windows; the sun made the glass and silver twinkle. Lucia glanced at her father's silvery hair, Bee's soft fair mane, David's sandy hair, rough on his stubborn skull. Let them alone! she cried in her heart. Let them *alone!*

"Here comes the postman!" said David, pushing back his chair. "Let's see if there's anything from Dad."

He went out, letting the swing door bang behind him, and came back with the mail.

"Four," he announced. "Two for you, Mother, and one for Bee, and one for me. V-mails. Newspaper for Grandpa and a letter for Sibyl, and some bills and stuff."

He and Bee opened their letters at once, but Lucia kept hers to read when she was alone. Old Mr. Harper opened his New York paper.

"Fair and warmer," he read. "High time, too. Most unseasonable weather we've been having. Let's see now . . . Things look very promising in Europe. Here's Monty . . . A good man . . . What's this? Ha! Body of Slain Art Dealer found on Simm's Island."

"Go on!" said David, looking up.

" 'The Horton County police report the discovery yesterday in an isolated swamp on Simm's Island of the body of Ted Darby, 34, whose name——' "

"Give it to me!" cried Bee.

"What?" said Mr. Harper.

"Give it to me!" she cried again.

"I want to read it," he began, but she snatched it out of his hand, and ran out of the room and up the stairs.

"What's the matter with her?" asked Mr. Harper.

"Probably someone she's heard of," said David. "She knows a lot of those arty people."

"She needn't have snatched the paper out of my hands," said Mr. Harper.

"She'll have a fine time now," said David. "She'll call up all the girls she knows. My *dear!* Have you *heard* about What's-his-name?"

"Nevertheless," said Mr. Harper, "she could have waited a few moments."

"Oh, you know how girls are with a nice juicy bit of gossip," said David, man to man.

51

Does he know anything? Lucia thought. Or is he just being loyal to Bee?

She did not permit herself to show any impatience or haste, but as soon as breakfast was finished, she went upstairs and knocked on Bee's door.

"It's me, Bee. Let me in, dear."

The key turned in the lock and Bee opened the door.

"Well, you win," she said, with that square, scornful smile.

Lucia went in, closing the door after her.

"I don't want to 'win,'" she said. "It's just——"

"You have won, though," said Bee. "I'm finished."

"Bee, you're *not!* Anyone can make a mistake."

"Not quite such a big mistake. I suppose what they've got in the paper is true . . . !"

"I haven't seen it yet."

"He was arrested, just before the war. He had some sort of little art gallery, where he sold obscene pictures. The police locked up the gallery but somehow he got into it before the trial, and daubed all over the pictures. Amusing, isn't it? What's more, he's already been divorced once, and his first wife accused him of swindling her out of all her money. I suppose you knew all this."

"No, I didn't, Bee. I didn't know anything about him."

"Then how did you know he was so—awful?"

"But when I saw him, Bee, I knew."

"How?"

"Well, I did . . ." said Lucia.

"But *how?* I saw a lot of Ted, and I'd never have thought he was—like that. I mean, he was so gay, and he seemed to be so careless. Not like anyone who'd plot things . . .
52

Mother, I'd like to know how *you*—caught on to him when *I* didn't?"

"But, Bee, I'm so much older——"

"But you've never been anywhere. You've never seen anything of life."

"That's rather silly, Bee. I'm married and I have two children."

"That's nothing," said Bee. "You told me how you met Daddy when you were still in school. I don't suppose you ever even *thought* of another man. You got engaged at seventeen."

"You're only seventeen yourself," said Lucia.

"It's a different era. Girls are different. They're not brought up in that sheltered way." She paused. "I want to get away," she said.

"What d'you mean, Bee?"

"I couldn't *stand* staying here!" Bee cried. "I don't want to see anybody I know. I'm never going back to that art school."

"Bee, you didn't tell anyone about Ted, did you?"

"Oh, not by name. But everyone knew I had a beau . . . I used to mention places we'd been—things like that. God! If anyone ever finds out that I fell for someone like Ted, I'll—I don't know. I'd rather be *dead*."

"Don't say that, Bee."

"That happens to be exactly how I feel. God!"

"Bee, don't swear, dear."

"Oh, what does it matter? When I think that I let him kiss me—*lots* of times . . . I tell you I'd rather be *dead*, than have people know that."

Her blue eyes looked dark, in her face that was white

53

as paper. She was stung to desperation by this pain, this shame.

"I want to get *away!*" she said.

"Bee," said Lucia. "Bee, darling, the only way to stand things is to face them, take the consequences . . ."

"You're talking like *Grandpa!*"

I feel like him, thought Lucia.

"I suppose you've told Grandpa about Ted?"

"I haven't told anyone. I never intend to. You ought to know that, Bee."

"Well, I don't! I don't know *what* your ideas might be. You might think it was your 'duty' to tell Grandpa and Daddy. To teach me a lesson, or something."

"If you can think that . . ." said Lucia.

"I know you always do what you think is *best* for me," said Bee. "But you don't understand me."

Lucia said nothing.

"Will you help me to get away?" Bee demanded.

"Yes," said Lucia. "Let me see the paper, will you, Bee?"

"You'll help me to get away—at once?"

"Yes. We'll talk it over later. I'd like to see the paper, Bee."

She took it into her own room, and sat down on the edge of the unmade bed. The details of Ted Darby's past did not interest her. She was looking for something else.

The body was discovered yesterday afternoon by Henry Peters, 42, electrician, of Rockview, Conn. While walking along the shore, Mr. Peters was led, by the insistent barking of his dog, to enter the marsh . . .

Lieutenant Levy, of the Horton County police, stated the death had been caused by a wound in the throat with some pointed instrument, from twenty-four to thirty-six hours previous to the discovery. The police are following several clues.

What clues? Lucia thought. If they trace it back to me, back to Father, then nothing could save Bee. And those letters . . . ? Those letters! If I could somehow raise five thousand dollars . . . But there'd be nothing to stop him from asking for more, later on. He could hold back some of the letters. I wouldn't know.

She left the paper on the bed and went over to the window. Maybe that was Lieutenant Levy I saw this morning in the launch, she thought. He looked rather nice. Suppose I go to him and tell him the whole thing? After all, none of us has done anything criminal. It was probably illegal to take Ted away like that, but I wasn't covering up a crime, just an accident. It would be dreadfully hard on Father, but he can take it.

Only not Bee. She had a vision of Bee, standing up in a court, looking so tough and scornful. But, at heart, so desperate and wretched. Miss Holley, you had asked this man to meet you in the boathouse? You had visited this man in his hotel?

No! Lucia said to herself. I don't want Bee to face things, and take the consequence of things. I'm going to get her away somewhere. Angela, in Montreal? Unless you have to have papers to go to Canada in wartime . . . Well, then, there's Gracie's camp in Maine. I could telephone Gracie, right now.

Only she couldn't. Her father might hear her telephoning, or David might. No privacy was possible for her. It never had been, she thought, wondering. All my life, people have known everything I did, everywhere I went. I don't mean that anyone's ever been snooping or suspicious, it's just that somehow I've always lived in such a sort of public way, right out in the open.

I'll go into the village and telephone from the drugstore, she thought. I'll——

Sibyl was coming up the stairs, creaking, sighing a little. Reluctant to speak to anyone, Lucia hurried to the bathroom, to hide in there, but the door was locked.

"Just a moment!" said Bee, in a loud, choked voice.

Lucia hurried out into the hall.

"I think I'll do a little weeding," she said to Sibyl.

"Yes, ma'am," said Sibyl.

Gardening had no appeal for Lucia. She did it because it was a duty to have a victory garden. She put on a big burnt-straw hat and her heavy gloves. She took up the basket with shears and trowel, and went out of the back door to the patch the local gardener had dug and planted for her.

She was not at all sure which sprouting things were weeds. It's queer, she thought. Father and Bee and David all take it for granted I know what I'm doing. Only Sibyl knows better. There was another implement in the basket, a stubby little rakelike tool with curved prongs. She did not know the name of it, or its purpose, but it was her favorite. You couldn't do much harm with this, she thought, kneeling in the hot sun and scratching gently at the earth.

Mr. Donnelly can stop at the drugstore, she thought. I'll pop in and telephone to Gracie and arrange for Bee to go there at once. I'll tell Father and David that Gracie suddenly needed another counselor. Sibyl can do up a couple of wash dresses for Bee, and she can take my little gray coat for the train. We can send the other things after her. I've got enough cash.

56

"Mother . . ." said David.

She looked up at him and saw him frowning.

"There's a man who calls himself Donnelly," he said. "Says he's come to take you out for a drive."

"Well, yes," said Lucia, rising.

"You mean you're going out for a drive *alone* with him?"

"Why not?" said Lucia. "He was here to tea yesterday."

"So I heard," said David. "Well, suit yourself. But I think it's a mistake."

There was no time to argue with David now. Lucia ran upstairs to wash and change her dress. A hat, she thought; it looks better, and she put on the new hat Bee had persuaded her to buy in New York, a sort of sailor with an edging of white eyelet embroidery on the brim. She put on white gloves, too, glancing in the mirror. It seemed to her that she looked altogether correct and dignified.

"What time for lunch, ma'am?" Sibyl asked as she reached the lower hall.

"Oh . . . one o'clock as usual, Sibyl," Lucia answered. "I shan't be gone long."

I'm just going to take a little drive with a blackmailer, she thought. It's—hard to believe.

Donnelly was standing in the driveway, with one foot on the running board of a superb roadster. He was wearing a dark gray flannel jacket and slacks of a lighter gray. He looked handsome, aloof, and distinguished.

"Good morning!" Lucia said.

"Good morning," he answered, not smiling, and helped her into the car.

He drove off, down to the highway, with nonchalant skill.

"Would you mind stopping at the drugstore?" she asked.

57

"We can't use our car until we get the next coupons; and things pile up so."

"Certainly. If you'll call the turns . . . ?"

"Next turn right," she said, "and then straight ahead."

Isn't he even nervous? she thought. Doing a thing like this—a crime that could send him to prison for years? Isn't he the least bit ashamed? When they reached the village, she caught a glimpse of them in the plate-glass window of the furniture store, and it was astonishing. The big, well-dressed, well-groomed man, and beside him a lady with gloves and a stylish hat. Nobody would *believe* it, she thought.

"There's the drugstore, on the corner," she said. "I'll only be a minute."

She was mistaken. It took a long time to get the camp in Maine, and it took still longer to get Gracie Matthews, the proprietor.

"I *think* Miss Matthews is out on the lake," said the polished, anxious voice that answered the telephone. "I'll send after her."

It was hot in the booth and there was a very unpleasant smell. Lucia's hands grew damp, sweat came out on her forehead and her upper lip. Oh hurry up! Hurry up! she cried in her heart. I don't want to irritate him by making him wait so long.

Gracie, when at last she came, was very trying.

"Certainly, Lucia. I'd love to have the child. But not today. We couldn't meet the train. The station wagon's laid up. Say Monday."

"I'd like—she'd like to come today, Gracie."

"But what's the hurry, Lucia?"

"It just came into her head . . ."

58

"Well, tell her it'll be just as nice on Monday."

"Can't you arrange for tomorrow, Gracie?"

"Well, I could!" said Gracie. "But why? I'll have to arrange with the Camp Weelikeus people to pick her up at the station, and I don't like to do that if I can help it. We'll have our own station wagon on Monday, and I don't see *why* she can't wait till Monday. It's Friday already."

"You know how it is when you're young."

"I do not!" said Gracie, with her usual vigor. "When I was young, I didn't *expect* people to cater to my whims."

"Bee hasn't been too well. I don't think this climate——"

"If there's anything wrong with the child, don't send her here, Lucia. I've got thirty-eight girls and no trained nurse. I'm short two counselors."

"Bee would love to be a counselor, Gracie."

"She wouldn't do at all!" said Gracie. "She doesn't know anything about handling people. Too self-centered."

"She's not," said Lucia, mechanically. "Well, if you won't let her come tomorrow——"

"All right!" said Gracie. "Let her come. But it's only for *your* sake, Lucia. Personally, *I* wouldn't give in to an adolescent whim."

They spoke a little, about trains, about equipment.

"Two blankets," said Gracie. "A pillow. And—are you writing this down, Lucia?"

"Yes," said Lucia, lying without a qualm.

It was a long list.

"And if she has any hobbies, stamp album, scrapbook, knitting, water colors; anything like that, tell her to bring them along."

"I will, Gracie. I do appreciate this."

"I think you're very foolish," said Gracie, "to give in to your family the way you do. You can take my word for it, Lucia, that they'd think twice as much of you if you'd stand up to them."

"Maybe you're right," said Lucia. "But thanks ever so much, Gracie. I'll write."

She hung up the telephone and opened the door of the booth. I've been ages . . . she thought. And I didn't want to irritate him. He did not seem irritated. He got out politely and helped her into the car. He set off again through the village and along a tree-shaded road unfamiliar to her.

"Have you the money ready?" he asked.

"I couldn't," she said. "I couldn't get into town to the bank without everyone asking questions. I just want a little more time."

He drove on in silence for a way.

"Things are changed," he said, "with Darby dead."

"Yes," she said. "Yes, I suppose so."

"That makes it worse for the girl," he said.

"Not much," said Lucia, evenly. "It couldn't be."

"It will be worse," he said, "with all that will come out at the trial."

"What trial?"

"They will try the man who killed Darby," said Donnelly. "It was a good job he did, but they will try him."

"If they catch him."

"There's no great mystery in it, at all," said Donnelly. "There's a dozen people know the man."

Oh, no! Lucia thought. They can't. They *mustn't* arrest the wrong man.

"They could be mistaken," she said.

"You mean there are others would be glad to see him

out of the way?" he asked, and for the first time she saw him smile, a bleak and fleeting smile.

"Or it could have been an accident," she said.

He turned the car up a side road and slowed down.

"There's a roadhouse along here," he said. "It is a good one. Respectable. Would you have lunch with me there?"

"Oh, thank you," she said, startled. "But I've got to be home to lunch. I really ought to be getting home now."

"Any way you like it," he said, and backed the car down to the road. "Will you have the money tomorrow?" he asked.

"Monday," she said. "I can't do anything until Monday."

"I wouldn't be bothering you so," he said. "Only there's someone else in it."

"Someone else . . . ?"

"My partner," he said. "If it was me alone, I would drop the thing altogether. I would let you alone."

It's the oldest trick in the world, Lucia told herself, pretending to have a partner to blame things on.

"If I don't get the money," Donnelly went on, "he'll be out again after it."

"Again?" she asked. "You mean it's Nagle—Mr. Nagle?"

"You're quick," he said, glancing at her sidelong, and the blueness of his eyes surprised her.

"He's a horrible man," she said.

"Do you think so, now?" he asked. "He's been a good friend to me. It was him gave me my start when I first came over here."

"Did you come from the other side?"

"From Ireland," he said. "I had a great idea of this country, from all I'd heard. I ran away from home when I was fifteen, and I shipped as a cabin boy, the way I'd get here. But it took me near three years. I got here, right enough,

61

on the first voyage, but the mate would not let me go ashore. He'd seen it in my eyes, maybe, that I was intending to jump ship. So there I was, standing on the deck, looking at the Statue of Liberty."

He fell silent, with the shadow of a smile on his face.

"Well, how did you get here?" Lucia asked.

"It would be tejus for you to hear," he said, modestly.

"I'd like to hear," she said.

That was true. She wanted to know what manner of man this was, so that she might deal with him better.

"Back we went, to Liverpool," he said. "I was down on the docks one day, looking for a ship would take me back here, when a stranger comes up, very civil. We talk for a while and then he says, 'Come and have a drink.' I was sixteen then, but I looked older. I never had had a drink and to tell you the truth, I was afraid of it, from all I'd heard. But I went along with him, to see what would come of it. The next I knew I was in a ship bound for Singapore. To China we went, to Japan. When we got back to Liverpool, my head was full of the wonders I'd seen, and I wanted more. I got another ship sailing east, Egypt, India . . ."

He was silent again for a time.

"It is a queer thing," he said. "When I'd the money to go traveling in style, I went back to those places. But they were not the same. Well . . . Maybe it was youth that was missing."

"But how did you get to New York?"

"There's no story to that," he said. "I saved my pay and bought a ticket."

And how did you get to be a blackmailer? she thought.

He must have been an adventurous and romantic boy, and how had he come to this?

"What did you do when you got here?" she asked.

"It's a thing you wouldn't believe," he said. "I knew I'd a cousin in Brooklyn. That's all I knew; no address, nothing at all but his name. I thought I could look him up, and off I went to Brooklyn, thinking it would be a small town. You wouldn't believe it . . . I walked up and down the streets, asking here and there: Did you ever hear of a Mr. Mulligan from County Clare? After a while I asked a policeman. There's a club near by, he says, for the men of County Clare. Go there, he says, and maybe you'll learn something. Well, my cousin was well known there. Someone took me out to the saloon he had, and my troubles were over, the first day I set foot in the country."

"Did you go to work for your cousin?" Lucia asked.

"No . . ." he said. "That wasn't quite the way of it. Y'see, he made book on the side——"

"What's that?"

"He took bets on the horse races," Donnelly explained. "He took me out to Belmont Park with him and I met a lot of his friends, and they'd put me on to one thing or another. Then I got in with the ward boss. I got in with everyone."

"But didn't you have a job? A regular job?"

"I did not," he said, with a certain pride. "I've never had a job in my life, since the three voyages I made."

"But didn't you ever want a regular job with a salary?"

"I did not," he said. "That's not in my nature."

And what is your nature? she thought. She could not understand him at all. She could not even imagine what his life had been, or what sort of world he lived in. He doesn't seem like a really *bad* man, she thought. Could I possibly talk him out of this?

But her own house was in sight now. There was no more time.

"I'll ask my partner will he wait till Monday," said Donnelly, "but I don't know . . . Are you sure you'll have it Monday?"

"Yes," said Lucia.

By Monday Bee would be gone. And I'll think of something . . . she told herself. Some way out of this.

When they turned into the drive, there was a high van drawn up before the house. Eagle Laundry. The driver was standing beside it, and Sibyl stood on the steps above him.

"Says he's only coming once a month," she said.

"A *month!*" cried Lucia. "But we can't possibly manage——"

"Best we can do," said the driver, a lean, dark young man in a visored cap. "Haven't got the gas, haven't got the tires, haven't got the men to make a pickup any oftener."

"I'll do it *myself,*" said Sibyl, with a sort of passion, "before I wait a *month.*"

"Okay!" said the driver and got back into his van.

He backed and turned and drove off. Donnelly got out and helped Lucia to descend.

"I'll get in touch with you," he said, standing hat in hand.

She was surprised to see him turn to Sibyl with a smile and a gesture like a salute.

Chapter Seven

"What's the *idea?*" Bee demanded. "It's not *like* you, Mother, to go running around with that man."

"I'm not running around," said Lucia. "He wanted to show me an old house. Historic. We'd better make a list, Bee, of what you'll need. Aunt Gracie said blankets and a pillow."

"I can't carry all that," said Bee. "And there aren't any porters any more. Anyhow, Gracie's sure to have some spares, she's so damned efficient."

"Bee, don't swear. You know how Daddy hates it. And Aunt Gracie."

"She's not an aunt, thank God."

"She loves you and David to call her 'Aunt.'"

"We haven't, for years. Personally, I'm not crazy about her at all. I wouldn't go near her gruesome camp, if I didn't have to get away from here."

Lucia was sitting on the bed in Bee's room, and Bee stood before her, barefoot, in an ivory satin slip, so lovely, and so remote. How much did she care for Ted Darby? Lucia thought. How much does all this mean to her? I don't know. She's very nervous. She didn't eat anything for lunch. But is she sad about it?

I *ought* to know. I ought to be able to talk to my own child.

"David took me over to the Yacht Club this morning," Bee began.

"But how could he? We don't belong to it."

"He knows people there. He's rather good at making friends. There was rather a nice crowd there, not all kids, either. I'd have had a nice time there, only I kept thinking all the time. Suppose any of them ever heard about Ted and me. It makes me *hate* him."

"Bee! He's dead."

"I hate him!" said Bee. "I'll never forgive him for the harm he's done me."

"Bee, what harm, darling?"

"He's made it so I can never trust a man again."

"He hasn't, Bee. Just think of your father and Grandpa and David."

"You don't realize," said Bee, "how rare they are. You don't realize how lucky you've been. Your life may have been stodgy, but at least you've never been deceived and humiliated. What's that Donnelly man like?"

"Oh, he's very pleasant," said Lucia. "Now let's get out your list, Bee."

"He's good-looking," said Bee. "But *I* think he's a wolf."

"Well, it doesn't matter," said Lucia. "You'll take your flannel dressing gown, of course."

"The thing is, *you* wouldn't *know* if he was a wolf."

"Certainly I should. I'm not an idiot."

"Mother, did you *ever* have anyone proposition you?"

"I shouldn't tell you if I had," said Lucia.

"That's where you make a mistake," said Bee. "Pretending to be superhuman."

66

"I don't pretend to be superhuman."

"But you do. You wouldn't let anyone see you shed a single tear when Daddy left."

"Why should I let people see me if I'm not happy?"

"It would be a lot better if you did. If you weren't so darned inhibited, I could *talk* to you."

Oh, Bee! Can't you talk to me? Lucia cried in her heart. I want that so. I do understand things.

David was springing up the stairs.

"Mother," he said, from the hall. "Someone wants to see you."

His voice was ominous.

"Oh, who, David?"

"He says Mr. Donnelly sent him. I'll stick around," said David. "Keep an eye on the spoons. He's on the porch."

"Try on that brown skirt of mine, Bee," said Lucia. "I'll be right back."

"Mother, what goes on?" Bee demanded. "Who *is* this Donnelly man anyhow?"

"I told you," said Lucia. "I'll be back in a moment."

From a window in the sitting room, Lucia could see the man on the porch, and her heart sank. He was the worst yet, far the worst, the most obviously shady and suspect. He was young, a boy, in a dark red sweater clinging tight to his skinny torso; he had a rough mop of black hair, and small black eyes set too close to a broad nose.

I suppose there's a gang, she thought. A whole gang of blackmailers. They'll keep on and on . . . Well, the first thing is to get Bee away. Then I'll see. Then I'll think.

Cold with dismay, she opened the door and went out.

"You want to see me?" she asked.

"Yeah," said the boy. "Regal Snowdrop."

"What?" said Lucia.

"Regal Snowdrop," he replied, impatiently. "Mr. Donnelly tole me to come. To pick up your laundry."

"Oh . . . laundry?" she repeated.

"Yeah. Laundry."

She was silent, trying to understand. This must be a sort of code, she thought. He must have come to get money, or a check, or something. And suppose he won't go away without it?

"Mr. Donnelly said tomorrow," she said cautiously.

"Well, he tole us today. Said we got to make dis a special job. Pick it up today, bring it back Tuesday."

"You *mean* laundry?"

"Well, jeez, lady, didn't I *say*? Laundry. What gets washed and ironed. Laundry."

"Mr. Donnelly sent you?"

"He said youse was having problems."

"But how can you take it?"

"I got a car here," he said, jerking his head, and she saw, parked down the drive, a very shabby little blue coupé. "Listen!" he said. "I haven't got all night, lady."

"No," she said. "I'll get it for you."

She went into the house, a little dazed, into the kitchen to Sibyl.

"There's a boy here for the laundry," she said. "They're going to send it back Tuesday."

"It's a new laundry, ma'am?" asked Sibyl.

It seemed to Lucia that Sibyl was looking at her in an odd way.

"Yes," she answered, in a matter-of-fact way. "It's the Regal Snowdrop. If you'll give it to the boy, please, Sibyl."

David was waiting in the hall.

"What gives?" he asked briefly.

"Why, nothing," said Lucia. "It's simply a boy for the laundry."

"Why hasn't he got a van?"

"I don't know. I don't care, either."

"What's the Donnelly man got to do with our laundry?"

"He knew of this laundry, and he wanted to be obliging."

"He can oblige me by keeping away from here," said David.

"Don't be silly," said Lucia, mechanically, and went up the stairs to Bee.

"Who was it?" Bee asked.

"Oh, it was a boy for the laundry."

"How did Mr. Donnelly get into it?"

"He knew about the laundry, and sent the boy."

"Well, why?"

"Why *not?* I'm tired of all these questions!" cried Lucia.

"Mother!" said Bee, shocked. "I never saw you like this before."

"Like what?" Lucia asked coldly. "Turn around, Bee, and let me see how that skirt is in the back."

This won't do, she told herself. It's not like me to get so irritable. Only I'm—I don't know. I feel tired, I guess. But I've got to keep hold of myself or they'll all notice.

They were all dangerous to her, her father, her daughter and her son. And Sibyl? I don't know, she thought. But I've got to be let alone, to handle this thing. I've got to think it out carefully. I'll get Bee away. And I wish I could get Father away.

It seemed to her that if only she could hide them some-where, in safety, she could cope with the growing menace of her problems. If they were away, I could think, she told

herself, and knew in her heart that she had not been thinking, that she had no plans at all. Nothing but this quite
useless, stupid impulse to put things off, to gain one more
day from Donnelly and Nagle. I couldn't possibly get hold
of five thousand dollars, she thought.

But if I have to?

No, it wouldn't do any good. Blackmailers never stop.
They wouldn't give me back all the letters. I couldn't know.
She was in her own room, sewing a sash on Bee's house
coat, a sweet little house coat, of dusty pink rayon, faintly
fragrant of perfume. It made her want to cry; she did begin
to cry a little.

But that had to be stopped. Someone would come and
see her. Someone always came. There was always a knock
at the door. Everyone had a right to come to her; that was
what she was for, that was her function, her reason for
being. There was never an hour that belonged to her.

The knock came and it was Sibyl.

"Mr. Harper's got a man from the police downstairs,
ma'am," she said. "He's asked him to stay to tea."

"From the police?" Lucia cried.

"Yes, ma'am," said Sibyl. "But I don't think there's anything to worry about. He came right to the back door and
he spoke to me first. Says he's going to all the people in
this neighborhood, got to see if anybody knew Mr. Darby."

Was that compassion in Sibyl's voice, and in her amber-
flecked eyes? Did she know anything? Or everything? Don't
ask her. Don't try to find out.

"Is—where's Miss Bee?" she asked.

"She went out walking with a young man, ma'am."

"*What* young man?"

"Only the neighbors, ma'am. Seems to be a *nice* young man," said Sibyl.

It was compassion in her voice, and understanding.

"A *nice* young man," she repeated.

"I'll go down," said Lucia.

"Yes, ma'am. Mr. Harper's pleased to have company for tea. He doesn't worry about the police, ma'am. Got nothing on his conscience."

So you know? Lucia thought. But she could not be sure, and she did not want to be. She washed, and brushed her hair, and put on a fresh dress, and hastened down to the sitting room.

"Oh, Lucia . . ." said her father. "This is Lieutenant Levy, from the Horton County police. Lieutenant, my daughter, Mrs. Holley."

The lieutenant had risen, a tall young man with big feet and big, rather outstanding ears. He was not in uniform; in a neat gray suit he was not formidable, his smile was friendly, his dark eyes were thoughtful and mild. But she was very greatly afraid of him.

"The lieutenant is making some routine inquiries," said Mr. Harper. "He's investigating a homicide."

That *you* committed, Lucia thought.

Chapter Eight

The postman came, while they were at tea, and there was a V-mail from Tom. Lucia kept it, unopened, in her hand. There was comfort in it, and in the thought of Tom, who was so definite about things, so uncomplicated. Here, I'll look after this, Lucia, he would say. And if he saw that she had dreadfully mismanaged things, he would not be angry, or reproachful, or impatient. I think you made a bit of a mistake right here, Lucia . . .

She was very thankful that Levy asked her no questions at all. He didn't even want to talk about Ted. But Mr. Harper did.

"I read about the case in the newspapers," he said. "Didn't mention it, because I didn't want to alarm you or Bee. Too near home, what? But it looks very like one of these gangster murders to me."

"Let's not talk about it," said Lucia suddenly, and more loudly than she meant.

"Certainly, m'dear. Certainly," said her father, instantly contrite.

It was as Sibyl had said, he was pleased to have company for tea. He's lonely, Lucia thought. He misses his office and his club. And he misses Tom so very much. They used to talk. He's lonely and he's getting old . . .

He was getting old in such a clean, fine way, his silver hair cropped close, his nails so neatly clipped, his necktie pressed that morning, a brown and a yellow check . . . I could cry, she thought, and was shocked at herself.

Levy asked her if she had read a certain book very popular just then.

"Well, no," she answered. "Have you?"

He had, and he talked a little about it. He's not—right, she thought. He's not like a policeman. Suppose he really isn't one? Suppose he's someone that Nagle sent?

Her home was invaded, it was no longer a safe refuge for her people. If I could only put Father on his guard somehow, she thought, so that he wouldn't say anything . . . But maybe he had already 'said something,' had, in his innocence, completely betrayed himself?

She looked and looked at Levy, trying to read his face. In vain. He looked mild, a little sad, nothing more. If he was a policeman, why did he stay and stay and stay, like this? To trap someone.

He stayed and stayed, and Bee came home. She brought a boy with her, and he seemed to Lucia a sinister boy, dark and unsmiling; his shoulders were too broad, he looked powerful and aggressive.

"Mother," Bee said, "this is Owen Lloyd."

Owen took her outstretched hand in a grip that made her wince. He then shook hands in turn with Mr. Harper and Lieutenant Levy.

"You're looking into that case over on the island, sir?" he asked Levy. "This Darby?"

Lucia was stricken with terror to see how white Bee grew. If Levy looked at her *now* . . . she thought.

"Oh, we have our routine," Levy answered. "We're visit-

73

ing everyone in the neighborhood, to see if we can pick up any information."

"My mother'll give you plenty, sir," said Owen. "She's been wanting to go to the police with her story. She says that early Wednesday morning she looked out of her window, and she saw a man and a woman, standing up in a motorboat between here and the island. Struggling, she says they were. She turned away to get her glasses and when she found them, and looked again, the man had disappeared, and the woman was heading for the island."

"Why didn't your mother come to us, Mr. Lloyd?"

"My father and I put her off it," said Lloyd. "We thought maybe she was mistaken, and she'd get herself all upset for nothing. She's pretty high-strung, you know."

"I see!" said Levy.

He finished his second cup of tea and rose.

"Thanks very much, Mrs. Holley," he said. "It's been very enjoyable."

"Stop in again, sir," said old Mr. Harper. "I'd be very interested to hear anything about this case you feel at liberty to tell."

"I will, Mr. Harper!" said Levy, earnestly.

Now it was the boy Owen who stayed and stayed, and Lucia stayed, too, until her father left to take his before-dinner stroll. Then she went up to her own room, longing for the solace of Tom's letter.

But it was one of his queer letters, filled with an almost wild hilarity. She had had two or three others like this and they had disturbed her profoundly. Tom never drinks too much, she thought. It's not that. Is it battle that makes him so excited?

She tried to think of her good-humored, nonchalant Tom

74

in battle. She recalled the battles she had seen in news-reels. Flames, smoke, hideous noises, whining, droning, screaming, shattering crashes. I can't . . . she thought. It's no use. He's too far away . . .

She sat on a chest by the window, in a curious apathy, until David came knocking at the door.

"Sibyl says you got a letter from Dad," he said. "What does he say?"

"Why, nothing very special, dear," she said. "Of course he's not able to tell anything much."

"Owen was in the Pacific zone," David said.

He glanced at Lucia, frowning a little.

"Well, if it isn't over pretty soon," he said, "it'll be my turn."

He had never spoken of that before, he said it now as if it were a question, as if he were asking her, what is this? What shall I think about life and war and death?

He looked so young, so slight. No! she said in her heart. *No!*

And who was she saying that to? She had no power to protect her own people, her own children. The walls of her home were falling down; there was no refuge.

"Have you got a clean shirt for dinner, dear?" she asked. "Give that one to me when you take it off. The collar . . ." She touched the collar at the back of his thin young neck. "It's a little frayed . . ."

"Oh, all right," he said with a sigh and went away dis-appointed.

Chapter Nine

Lucia sat up in bed to read over the letter she had written the night before.

DEAR TOM:

Bee is going to Gracie's camp for a week or two. I think it will do her good. It really is pretty dull here.

Dull . . . she repeated to herself, but she let it stand.

You ask how the car is standing up. We scarcely ever use it on account of tires and gas, so it will be in nice shape when you get back. I told Sibyl you sent her your best regards and she said to tell you she prays for you every night. She *means* it, too, Tom. I don't know what I'd do without Sibyl.

She leaned back against the pillows, thinking of Sibyl and what she might know. It was a sparkling morning, but she had no thought of going out. She had to stay here, right here, inside the house, so that nothing could happen. I will stop things, too, she told herself. I don't know now just what I'll do, but as they come up . . .

Nagle and Donnelly and Levy . . . Five thousand dollars . . . My jewelry! she thought suddenly. She had her diamond engagement ring, an emerald ring her father had given her on her twenty-first birthday, a string of pearls her mother had left her, her grandmother's diamond bracelet, all in the safe-deposit box in the New York bank. I could borrow on them, she thought. Or if it comes to the worst, I could even sell them.

To pay blackmail? Yes, she thought. It may be terribly stupid, but that's what I'm going to do. It'll keep those men quiet for a while, anyhow. It'll gain time.

And time must be her ally. She clung to that belief. She lived by it, now. Every day made the end of the war nearer, every day that no telegram came about Tom was a day gained. She lived as if holding her breath. Just get through this day.

She got a book and read it in bed, with stubborn determination. It was a mystery story she had got out of the lending library for her father, and she was not fond of mystery stories. Nobody in them ever seems to feel *sorry* about murders, she had said. They're presented as a problem, m'dear, her father said. What's more, they generally show the murdered person as someone you can't waste any pity on. *I'm* sorry for them, she said, I hate it when they're found with daggers sticking in them and their eyes all staring from poison and things like that.

Yet how little pity did she feel for Ted Darby! I really did that, she thought amazed. I concealed a body. Anyhow I took it away. And when I came back—after that—nobody could see anything wrong with me—anything queer. Maybe I haven't got so much feeling, after all. Maybe I'm rather too tough.

I'd better be, too, she thought, as she rose and began to dress.

Breakfast that morning had an unusual quality. She was surprised to find all her family so cheerful and talkative. Surprised but not pleased; it worried her. They were too innocent. They seemed this morning like victims, pitiably unaware of what darkly menaced them.

She saw the menace more vividly now than ever before. Her father standing in the dock. My dear, I don't like to be hurried, she'd heard him say all her life. But, once accused, he could be hurried. Question after question would be shot at him. She pictured him growing a little confused, indignant. She could imagine his overwhelming shame when he heard of Bee's folly. He and David. Tom would be different, she thought. He'd just be so sorry for Bee.

"Owen's mother wants to call on you," said David.

"Owen? Owen?" said Mr. Harper. "Oh, yes! Nice lad."

"He's twenty-three," said David. "And he was in the Army two years."

"His mother's a frightful nitwit," said Bee. "But she's rather nice. They're quite a nice family."

"Rolling in money," said David, complacently. "Absolutely rolling. I found them."

"Oh, you're a marvel!" said Bee, with scornful good humor.

"I know the art of making friends," said David. "Mother, the Lloyds asked me to lunch today. That all right with you?"

"Perfectly, dear," said Lucia. "Have you got a clean shirt?"

She went into the kitchen to consult with Sibyl.

"If that icebox man doesn't come today," said Sibyl. "I don't know how we're going to keep a thing over Sunday."

They stood in gloomy silence for a moment.

"I'd better get to market early," said Sibyl. "Better leave everything and get the nine o'clock bus."

"I'll do the marketing, Sibyl."

78

"No, ma'am," said Sibyl. "Better for me to do it Saturday. I'll go early and get back in time to iron those little things for Miss Bee." She thought for a time. "Best give me twenty dollars, ma'am."

"I'll send for a taxi," Lucia said. "And you'd better keep it, Sibyl. I'll pay it by the hour."

Bee wanted to go to the village, too; she and Sibyl set off in the cab. David had gone already; old Mr. Harper was taking his walk. Lucia put on an apron and was starting to wash the breakfast dishes when the telephone rang. She dried her hands and went to answer.

"Mrs. Holley, please," said a man's muffled voice.

"This is me," said Lucia.

"Donnelly speaking. I'd like to see you this morning for a few moments, Mrs. Holley. What time could I come?"

"Oh . . . !" she cried. "I'm afraid . . . You'd really better not come *here*."

"Well, I must see you somewhere, then."

"I don't know . . . I don't see . . ."

"Down at the railroad station, maybe. I am there now."

"I couldn't. I couldn't get away."

"I am sorry to bother you," he said.

"Can't you tell me what it is on the telephone?"

"It is not a good thing to be talking too much on the telephone," he said.

"I don't see *how* I can meet you *anywhere*."

"It is important," he said. "Else I shouldn't be bothering you. Is there someplace maybe near by where you can see me for a moment?"

"Wait," she said. "Let me think . . . There's the boathouse here. If you go by the shore road and then along a little path, you can get into it without anyone seeing you."

79

"What time will I be there?"

"Oh . . . It's very hard for me to say . . . I mean, I'll have to wait for a chance to slip out."

"I'll go there now," he said, "and I'll wait."

"Wait upstairs, please," she said. "I'll try to come right away, but I *might* be delayed."

"Don't worry," he said. "I'll wait."

She hung up the telephone and stood beside it, irresolute, flustered. There are such a lot of things . . . she thought. People are *idiots* to talk about getting married and being your own mistress, so much more free than women with jobs.

If Bee comes back and finds the dishes in the sink . . . Even unsuspicious Father would think that was queer . . . What reason can I give anyone for running out of the house?

"Oh, I don't know!" she cried aloud in angry desperation. "It's nobody's business."

She decided to finish washing the dishes, and leave them draining. Then I'll tell them, if they ask me, that I felt like being alone. I'll say I wanted to *think*. Why shouldn't I? Other people do.

She ran upstairs to powder her face and her anger increased, to see herself flushed and disheveled. Anger at them, her father, her children, and Sibyl. It's none of their business if I feel like leaving the house for a few moments. And the beds not made . . . I've got to make Father's bed. He's so neat. He'd hate to come back and find it not done.

Bee ought to make her own bed. Oh, Bee, my darling . . . ! Nagle and Mr. Donnelly, and maybe other people, horrible people, reading your poor silly letters. Trying to make money out of them . . .

This afternoon Bee would be going away, perhaps for weeks. Perhaps this trouble couldn't be kept away from her. I've got to make her bed, Lucia thought. Or she'd think I didn't love her.

She could not stop. She made David's bed too. She picked up, she tidied up the bathroom. David had left a ring in the tub. She took up the scouring powder and the rag. No! she told herself. I've got to see Mr. Donnelly and hear whatever it is. This is silly.

But she had to clean the tub. She ran down the stairs, and she nearly cried, because she wanted so terribly to empty the ash trays and straighten up the sitting room. She ran across the lawn and into the cottage part of the boathouse, hot, angry, miserable.

She went through the sitting room on the ground floor and up the stairs, and Donnelly stood on the landing waiting for her.

"I'm sorry I kept you waiting," she said briefly. "But I was very busy this morning."

"You hurried too much," he said. "You're out of breath and all. I did not mind waiting."

"Well . . . Let's go in here," she said, and led the way into one of the two bedrooms, a big room, dimly lit through the grimy windows, with two sagging couches against the wall, everything covered thick with dust.

Lucia sat down in a rocking chair with a torn and discolored antimacassar on the back, and Donnelly stood before her.

"Why is it the ladies don't carry fans any more?" he asked.

"Well, I don't think I ever did," Lucia answered.

"No. You're too young. I remember a long time ago, I
81

was in New Orleans and there was a girl there, French, she was, and dark like yourself, and she'd a little fan, purple, maybe. I don't know the names of those pretty, light colors."

He was trying to give her time to grow calmer, and she responded courteously,

"There's mauve," she said, "and lavender and violet."

"They are pretty names."

There was a silence. She rocked and the floor boards squeaked. Donnelly stood before her, arms at his sides, his head averted, immaculate and elegant in his dark suit and handsome olive-green tie.

"I am sorry this ever began at all," he said. "If I was in it alone, I'd hand you the letters and you'd hear no more about it."

"Well . . ." she said with a sigh.

"I told Nagle you said give you till Monday. He did not like that. It was all I could do to keep him from coming here himself."

"That wouldn't do him any good. It would only make things worse."

"That's what he wants. He wants to keep after you till you'll be desperate and get the money one way or another."

"But not *you*, of course!" she cried.

"Not me," he said.

A great anger was rising in her against Donnelly. He's a crook, she thought, and probably a very smart one. He's trying to trap me in some way. He's trying to deceive me. He's—I don't know what he's trying to do but it's something horrible.

"So Mr. Nagle's to blame for *all* of this?" she said, with a faint smile.

82

"Well, no . . ." Donnelly said. "No. I couldn't say that. When he first brought it up, I didn't make any objections."

"But now you've changed. You've got very high-minded about it."

"Now I wish to God I could stop it all," he said. "Only I cannot. Nagle is a man hard to handle. There'll be money coming to us from this deal we made. But things are bad now for the two of us, and he is nervous. He likes to have a bit of ready cash by him, in case anything'll be going wrong."

"But not *you*. *You* don't want this money, this blackmail!"

"I do not," he said. "Only I cannot hold Nagle off longer than Monday. Are you sure you can get the money that day?"

"Yes," she said carelessly, recklessly.

Bee would get away this afternoon, and there would be all Sunday to think things over, to make a plan.

"Will I come out here to get it?" he asked. "Or would you rather meet me in New York?"

"I'll meet you in New York," she said.

"When would it suit you?"

"I'll meet you outside Stern's on Forty-second Street," she said, "at noon."

She rose.

"There's one little thing more . . ." he said. "You'll only need bring forty-five hundred with you."

"Oh! How *nice* of Mr. Nagle!" she cried. "How kind and nice of him to let me off five hundred dollars!"

"I gave him five hundred," said Donnelly. "I told him

83

it was you sent it. I did that, the way he wouldn't be out here bothering you."

She looked straight into his face that was as it always was, handsome, strong boned, but blurred and veiled by something.

"I don't believe you," she said. "I don't believe any of this."

He said nothing and she went past him, out of the room and down the stairs. Liar! she cried to herself. Liar! I hate him!

She had never felt anything like this turmoil of the spirit, this anger. He's the one who brought the letters here. He's the one I'm to pay the blackmail to. And he says he did that. For me. Liar. Blackmailer. Contemptible crook. I hate him so . . .

She went back to the house, thinking of nothing but her anger. I will go to the police, she thought. I'll manage some way to keep Father out of it. The police will see to it that nobody ever knows anything about Bee's letters. They'll just arrest those men. That man!

She opened the front door and Bee came out of the sitting room. And at the sight of her child, all the other things rose in Lucia like a rushing tide. Getting Bee's clothes ready, packing, the lunch, the familiar feeling of things undone, things demanding attention.

"Oh, you're back, dear?" she said. "Did you get the things you wanted?"

"No," Bee answered. "But it doesn't matter. I'm not going to the camp, Mother. I sent Aunt Gracie a telegram."

"Bee! But why?"

Bee stood facing her, slight and lovely and curiously stern, all in white.

84

"I'm too much worried and upset about you," she said. "I'm shocked."

"What are you talking about?" cried Lucia.

"That man," Bee said. "The way you're acting with that man."

Chapter Ten

Lucia had felt irritated by her children now and then, and sometimes—not often—impatient. But this was anger.

"Don't talk like that," she said, curtly.

"How do you think I feel—we feel—David and I?"

"David would never be so silly and offensive."

"He feels just the way I do. When we found out that you'd sneaked out of the house to meet that man——"

"Don't say 'sneaked'!"

"You did! The moment we were gone——"

"I have things to talk over with Mr. Donnelly, and I'll see him when and where I think best."

"*What* things to talk over?"

"I certainly don't have to account to you," said Lucia. "And I'm not going to listen to any more of this. You'll have to go to the camp, as we arranged——"

"I'm not going. Not unless you promise me you won't see that man again. Ever."

"How can you dare to talk like that?" cried Lucia. "As if you had absolutely no confidence in your own mother."

"I met David in the village," said Bee, in a cold, even voice, "and that Halford kid gave us a lift home. You weren't in the house, and David thought maybe you'd taken

86

out one of the boats. So we went to see. We thought we heard voices in the boathouse, and we opened the door——"

"You stood there listening!"

"We didn't. We came right out. We were absolutely shocked."

"Then you're both very silly—and offensive. I don't want to hear another word about this."

"David and I consider that we have an obligation to Daddy——"

"Shut up!" said Lucia, and went past Bee, into the house and up the stairs to her room.

I shouldn't have said that, she told herself. It was vulgar and horrible. Only, I don't care. My own children turning against me like that. I can't believe David would have ideas like that. I'm going to speak to him now, this instant.

But she did not move.

I can't speak to David about such a thing, she thought. About meeting a man. It's impossible. But David couldn't possibly think I was 'shocking.' Suppose I did step out to the boathouse to see Mr. Donnelly for a few moments, because I had things to talk over with him . . .

Then she remembered what it was that she had to talk over with Mr. Donnelly. Oh, no! she cried to herself. Let the children be shocked. Let them be exasperating, and offensive, anything at all. Anything was better than that they should know the truth. David would never get over it, she thought, if he knew that his sister had written letters like that to Ted Darby. And Bee would never, never get over it, if she knew that that Darby man didn't really care for her at all. That he was just planning to make money out of her.

I said I'd get the money by Monday, she thought. Mr.

87

Donnelly said that if I didn't, he couldn't keep Nagle from coming out here. I can't let that happen.

Then I'll have to get the money. Four thousand, five hundred dollars. I've got eight hundred, about, in my account now, and there'll be the allotment check and Mr. Fuller's check next month. But I have to pay the rent and the food and the storage on our furniture, and all the other things. My jewelry? I don't know how much it's worth. Thousands, maybe. But maybe not.

Those people who make loans . . . That's the thing! She remembered seeing advertisements in newspapers; she remembered hearing something on the radio. Privacy, they said. Your personal signature alone.

I know how stupid and wrong it is to pay money to blackmailers. But that's what I'm going to do. I want *time*. Time to get Bee away. Time for—other things. I don't know just what. Only, if I keep that Nagle man away, even for a while, there's a chance of something happening. He might have to run away. Mr. Donnelly said so.

A sort of fever possessed her. Her anger against Bee was forgotten; she was desperately impatient for Monday to come, so that she could get the money, and pay Nagle, and have peace. For a time.

There was a knock at the door.

"Who is it?" she called, with an unusual sharpness.

"Me," answered David's voice.

"Well, do you want anything special, David?" she asked. "I've got a headache."

"It's important," he said, and she opened the door.

"Now, if you're going to begin to nag, David——" she said.

"I'm not," he said. "I think you're making a big mistake,

taking up with that fellow, but I told Bee I was darn sure there was no real harm in it. Just folly."

His extreme calmness was as exasperating and as humiliating as Bee's shocked indignation.

"I'm not going to be talked to like this by a boy of fifteen," she said. "I know what I'm doing——"

"All right! All right!" he said, soothingly. "I came to tell you that Mrs. Lloyd's downstairs."

"Who is Mrs. Lloyd?"

"She's Owen's mother. She's got another son, around my age, and a daughter. They're nice people. They've got two cars and a chauffeur. They've got a swell cabin cruiser."

"What does she want?"

"Why, I suppose she just wants to see you," said David.

"I can't see her now. This time of the morning—and I'm not dressed."

"You look all right," said David. "Anyhow, she won't care."

"No, I can't!" said Lucia. "I'll—tell her I'll come to call on her."

"Mother, she's *right here!*" said David. "I can't tell her you won't come downstairs."

David was shocked now, and, in a way, he was not to be blamed. I'm being—very queer, Lucia thought.

She stopped being queer, at once.

"I'll be very glad to see your Mrs. Lloyd, dear," she said. "I'll be down in a minute."

Mrs. Lloyd was a thin woman, with rouge daubed carelessly on her hollow cheeks, and light hair in a thick, careless bun at the nape of her neck. She wore a white blouse too big for her, with cuffs that half covered her hands, and a bunchy gray skirt, and emerald-green wedgies. But she

89

had a sweet voice, a sweet, triangular smile. Like a cat, Lucia thought. A mother cat, letting the kittens walk all over her.

"It's a *fearsome* time to come bothering you," she said. "But Owen and Phyllis and Nick got at me. I've been wanting to call—but really I never get around to anything." She paused. "I really don't know what I do all day," she said, with a sort of wonder.

"The days just go," said Lucia.

"Yes, *don't* they?" said Mrs. Lloyd. "Do you think you could possibly lunch with me at the Yacht Club some day soon? It's rather sweet there. You sit on the lawn—if it isn't *raining*, of course—and they bring little trays with fishes on them. *Painted* on them, I mean. A really very wonderful girl paints them. She supports her mother and her greataunt in a tiny little cottage, and she paints simply anything. You send things to her, or she comes to the house. I didn't seem to have anything to send her, so I put her in our sun porch, and she painted simply adorable little fishes all over, on tables, you know, and on the walls. She does flowers, too, if you ask for them. And she did a simply huge horse's head for Mrs. Wynn, almost *too* huge, I thought, right over the mantelpiece. Do you paint, Mrs. Holley?"

"Why, no, I don't," Lucia answered, soothed and pleased by this most amiable guest.

"I don't, either, but I'd love to. Or play the piano, or something like that. When the children were little, they went to the Dame Nature School, and they played in a little orchestra. All the children did. It would be rather lovely if everyone kept *on* playing in orchestras, all their lives, don't you think? But do you think you could possibly come to lunch at the Yacht Club?"

90

"I'd love to," said Lucia.

"Tomorrow, perhaps? We could have their Sunday brunch. And David says your father is here with you. We should so love to have him—and there's a bar in the club-house. He'd like that, don't you think?"

"I'm sure he would," said Lucia.

"Then may we call by, tomorrow? The station wagon will hold us all. Twelve, do you think? I've tried to train myself to sleep late on Sunday mornings, but I can't do it. I seem to be so *hungry*. And then, it's rather charming, somehow, to go prowling around in the house, with everyone else asleep. Do you think I might ask that policeman to lunch with us? If you like him, that is."

"Well, what policeman?" asked Lucia.

"That Lieutenant Levy. I think he's so kind. And it would be nice to have another man. I'm so glad that really sinister case is settled, aren't you? That man on Simm's Island, I mean."

"Settled . . . ?" said Lucia.

"They've caught the murderer, and I'm *very* glad, because my Phyllis is only nineteen, and I do hate the thought of a murderer in the neighborhood."

"Do you know what man they've arrested?"

"I really know quite a lot about it," said Mrs. Lloyd. "We had Lieutenant Levy in for cocktails yesterday and he told us. It's a horrible man, named Murray. Underworld, you know. He was an enemy of that poor Darby man, and they came out here together on the same train. Imagine, in that teeming rain! I was rather surprised, because *I* thought he'd been killed by a woman."

"Oh! Did you?"

"Yes. Nick went over to the island, with another boy.

Boys that age seem strangely gruesome, don't **you think**? Nick found this list there, in the reeds."

"A list?"

"A market list. Quite pathetic, somehow. I mean, grated cheese, two points, and things like that. You simply felt sure it was a *nice* woman, not black market, of course, with those points all written down. I thought it was probably someone goaded to frenzy."

"That's very interesting," said Lucia. "I'd love to see the list, if you'd let me."

"But I gave it to Lieutenant Levy. It did seem to be a clue, don't you think?"

"Oh, I do!" said Lucia.

It must have been one of my lists, she thought. An old one. I must have pulled it out of my pocket with the bandanna. And Lieutenant Levy's got it. He'll know ways to trace it back to me; he'll know I was there.

But they arrested a man—after they'd got the list. So they can't think the list is very important.

"This Murray they've arrested . . ." she asked. "Is he a criminal?"

"Oh, heavens, yes!" said Mrs. Lloyd. "He'd just come out of another prison. He's a dope-peddler, and what untold harm they do, don't they?"

"Yes, they *do!*" said Lucia, earnestly.

"I was rather surprised," Mrs. Lloyd went on, "because I'd felt quite sure those two women had had something to do with it."

"What two women?"

"Oh, didn't I tell you? Well, you know, the morning the poor man was killed, I got up frightfully early, about half-past five, and I went out on my little balcony. And I saw
92

a little motorboat, a little launch, like yours, you know, and two women were standing up in it, having a struggle."

But you didn't! Lucia thought. If there'd been another motorboat out, I'd have seen it. Certainly I'd have heard it. And there wasn't any. I could swear to that.

Mrs. Lloyd rose.

"I so look forward to our brunch tomorrow," she said. "You and your father and your two children. And shall I ask the policeman?"

"Oh, I think he's very nice," said Lucia.

David was not home to lunch, and Lucia sat at the table with her father and Bee, in a dream. It seemed to her that the world could offer nothing more desirable than Mrs. Lloyd's Sunday brunch. She had a remarkably clear vision of it in her mind; all of them sitting on a shady lawn, holding trays upon which fishes were painted, red and gold; Bee in her blue dress, she thought, and the sky pure blue, the calm sea a deeper blue. Father will enjoy it, she thought. And Bee . . . It's exactly the sort of thing Bee needs. There'll be Owen, and the daughter who's nineteen, and maybe other people will come. Maybe this is the beginning of a really happy summer for her.

"What did you think of Mrs. Lloyd?" Bee asked, with cold formality.

"I like her very much," said Lucia. "*Very* much. I don't know when I've met anyone I liked more."

"I don't think she's all that wonderful," said Bee, a little surprised, and still cold. "Of course, she's goodhearted and all that, but I think she's pretty silly. And irresponsible."

"'Irresponsible'?" old Mr. Harper repeated. "That's a strong word, m'dear."

"Well, I mean muddled," said Bee. "For instance, one

93

time when I met her in the village, she asked me if I'd seen *Life with Father*. I said no, and she said she'd seen it just the week before, and she told me things out of it. But what she told me about wasn't *Life with Father* at all. It was a boring little play I'd seen with Sammy before we came out here."

"Well," said Mr. Harper, "considering the sort of plays they produce nowadays, I can't say that I blame the good lady."

"Honestly, Grandpa!" said Bee.

She always took him up on things like that; she began now to defend the theater of her own day, and old Mr. Harper was quite as ready to praise, and to describe, plays he had seen in London, in his boyhood. Lucia waited impatiently for the first pause.

"Mrs. Lloyd's asked us all to brunch with them tomorrow at the Yacht Club," she said. "She specially wants you, Father."

"Me?" he said, with a short laugh. He was pleased.

"I think it would be very nice," said Lucia.

"Well, they do know how to have a good time, the whole family," said Bee. "They're all popular, too. There's always a lot going on in their house, people coming and going and the telephone ringing."

"Ha . . . shouldn't care for that, myself," said Mr. Harper.

"I love it," said Bee. "This house is like a graveyard."

That's meant for me, thought Lucia. All right; I know I'm not popular.

"They're calling for us at twelve," she said.

Now it was done. She was letting Murray stay in prison. Only over the week end, she told herself. I want Bee to get a little established with the Lloyds. I want them to see what she's really like. Then, later on, if they hear anything —about Ted Darby, or anything else, they'll see . . . Just this brunch, and then I'll tell Lieutenant Levy.

That Murray has been in prison before. A few days won't seem so terrible, to him. He's a criminal, anyhow. Being a dope-peddler is as bad as being a murderer. It's murdering people's souls.

I mustn't talk that way to myself. Like a cheap movie. I don't know anything about Murray, except what Mrs. Lloyd said, and maybe she is a little—irresponsible. All I really know is, that he's in jail for something he didn't do. I could get him out. And I'm letting him stay there.

That's a sin, she said to herself.

A car was coming up the drive; someone was mounting the steps. It's the police, she thought. They've traced that market list.

"I'll go, Sibyl!" she called, and pushed back her chair.

A small delivery van stood outside the house and the driver, a burly man in a singlet, stood leaning against the porch rail.

"Holley?" he asked.

"Yes."

"Package," he said, and went back to the truck, returning with a big bundle clumsily wrapped in brown paper.

"Well, but from where?" Lucia asked.

"Wouldn't know," he said. "I was tole to deliver it to Mrs. Holley."

He held it out to her and she took it, and was surprised by its heaviness. The driver turned away, got into his truck, and drove off.

"What is it, Mother?" asked Bee, standing beside her.

"It's probably something Sibyl ordered," said Lucia. "I'll take it into the kitchen. Go on with your lunch."

But Bee followed her into the kitchen; she began to pick at the string on the package when Lucia set it down on the table.

"Why are you so inquisitive?" cried Lucia. "*Do* go back to your lunch, Bee!"

Sibyl stood by the window, silent.

"Good lord!" cried Bee. "It's a ham! A simply huge ham!"

"Came from my nephew," said Sibyl. "Told me he'd send one, soon as he could."

"Without any red points?" Bee demanded.

"I've got plenty of red points, Miss Bee," said Sibyl, mildly.

Bee followed her mother into the hall.

"I hope Sibyl isn't mixed up in any black market business," she said. "I *despise* that."

"You ought to know Sibyl better than that," said Lucia.

"Well, just the same, I call it very queer," said Bee. "A simply huge ham arriving, and nobody asking for red points, or money, or anything."

Lucia sat down at the table again. I don't know where that ham came from, she thought. And I'm not going to think about it. Ever.

Chapter Eleven

Dear Tom: We've met some very nice people here, named Lloyd. It was David who found them, of course; he's like you about making friends. Mrs. Lloyd's asked us all to brunch with them tomorrow at the Yacht Club, and it ought to be fun. Mrs. Lloyd says they serve lunch on little trays with fishes painted on them by a girl . . .

This is nonsense, she thought. How can I write drivel like this to Tom? Tom—in a war? But I don't know what to write to him. If he knew what I'd done . . . What I'm do-ing *now*. Letting an innocent man stay in prison.

It's a sin. What I did about Ted Darby was illegal. I dare say it was foolhardy. But this is a sin. It's bearing false witness against your neighbor, not to speak when you know the truth. Suppose Mrs. Lloyd is mistaken, and Murray isn't a criminal and a dope-peddler? Suppose he's a per-fectly innocent man?

She had to get the letter finished, some sort of letter. But she was troubled by visions, very foreign to her. She imagined Tom standing on the deck of a ship that was rushing through the water; she could see his blunt-featured face raised to a sky sparkling with southern stars. She knew, in some way, that he was not thinking of her, but beyond that she could not go; she could not imagine the thoughts

97

of a man with battle and death before him and behind him. She felt desolately remote from him, as never before.

That's because of what I've done, she thought. It's made a separation.

She took up her pen and finished the letter, fluently, quickly, and pointlessly. It was late, and she took a bath and got into bed, and turned out the light. And then she had visions of Murray. He was shaking the bars of his cell and shouting. Before God, I am innocent! I am an innocent man! His head was shaved and he was wearing a shapeless gray uniform. I am an innocent man! he cried. But nobody believed him.

Suppose he kills himself? she thought, and sat up in bed, aghast. The prisoner hanged himself in his cell last night. The prisoner cut his wrists. The prisoner went violently insane.

I'll have to tell Lieutenant Levy now, she thought. But I'll have to tell Father first. And then we'll get Lieutenant Levy on the telephone, and they'll let Murray out tonight.

She went along the hall to her father's room; she stood outside it, barefoot, in her pajamas, her black hair loose on her shoulders. Then she heard him cough a little, an elderly cough. A lonely cough. Did he lie awake in the nights, and think of his wife, who had lain beside him for twenty years? Did he think of the days when his life had been vigorous and stirring, and not lonely?

I won't do it! she said to herself. Not at this hour of the night. I won't do it.

And when she got back into bed again, she made up her mind that she would not do it until after that brunch. All right! she told herself. I'll take a chance. A chance that Murray won't get desperate. I'm gambling with a human

98

life. That sounds like something out of a movie, but it's the truth.

On Sunday afternoon I'll tell Lieutenant Levy. No, I won't. On Monday morning I'll go to see that finance company, and if they won't lend me enough, I'll pawn my jewelry. I've got to get those letters back before the police get into this. It's going to be bad enough as it is, with all that shock and misery for Father. But I won't have Bee disgraced. I'm sorry about Murray. I'm so sorry . . .

Her visions of Murray so troubled her that she could not sleep; she got up and took two aspirins. You can see how people start taking drugs, she thought. Not from grief. I could bear it when Tom went away, when Mother died. It's this feeling of guilt, this horrible, shameful worry.

She waked later than usual; she dressed and went downstairs, and Sibyl was in the kitchen.

"Got the ham boiling," said Sibyl. "Then round about ten o'clock, I'll put it in the oven. Got some cloves left over, in a little jar. Got a little brown sugar. If you could spare a little sherry, ma'am?"

"Yes, of course," said Lucia.

She stood leaning against the doorway, heavy-eyed, oppressed. I suppose I ought to know . . . she thought. It's cowardly not to ask.

"Sibyl," she said. "Did your nephew really send that ham?"

"No, ma'am," Sibyl answered, without emphasis.

It seemed to Lucia necessary to go on with this.

"Well, have you any idea where it did come from, Sibyl?" she asked.

"No sense to look a gift horse in the mouth, ma'am," said Sibyl.

"Well, no . . ." said Lucia, and went into the dining room.

They took three newspapers on Sunday; one was especially for Mr. Harper; one had been requested by David, for certain comics he followed; the third was a sort of communal one. Lucia went through this one in haste, and found what she sought.

The Horton County police have arrested Joseph 'Miami' Murray in connection with the slaying of Theodore Darby on Simm's Island. . . . Five years ago Darby figured in the news as a dealer in pornographic art. . . . 'Miami' Murray has twice been convicted on drug-peddling charges. . . .

It's like one of David's comic strips, she thought. They're so *very* criminal. Why should people like Father and Bee have to suffer, just to clear a man like that Murray?

She had learned that answer by the time she was ten years old. Because it was right to tell the truth, and wrong to hide it. Because it was wrong to let anyone be blamed, unjustly, for anything. It was as simple as that. *Thou shalt not bear false witness against thy neighbour.*

That drug-peddler isn't my 'neighbor'! she cried to herself. And I'm not bearing any kind of witness against him.

She could not eat anything. She drank the two cups of coffee from the little pot Sibyl had brought in, and then she went into the kitchen.

"Sibyl," she said, "I think I'd like another cup of coffee."

"Never knew you to take three, ma'am."

I never did, Lucia thought. I never wanted to. Only, today I want to be—nice. I want to be gay and pleasant. I want the Lloyds to think we're a nice family.

100

A nice family? she thought. When Father killed Ted Darby, and Bee wrote him those letters, and I took Ted to the island, and now I'm paying blackmail. Why, if anybody knew about us, we'd be—outcasts.

Nobody's going to know, she thought. I'm not going to think about that Murray any more today. I've made my decision, and I'll stick to it. And not think.

She was curiously undecided about what to wear for the brunch. It was a problem which, as a rule, concerned her very little, only now she felt sure of nothing. She did not even feel like Mrs. Holley.

I want to look nice, she thought. But not too formal. And thinking about this, she was inspired to remember a picture in a magazine, and that was how she wished to look. She put on a black blouse with a high neckline and a white skirt; she looked in the mirror and was pleased with the debonair and somehow soldierly effect.

Mr. Harper was waiting for her in the sitting room.

"I suppose," he said, "that as long as these people have invited me, I'd better go. But I'm a bit past the age for enjoying alfresco meals." He laughed a little. "I prefer my tea—without ants," he said.

Lucia laughed, too. Oh, you darling! she thought, with a pang. You're dying to go. And you look so nice and handsome and pleased.

"Are the children ready, do you think?" she asked.

"Oh, yes. Yes. On the veranda, reading the news," he said. "Quite a little family excursion, eh? All four of us."

He's proud of us, Lucia thought, and it touched her almost unbearably. Everything about this day had pain in it, and, with the pain, a feeling of reckless triumph. She had got this day for them; she had bought it for them, at a

101

price she could not begin to compute. There could never be another day like it; it had, for her, the heartbreaking clarity of a lovely scene never to be revisited.

The Lloyds were bathed in this clear light. Mrs. Lloyd, her hair blowing wildly about her thin, rouged cheeks, sat among her children, with her sweet mother-cat smile, and they were gentle to her. There were Owen, and a vivid, pretty daughter, and a nimble boy of fourteen, all of them good-looking, polite, and at ease. More at ease, politer, gentler than David and Bee. Well, I dare say she's brought them up better, Lucia thought. But I do think David and Bee are more remarkable, somehow.

The brunch had style. A table was set ready for them on the terraced lawn overlooking the bright water; the chauffeur brought cocktails in a thermos jug.

"The bar doesn't open till one," Mrs. Lloyd explained. "And anyway, the ones you make at home are generally a little nicer, don't you think?"

"In this case, I agree with you," said Mr. Harper. "Smooth as velvet."

"I'm so *glad!*" said Mrs. Lloyd. "Lieutenant Levy doesn't seem to be here, does he? But he said he never could be sure."

"'A policeman's lot is not a happy one,'" Mr. Harper quoted, and he and Mrs. Lloyd both laughed at that.

Lucia could have listened to them and watched them all for hours. It's the loveliest day . . . she told herself. David was talking, with amiable condescension, to the younger Lloyd boy; Bee and the daughter Phyllis were talking together. It interrupted her dreamlike pleasure when Owen sat down beside her and began to talk, with an obvious effort.

102

He talked about himself. He was, he said, going back to Harvard, to take his senior year, and then there would be a job waiting for him in New York.

"It's a pretty good job," he said. "It's only three thousand to start, but the possibilities are practically unlimited."

"Oh, that's nice!" said Lucia.

He went on and on, in a curiously boring way for someone so young. He told her about his fraternity, about his Army record, he told her about sailing trophies he had won. I must say he's rather egotistic, Lucia thought. And then, suddenly, it occurred to her that he was telling her these things for a reason. He was trying to explain his qualifications as a suitor of Bee's. Oh, no! Lucia thought, in a panic. Bee's only seventeen, and he's much too young, too. No! He mustn't——

"There's the Lieutenant!" said Phyllis Lloyd.

The brunch had been cleared away by this time, and they all strolled down to the beach, a mild and amiable herd. They scattered there, the young people went away; Mrs. Lloyd gave all her attention to Mr. Harper, and Levy sat on the sand beside Lucia. She did not want him there. His presence made her remember everything that she wanted to forget. She wanted this day to be an interlude, all sunny and clear, and Levy made her remember Murray, in prison.

He talked to her in his quiet and gentle way; he talked about sea gulls and snipe and sandpipers.

"What a lot you know about birds!" said Lucia, politely.

"Well, since I've come here, I've got interested," he said. "I'm making a study of the shore birds, taking photographs of them, and so on."

That's an attractive thing to do, Lucia thought. Too nice for a policeman.

"Do you *like* police work?" she asked.

"Not always," he answered. "I started out to be a lawyer, you know. I was admitted to the bar. But police work appeals to me more."

"I should think it would be horrible," said Lucia. "Hunting people down, trying to get them punished."

"The function of the police is protection, Mrs. Holley," he said. "It's not punitive. I have nothing to do with punishing anyone. I enforce the law, that's all."

"I don't think so much of 'the law,' " said Lucia. "I think it's often very stupid and unjust."

"It's all we have, Mrs. Holley," he said. "It's the only thing that can preserve anything at all of our civilization. Whether it's religious law, or civil law, as long as it's something we've all agreed upon, and something we all understand—in advance——"

"*I* don't understand the law," said Lucia.

"You made it, Mrs. Holley," he said. "If we have any laws of which you don't approve, you have the right to work for their repeal."

"Yes, I know," she said, secretly rebellious.

"Women, above all, should value government by law," he said. "It's the one protection you and your family have against aggressive and predatory people."

"Oh, yes, I'm sure you're quite right," said Lucia.

She did not like him when he talked about his precious law, and she stopped listening to him. She leaned back, with both palms flat on the sand, and she allowed herself to relax. Far down the beach she could see her children, with the young Lloyds and some others they had met; she

104

could hear her father's voice, talking contentedly with Mrs. Lloyd. Nice friends for them to have, she thought. I'm very glad this happened, right now. It was an immeasurable comfort to her that it should be like this, a golden, tranquil day, friendly, and a little de luxe. No matter what happens to me, she thought, I'm pretty sure the Lloyds would stand by Bee and David and Father.

She believed that something was going to happen to her. She had no formed idea of what it would be; only it was as if, in a few hours, she was going to walk out of this sunny world into darkness. She was not frightened, simply resigned, and tired.

It's rather soothing to hear Lieutenant Levy droning on like this, she said to herself. I think he likes me. I'm sure he'd never suspect me of breaking any of his precious laws. He's—when you come to think of it, he talks like a grown-up David. Maybe David will be a lawyer. Or a policeman.

Then she realized that Levy had been silent for some time, and, like most shy people, she was afraid of silence. She glanced at him, and he was pouring sand through the open fingers of one hand, a fine, narrow hand; his head was bent, his face in profile was grave, even melancholy.

"I'd like to see a flamingo sometime," she said, anxiously. "They must be beautiful."

"They are," he said, looking up. "I've seen them, in Florida."

"Oh, you've been in Florida?"

"I went down there, after a man," he said. "However, I like our own birds better. Sandpipers . . . D'you often go over to Simm's Island, Mrs. Holley?"

"Why, no," she answered. "Only—once."

She hoped that this hesitation was not noticeable.

"We went there for a picnic," she went on, "but we didn't like it very much."

"Lots of sandpipers there," he said. "Did you find a fairly good place for your picnic, Mrs. Holley?"

"It was just a strip of beach."

"Most of the island is marshy," said Levy.

"Yes, it is," said Lucia.

"Still," he said, "there are a lot of inlets. It wouldn't be hard to get a boat well into the marshes."

She was afraid to look at him. A trap? she thought.

"But who'd want to?" she asked.

"To study the birds," he explained.

"Oh, yes!" said Lucia. "Yes, of course."

I don't think he means anything, she thought. I think he's too nice to want to trap me. Especially at a sort of little party like this. He's come here to relax and enjoy himself. Not as a policeman.

But he was a policeman.

He offered her a cigarette, and lit it for her and one for himself.

"My housekeeper's getting tough with me," he said, sadly. "She wants *me* to go to market for her."

"That's not right," said Lucia.

"She thinks I get preferential treatment," he said. "She tells me that whenever I take the list to the store, I get things she couldn't get."

"Well, it could be like that," said Lucia. "Someone in the police . . ."

"She says—let's hope it's not true, but she says they don't take enough points from me. Very unethical, that would be."

"I suppose it would be."

106

"For instance," he said, "how many points should I give for half a pound of Royal Grenadier cheese?"

"Twelve red points," said Lucia.

"Is it a good brand?"

"Oh, yes! We like it best of all."

He turned his head quickly.

"I see!" he said.

But he did not raise his eyes, to look at her. It was as if what he had heard was enough.

He did mean something. She had said something to make him prick up his ears.

Chapter Twelve

I've got to go in to New York this morning," Lucia said, at the breakfast table.

There was a silence; her family sat as if stunned.

"But, Mother! You never said a word . . . !" Bee protested.

"Well, why should I, dear?" said Lucia. "I've just got to run in, to look after some business."

"Business?" said her father. "I expect to be going in to town myself, later in the week. Maybe I could attend to things for you, m'dear."

"No, thank you, Father. It's just some little details."

There was another silence, and she resented it. Other people go to New York, she thought, and nobody's so amazed. I bet Mrs. Lloyd goes to New York whenever she feels like it. She made for herself a picture of Mrs. Lloyd at *her* breakfast table. Children, she said, I'm going in to New York this morning. Oh, are you, Mother? said her children.

"What train will you get back, Mother?" asked David.

"I don't know exactly, David. Early in the afternoon."

"If you'll make up your mind now," David said, "I'll meet you with the car."

"There's no sense wasting gas, when we're so short, David. I'll take a taxi."

"Very well," he said, stiffly.

"Mother," said Bee, "I think I'll go in with you."

"Well, not today, dear."

"I want to look at coats, little short coats. You can go ahead and attend to this 'business,' whatever it is, and I'll meet you for lunch."

"I'm having lunch," Lucia said, "with Mrs. Polk."

"For Pete's sake!" cried David. "What d'you want to see that old harpy for?"

Lucia regretted having chosen Mrs. Polk, a simpering white-haired lady of great culture, who had managed the lending library they had patronized in New York.

"You said she'd gone to Washington," said Bee.

Oh, let me alone! Lucia cried in her heart. Ask me no questions and I'll tell you no lies.

"Well, you wouldn't mind my being along, if it's only Mrs. Polk," said Bee.

"She said she wanted to talk to me about something rather special," said Lucia. "We'll go together someday very soon, Bee."

"But what could Mrs. Polk possibly want to talk to *you* about?" asked Bee. "You hardly know her."

"I wish you wouldn't keep *on* at me so!" cried Lucia. "I have absolutely no freedom at all! I can't do the simplest thing without all this nagging——"

She stopped short, well aware that she had shocked all of them, her father and her children. My disposition is getting horrible, she thought. Well, I'm sorry, but I can't help it.

"Will you telephone for a taxi, please, David?" she asked, with cold dignity.

All the way to the station, her anger occupied her mind.

Good heavens! Can't I even go in to town, without all this silly fuss? I'm not a child, or an idiot. I'm not a slave, either. I can go to New York whenever I think best, and I don't intend to be cross-examined by my own children. They ought to have confidence in me, and so should Father. Complete confidence.

But when she got on the train, she realized, with a faint shock, that what she ought to be doing, and must do, was to plan the day before her. First I'll go to the bank, she thought, and get my jewelry out of the safe-deposit. Then I'll go to that finance company. If I can't get enough from them, I'll have to pawn my things, to make up the difference. Anyhow, then I'll meet Mr. Donnelly and give him the money. Then I'll call up Lieutenant Levy. No. I'll have to warn Father first. Oh, how can I? How can I tell him he killed Ted Darby? They'll question him, and maybe they won't believe what he says.

They'll ask, why did you go to the boathouse to see deceased? I'll have to tell him not to mention Bee. I'll say I saw a light there, and I thought it was a prowler. That's a funny word, but everybody uses it. The lawn mower was taken by a prowler. There are prowlers in the neighborhood. I wonder if the police use it, write it down? John Doe, charged with prowling. I wonder if there are any women prowlers.

Stick to the point, you fool. Remember what this means. I could get Father to promise not to mention Bee, but I'd never, never be able to get him to tell a lie. He'd just be silent. Mr. Harper, why did you go to the boathouse? All by yourself, in the pouring rain? I refuse to answer that question, sir. Then we'll lock you up until you do answer.

110

Suppose they lock me up, too? For taking away the body. The children would be left alone. I know Sibyl would look after them, but think of the disgrace . . .

Oh, it can't be true! Things like this don't happen to people like us. I can't tell Lieutenant Levy. But I cannot let that Murray man stay in jail, not even one more night. Taking Ted away was breaking some sort of law, I suppose. But letting that Murray man stay in jail, when I know he's innocent, is really evil. It's a sin.

This was like a fever. Her thoughts came too fast; they merged one into another, in panic confusion. This won't do, she told herself. One thing at a time. First I've got to get the money, so that I can buy back poor little Bee's letters. That's the first thing. First things first. I can't afford to be so flustered.

When the train entered the tunnel, she looked at herself in the window, and she was dismayed. She had taken great pains with her dressing; a black suit, the little black hat with a veil, a white blouse, white gloves. Sophisticated, she had thought, and rather businesslike. But the image she saw in the black window looked idiotic; a white face, the collar of the blouse like a clown's ruffle, the little hat perching too high. Fool! she called herself. If I wasn't a fool, I wouldn't be in this position.

She took a taxi to the bank, and it was her misfortune that she kept on feeling like a fool, a clown. She felt that the man she spoke to was amazed at her and her request. Another man went with her, down to the strange, sinister vaults; a guard with a revolver in a holster opened the door for her and waited outside while she went in alone, to get out the jewelry. It was in a manila envelope, and on

111

it was written, in Tom's handwriting, "Lucia's jewelry."

Oh, Tom! Oh, Tom! Everything so carefully arranged for me—so that there wouldn't be any trouble—if you didn't come back . . . A loud sob came, and a sudden rush of tears; she fought them furiously; she dried her eyes and came out.

The distinguished elderly man who had escorted her gave her a form to sign. "*Thank* you!" she said, and hurried away.

She took another taxi to the offices of the Individual Loan Service Association, and now she had no illusion left of seeming sophisticated and businesslike.

"You want to pay off on a loan?" a drowsy, dark-eyed boy asked her.

"I want to get a loan," she said. "Make a loan. I mean, get one."

"Aw right!" he said, and went away, leaving her in a stately high-ceilinged hall set with Renaissance furniture. A young woman came out, and led her to a table, a young woman with round, rouged cheeks and modishly waved white hair.

"What amount did you wish to borrow?" she asked.

"Oh . . . Five thousand dollars," Lucia answered.

"That's quite a lot of money," said the white-haired young woman. "Where are you employed, Mrs. . . . ?"

"Holley," said Lucia. "I'm not employed anywhere. Not just now."

"What is the purpose of this loan, Mrs. Holley?"

"Well, I need the money," said Lucia.

"Doctors' bills? Paying off a mortgage?"

"Well, your ad says, no red tape."

"We have to protect ourselves, Mrs. Holley. Especially

112

in the case of such a large amount. Have you a weekly or monthly income, Mrs. Holley?"

"Yes."

"What is the source of this income, Mrs. Holley?"

"It's from my husband."

"Will you give me the name and occupation of your husband, please?"

"I'd rather not," said Lucia. "You said you'd lend money on a note. All right. I'll sign a note."

"How much is your income, Mrs. Holley?"

"Well, it's around five hundred a month."

"How much do you think you could repay every month?"

"Well . . . Fifty dollars?"

"Do you realize how long it would take you to repay five thousand dollars at that rate, Mrs. Holley?"

"Yes!" said Lucia, loudly.

"I'm afraid we couldn't consider it, Mrs. Holley. Unless you have collateral. D'you own any property? A car?"

"I've got a car."

"In your own name?"

Tom did that. The car's in your name, Lucia, so that if you ever want to sell it, or trade it in, you won't have any trouble. So that if he didn't come back . . .

"What's the make of your car, Mrs. Holley? How old is it?"

She had to go on with this, but she had no hope left.

"Well, why don't you do this?" said the white-haired young woman. "Drive the car in someday, and we'll get someone to look it over. Ask for me. Miss Poser."

"Your ad said, no delay."

"But we have to protect ourselves, Mrs. Holley," said Miss Poser.

113

Against *me?* Lucia thought. As if I was a crook?

"Well, how much do you think they'd let me have on the car?" she asked.

Miss Poser said it depended upon the condition of the car, and upon other things.

"But what's the most I could get?" Lucia asked.

If everything was satisfactory, it might, Miss Poser said, come to five hundred dollars.

"Five *hundred!*" said Lucia.

Miss Poser rose.

"You drive the car around sometime," she said, pleasantly enough.

It was a dismissal. For the first time in her life, Lucia was a person to be got rid of, a queer, troublesome, suspect person. Coming around here, trying to get five thousand dollars. Did you ever!

"Would you like to see some jewelry?" Lucia asked.

"Why, no. No, thanks," said Miss Poser.

She was obviously startled and uneasy.

"We don't make loans on personal effects," she said.

"I see!" said Lucia. "Well, thanks!"

She went over to Madison Avenue and walked uptown, looking in vain for a pawnshop. It's getting late, she thought. Mr. Donnelly won't wait. He'll go away. She signaled a taxi and got into it.

"D'you know where there's a pawnshop?" she asked the driver. "A—reliable one?"

"Sure," said the driver.

She was glad that he showed no surprise, not even any interest. It probably doesn't seem queer to him, she thought. He probably knows about society women and duchesses and people like that pawning their jewels. Only Father'd
114

be terribly upset. He has all those little jokes about hock shops, and cockneys hocking their Sunday clothes every Monday and getting them out on Saturday, and things like that. He'd hate me to be doing this.

I don't like it much, myself. But I don't care, if only they won't be rude to me. I didn't know I was so sensitive. It's rather disgusting, to be so sensitive. I thought I was pretty tough. But I'm not. Not when I get out in the world. Then I'm a nincompoop. If one of those reporters stopped me in the street and asked me what I thought about Russia, or something like that, he'd put me down as Mrs. Lucia Holley, Housewife.

Why is it 'housewife'? What would I call myself if we lived in a hotel? Nobody ever puts down just 'wife,' or even just 'mother.' If you haven't got a job, and you don't keep house, then you aren't anything, apparently. I wish I was something else. I mean, besides keeping house, I wish I was a designer, for instance. The children would think a lot more of me, if I was a designer. Maybe Tom would, too.

No! Tom likes me the way I am. Only, if I could be even a little different when he comes back? I don't mean bustling off to an office every morning. He wouldn't like that. But if I could go to an office or a store now and then, meet outside people. Have interesting little things to tell at dinner. Not be—just me, year after year . . .

"Here you are!" said the driver, stopping before a place on Sixth Avenue.

"Will you wait, please?" Lucia asked.

"Okay," said the driver.

She was frightened. It was such a queer little place, with a metal grille over the window in which was displayed

115

a crazy jumble of things, a mandolin, clocks, candlesticks, a fur neckpiece, an old-fashioned pearl stickpin in a box lined with purple plush. Do they put everything in the window? she thought. I'd hate my things to be there. Mother's pearls, and the ring Tom gave me. I hate this! I hate all this! It's worse than taking Ted over to the island.

It was dim inside the shop, and so queer. A dark, moon-faced young man in shirt sleeves came behind the counter; she thought he looked scornful, and she put on a manner of cold aloofness.

"I'd like to borrow some money on some jewelry," she said.

He said nothing. She opened her purse and took out the long envelope; she handed him the little boxes and he emptied them onto the counter.

"How much do you want?" he asked.

"Well, as much as possible," said Lucia.

The rings, the bracelet, the clasps, the necklace lying on the counter looked, she thought, like junk, worthless and dull. He gathered them up and took them to a little table by a window; he weighed them, looked at them through a glass in his eye, and she stood at the counter, waiting, in cold despair. It's my last chance, she thought. Whatever he gives me is all I'll have for Nagle, and it can't possibly be enough. Maybe he'll say ten dollars. Maybe he'll cheat me. I don't know. I don't care.

He brought the things back to the counter.

"They're very nice," he said. "The settings are nice."

She was startled by his words, and his tone, mild and kind.

"Pretty old, these two," he said. "I guess you think a lot of them."

116

Tears came into her eyes. All she could do was to ignore them, and keep on looking at him.

"Maybe you'd rather have a smaller loan," he said, "so it'll be easier to get them back?"

She shook her head.

"No, thank you," she said, unsteadily. "As much as possible, please."

"I can let you have six hundred and twenty-five on these," he said.

"Okay!" she said, suddenly and clearly.

"Or maybe we could bring it up to six-fifty," he said, looking down at the things.

"Thank you," said Lucia. "Can I get the money today?"

"Right now," he said.

"Will you—are you going to put them into the window?" she asked, still ignoring the tears on her cheeks.

"Oh, no!" he said. "That's only the things for sale." He glanced up. "Y'see, if you don't redeem the things, or you fail to pay the interest for a certain length of time, why, we're allowed to sell them."

"I see!" she said. "It seems—sort of pathetic, doesn't it? People's funny things."

"Sometimes," he said, "it's very pathetic. But mostly, well, you're doing a service. If anyone needs money in a hurry, well, here's where they can get it. There's been cases I know of where a man would have committed suicide if he couldn't get forty-fifty dollars quick. Then somebody'll come in here that would get put out in the street if he can't pay his rent. Well, the landlord won't take his fine watch. The landlord, naturally, he don't know the value of things. Then, say the next week, this man gets a good

117

job. Soon as he gets his pay, he's back here, redeems his watch, and all is well."

Lucia was very much touched. I like him! she thought. He's trying to make me see that it isn't horrible and comic to be a pawnbroker. He wants it to seem sort of romantic.

She wished to help him in this; she wanted to show an interest in his business.

"Do you ever get wedding rings?" she asked.

"Well, not so many," he said. "People have a lot of sentiment about them and a wedding ring hasn't got much actual value, as a rule. Although you'd be surprised how many women throw away their wedding rings."

"But why?"

"Well, they're getting a divorce, or they're mad at their husbands, or one thing or another, and they throw away their rings."

"I saw a baby's silver mug in the window."

"The father's a drunk," he said. "That's a bad case. Well, I'll get your money for you now."

He brought it to her, all in bills.

"Good luck!" he said.

The taxi driver sat in the cab, smoking a cigarette.

"Do you know where I could get any cigarettes?" Lucia asked.

"Lady," he said, "if I knew that, I'd be rich. I can let you have one."

"Thank you!" she said. "Now I'd like to go to Stern's, please, on Forty-second Street."

He gave her a cigarette; he struck a match and held it for her, and she leaned back, relaxed, savoring the cigarette with something like bliss. It's all over, she thought. I haven't got the money, and I can't get it, ever.

118

I wonder if this is a little the way people feel sometimes when they're going to die, she thought. When the doctor says there's no hope, and there's nothing you can do but just let go. It would be a rather good way to die, not fighting and struggling, just letting go.

She had a picture of herself at home, lying comfortably in bed, with everything over. Nothing to be done, about anything.

But the children! she thought. And Father . . . They'd have to send a cable to Tom . . . Oh, no! You never can stop fighting and struggling.

The cab turned into Forty-second Street, and looking at her watch, she saw that she was over half an hour late. Maybe Mr. Donnelly's gone, she thought. You couldn't blame him.

But he was there, standing outside the entrance, tall, outstandingly neat, in a dark blue, double-breasted suit and a gray felt hat; not smoking, not fidgeting, not glancing around; just waiting. He certainly doesn't look like a crook, she thought. He's quite distinguished looking. Quite handsome.

As she was getting out of the cab he came forward, hat in hand.

"We could keep the cab," he said. "There's a place in the Fifties I think you would like."

She settled back in the cab and as he got in beside her, he gave the driver an address.

"I haven't got the money," she said, at once. "I never can get it."

He was silent, and she turned to look at him; she found him looking at her, with his curiously clouded blue eyes.

"Be easy," he said. "Take it easy."

Chapter Thirteen

There was no reason to feel reassured by this, but she did feel so.

"This place where we are going," he said. "There's a small room in it we can have to ourselves. Unless you'd rather eat out with the other people?"

"Maybe we could talk better by ourselves," she said.

"That's what I'd thought of," he said.

It was strange, she thought, that she had no hesitation about lunching alone with him in whatever place he had chosen. She remembered things she had read in old-fashioned novels about private dining rooms, always the scene of some amorous adventure, a seduction, drugged wine, a conniving waiter. But Mr. Donnelly isn't like that, she thought.

The cab stopped before a little restaurant of rather smart appearance, with a dark blue canopy over the entrance on which was lettered Café Colorado; a doorman in uniform came forward to open the door of the taxi. Donnelly took a bill out of his wallet and passed it to the driver.

"All right," he said.

"*What?*" said the driver. "Well, thanks. Thanks a lot "

They went down a few steps, to a carpeted restaurant with lighted lamps on small tables, and at one end a bar with a mirror lined by blue fluorescent lights. The place was well filled with people; nothing at all queer about it, she thought. An elderly waiter came hurrying up to Donnelly.

"*Bon jour, madame, monsieur!*"

"Tell the boss I am here, will you?" said Donnelly.

"*Mais oui, monsieur!*" said the waiter, and hurried away.

Very promptly a man came across the room to them, stout and swarthy, with a black mustache and sorrowful eyes.

"Ah . . . !" he said. "Ze room, Marty?"

"*Parfaitement,*" said Donnelly.

"Zis way, madame!"

They followed him through the restaurant, and he opened a door beside the bar, leading to a dark little passage. At the end of this he opened another door.

"*Voilà!*" he said, with an air of pride.

"*C'est assez bien,*" said Donnelly, and went on talking in French, of which Lucia had only a schoolgirl knowledge. She gathered, though, that he was talking about the lunch, and that the other man was called Gogo.

The room itself made her want to laugh, it was so exactly like something from one of those old-fashioned books; a small room without windows, a round table right in the center, set for two, with a bowl of red roses in the middle; there was even a couch, covered with blue and gold brocade.

"*Alors . . .*" said Gogo, and bowed and smiled and went out, closing the door after him.

"I did not introduce him," said Donnelly. "I did not think you'd be wanting to know him."

"Well, why not? Is he—?" She paused for a word. "Is he—questionable?"

121

"He is a good friend of mine," Donnelly said. "Only, he's not the class you're used to."

'Class'? she thought. What 'class' would you call Donnelly? According to his own words, he came of peasant stock; he had had no education; he was a blackmailer and God knew what else. But he had a courtesy that was natural and effortless; his speech had a correctness, a rhythm like that of a carefully trained foreigner. I don't know what he is, she thought.

He drew back a chair for her.

"I ordered a Martini for you," he said. "Will that be what you like?"

"Oh, yes, thanks!"

"Will you have a cigarette?" he said. "While you're waiting?"

He lit one for her, and one for himself; he moved an ash tray nearer to her, and sat down across the table from her.

"You speak French very fluently, don't you?" she said.

"It is fluent enough," he said, "but I don't know at all if it is very good. I picked it up in Quebec."

"Did you live in Quebec?"

"I was in a monastery near there for more than a year."

"In a monastery?"

"It was in my mind, those days, that I'd study to be a priest."

"Oh! Did you change your mind?"

"I had no vocation," he said, and after a pause, "the world was too much with me."

It seemed to Lucia then that this big, stalwart man, of unimaginable experiences, was a creature infinitely more sensitive and more fragile than herself. She had thought that often about David, about her father, about Tom; she

122

had felt herself to be tougher, more flexible, better able to endure what must come.

"Didn't you ever marry?" she asked.

"I wanted to marry," he said, "but I never found a girl would suit me."

A slight resentment rose in her, against this male arrogance.

"You never found anyone good enough?" she asked.

"I did not," he answered, with simplicity.

The waiter came in then, with one cocktail on a tray.

"Aren't you having one?" she asked.

"I never take a drink till five o'clock."

"Why not?" she asked, a little sharply.

"There was a time when I drank too much," he said. "For three years I went roaring around, till I had the d.t.'s. It is a terrible thing. You'd never forget it. To Bellevue, they took me, and I saw the others that were in it. Old men, some of them, with their lives all drunk away and wasted." He paused. "Now I am moderate," he said.

"You've had quite a lot of experience . . ." she said, lightly.

"I have that," he said.

She sipped the cocktail, feeling an odd new strength in herself, a sense of power she had not known before. I can manage *him*, all right, she thought.

"You look very charming," he said. "It is a nice little hat you're wearing, and the white gloves, and all."

Then it all came back to her.

"I don't feel charming," she said, bitterly. "I've—failed. I can't get that money."

"You were trying?"

"I went to a loan company I saw advertised," she said.

123

"They said they lent money on your note, without any red tape. Well, they wouldn't." She was silent for a moment, remembering Miss Poser. She opened her purse and took out the manila envelope, into which she had put the money. "Here's six hundred and fifty dollars," she said. "That's all I can get. *All*."

"Did you draw that out of your bank?"

"No. I haven't anything in the bank except what I have to use. No. I pawned some jewelry I had."

"Give me the ticket," he said.

"But—why?"

"Give me the ticket," he said, with a ring in his voice.

"But why? I don't want to."

"Give it me!" he said, rising.

"No! I won't!"

He stood over her, his hand outstretched, and she was startled, and almost frightened, by the power of the man, the concentrated force in him. His face was not blurred now; the angle of his jaw was sharp; his eyes were clear and cold.

"Give it me! Get it out of your purse."

She took the ticket out of her purse, reluctant and angry.

"Well, why?" she demanded.

"I will get your things back for you," he said. "Every damn one of them."

"They're not important. I don't care about them."

He began walking up and down the room.

"I will get them back for you," he said.

"I don't care about them!" she cried. "I only want to stop that Nagle."

"I will do that, too," he said.

"Oh! But can you?"

124

"I didn't know how it was——" he began, when the waiter came in, with shrimp cocktails set in ice.

"Bring the lady another Martini," said Donnelly, and she made no protest.

He sat down at the table.

"I didn't know it would be so bad for you," he said. "Carlie—Nagle, that is, told me he'd looked into it. He said you'd plenty of money; your father, too."

"I haven't any money," she said. "Only what I have to use."

"It's a wonder they wouldn't give you some."

"They do! My father and my husband have always given me anything I wanted."

"It is not enough," he said.

"You mean I ought to have a little special fund—to pay blackmail out of?"

She could see that that hit him, hard, and she was glad.

"I don't care about those bits of jewelry," she said. "I only care about saving my daughter from a miserable scandal."

"I'm not worrying about your daughter. She would get over a scandal."

The waiter came back with the second Martini and set it before her.

"I'll have a talk with Nagle," he said. "I will try to make him wait till the money comes in from the deal we've got on. I'd pay him for you now, only the two of us are hard up, putting all we could lay hands on into this new thing. The trouble is, Nagle is always nervous if he hasn't a good sum in the bank. Drink your cocktail."

"I don't want it."

"Then eat your lunch."

"I can't."

"Look!" he said. "If I cannot keep Nagle quiet, then let him go ahead. He will take the letters to your father—"

"No! He can't! He mustn't!"

"Your father is a fine old gentleman, by what I saw. He will not be too hard on the girl."

"No! No!" she said. "My father *mustn't* know."

"You take it too hard. Let Nagle go ahead. It will soon be over—"

"No!" she cried, again. "You don't understand. Father can't know anything at all about Ted Darby."

She pushed back her chair, but she did not rise; she sat there rigid, thinking fast. If I tell Lieutenant Levy, Father'll have to know. Have to know about Bee and Ted; have to know that he killed Ted. And I can't let that Murray stay in jail. I've got to tell Lieutenant Levy, unless . . .

Unless somehow Murray could be got out of prison—without my telling the police.

"What is it?" Donnelly asked. "What is it worrying you?"

She glanced quickly at him, and the look in his face was clear to her. She did not care to put it into words for herself; simply she knew that she could trust him with anything at all. She knew that she could make use of all the strength and the force in him.

"Father would go straight to the police, if Mr. Nagle saw him," she said. "And if the police find out about my daughter and Ted Darby—"

"They would not care about that," he said. "When it is people like yourselves, they'd try to keep the girl's name out of it. Her letters have nothing to do with Darby's killing."

126

"But suppose they have?"

"They have not."

Her heart was beating in a quick, erratic way that made her breath come too fast.

"Suppose it wasn't Murray who killed Ted?" she said.

"I know damn well it was not Murray," he said. "Murray was framed."

"But he's in jail for it. He'll be tried for it."

"He will go to the chair for it," said Donnelly. "I would not lose a night's sleep over that. He and Darby, the two of them, were dirty, double-crossing——" He checked himself. "They are rats," he said.

"Murray can't be punished—executed—for something he didn't do."

"Don't worry about him. He is not worth it."

"Could you get Murray off, if you wanted?"

"I would not want to."

"But *could* you, if you tried? Please answer!"

"I might," he said. "Why do you want to know?"

The waiter came in, and hesitated, seeing the untouched shrimps.

"Wait a while," said Donnelly. "Is there a bell in it? There? Then take it easy till I'll ring for you."

The man went out, closing the door behind him.

"You could get Murray freed?" she asked.

"Maybe. Only I would not lift a finger to do it."

She had the most vivid image in her mind of yesterday's brunch, the blue water, the green trees, the sunny tranquillity; Mrs. Lloyd's smile, the way Owen had watched Bee. Bee, and David, and her father, and Tom so very far away, all of them so innocent, all of them threatened by these dark, horrible shadows from another world, Ted Darby, Nagle, Murray, criminals, all of them, cruel, dangerous as wild beasts.

"What is it worrying you?" Donnelly asked.

"Well . . . Suppose I told you *I* killed Ted Darby?" she said.

Chapter Fourteen

He gave her a quick sidelong look.

"No," he said. "You could not kill anyone."

"It was an accident. He was—I got angry at him, about the letters. I pushed him, and he fell. It was in the boat-house, and he fell into the launch, on the anchor. It killed him."

He gave her another of those sidelong looks, wary and alert.

"Swallow your drink," he said. "It will do you good."

She shook her head.

"I didn't know he was dead, until the morning," she said. "Then I found him there. Then I took him over to the island. It was . . . It was—" She paused a moment. "I had —to get him off the anchor. It was . . . And then I had— to get him out of the boat."

Her voice was unsteady, her mouth trembled. Remembering it was worse than the doing of it.

"You'll have to believe me," she said.

She looked up at him; their eyes met for a long moment.

"I do believe you," he said. "There's no saint in heaven would do more than you'd do for your family."

"I was—never going to tell anyone," she said. "But now —I can't let Murray pay for it."

"You can that," he said. "Murray's no good at all."

"That doesn't matter. I can't let him suffer for something that's my fault."

"You can."

"No," she said. "I won't. It's a sin."

"A sin?" he repeated, as if startled. "It's hard, now, to know what's a sin and what isn't."

"It's never hard," she said. "You always know in your own heart what's right."

"Ah . . ." he said. "It's not that easy. You have to look at all sides of it. Now, there's your family. They're good people. They do good in the world. What's the sense in sacrificing them for a rat like Murray? You have to think out what's going to do the most good."

"No," she said. "You have to do what's right, no matter what comes of it."

"There are many don't agree with that," he said. "There are many believe you have to study out what's going to do the most good in the end."

"That's——" she began, and stopped herself. That's Jesuitical, she had been going to say, but maybe that was his belief. "I can't see things that way," she said. "I can't let Murray stay in jail. No matter what happens to us. I'd rather be in jail myself."

"You'll not go to jail," he said. "Look, now. Will you not try to eat a little? I've ordered a steak, but if there's something else——"

"That man's in prison this moment—while I sit here."

"Look, now. It doesn't mean to him what it would mean to you. He's been in it before."

"Oh, can't you understand how I feel?" she cried. "I can't

sit here—eating . . . I don't know what to do. I don't know where to turn."

"Turn to me," he said.

She looked at him. He pushed back his chair and rose, and began to walk up and down the room again. He was a big man, and heavy, but his heel-and-toe walk was very light; his gleaming shoes seemed more flexible than anyone else's.

"It's my punishment," he said. "I've been a fool with my money, and worse. And now, when I need it, I haven't it. I'd give the eyes out of my head if I could pay off Nagle now. Or if I'd the money to pay Isaacs or Jimmy Downey to get Murray off." At the end of the room he turned and came back toward her. "Only don't be eating your heart out," he said. "I will do it."

"How?"

"I will work on Nagle," he said. "He knows we'll be getting this money before long, and I will pay him out of the share that's coming to me."

"Why should you?" she demanded, angrily. "Why should *you* pay blackmail to that horrible man, if he's your partner, or whatever you call him?"

"Well, you see," he said, "it was Nagle got the letters from Darby. Nagle thought up the whole thing. He has a right—"

"You can't talk like that! As if it was an ordinary business thing. It's—don't you realize it's a *crime?*"

He was coming toward her, so big, light-footed, his eyes blank. He was menacing. Then he wheeled round and went away from her.

"Yes . . ." he said. "Yes, you're right. God help me, I

131

hardly know any more what's right from what's wrong."

"Everyone knows."

"Yes," he said. "But I cannot go back on Nagle now."

"Even when you realize that he's a criminal?"

"I am a criminal myself," he said.

"You're not," said Lucia. "Not really."

"I've broken the law," he said. "I've done wrong enough. Only, God be praised, I never killed anyone." He was down at the end of the room now, with his back to her. "Only in the war," he said, "the first war, I mean. And the killing in the war is not accounted a sin." He was silent for a time. "But I wasn't easy about it," he said. "I was young then, and when I'd see some of the Boches—that's what we called them, in those days—when I'd see them lying dead in a field or maybe a forest, I'd think, was it me did that? And now, when you see the young lads going off again . . . You'd think the devil rules the world."

He came back to her.

"There's yourself," he said. "So good—and look at the trouble that's come to you. But I'll get you free of it. I'll work on Nagle, and I will see Isaacs or Downey, about getting Murray out."

"But how can they? Unless they find someone else?"

"Isaacs can get anyone off," said Donnelly.

"But what will you tell him? Will you have to say that you know someone else did it?"

"I will tell him nothing at all. He'll go to see Murray, and they will fix it up together." He paused a moment. "Will you trust me?" he asked.

"Yes . . ." she said.

"There is nothing I would not do for you," he said. "Nothing in the world."

She lowered her eyes, not to see the look in his face.

"Could we have the steak?" she asked. "I've got to be getting home."

He rang the bell at once.

"Did you ever get a ham?" he asked.

"Oh, yes!" she said, and added, "Thank you."

"There's a roast of beef on the way," he said. "And three pounds of bacon."

"Mr. Donnelly——"

"Yes?"

"I'd rather you didn't send anything more. It's—hard to explain them. And——"

"Yes?"

"Well, they're black market, aren't they?"

"I suppose you'd call them that," he said. "But there's no need for it to be on your conscience at all. They are a present to you."

"Thank you very much, but please don't send the beef. Please don't send anything."

"I'm afraid they're on the way, if they're not there already."

The waiter brought in the steak, French fried potatoes, peas, a salad; he moved saltcellars, emptied the ash tray, and went away.

"That Sibyl is a fine woman," said Donnelly.

"But you don't know her!"

"I had a bit of a talk with her yesterday, when you were not home," he said. "She is a fine woman."

"Yes. She is."

133

"I asked her to let me know if ever I was needed," he said. "I gave her my telephone number."

How could you be 'needed'? Lucia thought. But she did not say it.

"Eat, will you not?" he asked, anxiously. "You're pale. Eat a bit of the red meat. And take it easy. I will get Murray out of jail for you, and I will keep Nagle off your neck. He'll give you the letters back. Trust me, will you not?"

"I do trust you," she said.

He gave a sigh, as if a weight were lifted. But he did not eat, nor could she. This room without windows was quiet, too quiet; she felt unbearably restless. She did something unusual to her; she opened her purse and took out a little mirror and looked at herself.

She did not look flustered and frightened now. It was true that she was pale, her hair a little disordered, but there was something in her face she had not seen in it before, a sorrowful and quiet beauty. That's how I look to him, she thought.

Chapter Fifteen

They did not want the dessert; he waved it away. No check was brought to him; he left some bills on the table, and they went out of the room, through the restaurant, and into the street. He stopped a taxi and took her to the train.

"You'll be hearing from me," he said. "And you'll take it easy, will you not? I'll look after everything."

She stood silent, her lashes lowered. She knew that he was looking at her; she knew that she was dark, slender and lovely; she knew he was waiting for her to look up, and presently she raised her eyes.

"Thank you," she said.

"Could I come to the house?" he asked. "Just once more? Stop by, maybe, and bring a bottle of Scotch for your father?"

"I'm sorry," she said, "I'm very sorry, but—not possibly."

"Can I see you once more?" he said. "When I've settled all this, would you have lunch with me, the way it was today?"

She did not answer.

"Just the once, when it's all settled?" he asked. "I know how it is with you. You have your family and your—social position to think of. But if you'd give me just one more sight of you . . . ?"

There were people moving and hurrying all around them; a prodigious voice was announcing trains. But they were somehow isolated. He did not urge her any more; he simply waited, in a dreadful humility. The gate of her platform was opening, but still she stood there, with her lashes lowered.

Suddenly she held out her white-gloved hand, and looked at him.

"Yes," she said. "I'll be very pleased to have lunch with you someday."

She did not smile; they never smiled at each other. He held her hand for a moment, very lightly.

"Be easy," he said.

She went along the dim platform, in a silent, smooth-moving crowd; she got into a car. It was a smoker, and she decided to stay in it and have a cigarette. She sat down beside a man and opened her purse; she took out her pack, but it was empty; she felt in the corners; she turned it up-side down.

"Have one of mine!" said the man beside her.

"Oh, but really . . . ! When they're so hard to get . . ."

"Not hard for *me*," he said. "Take one! Take one!"

He lit it for her; a burly man with a red face and bright little blue eyes.

"This shortage'll be over in a week or so," he said. "But in the meantime it doesn't bother *me* any. I've got connections in just about every line of business *you* ever heard of. Why, only the other day, this fellow I know was squawking about an alarm clock. Couldn't find one anywhere. I'll get you one this afternoon, I told him. Hey, no black market stuff for me, he says. I don't use the black market, brother, I tell him. I use *this*."

136

He tapped his temple with his third finger and raised his thin brows; he smiled, with his lips closed. And he was trying to impress her. His little bright eyes flickered over her, not boldly, but with admiration.

"Here!" he said. "Let's change seats. You young ladies always like to sit by the window."

When he stood up, he put his hand into his pocket, and brought out two packs of cigarettes, Mr. Harper's favorite brand.

"Just slip these in your purse," he said.

"Oh, I couldn't!"

"Plenty more where they came from," he said. "You take them. You'll be doing me a favor."

He settled down cozily beside her.

"No, sir," he said, "I never married. I see you're wearing the badge of servitude." He laughed. "That's the way it goes," he said. "Every time I meet an attractive young lady, she's got a husband. Didn't bother to wait for me."

Now he got around to asking questions, and she had no objection to telling him that she had a husband overseas, that she had two children. Just like somebody in a magazine story, she thought.

"It's hard," he said, gravely, "it's very hard. Attractive young lady."

He's a wolf, she thought. But not a bad one. Sort of pathetic. She could see what he was getting around to now.

"I could meet you somewhere . . ." he said. "We could have a little dinner, go somewhere to dance. Do you good."

"I can't leave the children," she said. "I never go out in the evenings."

"Mistake," he said. "Great mistake. You could get one of these high-school kids to sit with the children."

He obviously pictured two small children, and let him, Lucia thought. She was surprised at herself for the bland enjoyment she found in his company. But she would not tell him her name.

"No," she said, looking into his eyes. "Really I can't."

"I'll give you my card," he said, "and if ever you change your mind—"

Mr. Richard Hoopendyke. Representing the Shilley Mfg. Co.

"Change your mind!" he said, rising when she did.

"Well, maybe . . ." said Lucia.

When she got out at the familiar station, it was strange to see the sunny afternoon quiet. It seemed to her that she had been gone so long, so very long; she felt timid about going home, as if she had in some way changed. She got into a taxi with two other people, a man and a woman, and they rode in grim silence. They don't like me, Lucia told herself. They think I'm queer. An Undesirable Acquaintance. Well, maybe I am.

She felt queer. She was the first one to get out, and she told the driver to stop at the corner; she walked down the road, feeling strangely solitary. Such a long day, she thought, and so much has happened.

But, after all, what really had happened? She had tried to get a loan, and failed; she had pawned her jewelry. And then I had lunch . . . she thought. There's nothing so wonderful in all that. Only, I never can tell anyone about it. Certainly not Father and the children, and not even Tom. Tom would know there wasn't anything wrong, but he wouldn't like it. Lunch in a private room. With a crook. Tom wouldn't like that man in the smoker, and neither would Father or the children. They don't think I'm like that.

The house seemed unwelcoming in the late afternoon sun. It's nice when someone comes out to meet you, she thought. When the children were little, they always rushed out. That was nice. But then I always had some little present for them.

And she was empty-handed now; she felt it. She was bringing back nothing. The front door was unlocked, as usual; she opened it and went in, and Mr. Harper spoke, from the sitting room.

"Lucia?"

"It's me, Father."

He was sitting in an armchair, with a book in his hand, an empty teacup on the table beside him.

"Oh . . . Sibyl gave you your tea?" she said.

"Never forgets," he said.

She came up behind him, and kissed his silver head.

"Ha . . ." he said, pleased. "Have a good day, m'dear?"

"Yes, thank you, Father."

"Shopping, I suppose," he said. "Your mother used to come home, say she was exhausted, shopping all day. I'd ask her what she'd bought, and half the time she'd say she hadn't bought anything at all."

He laughed, his eyes fixed upon nothing; as if in his mind he could see that absurd and beloved figure. Lucia handed him one of the packs of cigarettes Mr. Hoopendyke had given her.

"That's very nice," he said. "Very welcome, m'dear. By the way, that Lloyd boy was here. Wanted my permission to put my name up at the Yacht Club. I told him my sailing

139

days were a thing of the past. I shouldn't make much use of the club. But I didn't like to rebuff the boy. Nice lad. And the dues are no great matter. I told him to go ahead, if he liked."

He wants to belong to the club, Lucia thought. He's lonely. I don't keep him from being lonely. I haven't any time. I don't know what I do with myself, but I never have any time.

"You'll be on a committee inside a week," she said. "You always are."

"Nonsense!" he said. "At my age——"

"Nonsense yourself!" she said. "People always have such confidence in you, Daddy."

" 'Daddy'. . ." he repeated. She had not used that name for a long time, and it seemed to echo for both of them. Tears came into her eyes and she winked them away.

"I've got to see Sibyl," she said.

Sibyl was standing at the cabinet, in a dazzle of sun, breaking eggs, letting the whites slip into one fluted blue bowl, and the golden yolks into a green one. It was a delicate operation, and beautiful. She dealt with the egg in hand, and then looked up, with her tender, slow smile.

"Oh, you're back, ma'am?"

"Yes, I'm back. We're having the cold ham tonight, aren't we, Sibyl?"

"Thought I'd better cook the beef tonight, ma'am."

"The beef . . . ?"

"It came just in time," said Sibyl. "And I'll make the Yorkshire pudding Mr. Harper likes."

No questions about that beef. No questions, ever, about anything. But what does she *think?* Lucia asked herself.

Above everything in the world, she wanted to know what Sibyl thought.

"It was a present," she said.

"Yes, ma'am," said Sibyl.

"You must have been surprised, when the beef came," Lucia said.

"No, ma'am."

"Well, why not?"

"Mr. Donnelly told me he was sending it, ma'am. Asked me, what would Mrs. Holley like. Said he'd get anything you wanted, any time."

The words, in Sibyl's soft voice, had an impact that made Lucia catch her breath. Nobody should say that. Nobody should know that.

"I've told him not to send anything more," she said. "I've told him not to come here again."

"Yes, ma'am," said Sibyl.

Now drop it! Lucia told herself. Let well enough alone. But she could not.

"He's not the sort of person to have here," she said.

"He's unfortunate," said Sibyl.

"What do you mean, Sibyl?"

"Got in bad company," said Sibyl.

"He's a free agent. He could choose his company, like anyone else."

"We don't always know what we're doing, ma'am," said Sibyl. "Till it's too late."

"It's never too late to—change," said Lucia.

"That's what my husband says, all the time. But I don't think people change much."

"I didn't know you'd been married, Sibyl."

"Yes, ma'am. He's in jail, in Georgia."

141

"Oh, Sibyl!"

"Been there eighteen years," Sibyl said, "and got seven more to go. Unless he gets a parole. And he won't."

"And you're—waiting for him?" Lucia asked.

"Obliged to," Sibyl answered, somberly. "Bill never did me any wrong. Not that he knew of. When they took him away, I told him I'd wait for him, and I have."

"Eighteen years!" Lucia said. "That must have been terribly hard for you, Sibyl."

"Yes, ma'am," said Sibyl. "And I don't know if it was sensible, either."

"You mean you've changed your mind about him, Sibyl?"

"It just didn't do him much good," Sibyl said. "He's got a hopeful nature. Thinks he can come out of jail, when he's fifty-four years old, and start a fine new life for us. Gets more and more philosophical."

"Well . . ." Lucia said, anxiously. "That's probably a good thing, Sibyl."

"Maybe so, ma'am," said Sibyl, with courteous deference. "The philosophy Bill's got, it's that everything that happens is for the best. He doesn't study about injustice. He's not bitter, shut up there all the best years of his life for what wasn't wrong at all."

"What was it, Sibyl?"

"Bill was a sailor," said Sibyl. "I reckon that's why I married him; I was just so crazy to travel. Don't know how it got in my head, but even when I was a little girl, I used to think about it. Maybe it was out of books. The white people my mother worked for used to lend me books. I used to think, if I could ever get up to the frozen North, big, white fields of snow, those lights in the sky . . . And Paris. Bill told me it's all true about Paris. Colored people
142

can go anywhere, see all the sights. Bill said we'd get to take trips."

"Didn't you ever?"

"No, ma'am. First thing we got married, I started to have a baby. And he gave up going to sea. He got a job in the mill; said he wanted to be near me, case there was any trouble. I lost the baby, and there he was. We had some money saved, and he said we'd take a trip. Went to a steamship office to buy us a ticket. Man said they didn't want any niggers on their ships. Bill said it was the law that he could buy a ticket if he had the money. The man hit him, and Bill hit him back. Assault with intent to kill, they called it. But the man didn't die, and Bill didn't ever think to kill him. He just hit back. He had a knife on him, but he always did, ever since the days when he was at sea."

"Maybe when he gets out, you can take a trip."

"No, ma'am," said Sibyl. "Bill'll be fifty-four, and I don't know if he can get him a decent job. He's got kind of queer, shut up in that jail. I reckon I'll have to support him. Well, I can do it, if I keep my health."

"Well . . ." Lucia said. "You must have been a wonderful help and comfort to your husband, all this while."

"I don't know . . ." said Sibyl. "He's got that philosophical nature . . . If I'd said I wouldn't be waiting for him, he'd have found some other kind of comfort. And I'd have found some way to see the world."

Lucia was silent, deeply impressed by this glimpse into Sibyl's nature. All these years, while she had gone about her work so quietly and competently, there had been in her this passionate longing to see the world. I never had that, Lucia thought. I never specially thought about traveling. I never wanted anything like that. *What did I want?*

143

She had wanted a husband and children, and she had got them. Ever since she could remember, everything she had wanted had been given to her. If she had wanted a doll, a bicycle, a new dress, her parents had given it to her. The husband she wanted had appeared while she was still in school; the son and the daughter she wanted had come to her without too much pain and effort.

Was she, then, a creature uniquely favored? Or was she a creature, not favored, but scorned and dismissed by life, denied what other people had? There was David, filled with his uneasy hopes, Bee and her stormy follies, Tom going through the experience he could never share with her. Even Sibyl. Even Donnelly . . .

I'm like a doll, she thought. I'm not real. As she sat at dinner with her family, this sense of unreality became almost frightening. They told about things that had happened to them today, and it was all real, and crystal-clear, to be understood by anyone. But her day was like a dream; if she should try to describe it, who would believe or understand about the vaults, the loan office, the pawnshop, the private dining room, even Mr. Hoopendyke in the smoker?

She sat down to write to Tom, with the same sense of numbed unreality. Who was this, trying to write a letter?

DEAR TOM:

I don't know where you are. I don't know who I am. Tom, I'm in such trouble . . .

Take it easy, Donnelly had said. I'll get Murray out, he had said. I'll keep Nagle quiet. But she could not take it easy. She was caught in a current that was carrying her farther and farther from the shore.

Her restless dreams that night were all of the sea. She

144

dreamed that she was swimming, in a race with Mrs. Lloyd, and everyone she loved best was standing on the shore, watching. Mrs. Lloyd, in a little hat of purple violets, went through the water with incredible speed and ease, and Lucia went laboring after her, disappointing her own people so by her clumsy floundering.

She waked from that, and got up in haste, to look at the letter she had written to Tom, to make sure that she had not really written anything about 'trouble,' or even anything he might read between the lines. I don't think so . . . she said to herself. It seems to me just like my other letters. Just babbling.

She went back to bed, and she dreamed that she was in a rowboat, with an enormous rock on the thwarts. She pulled on the oars with all her strength, but she could not move the boat with that great weight in it. And she had to move; she had to hurry. At first it was because something was coming after her, out of the dark boathouse, something dangerous and dreadful. But, as she strained at the oars, she became aware that the danger was the rock itself. If she did not hurry, did not get to the place of safety, the rock was going to change into something else.

It was beginning already. Two things like ears were shaping on its top; it shifted a little, and she thought it sighed. Then it rolled toward her, and she waked, in a sweat of terror. There was a great wind blowing, and rain was driving in at the open window; there was a noise, as if the night itself were roaring.

She sprang up and closed her window and barefoot, in her pajamas, went out into the hall, to Bee's room. It was dark in there, and filled with the rushing wind, and her daughter lay there, unconscious, helpless. She closed that window, and went to David's room. He too was asleep, and the rain was driving straight on his back. She pulled off the damp sheet and covered him with a blanket, and he did not stir.

Tears were running down her face, it so pierced her heart to think of her children lying unprotected in the rain. She went along the hall to her father's room, and there was a light showing under the door; she knocked and he said "Come in! Come in!" in his steady old voice.

He was standing by the window in his flannel dressing gown, smoking a cigarette.

"'Oh, pilot, 'tis a fearful night,' what, what?" he said.

"Yes, it *is!*" said Lucia.

"What's this? What's this? Are you crying, m'dear?"

"It's just the rain. I was closing the children's windows."

"Sit down and have a cigarette," he said. "I've got that pack you brought me, m'dear. Here! Sit down here. Very comfortable chair."

Chapter Sixteen

I wish you'd ask Mrs. Lloyd to tea," Bee said at breakfast, with a hint of reproach.

"Well, I will," said Lucia. "I'll call her up after breakfast."

"There's the postman!" cried David, jumping up.

He went to the door, and came back leisurely, looking through the sheaf of letters he carried.

"Oh, hurry up!" said Bee. "Is there anything for me?"

"Take it easy!" said David.

"Mother, tell him to hurry up!" said Bee.

"*Take* it easy! *Take* it easy!" said David. "Four for you, Mother; two V-mails from Dad. One for you, Grandpa. Letter for me from Dad. And here's the vitally important mail for Miss Beatrice Holley. Letter from your alumnae association, letter from Boothbay—that must be Edna. Oh, gosh! Here's a letter from Jerry, Bee. Open it and let's see if he's still in China."

"When I'm good and ready," said Bee.

They all sat at the table, opening their letters. The V-mails from Tom looked queer, Lucia thought; his sharp, clear writing was unfamiliar in this diminished form. These were not the actual letters he had written; this was not the paper his hand had touched; these dwarf letters had been handled and read by heaven knew how many people.

147

Have written to David sending some snaps. I'd be very glad to get pictures of the house. Glad to think of you all there, out of the city. Don't worry about your letters being 'dull,' old girl. They're just what I want. They give me the feeling of our life going on, the same old way. I lived in heaven, but I didn't know it. End of paper. Love to you, kids, Granddad. Most to you.

In the second letter he wrote:

Like to hear all the little details. Other men tell me their wives complain of shortages, meat, butter, and so on. How are you getting on? You never say anything much, old girl.

Tom . . . she kept saying to herself. Tom . . . And she thought that if he were to walk into the room this moment, she would have nothing else to say to him. Only his name; only Tom.

"Will you call up Mrs. Lloyd now, Mother?" Bee asked. "If you don't, you'll forget all about it."

"I don't forget everything," said Lucia.

"Oh, Mother!" Bee protested, laughing.

"I don't find your mother forgetful," said Mr. Harper. "On the contrary. Remembers everything, it seems to me. You must realize, young lady, that a woman with a family and a house to look after has a great deal on her mind. Like an executive in an office."

"Yes, I know, Grandpa. I was only teasing her."

"Well . . ." said Mr. Harper, somewhat mollified. "You'll understand, one of these days, Beatrice, when you have a home of your own."

"Excuse me?" said David. "I promised to meet a kid."

"Wait a minute!" Bee said, and ran after him; Lucia could see them talking in the hall.

148

Their friendship pleased her beyond measure, but it was always a little surprising. She remembered a day, long ago, when they had been little more than babies, perhaps three and five. She had been writing a letter in the sitting room, and they had been in their nursery, with the door open. And, while she sought something to put into the letter, she had heard them talking. Those two baby creatures, that she had brought into the world, were living a life of their own, independent of her. They could talk to each other.

She had listened to them with rapture; it was a thing so thrilling that even now she remembered their talk. They had been making a baby plan. "You get your horse, David," Bee had said, "and I'll get Lilacker." That was her favorite, sacred doll, kept in a drawer; before this, she had always played alone with Lilacker; only now was the little brother admitted. Why, even if I died, they'd go on! Lucia had thought, delighted.

Why do you talk so damn much about "if you died"? Tom had asked her once. I can't say I enjoy it. Well . . . she had said. I don't exactly know. Maybe having children makes you feel like that. It doesn't make me feel like that, Tom had said. I've got insurance for you all; I've made the best arrangements I can. But I don't keep thinking about dying, all the time.

It's probably morbid, Lucia thought. It's probably some sort of enormous conceit. But it doesn't go away. When they were little, I used to feel that nobody else could understand how Bee felt about Lilacker. I used to think that nobody else would understand why David wouldn't say his prayers right. He just couldn't say "I pray the Lord my soul to take." He always said "keep." He didn't want anyone to "take" his soul. It frightened him. I'm still like that. I still think I'm the only one . . .

She telephoned to Mrs. Lloyd.

"I'd love to come!" said Mrs. Lloyd. "This afternoon? But I'm afraid Phyllis can't come; she has a dancing lesson. Would half-past four be too early? Because if I'm not home at *least* an hour before dinner, everything gets so queer. *Why* is it that just when dinner is served everyone locks itself up in a bathroom? They read; I know that. Or if they don't do that, they start making simply endless telephone calls. It must be psychological—but why *should* everyone be so psychological about not wanting dinner the moment it's put on the table?"

Mrs. Lloyd soothed Lucia; she liked her.

"Mrs. Lloyd is coming to tea," she told Sibyl. "Could you make some of those tiny biscuits, Sibyl?"

"Make popovers, ma'am," said Sibyl. "They don't take any shortening. Or we could have nice little ham sandwiches."

"Well, no," said Lucia.

She could not offer any of that ham to Mrs. Lloyd; it would be improper, even treacherous.

"Now, about the marketing?" she said. "I'll go this morning."

"Not much to get today," said Sibyl, with an air of satisfaction. "Got plenty of meat in the house. And now we can use more red points for butter."

She read off the list she had written.

"And if you'd stop in the gas company office, ma'am," she said, "maybe you could make them send a man about the icebox."

"I'll try," said Lucia.

150

She was surprised when Bee volunteered to go with her.

"I've got some things to get in the drugstore," Bee said. "Let's take the car."

"No," said Lucia. "I'd rather save the gas for sometime when we really need it."

They were both ready and waiting when the taxi came; Lucia in an old red and white checked gingham dress, stiffly starched, Bee in gray slacks and a white shirt, and that look she sometimes had of severely perfect grooming, her blonde hair pinned up under a blue bandanna, her arched, delicate brows a little darkened. She looked older this way; only when she turned away her head Lucia noted the sweet contour of her cheek, her childish neck.

"You're going to be disappointed, Mother," she said, "but I don't want to study art any more."

"I shan't be disappointed, dear."

"I'll tell you what I want to do, Mother. I want to go to Miss Kearney's, for her two-year secretarial course."

"Everyone says it's a very good school."

"It's the best," said Bee. "If you graduate from Kearney you're practically certain to get a job, no matter how bad conditions are."

"Well, I think that's a good idea, darling."

"Daddy won't think so," said Bee. "He'll kick like a steer."

"I'm sure he won't," said Lucia.

"Mother, honestly . . . ! You know how Father talks about career women. He's always saying that they miss out on all the best things in life."

"Well, you probably wouldn't want to be a career woman, dear."

"Yes, I do," said Bee. "I intend to keep on working after I get married."

151

"But if you have children——"

"I'd get a good nurse for them, and they'd be a damn sight better off than if I was home with them all the time."

"Don't swear, dear," said Lucia. "I don't see why they'd be better off. I don't see why a mother couldn't be as good as a nurse."

"Because the sort of mother who simply stays home and has no outside life can't help being narrow-minded," said Bee.

"Well, most nurses aren't so wonderfully broad-minded, that I can see," said Lucia.

"What's more, I think every woman ought to be able to support her children," said Bee. "Nobody knows what kind of world it's going to be, after this war. If you're going to take a chance and bring children into the world, you ought to be able to look after them, no matter what happens."

"Oh, yes . . ." said Lucia.

Anything rather than be like me, she thought. I'm simply a horrible example.

They rode in silence for a time.

"This new shampoo I'm going to get says it's specially good for dry hair," said Bee. "My hair's getting frightfully dry."

"You wash it too often," said Lucia.

This was a very familiar topic.

"I read an article about some women somewhere who wash their hair every single day," said Bee. "And they're famous for their beautiful hair."

"I never wash mine more than once a week," said Lucia, "and sometimes I let it go longer than that. And you'll have to admit that it's in pretty good condition."

"That's different," said Bee.

As if I were too old to *have* any hair, Lucia thought.

"I don't see why it's different," she said, coldly. "As a matter of fact, I've got rather remarkable hair. Hairdressers always speak of it. It's very thick, and it's very healthy."

Bee glanced at her.

"I know it is, Mother," she said, gently. "David and I always say so."

She kept on looking and looking at her mother.

"Don't stare so, Bee!" cried Lucia.

"Sorry, Mother," said Bee, and turned away her gaze.

They got out of the taxi at the market.

"I'll whip over to the drugstore, and come back for you," Bee said. "Will you be long, Mother?"

"Oh, hours, probably," said Lucia.

It was not, in theory, a self-service market, but it was understaffed, and the customers had been trained to go about and find their own things, to weigh the fruit and vegetables. Then you tried to get a place at the counter, to spread out the unwieldy hoard, and if you were not alert, people pushed in ahead of you and cut you off from your supplies; they planked down their things, and sometimes knocked yours off the counter. I hate this! Lucia thought. I wish I was immensely rich and arrogant, so that people *had* to be polite to me, no matter how they felt.

"No paper towels," said the clerk. "Try on Tuesday. No sugar today. Only cheese we got is pimento, and you're lucky to get that."

The telephone rang and he went away to answer it; Lucia was still waiting his return when Bee came for her.

The girl in the gas company's office was distrait and superior.

153

"Oh, hasn't the man been yet?" she said. "I'll check on it, to see if he came."

"He *didn't* come," said Lucia.

"Maybe you were out," said the girl.

"We're never all out."

"Well, maybe he's been busy with emergency calls," said the girl.

"Ours is an emergency," said Lucia.

"No," said the girl, flatly. "We don't call yours an emergency. I'll check on it."

"Will you let me know when to expect the man?"

"We don't do that," said the girl. "He takes the calls in turn."

The taxi driver was an unfamiliar one, and odious.

"They ought to leave us make a charge for them big grocery bags," he said. "If trucks get paid for bundles, why not us? But no. People fill up the cab with them heavy bundles that are hard on the springs and all, and when they get out, it's a ten-cent tip."

"Give him ten cents!" Bee whispered.

"No! I might have to take him again," Lucia whispered back.

He stopped the cab before the house and Lucia leaned forward to pay the fare and give him a quarter tip. He said nothing.

"I can't get the door open!" said Bee.

"Pull the handle *down!*" said he. "Pull it hard."

"I suppose it would kill you to open the door," said Bee.

"No," he said, "and it wouldn't kill you, neither."

"Hush!" whispered Lucia.

Bee got the door open and they descended, and carried the big bags into the kitchen.

154

"Master David said could we have lunch a little early?" said Sibyl. "He wants to go out."

"Why, yes," said Lucia. "Half-past twelve, Bee?"

"All right," said Bee, moving away.

Lucia was about to follow her, but Sibyl came to her side.

"Mr. Nagle's here, ma'am," she said, very low.

Lucia looked at her.

"Ma'am . . . !" said Sibyl. "Sit down! There! Drink some cold water, ma'am."

"Where is he, Sibyl?"

"Put him upstairs in the boathouse, ma'am. Nobody else saw him. Told him he might have to wait quite a while, till you got a chance to see him."

Lucia sipped the water, fighting against a dreadful weakness that weighed upon her. I can't, she told herself. I can't talk to him. I can't see him. I can't—I really can't do anything. If I don't go, he'll go away.

He would not go away. She was certain of that. If she did not go to him, he would come here, to the house. I'll have to see him, she thought. I'll have to.

A furious anger sprang up in her. What's Mr. Donnelly doing? she cried to herself. What does he *mean* by saying not to worry, that *he'll* look after things?

What the *hell's* the matter with him? she thought.

Chapter Seventeen

This anger helped her.

"I'll go and see him now," she said, rising.

The swing door opened and David came into the kitchen.

"Say, look, Mother!" he said. "Just glance over this, will you?"

"What is it, dear?"

"Take a look!" he said, holding out a sheaf of papers.

"But what is it, David?" she asked. "Won't after lunch do?"

"All right," he said. "Don't bother. I've got to post it right after lunch."

He was hurt.

"Oh, then I want to see it now!" said Lucia. "Give it to me, David!"

He hesitated, but only for a moment; he held out the papers again, neatly typed pages stapled together.

Ubu stood at the mouth of the cave and turned his shaggy head from side to side. Over his shoulders was thrown a rough garment of wolf-skin and in his hand he held a stone club weighing around fifteen pounds. The cave was on a mountainside and below him stretched the jungle, where roamed the saber-toothed tiger and other wild beasts who were the enemies of him and his.

156

"Is it a story, David?" she asked, glancing up.

"Sort of a good start, isn't it?" he asked. "I mean, you get interested in Ubu, don't you?"

"Oh, yes, you *do!*"

"I'll tell you what it's for," he said. "You know that Vigorex Gum program on the radio? Well, they're having a contest. Anyone under sixteen can send in a story, up to a thousand words, about any of the great inventions that changed the life of mankind. The first prize is a thousand-dollar War Bond. I bet you practically everybody will do stories about the printing press, telephone, things like that. Well, I've done the wheel. You'll see how I've worked it out."

"David, how interesting!" Lucia said. "Let's go into the sitting room while I finish it."

Nagle can just wait, she thought. Even if I was mean enough not to read David's story, I couldn't get out to the boathouse now. David would want to come with me—and what could I say?

Mr. Harper was in the sitting room, reading.

"When you've finished it, Mother," David said, "maybe Grandpa'd like to glance at it."

"Certainly! Certainly! What is it? A letter?"

"Well, it's a sort of story, in a way," David answered, laughing a little. "Don't worry, Grandpa. I'm not trying to be an author, or anything like that. I just thought I'd have a try for this prize."

Lucia sat down to read the story.

"Gosh, you're a slow reader!" said David.

"I know," said Lucia.

She was trying to make her distracted mind understand the words she read.

Ikko came out of the cave, bearing in her arms the infant just born, wrapped lovingly in the skin of a giant hare.

"Ikko! Look! Stone!" cried Ubu.

As Ubu stood watching the almost perfectly round Wonderstone rolling down the mountainside, into his brain was born the great principle of the Wheel. He saw how round stones like this could be used to transport the bodies of slain beasts . . .

"Lunch is served, ma'am," said Sibyl.

"Just a moment," said Lucia, and finished the last page. "It's *awfully* good, David."

"The thing is, is it interesting?" he asked.

"It's awfully interesting!"

"The deadline's the day after tomorrow," said David. "I didn't mean to be so late with it, but I couldn't get it right. I've got to mail it right after lunch, but I'd like Grandpa to take a look."

"I'll read it at the table, if your mother doesn't object," said Mr. Harper.

Bee came into the dining room, with a towel pinned over her hair like a Red Cross nurse.

"I tried that shampoo——" she began.

"Hush, dear!" said Lucia. "David's written a story——"

"I've read it," said Bee. "I must say I think it's pretty darn good."

"Remarkably good," said Mr. Harper. "Yes . . . The thing is, my boy, have you got all your facts straight? I mean to say, these prehistoric animals—they all existed in the same era?"

"Yes, sir," said David. "I looked them up in the library. I did quite a lot of research for this thing."

I think I have a fever, Lucia said to herself. I feel so hot.

158

I feel so—queer. I've got to see Nagle. Suppose he gets tired of waiting? Suppose he comes here?

As soon as he had finished lunch, David left the house, and Bee went out on the veranda, to dry her hair in the sun. I'll have to go by the back way, Lucia thought, and went into the kitchen. Through the window there she saw her father pacing leisurely up and down the lawn, hands clasped behind his back. I can't go that way, either, she thought. He'd ask me where I was going.

I must make up an excuse. I've got to get to the boat-house.

"Took some lunch out to Mr. Nagle, ma'am," said Sibyl. "Took him some of Mr. Harper's whisky."

"Oh, Sibyl, what a good idea! Was he—how was he?"

"He's quiet now, ma'am," said Sibyl.

As if he were a dangerous animal, quiet only for this moment.

"If you'll go up and lie down, ma'am," said Sibyl, "I'll tell you, soon as Mr. Harper stops his walking."

Lucia went up to her room, but she could not lie down, or even sit down. She stood by the window where she could see the boathouse.

Donnelly . . . she thought. He told me not to worry. What the hell's the matter with him? Damn him. He let this happen. He's no good. He's nothing but a crook, a liar. I hate him. Damn him.

She glanced at her watch, and panic swept over. Half-past one! It isn't good for Father to walk so long, at his age . . .

But that was his habit. On a stormy day, he would walk up and down a room for an hour or more. Oh, don't let him

159

do that today! Or make Bee come in. I've got to get out.

She kept her eyes upon her watch now. That's a mistake, she told herself. I ought to read—or mend something. This way makes the time seem twice as long. Twenty to two . . . He *can't* walk this long.

It was a quarter to two when Sibyl knocked at the door. "Mr. Harper's come in, ma'am," she said.

Lucia went past her and ran down the stairs, through the kitchen and out by the back door. Her father or Bee might be looking out of a window; they must not see her running. I don't want to run, anyhow, she thought. Nagle can just wait, damn him.

She walked across the grass to the boathouse and up on to the little porch; she opened the door and entered into the moldy dimness. There was no one in the room; there was not a sound to be heard. She closed the door and stood holding the knob.

"Mr. Nagle?" she called.

There was no answer. Is he—hiding? she thought. No. He's upstairs. Just sitting up there? If I go upstairs, suppose he's standing behind the door?

Suppose he tries to kill me? she thought.

That seemed to her quite possible. Nagle was mysterious to her as a creature from another planet; she did not think of him as a man, a human being; only as something wholly evil and dangerous. He's come for money, of course, she thought, and if he doesn't get any, maybe he'll try to kill me.

But suppose he wasn't there at all? Suppose he had got tired of waiting and had gone away?

Too good to be true, she told herself.

"Mr. Nagle?" she called again.

160

"Come up!" he called back.

The only thing to do was, to go quickly, without thinking. He was sitting in a wicker chair, in the upstairs sitting room, in shirt sleeves and lavender suspenders, his soft hat on the back of his head. The lunch tray was on the floor, and on the table beside him was a bottle of whisky and a glass.

"You took your time, all right," he said.

"I couldn't help it," said Lucia.

"All right," he said. "I've done all the waiting I'm going to do. It's ten thousand now—and I mean now."

"I can't get it."

"You can get it, off your father. I checked on him."

"No. I couldn't."

"You get it—or else."

"Or else what?"

"I take one of your girl's letters to this guy I know on a newspaper."

"Go ahead," said Lucia. "No newspaper would ever publish a letter like that."

"Wait a minute, duchess," he said. "Wait a minute. Who's talking about printing any letters? All I want is, to get this guy after you. Just let me tip him off there's a good-looking blonde mixed up in the Darby case, and he'll do the rest."

"What good do you think that's going to do you?" Lucia asked.

"Plenty, duchess. Plenty."

He wants to do me harm, she thought. He wants that, much more than he wants the money. He hates me.

And that, somehow, took away all her fear of him. He wouldn't dream of killing me, she thought, scornfully, looking at him as he sat there with his hat on the back of his head, drinking her father's whisky. I'd like to hit him, she thought. I'd like to hurt him.

"Well?" he asked. "What about it, duchess?"

"Nothing," she said. "I can't give you ten thousand dollars. Or even one thousand."

"All right," he said. "Then you and that blonde girl of yours get the first train out of here, and stay out of here."

"What a crazy idea!" said Lucia.

"Get the hell out of this town and stay out of it. Or you'll wish you was never born."

He's just bluffing, Lucia thought, surprised, and still more scornful. Just trying to frighten me. He can't really do anything.

"You needn't wait," she said. "You won't get anything."

"I'll go when I'm ready," he said. "Just now, I'm not ready."

"Suppose I call the police?"

"Go ahead! Go right ahead and call the police, duchess. I'm a friend of Ted Darby's. I know he was mixed up with that blonde girl of yours, and I'm here to see can I find out anything. So I give the cops one of her letters. And they'll make her talk."

Well, that could very well happen, if I called the police, Lucia thought. It's funny, when you think of it, but I really don't want the police getting into this, any more than he does.

"Well, duchess?" he cried.

"Stop calling me that!" she said, sharply.

"So you don't like it? That's just too bad, duchess. That's one mistake I never made, to get myself mixed up with one of you goddam society bitches."

162

"'Society'?" Lucia cried. "If you think I'm a 'society woman,' you're a fool."

"Oh, no," he said. "I'm no fool. I know your kind, all right. I seen friends of mine fall for them. You're just no goddam good, any of you. Any man that gets mixed up with one of you is finished. Look at Darby and——"

"Stop it!" Lucia said. "Get out of here!"

"When I'm ready, duchess. When I'm ready."

"You——" she began, and stopped, with a chill of terror at the sound of a step on the stairs.

Father? she thought. No, no! Oh, don't let it be Father!

It was Donnelly, tall and elegant, in a slate-gray suit, with a blue cornflower in his buttonhole.

"What's this?" he asked. "I could hear the two of you from outside."

"He's going to give the letters to a newspaperman——" said Lucia.

"Shut up!" said Nagle.

"Let her alone," said Donnelly. "What are you doing here at all, Carlie? It is a dirty, underhanded thing for you to do, when we had it all fixed up."

He spoke with severity, but not angrily.

"You got your money," he said. "Why wouldn't that be enough for you, Carlie? You'd no right to come here."

"Now you look here, Marty," said Nagle, rising. "If we got to have a showdown, we got to have a showdown. I come here, because some way I got to get this woman off your neck. You don't see it, but I do. She's going to ruin you."

"Let her alone," said Donnelly, still without anger. "It is a thing beyond your understanding, entirely."

"The hell it is!" said Nagle. "Look what she done to you already. A man like you, a man with a name—and yesterday you were passing the hat, getting a couple of hundred here, couple of hundred there. D'you think I want the money you got that way? Listen. We went in this together; we were cutting fifty-fifty. And when she won't come across, what do you do? Pass the hat—to pay *me*. Like I was holding you up. I am not. I don't want your money."

"Well, you took it," said Donnelly, "and you told me you'd let her alone. You are a liar, Carlie."

"So I'm a liar. Okay. I'm not going to let her alone."

"You will have to," Donnelly said.

Lucia moved aside, so that she could lean against the wall. The two men stood facing each other; Nagle was shorter, he was overweight, he looked older, but there was a powerful energy about him, in the pugnacious set of his head, in the way he stood, with his rear thrust out. And Donnelly was blurred, vague; he showed no energy, only that severe patience.

But he'll settle things, she thought. One way or another. She leaned against the wall, completely passive. There was nothing for her to do, or to say; for the moment there was nothing she need think about. The two men were talking, but she did not listen to them. She was waiting; she was resting.

Until a note in Donnelly's voice startled her. She glanced at him, and his blurred look was gone; he was wary, his head a little bent, like a listening animal.

"What did yez say?" he asked.

"You heard me," said Nagle.

They're afraid of each other, Lucia thought, seeing in Nagle the same alertness, the same bodily stillness. As if
164

the least little movement might make the other pounce.

"You told me Eddy and Moe were talking about it," said Donnelly. "Then it was you told them."

"It was not. Do you think you can go around in New York like you was invisible? You take her to Gogo's place. Champagne——"

"There was no champagne!"

"Okay, so there was no champagne. Okay. It was Pop that seen you there."

"Pop, was it?" said Donnelly. "And it was Pop told Eddy and Moe?"

"That's right," said Nagle. "It was natural that he'd tell them. She is the same woman they saw over in Darby's hotel, and Eddy and Moe were good friends of Darby's."

"Sure it was natural," said Donnelly. "Only that Pop is in Buffalo."

Nagle made a slight move, a shift of the feet.

"Maybe he wrote them a letter."

"He would not write anybody a letter. And he did not see me at Gogo's place. He went to Buffalo last Thursday. You are a liar, Carlie."

"Now, look here, Marty——"

"If Eddy and Moe were talking, it was you told them, Carlie."

Something was happening, something was changing in the two men who did not move.

"I did not tell them," said Nagle.

"You are a liar," Donnelly said again. "If they were talking, it was you set them on to it. I'll never forgive it you."

"All right. They were not talking. I only told you that to make you see what you were doing. You can't keep this thing hid; you can't do it. They'll find out, and it's going

165

to get them worried. You play around with this society bitch, and she gets you talking. Okay. One day you talk too much, and she turns you up. And the rest of us, too. For God's sake, Marty, drop her! You never let a woman throw you before. For God's sake, show some sense!"

"It's in your mind to set the others on her," said Donnelly.

"Then let her get the hell out of here. We——"

Donnelly struck, without any warning; his arm shot out straight from the shoulder, his fist caught Nagle on the point of the jaw, and sent him stumbling backward, with little running steps. He crashed into a chair and fell on the floor, with a thud that shook the house. As quick as a cat, Donnelly was on his knees beside him.

"Is he hurt?" Lucia asked, in a flat voice.

"No," said Donnelly. "Go back to your house."

He was bending over Nagle, and she moved, to see what he was doing.

"Marty . . . !" she cried. She tried to scream, but her throat contracted. "Marty . . ." she said, in a whisper.

"Be quiet!" he said, his teeth clenched. "Go home!"

She caught his arm, but it was like steel, like stone. His fingers were tight around Nagle's throat, and Nagle's pale eyes were bulging, his tongue showed between his gasping lips, his face was darkening.

"Marty . . ." she said, pulling at his arm with both hands. "Stop . . . I beg you . . . I beg you . . ."

She herself was choking. With her eyes fixed upon Nagle's awful face, she put her hands to her neck. She was choking and she was blind now, looking into blackness.

Donnelly lifted her onto the sagging couch. He raised her head and held a glass to her lips.

"Drink a little," he said. "It will help you."

166

The whisky had a rank, sour smell. She took a few sips; then she pushed the glass away, so violently that it fell out of his hand onto the floor.

"His glass . . ." she said.

She lay back, for a little time; then she sat up. Donnelly stood beside her, smoking a cigarette.

"As soon as you're able," he said, "go back to your house. Try now; can you get up?"

"Nagle . . . ?" she said, with a great effort.

"I will look after him."

"You killed him," she said. "You killed him. You choked him."

"I had to do it," he said.

"You killed him. You choked him——"

"Let you get back to your house now," he said.

"You killed him. You choked him——"

"Don't be saying that, darlin'," he said.

"How *could* you? How *could* you?" she demanded, beginning to cry.

"I had to do it. It was in his mind to set the two of them on you."

"Better . . ." she said. "Much better . . ." She was sobbing. "Anything—would be better—than that. Than *that.*"

"Look!" he said, sitting down on the couch beside her. "It is hard for you, but you'll have to have courage. You'll have to stop crying. Suppose, now, somebody was to call you, and you'd have to go downstairs?"

"O God!" she cried, in despair.

No matter what happened to her, no matter how she felt, her first thought must always be, how to face her world. Her little world, her children, her father.

"I'd like some more whisky, please," she said. "Could I drink out of the bottle?"

"You could," he said. "Only go easy."

She took a few swallows.

"Have you a cigarette?" she asked.

He gave her one and lit it for her.

"Thank you," she said.

"You're welcome," he said.

They spoke with formality, as they had in the past. She smoked for a time, sitting up straight, growing quieter, growing stronger.

"What will you do—with him?"

"Leave it to me," he said. "Go back now to your house, and if they ask you any questions, tell them this. Tell them you'd invited me to take a cup of tea before I'd be off to Montreal. Then, while you were out this morning, Nagle comes, asking for me, and you sent him off to the boathouse to wait. Well, after a while you get to wondering is he still there, and you walk out, and you hear the two of us, having an argument. You wait awhile, and then you're off, leaving us at it."

"All right!" she said, frowning. "But what are you going to do with him?"

"Say it for me once, will you not?" he asked. "I mean, the way you'll tell it, if they ask you any questions."

"No. I'll remember."

"Say it once, will you not?"

"Oh . . . I'll say I asked you to tea, and Nagle came, asking for you, and I told him to wait in the boathouse, and I heard you having an argument. Now I want to know what you're going to do with him."

"I will take him in your boat and row off with him."

168

"That's ridiculous!" she said. "There are always lots of people out on the water, this time of day."

"I will manage," he said.

"Not that way. There's no place you could take him."

"I will leave him here, then, where he won't be seen, and I will come back for him later."

"Here? No. Can't you think of anything better than that?"

"I cannot," he said.

"Then I will. The——" She looked up at him, frightened to see him blurred and vague again. "Don't you realize the danger you're in?"

"I will manage."

"Your plans are—simply idiotic. If you're found with him, you won't have a chance. I'm sure any doctor would know how he'd been killed. You want me to tell people I left you having an 'argument' with him. I suppose you mean to swear you killed him in self-defense. Well, nobody would believe that. Not when you choked him."

"I will manage," he said.

He stood there, so big, so slow, so vague.

"You're a perfect fool!" she cried. "You've got to get him away. I'll bring my car to the door, and you——"

"I cannot drive," he said.

"Yes, you can. You drove me——"

"I cannot drive now," he said. "My arm has gone dead on me."

"What do you mean?"

"My arm," he explained. "I cannot use it at all."

She noticed then that his right arm hung limp at his side.

"You've got to use it," she said. "That's all just psychological."

169

"How's that?" he asked, anxiously.

"It's just imagination. You can use it."

"It is a judgment on me," he said.

"What!" she cried. "You *can't* be so ignorant and stupid. I'm going to bring the car here, and you've got to get him into it, and take him away. You've got to leave him somewhere, and then go home. Nobody ever needs know what happened to him. *Don't* be so spineless! Aren't you man enough to fight for your own life?"

"I cannot move my arm at all," he said. "It was done to me, so I could not get away. Go back to your house now——"

"You fool! You idiot! You coward!" she cried. "Snap out of it!"

He did not answer.

"Then I'll get you out of it," she said.

Chapter Eighteen

Now look here!" she said. "I'll bring the car to the door and we—"

"No," he said. "I will not let you get into this."

"If you won't help me," she said, "I'll do it all alone. I'll get him down the stairs and into the car alone."

"Go back to your house," said Donnelly. "Leave me to manage my own way."

"I won't. You've got a chance, and you'll have to take it. I'll get the car, and you look around for something to—wrap him in."

"For the love of God, will you let me alone?" he cried.

"No. I won't. I'll do it all by myself if you're not man enough to help me."

"I will help you," he said, with an effort. He sighed, very deeply, and raised his head. "Have you a trunk, maybe?" he asked.

"Not here. But wait! There's that chest."

He looked where she pointed, at a long window seat, the top padded and covered with faded, moldering chintz. He went over to it and raised the lid.

"It will do," he said. "Only there are things in it, tools, and the like."

"Get them out," she said. "Oh, *try* to use your right hand . . . ! Here!"

She leaned over the chest, and brought out a trowel, two empty flashlight cases, a tangled mass of wire and rope and threw them on the floor; she was so fast, and he was so slow.

"Now we'll get him in," she said.

"You cannot!" said Donnelly, with a sort of horror.

"Oh, yes, I can!" she said.

"You don't know——"

"I picked up Rex—he was David's dog—I picked up Rex after he'd been run over. I carried him to the house," she said, proudly and arrogantly. "I can do anything I have to do."

"Not this," he said.

She turned then to look at Nagle. He was only a mound on the floor, covered with a dark green chenille tablecloth.

"Come on!" she said. "We've got to hurry."

Donnelly turned the chest over on its side.

"Hold open the lid," he said.

Using only his left arm, he pulled Nagle to the chest; he got him into it, lying on his back, with his knees raised high, because the chest was too short. He pushed the box upright, and Nagle shifted, with a faint thud.

"Now, while I'm getting the car," Lucia said, "do something with the tray and the whisky bottle. And the tools. Make the place look all right."

"I will," he said.

She ran down the stairs and opened the door. And out in the brilliant sunshine, terror seized her. Someone will see me, she thought. What can I say? What can I say?

She must not run. She must not look behind her. *Think!* Think of something to say to them. You must think.

She opened the garage door and got into the car. Think!

You can't get away with this. Someone is going to ask you where you're going. Someone will come to the boathouse. To see you and Martin dragging that chest down the stairs. What are you going to say?

She drove the car to the boathouse, and left the engine running when she got out. I *knew* I ought to save the gas, she thought. I knew something would turn up . . .

She opened the door, and saw Donnelly halfway down the stairs. He had wrapped the chest in the chenille cover and tied one end of it like the mouth of a sack; he held this in his left hand, letting the chest slide bumping down the steps ahead of him.

"That was a good thing to think of!" she said, pleased. "Now we'll get it into the car."

They could not. It was far too heavy for her, and he was of little use without his right hand.

"Can't you try?" she cried.

"God knows I would like to," he said.

They stood on the grass before the boathouse, with the chest at their feet, and they could not lift it into the car.

"Wait here!" she said. "I'm going to get Sibyl."

Sibyl was sitting in her neat, clean kitchen, reading a magazine. The sun was shining in, the wartime alarm clock ticked loudly.

"Sibyl," Lucia said, "help me, please. I've got to get a box into the car, and it's too heavy."

"Yes, ma'am," said Sibyl.

They walked to the boathouse, side by side.

"Mr. Donnelly's hurt his arm," Lucia said. "But I think we can manage, Sibyl."

It was very difficult, but they did manage. The chest was in the back of the car.

"Thank you, Sibyl," said Lucia. "You'd better get in front with me, Mr. Donnelly."

"*Mother!*"

It had happened. Bee was here, standing beside the car, her newly washed hair like silver in the sun.

"Mr. Donnelly wants to borrow an old engine I found in the boathouse," said Lucia. "He thinks he can fix it."

It was no trouble to say that. It was not necessary to think. The words simply came, when you needed them.

"But, Mother, where are you *going?*"

"To the station," said Lucia.

"But, Mother, Mrs. Lloyd'll be here——"

"Oh, I'll be back," said Lucia, carelessly.

"But, Mother, we can get a cab for—Mr. Donnelly——"

"No, dear," said Lucia. She started the car; they went down the drive and onto the highway.

"Holy Mother of God!" said Donnelly. "There was never another like you in the world."

"Can you think of any place to take the chest?"

"I don't know these parts at all."

"I don't, either," she said. "I haven't done any driving around. I suppose I'd better just go ahead . . . ?"

"You had. I'll keep my eyes open, for a lane or a byroad."

It's done, she thought. I got him out of it. She drove along, steadily, tranquilly, with an untroubled mind. The sweet air blew in her face; cars and trucks were rolling along the highway, each in its right lane, all so orderly. It's like riding in a procession.

It's done. I've got him out of it, the idiot. Sibyl will never say anything. Even if she knew . . . And maybe she does. I don't know. It doesn't matter. Anyhow, here he is.

174

Here he was, sitting beside her, riding along in the procession. The big parade . . . she said to herself. I got him out of it.

"You'd better really go to Montreal, right away," she said.

"I will," he said.

She glanced at him, and she did not trust him.

"You don't mean that," she said. "You haven't any intention of going to Montreal."

"I was just thinking . . ." he said, with humility.

A great pity for him rose in her. He was so helpless, so remote from her. He mustn't brood, she thought. I've got to get him talking.

There was only one thing in the world that *they* could talk about.

"Why did you come out here today?" she asked.

"Sibyl called me up. She told me Nagle was there."

"Why do you trust Sibyl so," she asked, "when you hardly know her?"

"It's a sort of idea I have," he said, with the same humility. "There's a kind of wisdom in her." He paused. "She is a realist," he said.

Strange word for him to use, she thought. Now he was silent again, and she did not like that.

"If you'd talk . . ." she said. "If we talked—about this . . ."

"I cannot talk at all," he said. "I'm sorry, but I cannot."

"We can't go on like this. We can't—just ignore it."

"I hope you'll forget it," he said. "Try, will you not?"

"Forget it?" she said, scornfully. "Not till the last day I live."

"I had to do it," he said. "You see, Carlie was a strange

175

man. He was a grand friend to the ones he liked, but there were not many of those. And if anyone did him a wrong, he'd never forget it. He was still talking about a teacher he'd had when he was a boy, over in Brooklyn. She's over eighty years of age now, but he was still trying to find a way to get back at her. He'd never have let up on you."

"But I never did him any harm!"

"He thought you did. He thought you wanted to break up the friendship there was between him and me."

There was a long moment's silence.

"There were other elements in it, too," he went on. "The first time he went out to see you, he came back very bitter. He was hurt."

"Hurt? That man?"

"He told me you looked down on him, you and your girl. He told me you were haughty to him. Like the dirt under your feet, he told me."

"I was afraid of him."

"Then you did not show it. Anyhow, he'd a great hatred for society women."

"*You* know better than to call me a 'society woman.'"

"It was the only word he had for it," said Donnelly, grave and gentle. "What they call 'the gentry,' in the old country. What he meant was, a woman with a standing in the world, a woman with a family, a good name. It was his conviction they'd always sell a man out, to keep what they had."

"He was a vindictive, ignorant man."

"Maybe," said Donnelly. "He always held it against his parents that they did not give him a good education, did not send him to college. They had him working for his father, that was a butcher, when he was fourteen, and it made him

176

bitter. He was a smart man. It is a pity he did not get a good education."

"Did you—like him?"

"I did," he said.

"But——"

"I had to do it," he said. "Once he had an idea in his head, he'd never let go of it. And he gave himself away. He let me see what he had in his mind. If he'd set Eddy and Moe onto you, it would be the worst thing could ever happen to you."

"Why? What could they have done?"

"You would not understand, the way you've never met anyone like those two, and never will."

"Are they—gunmen?" she asked, timidly, afraid of hurting his feelings, but desperately curious.

"They are not," he said.

"But—what are they?"

"You would not understand."

"You could explain," she said.

"I will not," he said.

After a moment, he spoke again.

"There's a lane to the left," he said. "What do you think of it?"

She slowed down the car, and looked along the road that ran downhill from the highway, a pretty lane, with trees meeting overhead. There were no buildings to be seen, no traffic.

"We might try it," she said.

"We don't want to waste any time," he said.

"Why? Why do you say that?"

"You ought to be getting home," he said.

That's a strange thing to say, she thought, startled. A strange thing for him to be thinking, when there's this other thing . . .

Nagle is here, she thought, with a shock. In the car. In that chest.

She was driving along this quiet lane, with a dead man in the car, a murdered man. If the least thing went wrong, it would mean—God knew what. We can't do this! she thought. This is madness. We can't possibly get away with this.

She glanced at him. His head was turned away; he was looking into the woodland that bordered the lane. Think what could happen to him . . .

"Mr. Donnelly . . ." she said, a little loudly, "we've got to talk about this. We've got to have a plan, a story. It'll have to be self-defense."

"Oh, I'll think of a story," he said.

"We've got to have the same story, don't you see?"

"There's no need for you to be thinking about a story," he said. "No one's going to bother you about this."

"That's silly. Something could go wrong, any minute. You've got to think this out, carefully."

"I will."

"But now! Lieutenant Levy's been to see me already about—Ted Darby. He might very well come again, and ask questions. He—I think he's very clever."

"Lieutenant Levy? The police, is it?"

"The Horton County police. Suppose he goes into the boathouse? He might find something there—something we hadn't thought about?"

"Look!" Donnelly said. "There's a bit of a lake, around the bend of the road. You can see it from here."

178

The road was level now, along the floor of a little valley. She accelerated.

"Slow down!" he said, mildly. "There is a curve ahead."

And a car came around the curve, a roadster, with two soldiers in it.

"They saw us!" she said. "They could identify us!"

"Don't be nervous," said Donnelly. "You're trembling."

"Let's hurry!"

The engine backfired, and she gave a sort of scream.

"Don't! Don't!" he said, in distress.

It backfired again, and stopped, and started. Donnelly leaned forward.

"Your gauge is broken," he said.

"I know."

The car stopped. She pressed the starter, and nothing happened.

"I'll get out and crank it," she said.

"It will do you no good," he said. "You're out of gas."

"God damn it!" she cried.

"Don't! Don't!" he said. "It's not like you."

"What can we do? What in God's name can we do?"

"We are fine," he said. "We couldn't have found a better spot. Let you be easy now. Here! Have a cigarette!"

"There's a car coming!"

"Let it come. They'll see nothing at all but the two of us, having a little smoke."

"The chest!"

"People are taking around queer things in their cars, these days."

"Oh, *don't* you see? All these people can say they saw us here. After they've found—that."

"They will not find it. Smoke your cigarette now, and I'll tell you what we'll do."

I'm shaking, she thought. I wasn't, before. But this is the worst. Just to sit here, until someone gets us.

"We can't get away with this," she said.

"Wait, now!" he said. "Listen to what I'm saying, will you not? We can get away with this, if you'll do your part right. You'll have to pull yourself together."

"What can I do? What is there——?"

"Come!" he said. "We'll walk a little way, up the road."

"Leave—that?"

He got out of the car; he held out his hand, his left hand, to her; she took it, and got out beside him. Still holding her hand, he began to walk away.

"Listen now to what you've got to do," he said. "You've got to do it right. If you don't, we're sunk, the two of us. You've got to go home, as fast as you can."

"And leave you—like this?" she said. "I won't."

"Listen, will you not? Your girl said there was someone coming to visit you. Mrs. —" He paused a moment. "Mrs. Lloyd."

"How can you remember that?"

"I'm a good one for remembering. If you don't go home, your family'll be worrying. If you're away out of it too long, they'll have the police looking for you."

"Oh . . . !" she cried, angrily.

"You wouldn't want that," he said. "You'll have to get home as quick as ever you can. Here's how you'll do it. We passed a filling station on the highway, just a bit before we turned off here. It is not a long walk. Go there, and tell them to send for a taxi to take you to the railroad station.
180

Don't say anything about your car being stuck. You could give a kind of idea that the man you were driving with began to make trouble."

"I can't."

"Ah, you can!" he said. "Look how you answered your girl, quick as a flash. Now, when you get home— Are you paying heed to me?"

"Yes."

"Forget the story about us having an argument and all that. It will not do now. Here's the story you'll tell. Are you listening, dear?"

"Yes."

"Sibyl told you Nagle had come and she had sent him into the boathouse to wait. Well, you'd seen Nagle before and you did not like him much. You thought he had something to do with the black market. So you didn't hurry out to see him. You let him wait, hoping maybe he'd go away. Have you got that clear?"

"Yes."

"Then there's myself. Was there ever an old engine in the boathouse?"

"Yes."

"As soon as you've a chance, get rid of it. Throw it down into the water. Well, you'd told me I could take the engine, to see could I fix it. So, after your lunch, when you thought Nagle would be gone, you went out to the boathouse, to have a look at the engine. And, sure enough, Nagle is gone. You did not see him at all. Then I come along, and you say you'll give me a lift to the station. Well, we're driving along, and you ask me where am I taking the engine, and I tell you to a sort of a boat yard where a friend of mine is going to work on it. You'll remember all this?"

181

"Yes," she said, resisting every word of the story in her mind.

"Well, I have hurt my arm, and in the kindness of your heart, you say you will drive me to the boat yard. The gauge in the car is broke, and you don't know the gas is low until the car stops on you. When that happens, you know you've got to get home, or they'll be worrying. You leave the car with me, to go on to the boat yard, and you take the train."

"And what about you?"

"I'll wait a bit, till you're out of it. Then I'll go along to the filling station and telephone a friend of mine in New York. He'll drive out, and he'll bring gas for me. He'll help me with the chest, and we'll drive back to New York. Then I will get a late train to Montreal."

"No," she said.

"Now, what do you mean, at all?" he asked.

"I can't . . . How is your arm?"

"It is better."

"Can you move it now?"

"A little, I can."

"Let me see you," she said.

She was startled to hear him laugh.

"And what's so funny?" she demanded.

"The way you talk to me."

"I'm sorry," she said, coldly.

"I like it," he said. "Only, don't you be worrying about me. I've been looking after myself a good long while."

"I know," she said. "But . . ."

She remembered him in the boathouse, so helpless, so vague. It is a judgment on me, he had said.

"I'd like to see you move your arm," she said.

182

"Well, maybe I cannot, just now," he said. "It comes and goes. But whatever it is, it is passing off."

"Suppose the friend you're going to call up isn't home?"

"I've plenty of others."

"It'll be a long time, hours, before anyone can drive out here from New York."

"Well, I've a nice shady spot to wait in. I've cigarettes on me, and a bottle of whisky in my pocket."

"You mustn't *drink!*" she cried. "That'll make you do wrong, stupid things. You mustn't touch it!"

"I wouldn't take too much," he said. "But a drop of good whisky . . . I was thinking you'd take a little yourself, you're that pale."

A car was coming from the direction of the highway.

"O God! He'll go right past my car!" she cried.

"Let him," said Donnelly.

"But if he sees the car there, with no one in it, he might stop. He might get out, and look in the chest——"

"Now, why would he be doing that, dear? He won't stop at all. You want to remember this. There's no one else in the world knows what's in that box, and if you do your part right, there's no reason why anybody would ever know."

She wanted to stop until the car had passed, but he took her hand and led her on, toward the highway. When the car had gone, he dropped her hand, and reached into a breast pocket.

"Here's something you might be glad of," he said, and held out three little capsules, bright yellow.

"What are they?"

"They're little sleeping pills," he said. "One will do you. Swallow one of them, and you'll have a good night's sleep."

"Do *you* take things like that?"

"I do," he said.

"It's a terribly bad habit."

"I don't like to be lying awake," he said.

She dropped the capsules into the pocket of her dress, and he brought out a wallet from another breast pocket. He flipped it open, and leaning it against his chest, he drew out some bills.

"You're not using your right arm!" she said.

"You've no money on you," he said. "You'd better take this."

She put the bills into her pocket without looking at them. They were getting nearer to the highway now.

"Send me a wire from Montreal," she said.

"I will," he said. "And take it easy. There's nobody else in the world knows about Nagle. He won't be missed for a day or two, the way he moves around so much. And it'll be longer than that before ever he's found. When he is found —and maybe that'll never happen—he won't be in the box. Nobody'll know where he came to his end."

Now she could see a big green truck going along the highway.

"The filling station's only a bit of a way, to the left," he said. "You'll go home now—and you'll remember the story, will you not?"

"I can't," she said, stopping short. "I just can't. I'm—tired, or something. I can't go on."

From a side pocket he brought out a bottle of whisky.

"You've got to go home," he said. "You know that, don't you, darlin'?"

"Yes . . ." she said.

"I didn't drink from the bottle," he said, anxiously. "Nobody's touched it at all since you had a swallow."

184

She took a sip, and it seemed weak, almost tasteless. She went on, one sip after another.

"I wouldn't take any more," he said. "It'd make you drowsy, maybe. It is good Scotch, the real McCoy. You know what to buy, don't you?"

"It's my father's," she said.

And, in speaking his name, amazement overwhelmed her. I *can't* be drinking Father's whisky—here! she thought. This can't be true. Not possibly. Not possibly.

"Now you'll go home, will you not?" he asked.

"Yes . . ."

"You've saved my life this day," he said. "I'd lost my wits entirely. I'd never have got him out of the place, if you hadn't saved me."

You killed him for me, she thought. So that I'd be safe.

"To your left," he said. "It's not far."

"Yes . . ." she said. "Good-by. You'll—be careful, won't you?"

"I will that," he said. "Good-by now, and God bless you."

Chapter Nineteen

She could see the house now, through the taxi window. She was coming back just as she had left, hatless, in the red and white checked gingham dress; she had no purse with her, no powder, no mirror, no comb. She did not know how strange, how dreadful she might be looking.

It seemed to her completely beyond her strength to mount the few steps to the veranda. The cab drove off, and she did not move.

The door opened, and Bee came running down to her.

"Mother!" she cried, in an unsteady voice. "I've been almost crazy with worry. Mother, what were you *thinking* of? Mrs. Lloyd waited nearly an hour——"

"We ran out of gas," said Lucia.

"But why did you go at all? *Why* did you go off with that man?"

"I don't intend to answer any more questions," said Lucia.

"All right! Just think—how I feel! I gave Mrs. Lloyd tea —and I tried to talk to her." Bee was crying now. "I kept telling her—you'd be back any minute. I said—something must have happened to the car—and that's what I kept thinking. An *accident* . . ."

186

"I'm sorry you were worried," said Lucia, and moved forward. "But I'm tired now, Bee. I want to wash——"

"Mother, there's liquor on your breath! Mother, you've been *drinking!*"

She stood facing her mother, her eyes dilated, tears on her cheeks.

"Don't you dare to talk like that," said Lucia, evenly. "If I choose to take a cocktail now and then, I intend to do so. And don't you dare to call it 'drinking.'"

I drank out of a bottle, in a country lane, she thought. I must be let alone.

"Let me pass, please," she said. "I want to rest a little, before dinner."

"Lieutenant Levy's here!" said Bee.

Let me alone! Let me alone! Lucia cried to herself. She waited a moment.

"I'm too tired now," she said. "Ask him to come back tomorrow."

"You've *got* to see him, Mother," said Bee. "He's a policeman. You can't put him off."

"Certainly I can," said Lucia. "It's nothing important."

"Mother," said Bee, "you've made things queer enough, as it is. When Lieutenant Levy asked me when you were coming home, I couldn't tell him. *I didn't know where you were!*"

"Well, why should you always know where I am?"

"*Mother!*"

That word was like a wave, like a tide beating against her. Mother! Where have you been? What were you doing? Open your door, when I knock. Answer, when I ask. Be there, always, every moment, when I want you. It's—inhuman . . . she thought.

"I'll see Lieutenant Levy," she said, briefly. "Tell him I'll be down in a moment."

Her father came into the hall as she entered the house. "Well, m'dear!" he said. "We were quite anxious——"

"Hello, Father!" she said, in a loud, cheerful voice, and went past him, up the stairs to her own room. She turned the key in the lock, and stood before the mirror.

She had thought of herself as bedraggled, grimy, pale, strange. But it was not so. Her hair was a little rough; there were faint smudges on her cheekbones, but, on the whole, she looked neat enough; a rather countrified housewife in a gingham dress.

She washed, and brushed her hair; she changed into a brown rayon dress with a ruffled peplum, ruffles on the sleeves. Fancy little number, David had called it, with disapproval. She did not like it herself, but what did it matter? She put on lipstick, more than usual, and, for some unrecognized reason, a necklace of green beads.

It's more about Ted Darby, she thought. I've just got to go through with it. Only, the whole Ted Darby episode seemed so far in the past, so unimportant. If it weren't for Father, she thought, I'd tell Lieutenant Levy the truth about it right now. There's nothing really horrible about it; nothing criminal.

Levy rose as she came into the room; he stood before her, tall, a little clumsy, with his big feet, his big nose, his big ears, yet with the mild, half-melancholy dignity that never left him.

"I'm sorry to bother you again, Mrs. Holley," he said. "But that's my job. I'm generally unwelcome."

"Oh, no!" Lucia said, warmly. "Not here! Smoke, if you like, Lieutenant."

"No, thank you," he said, and after she was seated, he sat down. "My housekeeper gives me a good idea of how hard things are for you ladies, these days," he said. "It must take the greater part of your day, just to get supplies."

"Well, you see, I have Sibyl," said Lucia. "She's wonderful."

"Does she do all the marketing?"

"Oh, I go sometimes," said Lucia. "But she's much better than I am."

"My housekeeper says you have to stick to one store, where they know you, if you want to get anything."

"Yes, you do," Lucia agreed.

I wish he'd get on with whatever he wants to ask, she thought. This is pretty boring.

But she appreciated his effort to establish a pleasant, easy atmosphere. It's the most sensible thing he could do, she thought, if he wants to get me talking, and off my guard. He had, she thought, a very good personality for disarming people, a slow, quiet voice, a gentle smile, a very courteous way of listening to every word you spoke. But she was on guard, and she would stay so; she would notice the first, the lightest change in his tone, in the drift of his talk.

He was talking on about his housekeeper; a Czech, she was, and a fine woman. She had been left a widow at twenty-five, in a strange country, with three children; she had brought them up, seen that they all got a good education. The two sons were in the Navy now; the daughter was married.

"But she keeps on working as hard as ever," he said. "The only thing that really upsets her is the shortage of soap. She was very apologetic about it, but she asked me to try, whenever I could, to get her a box of soap flakes. I haven't

189

been able to find any of the three brands she wants, in spite of my exalted position." He smiled a little. "In one store they offered to sell me something called Silverglo. D'you think it would do?"

"Well . . ." said Lucia, "I don't think there's any real soap in it, but it seems to get things clean, and it's certainly easier to get."

"Silverglo . . ." he repeated, and reached in his pocket.

He's going to take notes about it, Lucia thought, amused.

"Is this yours, Mrs. Holley?" he asked, holding out a dirty little scrap of paper.

She did not want to take that paper into her hand. She looked at him, but she could read nothing in his face.

"Will you look at this, please, Mrs. Holley?" he asked.

She did not want to look at it. She was afraid. But that would be the worst mistake I could make, she thought. To say—I didn't want to look at it.

She took the paper, still with her eyes fixed on his face. Then, with heavy reluctance, she opened it. It was an old market list of hers. Mrs. Lloyd had told her about a market list found by Ted Darby's body. *This one?* she thought.

Or was this just a trap, something subtle and complicated, designed to make her talk? But he can't make me talk, she thought, and I won't lie, either. That's what he wants, for me to lie, and get all mixed up.

"Why, yes!" she said, as if surprised. "It's an old market list of mine. Where in the world did you find it, Lieutenant?"

"It was found under Darby's body," he said.

That's supposed to shock me, she thought.

"Good heavens! On the island?" she asked. "We went over there for a picnic, and I must have dropped it."

"I don't think so, Mrs. Holley. Your picnic was nearly two

190

weeks ago, and this paper hasn't been out in any rain."

"It looks as if it had," she said. "It's frightfully dirty."

"Mrs. Holley, can you tell me on what day you wrote this list?"

"Not possibly," she said. "There are things that are on almost all my lists. Oranges, whole-wheat bread——"

"You'll notice that the list says 'Try Silverglo.' Does that suggest anything to you, Mrs. Holley?"

"No, it doesn't," she said. "I often put that down about things."

"I have information that the first advertisement for Silverglo appeared in the newspapers on the sixteenth. Does that refresh your memory, Mrs. Holley?"

"Why, no. I'm sorry, but it doesn't."

She saw what it meant. The list could not have been written before the sixteenth, and Ted Darby's body had been found on the eighteenth.

"Can you suggest any way in which this paper could have got on the island, Mrs. Holley?"

"Why, no, Lieutenant. When I've finished with a list, I don't bother with it. I throw it away, just anywhere. It could blow away."

Over a mile, across the water, straight to Ted Darby's body?

"Or someone—anyone could pick it up," she said.

"Yes," he agreed, politely, and waited. But she said nothing.

"Mrs. Holley," he said, "I understand that you took out your motorboat, early on the morning of the seventeenth."

"I don't remember dates, Lieutenant, but it's possible. I often get up very early. I like to."

"Did you, on this occasion, see anyone on the island?"

"I didn't look at the island," she said, airily. "I just went scooting past."

"Mrs. Lloyd has made a statement," he said. "She states that early on the morning of the seventeenth, sometime between five and six, she saw a motorboat in the bay, with two women in it. She has the impression that the two women were engaged in some sort of struggle. Did you see this boat with two women in it, Mrs. Holley?"

Lucia was silent for a moment, seized by astonishment. Maybe I'd better say I did see two women in a boat, she thought. It might help me.

But she could not do that. Her astonishment was turning into a curious anger. You can't let people get away with things like that, she thought. Mrs. Lloyd just says anything that comes into her head, and she can't *do* that.

"If there'd been another boat out," she said, "I couldn't have helped seeing it, or at least hearing it. Well, there wasn't any. Mrs. Lloyd may be nearsighted. I stood up once, to button my coat. Perhaps that's what she saw."

"She seems very definite about what she saw, Mrs. Holley."

"But she's mistaken," said Lucia. "I *know* there wasn't any such boat, with two women in it. Not between five and six in the morning. I *know* it."

Looking at Levy's face, she felt a curious fear. He was grave and patient, but he was not convinced. But can't he see what Mrs. Lloyd is like? she thought. She's sweet, but she's featherbrained. I dare say she thinks she saw two women struggling in a boat—but she didn't. I *know* she didn't.

It came into her mind that things like this must happen sometimes during a trial. Suppose you were being tried for

192

your life, she thought, and someone got up and made a statement like that? Suppose someone said—and really believed it—that they'd seen you in some place where you hadn't been? And maybe you couldn't prove you hadn't been there. Maybe all you could do was, to deny it.

She remembered David coming home from school one day, when he was a little boy.

"Miss Jesser said I scribbled in Petey's geography book," he had told her, pale, his eyes narrowed. "I didn't. But she won't believe me. I hate her! She's an old skunk!"

Lucia had gone to see Miss Jesser, but she had not been able to convince her.

"I don't want to make an issue of it, Mrs. Holley," she had said. "After all, it's not serious. At David's age, a child scarcely knows the difference between truth and falsehood."

Lucia had never been able to get any satisfaction for David. He had been falsely accused, and he had never been able to clear himself. Maybe he had forgotten about that—and maybe he had not. Maybe that happened to every child, at some time, leaving in every adult's mind the fear that she felt now, the fear of an utterly baseless accusation, coming like a bolt from the blue, and impossible to disprove.

"There wasn't any such boat," she said.

"Mrs. Holley," he said, "you understand that, no matter how reluctant I may be, it's my duty to enforce the law——"

"All laws?" she said. "Whether they're good or bad?"

"The laws in this country are made by the consent of the people. They can't be 'bad.' What the people decide for themselves is right, is, by that decision, right."

They were coming to something; she knew that. Every-

193

thing they said was leading to a destined end. He was driving her—somewhere, and she had to resist.

"You don't care how unjust a law might be to an individual?" she asked, scornfully.

"The law isn't necessarily synonymous with justice, Mrs. Holley. After all, we don't know very much about justice. And we'd need wiser men than we're likely to get, to apply justice to everyone. What we have is a code, a written code, accessible to everyone."

"D'you think that's so wonderful?" she demanded.

"Yes," he said. "You wouldn't admit that even God had the right to punish or reward, if He never let anyone know what the laws were."

His words frightened her, and silenced her.

"Mrs. Holley," he said, "I suggest that your daughter was with you in the boat, on the morning of the seventeenth."

"My *daughter* . . . ?"

"Darby was not killed in the place where his body was found, Mrs. Holley. We're certain of that. We also know that Darby was in your boathouse at some time. We've found his fingerprints on several objects."

"Anyone could get in there. Anyone. But you said—you said Murray . . ."

"We've let Murray go, Mrs. Holley. One of the smartest criminal lawyers in New York came out last night to take his case—and it wasn't a very good case, anyhow. He's out now."

"But my daughter . . . Why are you trying to drag her into this?"

"Your daughter is attempting to shield you, Mrs. Holley.
194

That's obvious. I've questioned her, and she was extremely evasive."

"And what's she supposed to be shielding me from?" Lucia asked.

"Mrs. Holley, it's my duty to inform you that you are not obliged to answer my questions. It is furthermore my duty to inform you that anything you say may——"

"Don't *talk* like that!" she cried.

He rose, and stood before her, and he was so immensely, toweringly tall that she could not see his face.

"Mrs. Holley. I have evidence that Darby was in your boathouse. I have good reason to believe that he was killed there and his body later removed to the island. I have reason to believe that this afternoon Donnelly assisted you to remove from the boathouse some object or objects which you feared might tend to incriminate you."

"No," Lucia said. "No, I didn't."

"I haven't applied for a warrant, Mrs. Holley——"

"A warrant?" she cried. "For—me?"

"I'd certainly be justified, Mrs. Holley, in holding you, and your daughter for questioning. You're both withholding information."

"My daughter . . . ?"

"Your daughter is very evasive, Mrs. Holley. She told me that Donnelly had come here to see her. She gave me to understand that he was infatuated with her, and was attempting to win your good will, for that reason. Further questioning made it plain that she knows nothing at all about the man. She doesn't know his first name, for instance, or his address. She 'can't remember' where or when she met him. She then told me the same story about Darby.

195

That if he had come here at any time—which she didn't admit—it was to see her." He paused. "How long have you known Donnelly, Mrs. Holley?"

"Oh, not long. He's—just an acquaintance."

"How did you make his acquaintance, Mrs. Holley?"

"Well, I *think* some life-insurance agent introduced him."

"Do you know what Donnelly's occupation is, Mrs. Holley?"

"No," she said. "No, I don't."

"He was arrested five times in connection with bootlegging and rumrunning, during prohibition. At present, the O.P.A. is interested in him. There's good reason to believe that he's active in the black market, particularly in meat."

"But he hasn't done anything really—criminal, has he? I mean, robbery, or——?"

"Mrs. Holley," said Levy, "your attitude is surprising. If you don't consider black market activity, in wartime, a criminal offense——"

"I *do!*" she said, quickly. "Of course I do!"

"Mrs. Holley," said Levy, "I shall have to ask you what you and Donnelly removed from the boathouse this afternoon."

She sat very still. She did not realize that she was holding her breath until it burst out in a faint gasp.

"An engine," she said. "An outboard motor."

"That's what your daughter told me," he said. "When I asked her where you were, she told me you'd driven Donnelly to the station, taking with you an outboard motor. I made an opportunity to visit the boathouse, and the engine is still there."

"There were two."

"Did the landlord give you an inventory of the contents of the boathouse, Mrs. Holley?"

"Yes. Yes, I think so. But I don't exactly remember where it is. I can *find* it, of course, later on . . ."

"Why did you put the engine in a chest, Mrs. Holley?"

"Well, I always like to put things in boxes . . ."

The end of the tether, she said to herself. You go as far as you can, and then the rope is stretched tight and you can't go on.

"Where did you take this chest, Mrs. Holley?"

"Well, we were going to take it to a boat yard, but we ran out of gas, and I came home by train."

"Where did you leave Donnelly?"

"In the country. In a lane."

"What part of the country?"

"I don't know exactly."

"What station did you take the train from?"

"It was—I think it was called West Whitehills."

"When is Donnelly going to return your car, Mrs. Holley?"

"Well, very soon, I guess."

"I'll have to question Donnelly, Mrs. Holley. Will you give me his address, please?"

"I haven't got it."

"How do you communicate with Donnelly, Mrs. Holley?"

"Well, I don't."

"Has any member of your family his address?"

"No. I'm sorry."

"Mrs. Holley, I suggest that you and Donnelly removed evidence pertaining to Darby's death."

"No! Really we didn't. I promise you we didn't."

You get to the end of the tether, but nothing hap-

197

pens. The rope doesn't break; it doesn't choke you to death.

"I can't accept your story about this engine, Mrs. Holley. You've given me no satisfactory explanation for the presence of your market list under Darby's body. Neither you nor your daughter has given me any plausible explanation for Darby's presence in your boathouse. I'll have to ask you to come with me to the District Attorney's office."

"Well, but—when?"

"Immediately."

"But it's almost dinnertime!"

"I'm sorry."

"But—when would I get back? I mean, what time shall I tell Sibyl to put dinner on?"

"I don't know, Mrs. Holley."

"An hour?"

"It would be better not to count on that, Mrs. Holley."

"You mean . . . ? You don't mean—they'd keep me?"

"That's a possibility, Mrs. Holley."

"You mean—arrest me?"

"I think it's a possibility that the District Attorney may consider it advisable to hold you for further questioning."

"Hold me? In prison?"

"It's a possibility, Mrs. Holley."

"I can't," she said, flatly. "I can't possibly just walk out of the house like this, and go to prison. You don't realize . . . I've got my children and my father . . . Perhaps you didn't know that my husband's overseas, in the Navy?"

"Yes. I knew that, Mrs. Holley."

"Then don't you see . . . ? Don't you see what it would do to them all? I *can't* . . . Don't you see? They can't—just sit down to dinner . . ."

198

She rose; she clasped her hands, to keep from seizing his sleeve.

"Please!" she said. "You understand human nature. You *know* I didn't kill Ted Darby. You don't want to bring such disgrace and misery—to all of us——"

"Mrs. Holley," he said, "you've been consorting with a known criminal——"

"'Consorting'?" she repeated, looking into his face.

"That's the usual expression," he said, returning her look steadily.

He thinks we're lovers, she told herself. Everyone will think so. The police will find out about that lunch. About everything.

But nobody knows anything about Nagle; maybe they never will. Maybe if I tell the truth about Ted Darby now, it will be the end. Only I've got to warn Father.

"Lieutenant Levy," she said. "Let me have until tomorrow morning. I beg of you."

"It's not possible, Mrs. Holley."

"I'm—so tired," she said. "I can't put things very clearly. If I can just have a good night's sleep, then tomorrow I'll —tell you."

"Tell me what, Mrs. Holley?"

"About Ted Darby," she said.

"You admit that you know the circumstances of his death?"

"Please," she said, "please just let me have until tomorrow morning."

"That's impossible, Mrs. Holley."

"It has to be that way," she said.

Because I won't let them spring it on Father, she thought. It'll be hard enough for him, no matter how careful I am

199

about telling him. He doesn't even know that the man he met in the boathouse was the horrible Ted Darby he read about in the newspapers. He'll——

"Mrs. Holley," said Levy, "I don't think you understand your position. It's extremely serious. You've admitted that you have knowledge of Darby's murder——"

"It wasn't a murder."

"Of Darby's death. By admitting this knowledge, Mrs. Holley, you've rendered yourself liable to arrest."

"Look!" she said, with desperate earnestness. "Lieutenant, let's just talk, like—people. You *know* I'm not a murderess. I should have told you the whole thing before, but I had a reason—it seemed to me a good reason. I'll tell you everything tomorrow morning. As early as you like."

"Why not now?"

"I need a good night's sleep. I'm—really, I'm so tired . . ."

He moved away, his hands clasped behind his back.

"Mrs. Holley," he said, after a moment, "I'll postpone questioning you any further until tomorrow, if you'll get Donnelly here tonight."

Chapter Twenty

She walked over to the window, and she was startled to see how it looked out there in the world; everything bathed in a clear lemon light; the coarse grass looked yellow, the leaves on the young trees were a translucent green, and trembling strangely in the strange light.

He's gone now, she told herself. He's on the train, going to Montreal.

But in her mind she could see him only in the lane, as she had left him, tall and neat, his right arm hanging useless by his side. And that's the bargain, she thought. I'm to sell him out. I'm to get him here, and hand him over to the police.

There were footsteps overhead; a door closed. Father, she thought. I suppose Bee's upstairs, too. And David? It's nearly time for dinner.

"Mrs. Holley?"

Levy's tone was courteous and patient; too patient. It's ridiculous for him to wait like this, she thought, with a sudden anger, when he could make me give him an answer.

"I don't know where Mr. Donnelly is," she said, evenly.

"Then I'm afraid we'll have to be getting along, Mrs. Holley."

"You can let me have my dinner, can't you?"

"I'm afraid not."

She turned to face him. The room was growing shadowy, and that made him look very pale, his hair very black.

"I didn't think *you'd* behave like this," she said.

He said nothing.

"Why don't you find Mr. Donnelly for yourself?" she demanded. "If you're so anxious to see him."

"I've tried. But the New York police have lost track of him, temporarily. They'll trace him, of course, but I'd like to see him now."

"You'll arrest him, won't you?"

"I want to question him, Mrs. Holley. If his answers are satisfactory, he'll have no further trouble."

He's been arrested five times, Lucia thought. And they never could convict him. He knows how to look after himself. And they won't ask him about Nagle. Why should they? Nobody can know yet that anything's happened to Nagle. The rest of it isn't dangerous for him. Lieutenant Levy will only ask him about Ted Darby, and he can easily clear himself. He must have an alibi for that evening; certainly he wasn't here.

And about the chest? He'll certainly have got rid of that, long ago. And nobody can possibly know about Nagle yet. No. Martin will say what I said. That it was an engine. He'll be able to answer all Lieutenant Levy's questions—much better than I can. He's been arrested five times, and they couldn't hold him. *He* knows how to look after himself.

She heard the screen door in the kitchen bang, and David's voice, loud and hearty.

"Hello, Sibyl! What's with dinner?"

"Lieutenant Levy's talking to your mother just now," Sibyl answered, in her gentle voice.

202

"Aha!" said David, pleased. "He's a smart cooky. I bet he cracks this case. Any coke in the icebox, Sibyl?"

"No, Master David. Can't get any."

"Well . . ." said David. "Maybe I'll mix up a chocolate malted."

"Spoil your appetite!"

"It never does," said David.

"I'll mix it for you," said Sibyl.

All the little sounds were strikingly clear to Lucia. That was the bowl being set down on the kitchen cabinet; here was the egg beater clattering, and catching, and starting again. David, she thought, would be sitting on the edge of the kitchen table, happy to be home.

I can't spoil this for David. For all of them. I *will not* go off now, just at dinnertime, to the District Attorney's office. And maybe not come back tonight—not for days. And let them hear—let everyone hear—that I consorted with a known criminal . . .

I'd do anything, to keep that from happening.

He would keep it from happening, if he came. He'd know how to answer Lieutenant Levy, and the District Attorney. He'd know how to help me out of this, if he came. He'd put that first.

"Mrs. Holley, I'll have to have your decision," said Levy.

The egg beater had stopped; she heard the oven door open and shut.

"Yes . . ." she said, and went out of the room, along the hall to the kitchen.

"Hello, David, dear!" she said. "Sibyl, will you come into the sitting room for a moment, please?"

"Sibyl's going to be grilled, is she?" asked David. "Well, watch your step, Sibyl!"

Sibyl smiled at him softly, and followed Lucia back to the sitting room.

"Sibyl," said Lucia, "do you happen to know Mr. Donnelly's telephone number?"

Sibyl looked at her; their eyes met. If she said no, that would be fate.

"Yes, ma'am," said Sibyl.

"You might call him now," said Levy. "Say that Mrs. Holley would like him to come out this evening, as early as possible. Don't mention me."

"No, sir," said Sibyl.

The telephone was on a little table in the hall, just outside the sitting-room door; they could both see her as she sat down on the chair and dialed. Her face looked composed and sorrowful, with her eyes lowered. She's dialing a wrong number, Lucia thought. She likes Martin, and she knows this is a trap for him.

"Hello?" said Sibyl. "May I speak to Mr. Donnelly, please? . . . You expect him in soon? Well, will you please tell him Sibyl says will he please come out to see her this evening, soon as he can? Thank you, sir."

"He's not home, ma'am," she said, rising. "But I left a message."

"With whom?" asked Levy.

"Don't know who it was, sir."

"You might give me the number, please," said Levy, and Sibyl repeated a number which he wrote down in a notebook.

It's a wrong number, Lucia thought. Sibyl wouldn't do this to Martin.

Anyhow, he's gone now. He's on the train now, going to Montreal. He's not coming here. He's gone.

"Thanks," said Levy, putting the little book back into his pocket. "Then I'll see you tomorrow, Mrs. Holley. Good night!"

"Good night!" Lucia answered.

As soon as the door had closed after him, Lucia hurried to the kitchen, almost breathless with impatience to hear what Sibyl would have to say.

"Sibyl . . . ?"

"Yes, ma'am?"

Their eyes met, and Sibyl's were unfathomable, dark, sorrowful and steady.

"Sibyl . . . Do you think he'll come?"

"Left the message, ma'am."

But did you, really? Lucia thought. Or did you just pretend to? You like him. Would you really get him out here —for a policeman?

She stood looking at Sibyl, and she could not ask her that question.

Anyhow, he's gone. He's on the train to Montreal.

"Shall I ring now, ma'am?"

"I suppose so," said Lucia.

She thought that Sibyl enjoyed sounding the gongs in the hall, a series of four strung on a red silk cord; an old thing, that had belonged to Lucia's mother. David and Bee had loved the chimes in their childhood; it was a part of their family life; they had brought it along as a matter of course.

The setting sun made a gold dazzle on the glass of the front door, but the brilliance did not reach Sibyl; she stood in shadow, with the little padded wooden stick in her hand. She struck the lowest and deepest gong, and went on, up to the fourth, then down, then up once more; the notes

205

hummed through the house. And it was like a charm; old Mr. Harper at once came out of his room, then David opened his door; before they had reached the hall, Bee was coming down the stairs.

I want Tom here! Lucia said to herself, in passionate rebellion. I want them all here, all safe. It was an impious wish, a rebellion against heaven, against life itself. She knew that. But she would try, she would fight, to turn away the tide from her doorstep.

She felt that she could do anything. She could sit at the table, she could even eat a little. That was because she had set a limit to her ordeal.

At nine o'clock, she told herself, I'll say I'm tired, and I'll go upstairs. And I'll take one of his pills and go to sleep.

Bee and David were 'queer'; she noticed that at once. They were unusually silent; they were disapproving of her. Let them. They would get over it. Her father talked, and she responded, soothed by his kindly vagueness. He had never disapproved of her. If he had noticed any of her strange goings-on lately, or if anyone were to tell him of still stranger goings-on, he would dismiss it all. She was his daughter; she was the irreproachable wife and mother, the wise and prudent housekeeper. The worst he would ever admit against her was, that perhaps she had been somewhat lacking in judgment.

But her husband and her children did not consider her beyond criticism. She belonged to them; whatever she did affected them; their pride, their good name in the world lay in her hands. They would give her love, protection, even a sort of homage, but in return for that she must be what they wanted and needed her to be.

They all went into the sitting room after dinner. Bee sat

206

down at the desk to write a letter; David took up a science magazine; old Mr. Harper proposed a game of cribbage. It was only a little after eight, but Lucia could not keep to her self-imposed limit of nine o'clock.

"Father," she said, "if you don't mind, I think I'll just write to Tom, and then go to bed."

"Very good idea!" he said. "Have you anything to read, m'dear? I have this book from the lending library, very amusing; light touch. This family in a cathedral town in England——"

"I'm sure I'd like it, Father, but I don't think I'll read anything tonight. I think I'll go right to sleep. Good night, Father. Good night, children."

David rose, and kissed her cheek; it was a stern kiss, but at least he accepted her.

"Good night, Mother," said Bee, not even raising her head from her writing.

You're unkind, Lucia thought. But that's because it's much, much harder for you than it is for David. He just thinks I'm being silly and trying, but you feel that there's something more, something dreadful, and you're frightened. I'm sorry . . .

It was necessary to write Tom's letter quickly, while she could. Her room was tranquil in the lamplight; a soft salt wind blew in at the open windows.

Dear Tom.

It was as if something stirred behind a curtain.

Dear Tom. The weather. Dear Tom. Oh, Tom, *come alive!* Be real. Let me remember how you were, let me see you. Let me feel something about you. Anything. You mustn't, you can't be this far away, so that you're not real.

But there was no feeling in her, for anyone. She was in

207

a hurry to get to sleep, that was all. Folded in the back of the writing tablet she found an old letter to Tom that had not seemed good enough to send. She copied it, almost without change. There were little domestic details; there was a reminder of a day they had spent together at Jones Beach, long ago, when the children were little. It had been a special day, specially happy, but it evoked no feeling in her now. That young, happy Tom and Lucia were no more than bright little dolls.

She addressed the envelope and stood it up against Tom's picture, where every night an envelope stood. She had wrapped the yellow capsules in a paper handkerchief and put them into a bureau drawer. She took one out now, and swallowed it with a glass of water. I don't even know what it is, she thought. I don't know what it will do to me.

Only it would do her no harm. She was not afraid of anything from his hands. She undressed, and bathed, hurrying, for fear sleep would suddenly overcome her. I might fall down, she thought; I might fall asleep just anywhere, and in the morning, they'd find me on the floor. How long will it last, I wonder? So that they'll have trouble waking me up in the morning?

It worried her to think of that, of being drugged and 'queer' in the morning. Especially when I've got to tell Father about Ted, she thought. But nothing really mattered except getting through this night, sleeping through it, utterly unconscious. There's nothing to stay awake for, she thought. It's out of my hands now. I let Sibyl give that message. But he won't come. He's on his way to Montreal now.

She got into bed and lay there, propped up on two pillows, the lamp still lighted. She took up a book, but that
208

was no good. What's the matter with that pill? she thought, impatiently. Why doesn't it start? I'll give it twenty minutes more, and then, if nothing's happened, I'll take another.

She closed her eyes, and a face was forming before her; she watched it anxiously. It was a familiar face, bony, wearing pince-nez, and a simpering smile. Now, who's that? she thought. I ought to know. Why, yes; it's Miss Priest, our English teacher. But didn't I hear from someone that she'd died? Well, has she come to give me a message?

"Miss Priest?" she asked, apologetically.

No answer. Lucia sighed, and put the pillows down flat; she stretched out her legs, relaxing. Miss Priest, she thought, trying to remember something. About school, was it? I don't care whether I actually sleep or not, she thought, as long as I can relax like this. And not worry.

Sibyl's voice was hissing in her ear.

"I'm asleep!" Lucia said, angrily. "Let me alone!"

Hiss, hiss, hiss. Misss-ess Holley.

"Let me alone, Sibyl."

"Mrs. Holley, he's here, ma'am. Got to hurry."

Holley. Here. Hurry. Hiss, hiss, hiss.

Sibyl laid a cold, wet washcloth across her forehead, drew it across her eyes.

"Again!" Lucia said.

She opened her eyes and sat up.

"Got to hurry, ma'am. He's here."

"I can't hurry, Sibyl. I took a pill. I was asleep."

"I'll help you, ma'am."

This was a dreadful way to feel, so leaden, so confused. And so indifferent. She sat in a chair while Sibyl put on her shoes and stockings and pinned up her hair.

"What time is it, Sibyl?" she asked.

"Nearly two o'clock, ma'am."

Lucia began to cry a little.

"I didn't get to sleep until after nine," she said. "I haven't had—enough sleep."

"You can go back to sleep later, ma'am."

The dimly lit hall frightened her; she held back, in dread that one of those closed doors would open. But Sibyl took her hand and led her to the stairs; she went down carefully, on wooden feet, still holding Sibyl's hand. They went through the dark kitchen and out onto the back porch, and it was black as pitch there.

"It's raining!" she whispered.

"Just a little bit, ma'am," Sibyl whispered back. "Got to be very quiet now, ma'am."

There was a man moving along the drive; Lucia saw the dull gleam of his raincoat as he passed within a few feet of them.

"Now!" Sibyl whispered.

They went, half running, across the grass, to the boathouse. Sibyl opened the door and they entered, and it was pitch-dark in there, and there was a cold, musty smell.

"This way, ma'am," Sibyl said.

She opened the door that led to a little pantry without a window, and the light from the unshaded bulb that hung from the ceiling was dazzling. He was there.

"It was kind of you to come," he said, with formality.

This was not a dream, and she was not leaden and drowsy now. He was most immaculately neat, in his dark suit and dark tie, his arm in a black sling; he was not blurred now, but sharp and clear. He was completely a stranger to her, and she was cold with fear at the sight of him.

210

This brilliant little room without a window was a trap, that she had got him into. And now she was shut up in it with him. This was the meeting that she had dreaded more than anything in the world.

"I wouldn't have bothered you," he said, "only my arm is broke on me."

"Broken?" she cried.

"Broken," he repeated, apologetically. "If it wasn't for that, I'd have mailed you the things, with a bit of a note, to explain. Only the way it is, I cannot write."

"Have you had your arm set?"

"That'll come later. Look, will you, what's on the shelf?"

"You can't go on like this! It must hurt you—horribly."

"I don't think of it," he said. "Don't worry. It'll be cared for, later. Look, now, what's on the shelf."

But she kept her eyes upon his face, that had so strangely gay a look.

"Look, now!" he said. "Here's your girl's letters, every last one of them."

He picked up from the drainboard a little bundle of envelopes in an elastic band.

"You'll have no more worry about them," he said. "And here . . . Won't you look? Here's your jewels." He smiled a little. "They're not so grand as I'd been thinking."

"Martin . . ." she said.

The dam was giving way, the great wave was mounting, to engulf her.

"Martin," she said, "your arm is broken. Martin, you must get away, quick."

"There's no great hurry."

"There is! There is! There's a policeman——"

"He is just patrolling. I saw him before, and I kept out

211

of his way while I knocked on the kitchen window and Sibyl came out."

"Martin . . . I'll take you in the rowboat—farther down the shore. Hurry! You must hurry! The policeman might come here."

"He wouldn't be bothering with me."

"But that's what he's here for! I'll take you in the rowboat. I'll get you away, somehow."

"The cop's not looking for me."

"But, Martin! Lieutenant Levy knows about the message——"

"What message?"

He doesn't know, she thought. And if he finds out . . .

"What message was it?" he repeated. "I want the truth of it."

He was looking at her, in a narrow, thoughtful way, as if he were making up his mind. She could not speak; she could not turn her eyes away from him.

"You sent me a message?" he said. "What was it?"

He waited a moment.

"So that's the way of it?" he said. "You turned me in."

"Martin . . ." she said.

He gave a long sigh.

"Ah, well . . ." he said. "That's what poor Nagle meant, y'know."

Chapter Twenty-one

She could not understand the words; only the tone, that had in it no trace of bitterness or reproach.

"You could not help it," he said. "Levy got after you, did he?"

"It was only about Ted Darby," she said. "He doesn't know about anything else. He only thinks we took something away—evidence—about Ted. Nothing else. Nothing —that could really hurt you. I wouldn't—you know I wouldn't . . . Never about—the other. Never!"

"My poor girl," he said, "you couldn't help yourself at all. That's what Nagle meant, y'know. A woman like yourself will always have to be thinking of her family and her good name first."

"No. Not about—the other. I'd never give you away. Never!"

"Sure, I believe you," he said.

"You don't. I can see that you don't. You think——"

"Look, now! Would I forget the way you helped me get him out, in that chest? Would I forget the courage you had, and the spirit, answering your girl as quick as a flash? You've been good to me."

"No," she said. "I haven't."

"Well, I'm satisfied," he said, with a flicker of that strange

213

gaiety. "Sit down now, will you not? There's a few things——"

"No! You've got to get away now—this instant—in the rowboat."

"You will have to listen, my poor girl," he said, "for my mind is made up."

"You must go!" she said.

"There's no chair in it," he said, glancing around the pantry. "Well, I'll be quick. There's no one ever need know Nagle was in the chest, and the chest itself is burned to ashes. You've only to say you don't know what I had in the chest at all, or where I took it."

"Where is Nagle?"

"It's better you don't know that. Anyhow, he is far from here, and there's nobody knows he was ever in the boat-house but the two of us, and Sibyl. Your car's in the garage by the station. I sent a young boy with it. There's nothing to tie you with Nagle."

"And what about *you?* What are *you* going to do?"

"I can't get away with it," he said, "if the cops are look-ing for me here."

"You can! I'll take you in the rowboat."

"No," he said, "I can't get away with it. And well I knew it, from the start."

"Martin, even if they did catch you tonight, they'd only ask you questions about Darby. They don't know about Nagle."

He took out a pack of cigarettes and shook one into his hand.

"Will you give me a light, please?" he asked. "It is hard——"

"Aren't you *going?*"

214

"A few drags . . ." he said, apologetically. "It is a comfort."

She struck a match and held it out for him.

"Martin," she said, "you're not being—sensible. You *can* get away. If I take you in the rowboat——"

"I'll not go in the boat with you," he said.

"Then go by the road. We'll watch, Sibyl and I, until the policeman's on the other side of the house, and then you can get away."

"Sure!" he said, absently, drawing on the cigarette.

"Martin!" she cried. "You've got something in your mind! Something silly."

"A life for a life," he said. "That's the way of it."

"It doesn't have to be—unless you just give up. Martin, aren't you man enough to fight for your life?"

"There are things you can't fight," he said. "Carlie and I, we were friends for near twenty years. It never came into his head I'd do that to him. Surprised, he looked, like——"

"Stop! Don't talk like that! You——" She stopped for a moment, appalled by the look on his face, the blankness. "Don't be a fool! Pull yourself together. You've got to fight for your life."

"And what kind of life would it be at all, with never a moment's peace, day or night? I'd never lay my head on my pillow that I wouldn't see Carlie——"

"Shut up!" she said, furiously. "You did it for me."

"That was the same as doing it for myself," he said. "There is no merit in that."

"Snap out of it! You can get away—if you'll stop being such a dope."

He was looking down at her with a smile.

215

"Stop that smiling!" she said. "There's nothing to smile about. For God's *sake,* will you pull yourself together and *think?*"

"I will," he said, readily.

"And you'll go to Montreal?"

"I will try."

"Don't say that. Don't think that way. Say you will go to Montreal."

"I will," he said.

"I don't trust you! You've got something in your mind. You think that because I sent—because I had to send that message—you think it's fate, or something."

"It is not fate I believe in," he said.

She was silent, in a furious effort to find the right words, to reach him, to rouse him.

"Martin," she said, "you've managed so well, up to now. You've burned the chest; you've—managed everything. You won't go to pieces now, when the worst of it's all over?"

"Oh, I won't," he said. "Don't you be worrying, dear."

"Martin, you don't—you can't believe—what Nagle said . . . ?"

"I do not," he said.

She was leaning against the drainboard, supporting herself with one outstretched hand. He laid his hand over it.

"Good-by now," he said.

"Martin . . ."

But he had opened the door and gone into the dark room beyond. She moved after him, groping, lost in the blackness. The front door closed softly.

"Sibyl?" she called, sharply.

"Yes, ma'am?"

"We ought to——"

216

Ought to do what? She made her way across the room and opened the door. It was lighter out there, and she saw Donnelly moving quickly across the grass, going toward the highway. Then a flashlight swung in a half circle, and she shrank back against the house.

Now there would be a shout. Now there would be a shot.

The flashlight swung again, and she had a glimpse of stunted bushes that seemed to slide along the beam of light. The water lapped softly against the boathouse; the rain made a whispering sound.

"Now, ma'am?" said Sibyl, close to her ear.

It was a dreadful thing, to cross that dark, open space. The flashlight would catch them, and they would be paralyzed by it; they would stand frozen.

It was a dreadful thing to go up the stairs. A door would open, a voice would call to her.

"I'll help you get to bed, ma'am."

"No, thank you, Sibyl. No, thank you."

Her own lamplit room was not safe. Someone could knock; someone could open the door. She undressed in frantic haste, and threw all her damp clothes into the closet; she put on her pajamas and lay down on the bed.

She lay very still, waiting for the shot to ring out, for the sound of footsteps running up the stairs.

Chapter Twenty-two

She waked in a gray twilight, and looked at her watch. It was half-past four. That's too early, she said to herself, and frowned, worried by the words. What was it about 'too early'? Something important. Too early . . .

Come as early as you like tomorrow morning, she had told Levy, and this was tomorrow morning. I'll have to talk to Father first, she thought, but not just yet. I can sleep a little longer.

She had a dream, about Sibyl. Sibyl was living in a little shack, by the edge of a swamp, and the sheriff and his men were coming to get her husband. But that was all right, because she knew it was only a dream. The swamp was a dream swamp, a jungle of tall, dark trees festooned with strange white moss that rustled like paper. The sheriff and his men had brought bloodhounds with them, and they went into the jungle-swamp, splashing through water. She could not see them now, but the hounds began to bay, and it froze her blood.

She heard a high, squealing whistle. That's a bazooka gun! she thought. Oh, Tom, be careful! Now she knew that it was Tom in the gloomy swamp, hunted by dogs, and his leg was broken. She tried to run to him, and she could

218

not stir; she tried to call to him, and her voice was strangled. Some gasping little sound came, and waked her.

There was the same gray twilight in the room, and the house was very quiet. But it was after seven, by her watch. I'll have to talk to Father, she thought, and got up. A sick dizziness came rushing up, spinning round and round, from her feet into her head; she fell back on the bed, and the bed rose from the floor and spun, in a great swoop.

When that stopped, she was afraid to move, for fear it would start again. She still felt sick, and too tired, too weak to lift her head. I can't talk to Father, she thought. I can't get up. They'll have to let me alone for a little while, until this goes away.

There was a knock at the door, and Sibyl came in with a tray. She set the tray down, and came over to the bed; she helped Lucia to lie back against the pillows; she drew the sheet neatly up over her chest.

"Thought you'd like some breakfast, ma'am."

"Sibyl . . . Have you heard anything?"

"No, ma'am."

"Did you look in the newspapers?"

"Yes, ma'am. There's nothing."

"Sibyl, I'd like to rest for a while."

Sibyl poured her a cup of coffee.

"If you'll just tell the others that I'm tired, and that I'd like to rest until lunchtime . . . If you'll just see that no one disturbs me, Sibyl . . ."

"I'll tell them, ma'am," said Sibyl, with no spark of hope.

"Can't you see to that for me?" Lucia demanded, ready to cry.

"I'll tell them, ma'am. That's all I can do," said Sibyl.

There was nothing sympathetic in her tone; her face was

completely inexpressive. Tears were running down Lucia's cheeks as she drank her coffee. Sibyl's absolutely heartless, she told herself. She could see that I got a little peace and quiet, if she wanted.

The coffee made her feel better. No, she thought, Sibyl's not heartless. She's a realist, that's all. She knows you have to do things. I'll lie here until Lieutenant Levy comes. Then he can wait downstairs until I've talked to Father. He can just wait. Do him good.

She drank two cups of coffee, and lit a cigarette. But it was curiously bitter, and she put it out. I really don't feel at all well, she thought. I think I'm on the verge of a breakdown. What, exactly, was a breakdown? Aunt Agnes had a nervous breakdown. Lots of people do. Maybe this was it, this bodily weakness and weariness, this refusal of the mind to think or to feel. This is how sick animals feel, she thought. When Tom's collie was sick, he always wagged his tail when Tom spoke to him. I used to think he hated to do it. Toward the end, he didn't even open his eyes; just gave one little thump with his tail. Because he felt he had to, on Tom's account. I always thought he didn't like Tom to pat his head and say, "Good old scout, aren't you? Aren't you, Max? Good old scout, aren't you?" Enough to drive you crazy, when you're dying.

She lay with her eyes closed, and thought about dogs, and then about cats. People don't make such exorbitant demands upon cats, she thought. Nobody expects them to grin and pant and wag their tails and be overjoyed every time anyone speaks to them. No . . . People feel rather flattered if they can make a cat purr.

Birds . . . she thought. Why should everyone think that a skylark was so full of rapture? I think birds are fright-

220

fully fussy and worried. People say 'nervous as a cat.' I think 'nervous as a bird' would be much better. When you think of birds, hopping around, and chirping, and looking for food all the time . . . They push each other, too. I've seen them. They're rude, birds are.

There was a knock at the door, and she began to cry.

"Come in!" she called, drying her eyes roughly on the sheet.

It was David. He stood in the doorway, slight, too slight, in slacks and a blue shirt, and he was not smiling.

"I hear you're not feeling so fine," he said. "What's the trouble?"

"I'm tired, that's all," said Lucia.

"Well, I hadn't noticed you'd been doing such a heck of a lot lately," he said.

"Everyone gets tired, sometimes," said Lucia, nettled by this tone. "And, after all, I'm not fifteen, David."

"You look funny," he said. "I think we'd better get a doctor."

"No!" said Lucia. "I'm not going to have a doctor. All I need is a little rest."

"Well, I think you look funny," said David.

She fought against her anger; she reasoned with herself. It's always like this, she thought. Even Tom is sort of furious if I get sick. What have you been *doing* with yourself, to get a cold like this?

"I'll be all right, David, after a little rest," she said.

"Well . . ." said David, "I don't want to bother you, but there's one thing I'd like to ask you. What's happened to our car?"

"It's in the garage by the station."

"Well, I hope it is," said David.

"I *know* it is," said Lucia.

"Well, I hope so," said David.

Lucia closed her eyes, so that she need not see his irritating face.

"Mother?" he said, and when she did not answer: "*Mother?*" he said, in a different tone, in a panic.

"Oh, what *is* it, David?"

"Well, when you closed your eyes . . . I thought maybe you felt faint, or something."

She remembered him, when he was a little boy, shaking her by the shoulder, waking her out of a sound sleep, crying "Mother!" in that same tone. "What *is* it, David?" she had asked.

She remembered how he had looked, thin and wiry in his striped pajamas, his black hair ruffled. "I thought you were dead," he had said.

"I'm sorry I worried you, dear," she said. "Don't worry any more. I'll just rest for a while, and then I'll be perfectly all right."

She smiled at him, and his face relaxed.

"Okay!" he said. "Want anything from the village, Mother? Any medicine, or anything?"

"No, thank you, dear. But ask Sibyl what she wants."

It's going to be dreadful for David, she thought, when the story comes out. He wanted his mother to be not only conventional, and beyond measure respectable, but practically invisible. He had been disturbed even by her going out in the motorboat earlier than was the custom for mothers. How would it be when he learned what she was doing with the boat? And if he learned about Donnelly?

He had gone out of the room now, reassured about her health, but he left her miserably agitated, all the vague calmness gone. Now Bee will come, she thought. Bee was frightened yesterday. I know how she felt. When I was seventeen, if my mother had gone driving off with a strange man, leaving a guest she'd invited to tea, coming back so much later, and smelling of whisky . . . I'd have thought it was the end of the world. And I didn't explain anything to her.

Explain? *Explain?* But did I really do that? Did I help to put Nagle into that chest?

Oh, the chest is the worst! Far the worst. I drove the car, and I never even thought about the chest. He was there, in the chest, and I wasn't even sorry for him. Suppose he wasn't really dead? O God!

Sweat came out on her forehead. How do I know he was dead—when we put him——?

There was a knock at the door.

"May I come in, m'dear?"

"Oh, come in, Father!"

"Resting, eh?"

"Yes, I am, Father."

"Very good idea. Keeping house, in times like these— great strain. You need a rest, now and then."

"Well . . ."

"There's one thing, m'dear," he said, standing beside the bed. "I don't want to disturb your rest, but I dare say you can solve the mystery with one word."

"What mystery, Father?"

"Thing is," he said, lowering his voice, "I had a bottle of Scotch, in the sideboard. Hadn't even opened it. Well, dashed if it hasn't disappeared!"

"You've got another bottle, haven't you, Father?"

"Oh, yes. Yes. Plenty. But that's not the point, m'dear.

223

I put that bottle in the sideboard myself, day before yesterday. And it's gone. I don't like to ask Sibyl about it. Colored people are sensitive—and you can't blame them. Shouldn't like her to imagine I was accusing her."

"She wouldn't think that, Father. She knows how we feel about her."

But Sibyl did take his whisky! she thought, remembering. And I drank out of the bottle. And Nagle . . .

"It occurred to me . . ." he said. "D'you think Bee might have offered drinks to some of her friends?"

"She'd never *touch* your whisky without asking you, Father. And she doesn't drink whisky. Only a little glass of sherry, once in a great while. Bee isn't like that, Father."

"No, no. Naturally. Don't worry. Rest. Enjoy yourself. Don't worry about anything."

He laid his hand on her forehead.

"Headache?" he asked. "Any aches or pains, m'dear? The great thing is, if there's anything starting, to nip it in the bud."

She looked up at him, into his steady blue eyes that had never looked at her except with affection and trust, and tears rose in her own.

"I'm—just tired . . ." she said, very unsteadily.

"Come, come!" he said, in alarm. "That's not like you, m'dear. Nerves . . ."

She forced a smile; she could feel how stiff and forced a smile it was, but it satisfied him.

"That's better!" he said. "I'm going to write to Tom today. Going to tell him how you keep the flag flying, eh?"

When he had gone, she cried . . . She wanted to cry wildly and violently, but only a few slow tears ran down
224

her face. Why doesn't Bee come? she thought. I want Bee to come.

She was asleep when Sibyl brought her lunch tray.

"Is Miss Bee home?" she asked.

"Yes, ma'am. Went down to the village with Master David, and they came back in the car."

"Sibyl . . . Haven't you heard anything?"

"They brought back an evening paper, ma'am. It's in that."

"What is it? Did they get him?"

"I'll bring you the paper, ma'am, soon as they start their lunch."

"Tell me."

"I'll bring you the paper, ma'am."

She waited, waited, waited, not even looking at the tray.

"Can't you eat anything, ma'am?"

"No. Let me see, Sibyl."

SLAYER CONFESSES UNSUSPECTED CRIME

QUESTIONED IN DARBY CASE, SUSPECT ADMITS FEUD MURDER

Early this morning, the Horton County police got not only a full account of the accidental slaying of Ted Darby on the 17th, but also the surprise confession of a murder wholly unsuspected by them.

At 3 A.M. a police car picked up Martin Donnelly, 42, who gave his residence as the Hotel De Vrees, New York City, and took him to headquarters for questioning in regard to the Darby case.

DARBY DEATH ACCIDENTAL

In a statement to press representatives, Lieutenant Levy, of the Horton County police said that Donnelly's account of

Darby's death tallied with medical reports and other factors. The two men had, according to Donnelly's account, engaged in a quarrel, on the private pier of one of the Glendale Beach palatial estates, which Donnelly was unable to identify. In the course of the quarrel, Donnelly stated that he had pushed Darby off the pier, and had then gone back to his car, in which he had slept until morning.

Alarmed then by Darby's continued absence, Donnelly stated that he returned to the pier, where he found Darby's body impaled on an anchor in a motorboat. He ran the boat over to Simm's Island, four miles or so offshore, and concealed the body in a marsh.

CONFESSION A SURPRISE

"We were wholly unprepared," Lieutenant Levy told press representatives, "for the confession which followed. Donnelly stated, voluntarily, that on the previous day he had strangled and killed Anton Karl Nagle, 57, believed by New York police to have been an associate of Donnelly's in black market activities.

Following Donnelly's directions, police found Nagle's body in a lake . . .

"Sibyl!" cried Lucia.

But Sibyl had gone, and she was alone.

Martin, you fool! You wicked, wicked fool! You can't get out of this. And you don't want to. You wanted to be arrested. You wanted to confess. You want to die—in the electric chair.

Well, I won't let you. I'll tell Lieutenant Levy the truth about Ted Darby.

That won't do any good. Ted Darby doesn't matter now. It's Nagle. He did that for me. Martin, you fool! You fool,

226

to choose that dreadful death. You didn't trust me. You thought I'd give you away. Again.

I've got to talk to him. I've got to see him. And I never can. Never, never again. But it can't—

"Lieutenant Levy is here, ma'am," said Sibyl. "Shall I bring him up?"

"No, no! He can't come up here. No. Ask him to wait. I'll be down in a moment. No . . . Ask my father to come here, please."

"Mr. Harper's stepped out, ma'am."

This is too much. This is too much, Lucia thought. She got up, and tried to dress in haste, but her hands trembled so, her heart beat so fast. What dress? she thought, opening the closet door.

She took down the brown dress, and hung it up again. She took down a clean pink cotton dress, and that was not right. O God, I've got to hurry! What dress? She picked out two others, and laid them on a chair, and they were not right. O God, what shall I do? I've got to find the right dress . . .

There was a gray flannel skirt in the closet, with the hem half unripped. That was the right thing. With shaking hands she opened her preposterous sewing basket, a jumble of thread, darning silk, shoulder pads, bits of ribbon. She threaded a big darning needle with gray silk, and stitched up the hem, so badly that it was in puckers. She put on the skirt, and a white blouse, and forgetting to glance in the mirror, she went out of the room and down the stairs. She thought she heard Mrs. Lloyd's voice, but that was impossible.

She stopped in the hall outside the sitting room, and it was Mrs. Lloyd in there, sitting on the edge of a chair. She

227

was stylish today, in a high black hat from which a cyclamen veil floated, and she was just drawing off a cyclamen glove. But Lieutenant Levy was not there.

He's in the dining room, Lucia thought, and was moving away when Bee called to her.

"Mother!"

"I'm sorry . . ." Lucia said. "I'm sorry, but I've got to see Lieutenant Levy."

"He's gone, Mother. Mother, Mrs. Lloyd is here."

"I know. But——"

Bee crossed the room and took her mother's hand.

"Come and sit down, Mother."

It was inhuman of Bee to ask her to sit down and talk to Mrs. Lloyd. She hung back, like a rebellious child, but Bee drew her forward.

"I'm afraid *I* drove Lieutenant Levy away," said Mrs. Lloyd.

"Oh, no!" said Bee. "He said it wasn't anything important. He just stopped by, to tell Mother that the Darby case was closed."

"I've been to a meeting of the hospital committee," Mrs. Lloyd said, "and everyone was talking about this case. The Donnelly man was absolutely desperate. He fought off the police like a tiger, for hours, and they had to shoot him in the leg before he'd give in. Mrs. Ewing heard the shots."

"I'm afraid Mrs. Ewing's mistaken," said Bee. "Mr. Donnelly didn't even try to get away."

"But these gunmen always seem to defy the police, don't they?"

"Mr. Donnelly isn't a gunman," said Bee. "You see, we know him."

228

"You *know* him?" said Mrs. Lloyd, fascinated.

"Yes. And we liked him, Grandpa, and David and me, and Mother . . ."

"Then weren't you appalled, when you found out what he'd done?"

"No," Bee said, rising. She sat down on the arm of the sofa beside Lucia, and laid her hand on her mother's shoulder. "We're just terribly sorry."

Her hand lay heavy on her mother's shoulder.

"He had lots of nice qualities," she said. "Only, the war makes people do—queer, horrible things." Her voice was a little unsteady now. "Especially middle-aged people."

"Oh, do you think so?" Mrs. Lloyd asked, a little surprised.

"Yes!" Bee said, vehemently. "It's psychological. Middle-aged people feel—sort of left out. As if everything was finished for them. They get a sort of craving for adventure . . ."

It was not Donnelly she was defending; it was her mother. She had tried to understand Lucia's bewildering and frightening behavior; she was trying now to present it as the foolish, but pitiable, last fling of a middle-aged woman. Lucia glanced up at her, and their eyes met.

"Mother," Bee said. "I'm sorry you felt so tired, but I thought I wouldn't bother you."

She had forgotten Mrs. Lloyd, so important in her scheme of life. All she wanted now was, that Lucia should know she understood, that she loved her.

"I'll look after the housekeeping for a while," she said. "And you can take things easy, Mother."

Be easy . . .

"Excuse me, ladies!" said Mr. Harper. "But the young fellow from the gas company wants to see the contract, Lucia."

"What contract, Father?"

"He says the owner of the house has a contract for maintenance. He must have left it with you, m'dear."

"I don't remember seeing it, Father."

"Well . . ." he said, indulgent and resigned, "if you can't find the contract, m'dear, we'll have to pay, and pay through the nose, for these repairs to the icebox." He smiled at Mrs. Lloyd. "I'm afraid you ladies don't take contracts very seriously," he said.

"I'm frightful about losing things," said Mrs. Lloyd.

This is my life, Lucia thought. The things I dreaded aren't going to happen, the shame, the disgrace. I don't know whether Lieutenant Levy believes Martin's story about Ted Darby, but anyhow he's going to accept it. Nothing's going to happen to me.

This is my life, going on just the same. I haven't hurt the children, or Tom, or Father. I haven't shocked people like Mrs. Lloyd. The man is here to fix the icebox, at last. This is how I'll go on.

And all that had happened to her would be, must be, pushed down, out of sight; the details of daily living would come like falling leaves to cover it. I don't really know what's happened to me, she thought, in wonder. I haven't taken time to think about it.

Maybe I never will. Or maybe, when I'm old, and have plenty of time and quiet . . .

Sibyl came in, with tea and cinnamon toast. The butter on the toast was margarine, colored yellow; the cinnamon was artificial. Lucia had read the label on the little tin with

230

an unreasonable interest; she remembered some of it now. Imitation cinnamon. Cinnamic aldehyde. Eugenol. Oil of cassia, quite a lot of other things, too.

But nobody knows the difference, she thought. Only Sibyl and me.

The Innocent
Mrs. Duff

The Innocent
Mrs. Duff

A NOVEL OF SUSPENSE

by
Elisabeth Sanxay Holding

INTRODUCTION BY PETER SCHWED

Academy Chicago Publishers

Published in 1991 by
Academy Chicago Publishers
213 West Institute Place
Chicago, Illinois 60610

Printed and bound in the USA

Library of Congress Cataloging-in-Publication Data

Holding, Elisabeth Sanxay, 1889-1955
   The blank wall : a novel of suspense ; The innocent Mrs. Duff : a
novel of suspense / by Elisabeth Sanxay Holding ; introduction by
Peter Schwed.
      p.   cm.
    ISBN 0-89733-366-7
    1. Detective and mystery stories, American.   I. Holding
Elisabeth Sanxay, 1889-1955.   Innocent Mrs. Duff.   1991.
II. Title. III. Title: Innocent Mrs. Duff.
PS3515.03418A6   1991
  813' .52--dc20   91-31464
                                                              CIP

Cover art by James "Ozzie" McMahon
Cover design by Julia Anderson Miller

Introduction

The financial crash of 1929 changed the lives of a great many people. In the case of Elisabeth Sanxay Holding, it stopped her from writing long, serious, critically acclaimed novels, and forced her into a new career, penning shorter, suspenseful mysteries. The reason was simple. An author back in those grim days had great difficulty in selling the sort of book that Mrs. Holding had written so brilliantly through the 1920's, either to a magazine for serialization or to a book publisher, but a regular market continued to exist in both areas for mysteries. And Mrs. Holding had two small daughters to support.

The half dozen books that she had written previously, starting in 1920 with *Invincible Minnie,* displayed a style that stood her in good stead the rest of her writing life. That went on for another 25 years, in the course of which she wrote just about a book a year. *The New York Times'* review of one of her early novels (*The Silk Purse*) said:

> She has managed to make every one of her characters, however unimportant, important. They are as real a collection of people as ever said yes when they wished to heaven they could say no. Like real people, they talk when they should be silent, are silent when they

should say something, and, with the best intentions in the world, quietly wreck each other's lives.

This same unusual talent for depicting believable characters informed all of Mrs. Holding's subsequent work, and she was a forerunner — very possibly the forerunner — in the creation of the story of suspense, as opposed to the conventional mystery.

All of Elisabeth Sanxay Holding's suspense novels were first published in hardback form, and then reissued a year or so later in paperback. Most of them were chosen by mystery and detective book clubs, had foreign editions, and a few also were serialized in national magazines. But the fate that befalls practically every novel eventually befell Mrs. Holding's prodigious output. The books were allowed to go out of print, and stayed that way for some years.

They achieved a renaissance early in the 1960's when a collection of Raymond Chandler's letters (*Raymond Chandler Speaking*) was published both in the United States and in England; included in it was a letter that Chandler wrote to his British publisher, Hamish Hamilton:

> Does anybody in England publish Elisabeth Sanxay Holding? For my money she's the top suspense writer of them all. She doesn't pour it on and make you feel irritated. Her characters are wonderful; and she has a sort of inner calm which I find very attractive. I recommend for your attention, if you have not read them, *Net of Cobwebs, The Innocent Mrs. Duff, The Blank Wall.*

By this time, Mrs. Holding had died and I, then a book publisher myself and Mrs. Holding's literary executor, saw a chance to revive her books for the benefit of her two heirs, my sister-in-law and my wife. Accordingly, armed with the Chandler letter and a number of excellent reviews of all her books that I had collected, I interested a reprint house, Ace Books, in re-issuing more than a dozen of Mrs. Holding's novels, two in a volume, much like the present book you hold in your hand.

That was very satisfying, but after a while time once again took its toll, the books were allowed to go out of print, and Mrs. Holding's work has not been available in the bookstores for the past quarter of a century. So it is with real gratification that my sister-in-law, Skeffington Ardron, my wife, Antonia, and I see two of her best suspense novels being put out again now by Academy Chicago. You will note that both *The Blank Wall* and *The Innocent Mrs. Duff* were cited by Raymond Chandler as being among the author's best, and *The Blank Wall* was the prime selection chosen by Alfred Hitchcock for his classic anthology, *My Favorites in Suspense* in 1959, which included twenty short stories by other masters of the genre; but *The Blank Wall* was the only full-length novel. That fact elicited from James Sandoe, in his lead review in the *Herald-Tribune Book Review*, the statement that *The Blank Wall* was "by that astonishing artist, the late Elisabeth Sanxay Holding, whose evocation of nightmare was and still is unique, as reprint publishers might recall to their benefit."

Well, Academy Chicago has recalled it, and a major beneficiary will be you, the reader.

PETER SCHWED
NEW YORK CITY
1991

Chapter One

"My God!" Jacob Duff said to himself, standing stripped before the bathroom mirror. "I'm putting on weight!"

He was a big man, and very well-built, with broad shoulders and narrow flanks; it shocked him to study that thickening around his middle. And his ruddy, handsome face showed a sagging about the jowls. My God! he thought. I'm only forty-two. There shouldn't be anything like *this* . . .

Reggie began singing in her bedroom. Oh, shut up! he cried in his heart. You can't carry a tune. You know that; you know how it gets on my nerves, and still you keep on. Shut up!

He opened the door into his own bedroom and closed it behind him with a slam. That stopped her. But she'll do it again, he thought. There's nothing, absolutely nothing I ask her not to do that she doesn't keep on doing.

He began to dress, and this morning he admitted what for some time he had been trying to ignore: that the waistband of his trousers was tighter, was too tight; his back bulged a little between the shoulders. This made him miserable. It's *her* fault, he thought. She doesn't have the right sort of meals. As far as that goes, she doesn't have any-

1

thing right. We've been married nearly a year, and she hasn't learned one damn thing. She never will, either. She doesn't even try.

He heard her come out of her room into the hall. She knocked at his door.

"Ready, Jake?"

"Not yet," he answered. "You go ahead."

He knew exactly how it would be. She would go running down the stairs and into the dining-room, and she would say 'hello' to the housemaid. That was another thing he had asked her, again and again, not to do, but she kept right on, saying hello to everyone. To the chauffeur, to the cook, to the doctor, to anyone he was fool enough to invite into his house. Oh, hello!

I'm ashamed of her, he thought. I admit it. That time I brought Copeley in for a drink, she said 'hello, hon', to me. I caught him grinning. Everybody—servants, everybody laughing at her behind her back. And at me, for marrying her.

He hated the thought of going downstairs. I never have any appetite for breakfast any more, he thought. I used to look forward to breakfast, when Helen was alive. Good God! After being married to a girl like Helen for four years, *how* could I have married Regina Riordan? The name ought to have been enough for me. Reggie. A photographer's model.

He had to go downstairs. She was sitting at the table, and she was wearing another of those negligées she fancied: blue satin, with a little scalloped cape.

"Oh, hello, Jake!" she said, with that dazzling smile. A model's smile, he thought.

"Morning," he answered. "Reggie, I've asked you time after time if you'd kindly get dressed for breakfast. If you

2

can't make the effort, then have your breakfast in your room."

"I know," she said, anxiously. "I've been trying to get some nice little porch dresses, but I honestly haven't seen anything worth buying."

"Porch dresses? What are they?"

"Oh, little ginghams, you know. Little checked dresses, or percales, things like that."

He knew they would be wrong. Helen had never had things like that.

"Why can't you wear your ordinary clothes?" he asked.

"Oh, I got it so drilled into me not to sit around in my good clothes," she explained. "At the studio we always—"

"Hush!" he said, as the maid came in through the swing door.

"The cook was able to get some bacon yesterday, Jake. You like bacon and eggs—"

"None for me, thanks. I'm going on a diet."

"Oh, Jake! Did the doctor say—?"

"Yes," he said, to keep her quiet. "Only black coffee and orange juice this morning. Where's Jay?"

"Oh, Miss Castle said he got something in his eye. They'll be right down. Honestly, Jake, I hate to sit here eating when you're not taking a thing."

"Thanks," he said.

Anyone else would see that I don't feel like talking, he thought. But not Reggie.

"Aunt Lou asked me to stop in and see her this morning," she went on. "I thought I'd take Jay."

"You'd better leave Jay to Miss Castle. That's what she's here for."

"I know. But—"

3

"I'd very much rather you didn't drag the child around with you."

"Well, I always consult Miss Castle, Jake."

I'd rather you never had anything to do with my son, he thought. I don't like him to go anywhere with you. I don't like him to see you here in that tawdry thing. He glanced at her across the table. She's beautiful, he thought, with distaste.

She looked taller than she was, being so slight. Her face was thin, with faint hollows under the high cheekbones, but heaven knew she was healthy enough; never sick, never tired. Like a peasant. Her eyes were dark-blue, with thick black lashes, her hair was black, her skin had a delicate rosy glow.

Jacob Duff, junior, came clattering down the stairs and into the dining-room, a thin little boy of seven, with neat fair hair and a debonair manner.

"Hello, Daddy!" he said. "Hello! Reggie!"

"I've told you not to say 'hello'," said Duff, angrily.

"Well, good-morning," said Jay, without interest, and drew back Miss Castle's chair for her.

"Good-morning!" she said, with a smile and a slight inclination of the head.

She was an Englishwoman of thirty-five or so, handsome in a calm and disinterested fashion. She wore no make-up but a little powder; her thick light hair was cut and waved in unbecoming scallops; her white blouse with an artless little round collar did not suit her strong-boned face. But she's not interested in being 'alluring' and 'glamorous'—and cheap, Duff thought. If she chose to use lipstick and all the rest of it, she'd be a damn sight better looking than Reggie. Better figure, too. More womanly.

4

"I hear Jay's going to visit his auntie this morning," she said.

"I don't want to go!" said Jay, loudly.

"Don't shout like that!" said Duff. "And don't say things like that, either."

"Well . . ." said Jay, sulkily, and he pronounced it 'wull'.

"None of that," said Duff. "None of your 'wells', when you're told to do something."

"Told to do *what*?" asked Jay.

"Jay!" said Miss Castle, in mild rebuke.

"Well, he didn't tell me to do anything," said Jay. "I just said I didn't want to go and see Aunt Lou. Is that anything so bad?"

"Leave the table, sir!" said Duff.

"All right—sir!" said Jay, and jumped up nimbly.

"Go up to your room and stay there until you've learned some manners," said Duff.

"Learn 'em out of a book?" asked Jay; then, at the sight of his father's face, he giggled and ran scampering up the stairs.

Miss Castle went on quietly eating her breakfast, but not Reggie.

"It's just one of his wild fits," she said. "He's such a high-strung little fellow."

"Thanks," said Duff. "Thanks for explaining him to me."

"Well, I didn't mean it like that, Jake. I just meant he doesn't really mean to be rude. He's always as good as gold with Aunt Lou."

"Yes . . ." said Duff. "If you ladies will excuse me, I'll just glance at the news."

5

He was glad to put up the newspaper, to block out Reggie's face. *Aunt Lou!* he thought. The idea of a girl like Reggie being in a position to call her that. It's my fault. I realize that. But what was I thinking of, to do a thing like that?

His aunt, Louisa Albany, was a figure of overpowering importance in his life, and always had been. He was her heir; he would some day inherit a very nice little fortune from her, but her importance, to him, was not derived from that. It was her personality, her character, her tradition. His respect and admiration for her were beyond measure.

She could have stopped this, he thought. When I first brought Reggie to see her, if she'd said one word. . . . Of course, she'd never met anyone like Reggie; you couldn't expect her to understand that type. She simply thought I'd be happier if I married again. She was simply thinking of my welfare.

But if she'd only realize now . . . I don't like to say anything outright to her, but if she'd only see for herself. She knows me; she knows what my life with Helen was like. I don't know how she can help seeing. It's beginning to affect my health. I'm sleeping badly—and putting on weight like this isn't healthy.

"Couldn't you have one little corn muffin, Jake?" asked Reggie. "They're as light as feathers."

"No, thanks. To tell you the truth, I don't think all this heavy, starchy food is a good thing for anyone."

"*I* can't eat them," said Miss Castle. "I think your hot breads are delicious, but if I start the day with them, I'm quite dull all morning."

Duff glanced at her, and their eyes met for a moment.

Then she smiled and looked away, but Duff had already got her message. She understands! he thought, with a sort of wonder.

"Look!" said Reggie. "I'll just run up and put on a dress and drive to the station with you, Jake."

"I'm sorry, Reggie, but I've got to pick up three or four men this morning."

"Oh, well . . . !" she said. "Then how about Jay and I meeting you for tea somewhere, after we leave Aunt Lou's?"

"Jay is to stay in his room all day," said Duff.

"Oh, Jake, honestly—!"

"My dear girl, I happen to be the child's father. I understand him better than you ever could. I'm not going to have him behaving like a common little brat."

"But, honestly, Jake, he didn't do anything—"

"If Miss Castle thinks I'm being harsh or unreasonable—" he said, and again he glanced at Miss Castle, and again she smiled at him.

"Suppose we wait and see what Jay has to say for himself, later on?" she suggested. "I'll go up and have a talk with him presently."

"Very good idea," said Duff.

We speak the same language, he thought. God, what a relief! She's got some sense and breeding and dignity. She's a handsome woman, too; knows how to carry herself. Reggie looks like a rag-bag in that thing.

He pushed back his chair and rose, and now was the time for him to kiss Reggie. He did not want to. It's a silly, meaningless habit, he thought.

"Well, au revoir!" he said.

"Hi! Wait!" cried Reggie, and jumping up, she ran to

7

him. She put her hand on his arm and looked up into his face with her wide, gay, model's smile.

"You forgot to kiss me good-bye!" she said. "I guess the honeymoon's over."

And you think that's a joke, do you? thought Duff.

Chapter Two

The car was waiting; Nolan, the chauffeur, opened the door for him.

"Good-morning, sir," he said.

"Good-morning," said Duff. "We'll stop for Mr. Vermilyea, that's all."

"Yes, sir," said Nolan.

Duff lit a cigarette and leaned back. This car-pool business was a nuisance, he thought. And Johnny Vermilyea's a nuisance, too. If he weren't so lazy, he'd walk to the station.

The three other men who had gone into the pool with him were pretty well eliminated, now that he had begun taking the nine-twenty. They had to go earlier. Only Vermilyea didn't care what train he got. Any time that suits you, old man, he said. Any time, any time. He was sauntering across the driveway in front of his big house, very dapper in his dark suit, which was, according to Duff's standards, too snugly-fitting to his muscular body. With his red face, his big nose, his little bright eyes, he looked like Mister Punch.

"Hello, hello, hello!" he said. "Here we are." He got into the car. "Wonderful weather for April."

"Yes," said Duff, without enthusiasm. "But this commuting business gets me down. I'm not used to it. To tell

9

you the truth, I don't like suburban life. Born and brought up in New York."

"I couldn't live in the city," said Vermilyea, earnestly.

He was certainly close to forty and he lived, Duff thought, a ridiculous life, with his aged parents, in that big old house. His father had retired at seventy, and Vermilyea had become president of the Vermilyea Steamship Company. I'm more or less a figurehead, he would tell anyone, candidly. I've got some first-rate fellows there who do all the work.

Three nights a week he served as an orderly in the Vandenbrinck Hospital, and his leisure time was chiefly given up to Drives, drives for the Red Cross, the Community Chest, War Bonds; he was forever appearing at your house, trying to collect money. Duff found him boring, but after all he was a Vermilyea of Vandenbrinck; he had gone to a very good prep school, and, though not to Harvard, to Princeton.

This was the wrong sort of suburb to choose, Duff thought. I should have gone to one of those flashy new places—where Reggie might have fitted in. But I was thinking of Jay. I was thinking of Jay when I married her, too. I thought she'd be good for him, make a home. She's ruining the boy. She's making life hell for me. I'm putting on weight . . .

I want to get weighed, he thought. I want to see . . . He answered Vermilyea absently, while he tried to think where he had seen scales. At the club, of course, but he had not been there for months; people would ask him questions, make jokes about his marriage. In drug-stores? he thought.

The car stopped in the circular drive behind the railroad station.

"Five-twenty, sir?" Nolan asked.

"Yes," said Duff, and crossed the platform with Vermilyea.

"Darn good-looking fellow," Vermilyea observed.

"Who?" asked Duff.

"That chauffeur of yours. Mrs. Laird was speaking about him the other day."

"Speaking about *Nolan?*" said Duff.

"Yes," said Vermilyea. "She was saying it was a pity she couldn't get him for this play she's putting on for Overseas Bundles."

"Can't she find anything better to gossip about than other people's servants?" Duff demanded.

"Wasn't gossiping, old man. Just—well, here we are! Here we are!"

They got into the club car, and there were a couple of fellows Vermilyea knew. They wanted to play gin rummy.

"Sorry," said Duff, "but you'll have to count me out. I've got a head this morning."

"Oh! Big night?" one of the men asked.

"Could be," said Duff.

A big night, he thought. That's a good one. Directly after dinner he had gone into his study; he had sat there all alone all evening, reading, or trying to read, his late uncle Fred Albany's book, *Big Game and Small.* He had two or three whiskies, or maybe four, simply in order to get sleepy. He did that every evening now; he had to do it, or he could not sleep.

But it's not a good idea, he thought. I mean to say, drinking alone. Not good for morale. Not good for your health. I don't feel well, and that's a fact. But what the hell *can* I do in the evenings? I can't sit there talking to Reggie; there's nothing to talk to her about. Nobody ever comes

11

to see us; there's no place to go. If I could take a room in a hotel in town . . .

Duff and Vermilyea and another man were all going downtown; they shared a taxi. Once I've started working, I'll feel better, Duff thought. But, unfortunately, there was little or no work for him to do that morning. He was the junior partner, as his father had been, in the firm of Hanbury, Martin and Duff, Surgical and Dental Appliances; they were working almost entirely on Government contracts now, and Duff left all that to Hanbury. I don't like all this red tape, he said. I don't like all these regulations, all this red tape.

There's no need for my coming in to the office five days a week, he thought, and I wouldn't do it, except for the sake of getting out of that house. But if I stay home, there's Reggie, trailing around in a wrapper, and the servants doing just as they damn please. No order, no system, no peace and quiet. When Helen was alive, everything went like clockwork. If I called up and said I'd like to bring someone home to dinner, I could absolutely count on everything being exactly right. But now . . . !

They had taken in so many new people that his secretary had to work in his private office half the time. She began to type, and the noise was exasperating.

"I'm going to step out for a cup of coffee, Miss Fuller," he said. "Back in a few moments."

He wanted to find a pair of scales. Funny, he thought, that you always say a 'pair' of scales. You couldn't ask anybody where to find scales; simply calling attention to the fact that you'd gained a few pounds. So he went into the drug-store in the lobby of the building. There were scales there, two kinds, the old-fashioned reliable kind

with weights on a bar, and the other kind, that gave your weight printed on a ticket, in privacy. He chose the privacy. He put in a penny, and out came the little ticket.

"My God!" he cried to himself. "It's not possible." He stepped upon the trembling platform again and put in another penny; out came another ticket with the same figure on it.

No matter who might be watching him, he had to try the honest old-fashioned scales. He set the weights for what he had last weighed; five pounds more, ten pounds more, fourteen.

Fourteen pounds more than he had ever weighed in his life. It made him feel actually sick. I need a drink, he thought. Then I'm going to turn over a new leaf. Diet, exercise, and so on.

There was a bar down the street where he sometimes went after five for a cocktail. He had never entered it at an earlier hour; he could not remember ever having taken a drink at eleven o'clock in the morning, and he was ashamed to be seen going in there.

But there were plenty of men at the bar, and they looked all right, prosperous-looking fellows, well-dressed; they seemed perfectly matter-of-fact about an eleven o'clock drink. He ordered a straight rye, and drank it standing at the bar. It wasn't quite enough, and he ordered a second.

That turned out to be just what he needed. Sitting on the stool, in the dim, quiet bar, his mind began to work, quickly and clearly. This weight, he thought; I can get rid of that, easily enough. Go to one of these gyms, sweat it off in a couple of weeks. No. That's not what's worrying me. It's the whole setup. Reggie. I don't see why I should

13

sacrifice my whole life for her. She married me for money and social position; nothing else. For all I know—

A thought came to him that was like a flash of light. Darn good-looking fellow, Vermilyea had said. Mrs. Laird had talked about Nolan's good looks. Had everybody in the neighborhood been talking about his handsome chauffeur?

I'll just put on a dress and drive down to the station with you, Reggie had said. Then she would have driven home alone with Nolan. And she had done that, a dozen, a score of times. He began to remember other things now. The way she said 'hello' to Nolan, with her wide, dazzling, model's smile.

I've been sleeping in that other room for nearly two months now, he thought, and she hasn't said a word. That simply isn't natural—unless there's somebody else. That would be absolutely typical of her, to disgrace me—with a chauffeur.

But she's not a bad girl, he thought.

On the contrary, he had found her altogether too good, too innocent; it had been like marrying a schoolgirl. He remembered the miserable embarrassments of their honeymoon. When the bellboy had opened the door of the hotel suite in Montreal, she had given a squeal of delight. Oh, Jake! Isn't this grand?

Helen had felt as he did; they had both determined that no one should know they were a honeymoon couple, and they had gone to Havana, and nobody had known. But not Reggie. Reggie had *told* people. She's absolutely insensitive, he thought. She doesn't realize that she's killed all the love I ever had for her. But she's not a bad girl.

Not yet. At least, I don't think so. But she could behave in a way to make a hell of a scandal with that fellow Nolan.

14

Anyhow, I can't stand any more of this, and I'm going to tell Aunt Lou so, frankly. I'll provide for Reggie, of course. Generously. I'm not interested in a divorce, either. I simply want to get away from that setup. I cannot stand it any longer.

Chapter Three

When her husband died, Mrs. Albany had sold his house on Ninth Street, and she lived now in an apartment-hotel not far from Washington Square. She lived, as always, with old-fashioned stateliness, combined with her own particular dash. When Duff rang the bell of her suite, the door was opened by a colored maid in a trim uniform, who led him into the sitting-room filled with the hideous Albany furniture, pictures and ornaments.

"I'll see if Mrs. Albany is at home, sir," said the maid, and withdrew.

It made no difference that he was Mrs. Albany's nephew and heir. He would have to wait, like anyone else, and if Mrs. Albany were taking a nap, or if she were engaged with the manicurist, or if she were not disposed to receive guests, he would be dismissed, like anyone else. I have no regular hours At Home, in war time, she had told her nephew. If people want to see me, they must telephone ahead, or take their chance.

Rose, the maid, came back.

"Mrs. Albany is At Home, sir," she said, and went away, without a smile.

Louisa Albany came in promptly, a tall and very thin woman, with frizzy hair dyed a strange, pale red; she had

16

rouge on her hollow cheeks and on her thin lips; she wore a blue satin blouse with a high collar, and a short black skirt. You could say, with truth, that her face in profile was like a camel's; you could say she was a hag. But it was none the less undeniable that she had an air; she had style, even elegance.

"Well, Jacob?" she said, in her clear, superior voice. "Sit down! I haven't seen you for some time."

"I've been rather busy. How are you keeping, Aunt Lou?"

"Very well indeed, thank you. You're putting on weight, Jacob."

His face grew hot.

"I'll soon get rid of it," he said. "I've started on a diet."

"Then I shan't offer you a cocktail," she said.

"That won't do me any harm."

"It will," said she. "You can't touch alcohol when you're reducing. Your Uncle Fred often had to go without a drink for weeks, when his weight got up. He had a perfect horror of getting fat."

"Naturally," said Duff. "Look here, Aunt Lou, I'd really like a cocktail. I'm a bit upset."

She looked at him for a moment.

"Then you shall have one," she said. "I'll make it myself."

He watched her as she crossed the room to the kitchenette across the hall.

"Ice, Rose," she said.

"Yes, madam," said Rose, who never smiled.

There was a strange, and, to Duff, an irritating harmony between Mrs. Albany and Rose. They worked together now like two professional bartenders.

"Martinis," said Mrs. Albany.

On a shelf there was a fine array of bottles, with jiggers of two sizes, swizzle sticks, glass mixers. Rose washed a

lemon, and cut curls of peel; Mrs. Albany moved about neatly. Rose put a glass mixer and two glasses on a tray and brought it into the sitting-room.

"What are you upset about, Jacob?" Mrs. Albany asked, when they were alone.

"I simply can't go on like this," he said. "My life is hell."

She took a sip of her cocktail. "Light a cigarette for me, Jacob," she said. "Thank you. Is this all about Reggie?"

"Yes. I don't know how to make you understand. You're absolutely blind about that girl."

"No, I'm not," said Mrs. Albany, simply. "She has her faults. I was telling her today—you knew they came in to lunch?"

"They?"

"Yes. Reggie and Jay."

"*Jay?*"

"Don't shout so, Jacob."

"I said the child was to stay in his room—"

"Well, probably your Miss Castle didn't think that was a good idea."

"When I give an order, in my own house—"

"Pooh!" said Mrs. Albany. "That's no way to talk. No . . . I was speaking to Reggie about her housekeeping. I told her she'd better go and take one of those courses. I told her about this finishing-school—junior college, they call it now—where she could learn how to do things properly."

"It's a lot more serious than a matter of housekeeping. She doesn't care a damn for me."

"Yes, she does. She's very fond of you, and very anxious to make you happy."

He had finished his cocktail. He set the empty glass on the table and glanced at Mrs. Albany, but she took no notice.

18

"Mind if I help myself?" he asked. "They're excellent. Excellent. Aunt Lou, I'll tell you something that may make you realize. For nearly two months we've—" He hesitated. "We've been occupying separate rooms."

"Reggie didn't mention that. What was the quarrel about, Jacob?"

"There wasn't any quarrel. One night I didn't feel at all well, and I went to sleep in one of the guest rooms. And the next night, it was simply taken for granted. Bed turned down in there, my pajamas laid out. And it's been that way ever since. Reggie's never said a word."

"It's for you to speak of it," said Mrs. Albany, severely. "That's no way to treat your wife."

"No . . ." he said. "There's nothing left of our marriage. No companionship, no home life, no social life, nothing."

"Jacob," said Mrs. Albany, "Reggie is young, very young, and she has not had advantages. But she's an affectionate, loyal, good girl. She's devoted to little Jay. If you'll give her the help and guidance it's your duty to give her, she'll make you a splendid wife."

"Not she! She won't do a single thing I ask her. She doesn't learn anything."

"That's unjust. She's learned to dress in very good taste."

"That's because you buy her clothes for her."

"No. She gets things for herself now. And she's always reading little articles, about etiquette, and so on, and keeping up with the new books. And she works faithfully as a Nurse's Aid in the hospital."

"Mind if I finish up the cocktails?"

"Yes, I do mind," said Mrs. Albany. "I only made two each, and I want that for myself."

"Then d'you mind if I get a drink from the kitchen?"

"Yes, I do. You've had plenty."

19

"I'm upset!" he cried. "The whole thing is hell. And when I think of Helen—"

"You never cared so very much for Helen."

"I respected her."

"She saw to *that*," said Mrs. Albany. "Helen knew how to hold her own. And Reggie doesn't.

"Look here, Aunt Lou, I really need another drink."

"Don't ever let me hear you say you 'need' a drink."

"Well, I do!" he said. "I can't go on, with things as they are. I'll have to get away, take a room in town—"

"Out of the question!" said Mrs. Albany. "You can't desert that poor girl for no reason at all."

"All right!" he said, rising. "Suppose I told you I'd heard some very unpleasant talk about Reggie?"

"What sort of talk?"

"She's pretty free and easy with Nolan—"

"Jacob," said Mrs. Albany, "you ought to be ashamed of yourself for listening to gossip about your wife. What's more, you know as well as I do that there's not a word of truth in it. You know Reggie's absolutely incapable of anything of that sort."

"Good God!" he cried. "You have no sympathy for me whatever, no understanding. Reggie is 'incapable' of anything wrong, but I'm—I don't know what. A monster. I never knew you to be so utterly unjust."

That disturbed her.

"I don't mean to be so," she said. "I know Reggie has a great deal to learn, and I know you're not happy, Jacob. But—to be frank, Jacob—I don't think you ever could be happily married."

"What? Why not—if I found the right woman?"

"You don't know how to be married, Jacob. You don't like it. You're not domestic. A man's man, as they say."

"And what about Uncle Fred? He didn't spend—didn't want to spend four months of the year at home."

"He wanted me with him, wherever he went," said Mrs. Albany. "He was—very companionable."

"And I'm not?"

"I don't mean to be carping and fault-finding, Jacob," she said, and she was a little anxious now. "But I'm sure that, if you'll try, you can make this marriage a success. Reggie does everything she can to please you—"

"That's where you're wrong," he said.

"No . . ." she said. "Jacob, give her a chance. Try to make her happy—"

"Good God!" he cried. "When you think of what I've given that girl—!"

"Jacob," said Mrs. Albany, "that's sheer vulgarity."

Their eyes met.

"I think I'd better be going," he said, coldly.

"Perhaps . . ." said Mrs. Albany, with a sigh.

When he went out into the little hall, she followed him.

"I dare say it's hard," she said. "But now that you're getting older, it will be easier to settle down. As time goes on." She hit his shoulder with her bony hand. "Think of Jay," she said. "Try to make the best of things, Jacob."

He stood waiting for the elevator, sunk in a bleak depression. If *she'd* stood by me, he thought, I might have been able to stand it, to go on. But she's hypnotized by Reggie. Now I can't stand it. Now I can't go on.

Chapter Four

He stopped in at a bar and got a drink; only one, that was all he wanted.

The bartender set a plate of cheese crackers and pretzels before him.

"Not for me, thanks," said Duff. "I'm on a diet."

"Well, there's plenty of us on diets now," said the bartender, somberly, "simply for the fact that the red points we will get so little."

"Compared with the rest of the world," said Duff, "we're damn lucky. The thing is, some people say alcohol puts weight on you. What do you think?"

"Well, it does with some," said the bartender. "With others it don't. It all depends on what constitution you got."

"That's probably it," said Duff.

He felt somehow reassured by this little talk. I know people who drink, he thought, drink excessively, and they're thin as rails. He knew he was going to need a few drinks at bedtime, to get some sleep, and he did not want to think that that might undo the benefits of the day's dieting. Black coffee and orange juice for breakfast, a lamb chop and a salad for lunch—nothing else. It won't take long, at this rate, he thought. And after all, fourteen pounds isn't so much, on a big frame.

He missed the five-twenty. Won't hurt Nolan to wait

a while, he thought. God knows he has little enough to do these days, with no gas to run the cars. I don't know about Nolan and all that gossip . . .

He sat in the smoker, in a front seat, hoping not to see anyone he knew. He wanted to think about Nolan. Where did I first hear that gossip about Nolan and Reggie? he thought. But he could not remember. It's probably all over the place, he thought. You can't deny that Aunt Lou's a woman of the world. She travelled everywhere with Uncle Fred, met everybody. But she doesn't know anything about a girl like Reggie. Never met that type.

Well, he thought, with a sigh, there's nothing to do but wait. In the course of time she's absolutely certain to do something that will make Aunt Lou realize . . . Or she'll get sick of living like this, and she'll leave me. That would be the perfect solution.

The sun was low when the train stopped at Vandenbrinck; the river was pearly grey under a sky without color. The whole scene had, for him, a desolate look. I've had some of my happiest hours alone, he thought. In the North Woods, the Adirondacks, sailing. It's either that, or the big cities. But this suburban setup makes me sick.

The car was waiting, and Reggie was in it. Her beauty surprised him, for when he thought of her, he forgot that: the delicate loveliness of her thin young face, the grace and fineness of her body. She *looked* entirely right, too, in a navy-blue linen dress, her shining black hair brushed back from her face. She looked like a quiet, well-bred young girl. But who knew better than he that she was not?

Nolan was standing in the road, smoking; he threw away his cigarette and hastened forward to open the door of the car. And for the first time Duff really looked at him. Why, he's like a damn movie actor! he thought, outraged.

23

Black, wavy hair, Nolan had, that sprang up from the temples, fine black brows over deep-blue eyes; he was of medium height, and slender, but in his very upright carriage, the set of his head, there was a vitality a little aggressive.

"Hello, Jake!" said Reggie.

He gave her something like a smile and got in beside her.

"The chairs have come!" she said.

"What chairs?"

"Why, don't you remember, Jake? You said I could order those dining-room chairs, over four months ago?"

"That's nice," he said.

"I went in to lunch with Aunt Lou, Jake, and she had an awfully good idea. About me taking a Homemaker's Course. I went to the Haverdean Junior College about it. Of course, it's sort of late in the year, but Mrs. Haverdean said that if I started right away, I'd get a good two months, and I could take some private lessons. And next year I could start when the school opens."

"Do you want to do that?" he asked.

"I'm crazy to."

"You would be," he said.

"How do you mean, Jake?" she asked.

"I think you would be crazy, to go to a school like that —with young girls."

"Well, I'm not so terribly old, Jake. Twenty-one."

"It's not that."

"But then what, Jake? You mean because I'm married?"

"That's one reason."

"But Mrs. Haverdean says they've got other married girls—"

24

"Please don't talk about 'married girls'. I'd rather not go on with this. If you can't see for yourself how unsuitable, how—damn ridiculous it would be for you to go to Haverdean—"

"You mean, about them being society girls?" she asked. "Well, Aunt Lou said that would be all right, Jake. She said I'd make some nice friends."

"Do you *want* to have schoolgirls for friends?" he asked.

"Well . . ." she said, with a doubtful smile.

They were both silent then. It's all very well for Aunt Lou to say that I didn't love Helen, he thought. I wasn't infatuated with her; I admit that. But we got on together. We spoke the same language. Helen was a woman, not an ignorant, childish—ninny.

They had turned into the driveway: the burgeoning trees threw long shadows on the lawn, the windows had a fiery dazzle from the setting sun. It seemed to Duff that the place had a strangely deserted look. Not like a home at all, he thought. The housemaid opened the door, and they went in, to a blank silence. Never any stir here, no preparations for guests, no telephone calls.

"Where's Jay?" he asked.

"Miss Castle sent him to bed early, because he was rude to you at breakfast."

They went up the stairs together, and, without a word, separated, going to their separate rooms. If she was human, Duff thought, if she was a *woman*, she'd ask me to come back to her. But she never says one word. Good God, what is she?

There was nearly an hour to fill before dinner. Duff washed, and went quickly downstairs. He was pleased to find Miss Castle in the sitting-room, and he thought she

25

was pleased to see him. She looked very nice, he thought, in a long-sleeved white blouse, her hair so neat. A handsome woman; a real woman.

"I thought a cocktail wouldn't come amiss," he said. "Will you join me, Miss Castle?"

"Oh, thank you!" she said.

He rang for Mary, and told her to bring ice cubes, gin, French vermouth, and bitters.

"And be as quick as you can," he said.

That needed explaining to Miss Castle.

"When I do take a cocktail," he said, "I like it fifteen or twenty minutes before dinner. Not right on top of the meal."

"I'm sure that's more artistic," she said. "Do you know, when I left England, six years ago, I'd never had a cocktail? Sherry, sometimes, before dinner, and once in a great while, a brandy afterward."

"If you'd rather have sherry—?"

"Oh, thank you, but I quite enjoy a cocktail now and then. If one's at all depressed or out of sorts . . ."

He did not like to think of Miss Castle being depressed; he wanted her to be serene and happy under his roof.

"I hope Jay doesn't give you too much trouble," he said.

"Oh, no! He's a very interesting child. But there *is* one thing . . . I don't think Nolan is a good influence, Mr. Duff."

"Nolan?" he said, startled. "Does the boy see much of Nolan?"

"He's always running off to the garage. He's quite devoted to Nolan. Of course, it's easy to understand. Nolan tells him these stories of his life in the Marines."

"I didn't know he'd been a Marine."

26

"Oh, yes! He was two years in the Pacific islands."

The clock on the mantle struck half past six; Duff frowned and rang again for the housemaid.

"What's your opinion of Nolan, Miss Castle?" he asked.

"Not very high, I'm afraid."

"I'd like very much to know just why."

"It's difficult to put these things into words . . ." she said. "I don't think Nolan is—trustworthy."

"Have you had any trouble with him? Has he been impertinent to you?"

"Oh, no, never!" she said. "I shouldn't quite call Nolan impertinent. It's simply that he's so—" She hesitated. "So extremely independent," she said. "Or perhaps cynical would be a better word."

"Have you forbidden Jay to go to the garage?"

"No," she said.

He rang the bell in the wall again, kept his finger on it.

"I'd like to know why not," he said.

"I have the greatest admiration for Mrs. Duff's ideas," she said. "She's truly, sincerely democratic. I wish I'd been brought up with a little more of that, myself. I think that spirit is increasing at home, in England. And really it's not because Nolan's a chauffeur that I object to him. It's because of his—character."

"And Mrs. Duff stands up for him?"

"I shouldn't put it quite that way," she said. "It's simply that Mrs. Duff is so very honest—"

The housemaid came in now with the tray.

"You've forgotten the bitters," said Duff. "Hurry up with it, will you?"

"I didn't see any bitters, sir. I read the names on all the bottles—"

27

"Let me get it!" said Miss Castle, rising.

"No, no!" said Duff. "Sit down, Miss Castle. You come with me, Mary, and I'll show you . . ."

He got the bottle from the pantry, and when he returned to the sitting-room, Reggie was there.

He remembered that when he had first seen her the thing that had most charmed him had been her look of exquisite cleanliness. Flower-like, he had called it. Very well; she was flower-like now, in a black-and-white checked evening dress with a long skirt and a prim little bodice buttoned up to the neck, her black hair soft about her pale, clear face; her blue eyes brilliant.

But it failed to charm him now. He knew how it would be to take her in his arms. She would nestle against him, feeling boneless; there would be a faint scent of talcum powder about her; she would be pleased with his love-making, as a kitten may be pleased at being picked up. And, like a kitten, she was happy when let alone.

Does she let Nolan make love to her, in that same way? he thought.

He mixed the cocktails and poured out two; none for Reggie. 'I've never had a drink in my life,' she had told him in the beginning, 'and I guess I never will. I've seen too much of it, right in my own family.' She had told him a tale about an Uncle Vincent, who had begun to drink and had ruined himself. It was just the saddest thing, she had said.

"Dinner is served, madam," said the maid.

"Can you put it back ten minutes, Reggie?" Duff asked. "We'd like to finish our drinks in peace."

"Oh, yes!" said Reggie. "Mary, will you tell Ellen, please?"

But the drink was spoilt now; there was none of that pleasant feeling of relaxation.

"There's a dividend here for you, Miss Castle."

"Oh, no, thanks! One is just right for me."

So he had to finish up what was in the shaker, and much too quickly.

"Well, is it all right to have dinner now, Jake?" Reggie asked.

"Certainly," he said.

He had no appetite at all. But that's all to the good, he thought, with this new diet. Reggie and Miss Castle went past him into the dining-room and he followed them.

"What do you think of them, Jake?" Reggie asked. "The new chairs?"

He thought they were terrible: a sort of bogus Windsor style, with cane seats and cane insets in the backs.

"Very nice," he said.

He drew back her chair for her; Miss Castle was already seated, and he went to his end of the table. The new chair was not only ugly but uncomfortable; the seat was too narrow, the arms constricting. He did not like the soup set before him.

"It's a meatless day," Reggie said, "but we've got some nice creamed sweetbreads—"

"Not for me, thanks," he said. "I'm on a diet. I told you so, this morning."

"Well, what can you eat?" she asked, anxiously. "Scrambled eggs, Jake? Or—"

The cane seat of the chair gave way. As he seized the arms and tried to rise, he fell over sideways, caught in the chair. Reggie came running to him.

"Oh, Jake!" she cried. "Oh, gosh! Are you hurt? Oh, Jake, I'm terribly sorry!"

Now he hated Reggie.

"No, thanks," he said. "I don't want anything more."

"But, Jake, you haven't eaten a thing—!"

"Nothing more, thank you. I've brought home some work to do. Good-night, Reggie. Good-night, Miss Castle."

He went off to that study, a ridiculous room, and locked the door. He took up Uncle Fred's book, but his hands shook so that he could not hold it. He had a bottle of whiskey in a drawer of the desk; he brought it out and poured himself a drink.

All right! All right! he told himself. I'm going to put the whole thing out of my mind. It's nothing.

Only, Miss Castle had seen him. Very well. She wouldn't think anything of it. A little—contretemps. Could happen to anyone. It's nothing. Simply, if you're a little overweight, you're—sensitive about a thing like that.

Damn those chairs! It takes Reggie to buy such flimsy, tawdry stuff. Damn. All right! Damn Reggie. Everything's finished between us, as far as I'm concerned. Even Aunt Lou could see that now, if she were here. I've got to get out.

There was a knock at the door.

"Yes?" he said.

"It's me, Jake."

"I'm very busy just now, Reggie."

"Just a minute, Jake! Please!"

He put away the bottle, and hid the glass under the desk, and unlocked the door.

"Jake, I'm so terribly sorry about what happened."

"It's nothing. Absolutely nothing, my dear girl."

30

"Jake, I'm so sorry. I guess those chairs just weren't any good."

"It's nothing. Let's not talk about it."

"Jake, could I sit in here with you for a while, and just read?"

"Thanks, but I have some rather important business papers."

"Could I type for you, Jake?"

"No, thanks. No typing to be done."

"Jake . . ." She laid her hand on his arm. "I just hate for us to get like this."

Then do something about it! he cried in his heart. Do something to stir me, to make me care again. Don't stand there—like a damn flower . . .

"Haven't you been feeling so well lately, Jake?"

"Never better," he said.

"I've been worried about you, Jake."

"And why?"

"Well, you hardly eat a thing, Jake." She paused. "I was talking to Aunt Lou today, Jake. About when you were a little boy. She said you always were terribly hard to—amuse. She said you always got bored so easily." She paused again. "I thought maybe you were sort of bored now, Jake," she said.

"Oh, certainly not!" he said, with bleak politeness.

"Because if you are, Jake, couldn't we do something about it?"

We? You could. You could be even a little exciting, a little seductive.

"Could we go out more, maybe? To shows, or night-clubs, or whatever you like?"

"Thanks, Reggie, that's a very nice idea. Later on, perhaps."

31

"Jake . . . We used to love each other . . ."

"Certainly. We do now. But at the moment, I'm pretty busy. If you'll excuse me—"

"Well, good-night, Jake," she said, and kissed him on the cheek.

One of her damn flower-kisses, he thought. I'm not going to go on like this. I can't stand it, and I won't.

Chapter Five

He waked in the morning, feeling strangely ill. When he got out of bed his legs were so weak he could scarcely stand. There was a grinding pain in the pit of his stomach.

This is no hangover, he said to himself. Anyhow, I didn't drink so much last night. No. This is something else. Something serious.

He was afraid to take a cold shower, feeling like this. He dressed as quickly as he could, but his hands trembled horribly. When he brushed his hair, one of the brushes somehow twisted in his hand and hit him a whack on the head. He had a very bad time with his necktie.

This is no hangover, he thought. I've had plenty of them in my day, and this isn't one. I'm going to take a drink, but it won't help me much. Not with this thing, whatever it is.

He had the good luck to get downstairs without meeting anyone. He remembered that the bottle in the study was empty, and he had to go to the cellarette in the dining-room. That was almost too much. Mary might come in, Reggie, Miss Castle, Jay, anyone, and see him taking a drink—before breakfast. The thought of it made him sweat with fear and dismay.

But I've got to! he cried to himself. I can't go on this

way. He opened the cellarette in the sideboard, he unscrewed the top of a bottle, and he had poured himself a generous drink before he noticed that it was gin instead of whiskey.

"Oh, damn!" he said, aloud.

But then an idea came to him. He put the bottle back and filled up the glass, already half-full of gin, with stale water from the carafe; he carried it into his study and closed the door. He scribbled some meaningless figures on the pad before him; he sipped his drink, and lit a cigarette. He knew Reggie would come knocking at the door, and she did.

"Come in!" he said, absently.

"Oh, Jake! You shouldn't smoke before breakfast, hon!"

"Just a minute . . ." he said, in the same absent tone, and wrote down some more figures. He lifted the glass and took another swallow. "I'll be with you in a moment, Reggie."

Anyone would take it for granted that what he had was a glass of water. You don't expect to see a man drinking gin at eight o'clock in the morning. Normally, he thought, I'd say it was a pretty bad sign, pretty serious. Only I'm so damn sick . . .

Only he wasn't. That strange weakness, the pain, the trembling, were all passing away. His brain became clear, and he remembered the plan he had made the night before. It was a good plan, and he intended to carry it out at once.

He went into the dining-room, and for the first time he noticed that it was raining outside; there was a grey, dull light in the room. Reggie was wearing a black dress with long sleeves; she looked, he thought, like a shop-girl.

"Jay . . . !" said Miss Castle, and Jay stood up.

34

"G'morning, Daddy!" he said, and sat down again, so hard that his chair slid back a little.

"Good-morning," said Duff. "Good-morning, Miss Castle."

"Good-morning, Mr. Duff."

He liked all this good-morning good-morning ritual; he liked the looks of Miss Castle, in her white blouse and grey skirt, with the healthy color in her cheeks. And Jay, he thought, was a rather remarkable child. Not exactly handsome, but even now, at this age, he looked like Somebody.

"You can eat plain boiled eggs, couldn't you, Jake?" asked Reggie.

"No, thanks," he said. "I'm a little off my feed. Need a change, probably. Tell you what, Reggie. If you haven't any engagements, suppose we go out to the shack for the week-end?"

"Oh, I'd love it!" she said.

"Good! You can drive out this afternoon, and I'll come straight from the office. We can eat dinner at the Yacht Club, to save you trouble."

"Oh, let's eat home! I'll get things on the way. I love to cook, Jake."

"Nolan can wait there until I come," he said. "I don't care to have you there alone. It's pretty deserted, this time of the year."

"All right, Jake," she said.

He drank a cup of coffee and ate a slice of toast.

"Kin I go now?" Jay asked.

"No," said Duff. "You're to stay at the table until other people have finished."

Jay leaned back in his chair and folded his arms.

"Unfold your arms," said Duff.

"Well, *why*? What's bad about *that*?"

35

"Do as you're told," said Duff.

Jay stretched out his arms straight from the shoulders, and looked at his father sidelong.

"Sit properly!" shouted Duff.

"Well, *how*? *I* don't know how you mean!"

"Then I'll teach you. You need a good thrashing."

"I do not!" said Jay, and began to cry.

"Come, Jay!" said Miss Castle, and taking his hand she led him out of the room.

"Honestly, Jake, he doesn't mean to be naughty," said Reggie. "It's only—"

"Would you very much mind not explaining my own son to me?" he said, pushing back his chair. "I know exactly what's wrong with Jay."

And it's you, he thought. He used to be a very well-behaved child; people spoke of it. But you encourage him to spend his time with the servants; you send him out to the garage. To Nolan.

I've got to get rid of Reggie, he thought.

He did not care for the thought in that crude form. I mean, he said to himself, that I want a separation. We're not suited to each other in any way, and it is ruinous for the child. *She* can't be so very happy, herself. Perhaps if I simply went to her and proposed a separation, she'd agree. But Aunt Lou would make such a hell of a row about it. Give Reggie a chance. The poor girl. All that. She *won't* see.

So I've got to go through all this unpleasantness, he thought. His plan of last night was indeed detestable to him. It's not the sort of thing a gentleman does, he thought. But what else can I do? I haven't been into her room for nearly two months—and that doesn't seem to bother her. I never bring anyone here. I never take her anywhere. If

she wasn't so damn stupid and common‚ she'd have seen . . . And, at that, maybe she does see. It's a nice life. Plenty of money, plenty of clothes. Mrs. Jacob Duff . . .

He hated the house and was glad to get out of it, but he hated the office too.

"I'm just stepping out for a cup of coffee," he told Miss Fuller at eleven o'clock.

He went to another bar this time, so that this little pick-me-up would not look habitual. And in this place he came across a fellow he knew, Sammy Poole.

"Hello!" Duff said, with an air of immense surprise. "What are *you* doing here, this time of the day?"

"Oh, I come every morning," said Sammy.

He did not seem to see anything out of the way in it. He seemed very healthy, too; he played golf, he went to a gym, and so on. Duff did not make the explanation he had been ready to make. If Sammy could take this for granted, so much the better. He had two drinks, just two; he was never going beyond that. Then he went back to the office.

I don't know, he thought. Maybe I'll cut lunch out entirely. You're bound to lose weight that way.

He dictated some letters, he saw two or three people, he talked to Hanbury.

"Mr. Duff," said Miss Fuller, "will it be all right if I go out to lunch now? It's after two."

"Oh, certainly, certainly!" he said. "Go right ahead. I didn't realize the time."

When she had gone, he had nothing to do, and he felt very sick again. He went out to the first bar, and it upset him. I can't go running in and out of bars all the time, he thought. It doesn't look well. I ought to keep something

37

in the office, in case I want it. Plenty of fellows do that. Only Miss Fuller's in and out, all the time.

He felt a little better when he got back. At four o'clock he called Vermilyea.

"Don't hesitate to turn this down, old man," he said. "But here's the setup. My wife's gone down to our place on the shore, and I want to join her. But the garage people can't fix me up with a car. Can't—or won't. It's a hell of a trip by train, with those two changes, so I thought that, if you had enough gas, maybe you'd drive me down and stay overnight."

"Very pleased to, Duff," said Vermilyea. "What time?"

"I can't get away very early," Duff said. "I'm up to my ears in work. About seven, say?"

"There's a train leaving Grand Central at six-twenty-two," said Vermilyea. "How would that do, Duff? I could meet you at the Vandenbrinck station."

"Fine! Fine!" said Duff. "I appreciate this, Vermilyea."

Then he called up the shack, and Reggie's voice answered.

"I'm sorry, Reggie," he said, "but something's just turned up. This man's coming from Washington, and I've got to wait. I'll take a room in a hotel for the night, and I'll be out early tomorrow morning."

"Oh, I'm sorry, Jake!"

"And tell Nolan to stay," he said. "I don't want you out there alone."

"All right, Jake," she said. "Take care of yourself, and I'll see you tomorrow."

He disliked his plan more and more. But if Reggie's behaving properly, there'll be no harm done, he thought. And if she isn't . . . then I needn't have any compunction.

He knew Reggie well enough to feel almost sure she

would be doing something that would look wrong. Something that would shock Vermilyea. For she had no dignity, no discretion.

Pictures came into his mind. Suppose they were to find Reggie and Nolan sitting side by side on the front steps, talking and laughing? Drinking soft drinks out of bottles? He imagined himself telling this to Mrs. Albany. You can realize how I felt, he would say, arriving there with a fellow like Vermilyea, and finding my wife and the chauffeur . . .

If they'd only be making love . . . ! he thought. No matter what I find, I shouldn't make use of it. I'd still let her get the divorce. I'll provide for her decently. It's simply that I want somebody to realize what she really is. Aunt Lou, above all.

Vermilyea was waiting for him on the Vandenbrinck station.

"You're looking a bit seedy, Duff," he said.

"I'm dog-tired," said Duff.

"Take a little snooze, on the way out," said Vermilyea. "Nice night, after the rain this morning."

Duff leaned back in the dark car and closed his eyes. There couldn't, he thought, be a better witness than Vermilyea, a man of honor, a gentleman, who would understand all the implications of what he was going to see. Mrs. Duff and the chauffeur, sitting on the steps, drinking pop out of bottles, his arm around her shoulder.

It was worse than that, though. There was a merry-go-round on the lawn outside the house, and Reggie sat on a coal-black horse, with Nolan behind her, holding her round the waist; they went round and round, laughing, to very loud music. Fortunately Aunt Lou was with him, and she could see for herself how it was.

"*The whole neighborhood's complaining*," he told her. "*But* she *doesn't care.*"

He opened his eyes and they were in the main street of the village, with a radio playing loudly somewhere.

"Oh, look here, Vermilyea!" he said. "Mind going back just a couple of blocks? I want to stop at the liquor store. There's nothing in the house."

The man in the store knew him well, from the days when he had used to come down here with Helen.

"You're starting early," he said. "There isn't anybody else has come down yet."

"I've been working pretty hard," said Duff, "and I thought I'd like a little sea air."

"Nothing like it," said the man.

"Might as well stock up. Two bottles of rye—and I might as well take a couple of bottles of gin. A lot of people seem to like gin drinks, Martinis, Tom Collinses, and so on. Personally, I don't like gin."

He wondered a little why he had said that and why he was talking so much. It's because I'm upset about this thing, he thought. He got back into the car with a big paper bag, and Vermilyea started off again. They turned in to the Shore Road, and there was the sea, pale under the starry sky. Some ten feet below the road and fronting the ocean was that solid and comfortable little bungalow which he and Helen had always called 'the shack'. It was the only lighted house to be seen.

"I hope Reggie got my wire," said Duff. "I couldn't get her on the telephone, so I sent her a wire to say we'd be along."

"Certainly hope so," said Vermilyea. "I shouldn't like to cause Mrs. Duff any inconvenience."

"Better leave the car up here," said Duff. "Nolan will

take it down to the garage. It's a rather tricky bit of road."

Vermilyea parked the car at the side of the road, and Duff led the way, down a flight of wooden stairs to the beach. His knees felt weak; he felt cold and wretched. Suppose we find something—outrageous? he thought. Suppose she's got Nolan in her room? Well, Vermilyea would never talk. Nobody else would know.

He mounted the three steps to the veranda and looked in at the sitting-room window. Nolan, in his shirtsleeves, was doing something to the radio, a cigarette in the corner of his mouth. Reggie sat in a wicker armchair, with Jay on her lap.

Chapter Six

"Oh, hello, Jake!" cried Reggie. "Hello, Mr. Vermilyea!"

"Hello!" Vermilyea answered, smiling broadly.

"Nolan, get Mr. Vermilyea's car into the garage," said Duff. "Jay, you ought to have been in bed hours ago. What's the child doing here, anyhow, Reggie?"

"Well, he wanted to come," she said.

Duff was struggling against a furious anger that was beyond his understanding. Anger against Nolan, who was leisurely putting on his jacket, against Reggie in her black dress, even against Jay.

"Go to bed at once, Jay," he said.

"Well, I'll have to change him in to the guest room, Jake," said Reggie. "I didn't know you were coming, and I was going to keep him in with me."

"Didn't you get my wire?"

"Why, no, I just—"

"Don't change your arrangements," said Duff. "I'll share a room with Vermilyea. Only get that child to bed."

He was very nearly shouting, and that wouldn't do. He must get himself in hand.

"Sit down, Vermilyea!" he said, with great heartiness.

42

"Sit down! Sit down! We'll have a drink. What's yours, **gin,** or rye?"

"Rye, thank you, Duff."

"Personally, I don't care for gin," said Duff.

No sense in saying that all the time. He went into the kitchen, and there were no ice cubes in the refrigerator; no soda. He opened a bottle of gin and poured himself a drink, and put the bottle back in the paper bag. Then he opened a bottle of rye and brought it, with two glasses, into the sitting-room.

"Sorry to say there's no ice, old man, no soda."

"That doesn't bother me," said Vermilyea.

"I'll get some water," said Duff, and returning to the kitchen, he drank the gin and rinsed out the glass.

"Cigarette, old man?"

"I'll use my own, Duff. They're worth their weight in gold, these days."

"Here! Here! Take one of mine!" said Duff. "I've got plenty, at the moment. My aunt, Mrs. Albany, gave me two cartons last week. Remarkable woman."

"So I've heard. Roger and Elly Pendleton know her."

"Remarkable woman," Duff said. "Sixty-five years old, and still—remarkable. Used to do a lot of big-game hunting with her husband, y'know, and I believe she could do it now. Y'know, when I was a kid, I used to like it better than anything when she'd come out to see me in school. She'd bring a souvenir—from Africa, India, wherever she'd been, and she'd have stories to tell that were better than any book you ever read. The other kids would all gather round . . . A thorough sportswoman. Thorough."

"Very interesting, Duff."

Duff told a story about Mrs. Albany and a rhinoceros.

"Well, by Jove . . . !" said Vermilyea.

"My uncle used to say he'd rather have her beside him in an emergency than any man he'd ever met."

"That's certainly a fine compliment," said Vermilyea.

"Yes. True, too. Another spot, old man?"

"Just a small one, Duff. You're not taking any?"

"Well, no," said Duff. "To tell you the truth, it's apt to make me wakeful if I take a drink around bedtime."

"It's just the other way with me," said Vermilyea, seriously. "It's a very rare thing for me not to go to sleep as soon as my head touches the pillow, but if it ever does happen that I can't sleep, a jigger of whiskey will always send me off."

"You're lucky," said Duff.

He was waiting for Reggie to come back. At least she'll have manners enough to say good-night to Vermilyea, he thought. But eleven o'clock came, and Vermilyea was politely covering a series of yawns.

"Shall we turn in now?" he suggested.

From his overnight case Vermilyea brought out pajamas, dressing-gown, slippers, a few toilet articles, a razor, everything of the best quality and absolutely right. God, what a relief to be away from Reggie, with her flimsy things strewn all around!

Vermilyea was breathing calmly in his bed in the dark room, asleep already. And what had he thought of that scene, that nice, cozy, domestic scene? Mrs. Jacob Duff, and the chauffeur in his shirtsleeves and a cigarette in his mouth.

Why did she bring the child here? he thought, his anger rising and rising. She's ruining him. Encouraging him to hang around with the servants all the time. God knows what he's picking up.

After a while he rose and went barefoot into the kitchen.

44

He poured himself a drink of gin, a good one, too. I've got to get some sleep, he thought.

He went back to bed, and now he was able to sleep, in the cool breezy dark.

When he waked in the morning, Vermilyea's bed was empty. He heard voices near, he heard Jay laughing, and Reggie. She's turning the child against me, he thought. When Helen was alive, he'd run to meet me, as soon as I came into the house. Only four years since Helen died? I can't realize it . . . Aunt Lou could have stopped this—disastrous second marriage. Only time I've ever known her to use poor judgment.

He felt sick, very sick, but he had expected to be. I was a damn fool not to bring a bottle in here last night, he thought. Now if there's anyone in the kitchen, I can't get a drink.

Yes, I can, he thought. He got out of bed and put on his dressing-gown and slippers. He went straight to the kitchen. In the dining-room Reggie and Vermilyea and Jay were all sitting at the table.

"Good-morning, everybody!" said Duff.

"Jay!" said Reggie, in nervous imitation of Miss Castle, and Jay stood up.

"Mrs. Duff's giving us a wonderful breakfast," Vermilyea said. "Wonderful! I only wish I had more time. But for a wonder I've got to show up at the office fairly early."

The big paper bag was on the sink-board. Duff picked it up and carried it into the bedroom; he did not explain, he did not have to explain. He had a drink of gin poured out and standing on the dresser when Vermilyea came in to get his bag.

"I've enjoyed this very much, Duff," he said. "You're a lucky man."

45

"Oh, very!" said Duff.

No sooner had Vermilyea gone than Reggie came knocking at the door.

"Come in!" said Duff, with a sigh.

"I just wanted to know if you'd like some little sausages, Jake," she said.

"No, thanks, I shouldn't."

"Jake," she said, "now that we're down here—now that we've got more time together—couldn't we have a good long talk?"

"About what?" he demanded.

"About—whatever it is that's gone wrong between us." She had never taken the initiative before, never had questioned him. He was not prepared for it; he did not know how he wanted to answer her.

"I'm afraid we haven't much time," he said. "I've got to go in to the office this morning."

"Oh, I thought we were going to stay here over Sunday. I told Jay so. He'll be disappointed, poor little fellow."

"I'm sorry," said Duff, briefly.

Why didn't she go away? She was obviously nervous, one hand picking at her dress, a warm color in her cheeks; she did not look at him. She's guilty! he thought.

"Jake . . ." she said. "Jake, honey, what's *happened*?"

"What d'you mean? What are you talking about?"

"Things seem to have gone—all wrong between us," she said, and there were tears on her cheeks. "I guess all married people have their ups and downs—but I thought that if we could just clear things up—if we could have a good long talk, Jake . . ."

"My dear girl," he said, "this is hardly the time. I haven't had so much as a cup of coffee, and—" He paused. "I'm not feeling any too well," he said.

"I knew that!" she said. "For quite a while I've thought you seemed queer."

"Tactfully put," he remarked.

"I didn't mean to be tactless. It's only that—"

"D'you mind if we postpone this?" he asked. "I'd like to finish dressing and get some coffee."

She went away then and he finished his dressing and his drink in haste. But instead of going to the dining-room, he went out of the house, to the garage. The door was open, and Nolan stood there, smoking.

"Morning, sir!" he said, alertly.

"Good-morning," said Duff. "We'll be leaving in an hour. And after you've driven us home, I'll pay you whatever is due you, and you can go."

"And why is that?" asked Nolan, with interest.

"I don't care for your manners," said Duff. "I don't care to find my chauffeur in my drawing-room, in his shirt-sleeves, smoking a cigarette."

Nolan drew on his cigarette.

"I know a frame-up when I see one," he said.

Everything in Duff drew together against this blow.

"What are you talking about?" he asked.

"I've been around," said Nolan. "You tried to frame me and your wife."

"Keep quiet!"

"For the time being, I will," said Nolan.

Chapter Seven

Nolan's going to blackmail me, thought Duff. Or try to, anyhow. But he can't prove anything. Can't prove I didn't send a wire to Reggie—or anything else. Only I don't want him putting any ideas into Reggie's head.

That thought made him sweat with dismay. If Reggie should turn on him, accuse him of this contemptible thing . . . I couldn't stand that, he thought. It was a mistake, anyhow. I'm sorry I ever tried it. It's not like me.

And if Vermilyea ever knew . . . ? All right, Duff thought. I'm sorry. It was a bad idea, the sort of thing a gentleman doesn't do, or even think of. But I don't see how Vermilyea ever could find out. Who'd tell him? He wouldn't believe it, anyhow.

But Reggie might believe it, if Nolan told her. She and Nolan, no doubt, spoke the same language. Very likely they both knew of instances like that, a suspicious husband coming home, when he had definitely said he would not be home. It was such a damn vulgar thing for me to do, he thought.

"Is the coffee all right, Jake?" she asked.

"Very good. Very good indeed."

That pleased her.

"I'm terribly glad you like it, Jake," she said. "I honestly

48

think I could get to be quite a good cook. I know I'd love it. Only, living around in furnished rooms the way I did before we were married, I never got a chance."

"No, of course not. Can you be ready in half an hour, Reggie?"

"I'll just wash up the dishes, Jake—"

"Don't bother. Mrs. Anderson comes in once a week to air the place. She'll attend to them."

"Honestly, I'd rather, Jake," she said. "I'd hate to go and leave dirty dishes. It'll only take a moment."

"Well, if you'd rather—" he said, and his indulgent tone brought out her wide, dazzling smile.

I'm going to behave differently, he thought. Not going to be irritable. And if Nolan does try to put any ideas into her head, she won't believe them. Anyhow, it wasn't a frame-up. I simply wanted to see if that fellow was too familiar and free-and-easy when I wasn't around. Very well. I did see.

He went into the bedroom to pack, and as he took the three bottles out of the paper bag, he frowned to see how much gin had gone since last night. Of course, the stuff evaporates, he thought, but even at that, it's too much. I'm cutting down.

Reggie was still in the kitchen and Jay was with her, drying the dishes.

"Soldiers dry dishes!" Jay said. "Reggie's a train nurse, and I'm a soldier."

Duff very much disliked the child's calling her 'Reggie', but he had never been able to think of a reasonable substitute. He didn't like to see Jay drying dishes, either; the whole atmosphere was displeasing. When he and Helen had used to come here, they had always brought a maid along; everything had been informal, but not like this.

49

"I've nearly finished, Jake," she said. "I just want to leave things nice and neat."

"I see! I've been thinking, Reggie . . . I'll be finished early at the office. Suppose you come in to town by train with me, and Nolan can drive Jay home. You could do a bit of shopping, and then we could meet somewhere for lunch?"

"Oh, I'd love it!" said Reggie.

"I want to go to New York, too," said Jay.

"Not today," said Duff.

"But I'll bring you a surprise," Reggie told the child, and he seemed satisfied.

Nolan drove them to the station and they got on the train.

"I want to speak to you about Nolan, Reggie," said Duff. "You don't realize how insolent the fellow is."

"Honestly, he's never said anything—"

"I was shocked," said Duff, "when I saw him there in the sitting-room."

"But he was just fixing the radio. I asked him to, Jake."

"I don't suppose you asked him to take off his coat and light a cigarette, did you?"

"Well, no. But I don't think he meant to be fresh."

"He's a good deal more than what you call 'fresh', my dear girl. I'm going to let him go."

He watched her covertly, to see how she took that, but he could see no emotion in her thin, gentle face.

"Well," she said, "I guess he can find another job, easily enough."

"That doesn't interest me," said Duff. "He'll certainly get no reference from me."

"But, Jake, that seems kind of hard on him."

"My dear girl," said Duff, "he's a dangerous man."

"Dangerous, Jake?"

"Yes," said Duff. "I don't want to go into details, but he made an attempt to blackmail me."

"Oh, Jake, how could he? What about?"

"Let's not talk about it, Reggie. Fortunately, I knew how to deal with him."

"But, Jake, what could he possibly try to blackmail *you* about?"

Duff was silent for a moment.

"I'm not going to tell you, my dear girl," he said, presently.

"Jake! Was it something—about me?"

"I'm not going to talk about it any more," he said, and patted her hand. "It's finished."

"Jake, if I did do something that looked wrong some way, I'm *terribly* sorry."

"Don't worry, Reggie," he said, with his hand over hers.

All right! he thought. Now let Nolan go to her with his tale about a frame-up—and see where it gets him.

He saw Reggie into a taxi at the Grand Central, and went off, in another cab, to his office. Eleven o'clock came, and he was pleased that he had not the slightest desire for a drink. I certainly shouldn't want to make a habit of that, he thought.

He was to meet Reggie at one, in a midtown hotel; he got there a little early and stopped in the bar for a double Martini. A cocktail doesn't hurt you, he thought, as long as you eat directly after it. Although, if I'd been having lunch alone, I shouldn't have wanted a drink. Only, it's so damn hard to *talk* to Reggie. She has nothing to say for herself. She's never been anywhere, never seen anything.

When he entered the restaurant, Reggie was waiting for him, and he felt a slight shock at the sight of her beauty

51

and her air of distinction. She was wearing a new costume, a grey suit that brought out the long fine lines of her body, a blue blouse, a blue turban with a white band that encircled her broad and candid brow like a coif; grey gloves, a blue pocketbook. Dressed so, with her head set so well on her slender neck, her straight back, her way of sitting so quietly and easily, she looked aristocratic.

This irritated him, and so did her smile when she caught sight of him.

"Hello, Jake!" she said. "How do you like my outfit?"

"Extremely nice."

"I telephoned to Aunt Lou and she came with me."

"Well, you did a very fine job together," he said.

The headwaiter led them to a table with which Duff could find no fault. He took up the menu and studied it.

"You order for me, Jake," she said. "You know what's nice."

"There's nothing nice here," he said.

"Why don't you have a cocktail, Jake, to give you an appetite?"

"It's not a good idea, to drink in the middle of the day."

"Well, but just for once—?"

"All right!" he said, with a good-humored laugh. "A dry Martini, waiter. Or you'd better make it a double. That saves time," he explained to Reggie. "As long as you're not drinking, you naturally don't want to sit here and watch me."

"I don't mind, Jake. Jake, Aunt Lou was asking me how things were."

"What things?"

"I mean, if we were—sort of settling down better. And I told her *yes.*"

"Oh, did you?"

"Yes. You were sweet to me, Jake, about whatever it was Nolan tried—"

"You didn't tell Aunt Lou about that, did you?"

"Oh, no! I just said I thought things were going better, and she was terribly pleased."

"I see!" he said, absently.

I did the right thing, he thought. It's better, in every way, to have things pleasant and friendly between us. If Nolan goes to her now with his fantastic tale, she wouldn't believe a word of it. Only, I'm not going in for any love-making.

"Reggie," he said, "if I haven't seemed very lover-like recently, it's because I haven't been well."

A burning color rose in her cheeks.

"Oh, well, but, Jake . . ." she said. "Marriage isn't just—that. I mean—that . . ."

Good God! he thought. It's revolting. She's like a sixteen-year-old girl in a convent. It's impossible to talk to her about anything.

"We'd better order now," he said. "I told Nolan we'd get the two-fifty."

He had a little nap on the train, and when he waked he felt greatly refreshed. Nolan was waiting on the platform, handsome and alert, as they drove to the house, Duff kept his eyes upon the fellow's strong young neck, kept his thoughts upon the fellow's insolence.

"I'd like a word with you, Nolan," he said, when the car stopped.

"Very well, sir," said Nolan, and followed him into the study.

"Close the door," said Duff. "Now, then. I'll pay you whatever's coming to you, and you can clear out."

"Very well, sir," said Nolan.

"And don't use me for a reference."

"That suits me," said Nolan.

His bright composure nettled Duff. Somehow this interview was not going as it should.

"What's more," he said, "if I hear of your repeating that slanderous lie to anyone, I'll take steps."

"What steps?" asked Nolan.

"I've warned Mrs. Duff, so that if you make any attempt to repeat that lie to her—"

"If I was going to tell anyone about that frame-up," said Nolan, "it wouldn't be Mrs. Duff."

I must not ask him who it would be, Duff told himself. As if I were anxious.

But he had to know.

"Is that so?" he said, with a scornful smile. "The tabloids, I suppose."

"No. Mrs. Albany," said Nolan.

That was like a blow in the midriff. Now he had to fight.

"D'you imagine you could collect money from Mrs. Albany on the strength of a preposterous lie like that?"

"We weren't talking about collecting money. The point is," said Nolan, "if I wanted to find someone who'd believe that story, I'd choose Mrs. Albany. Once she heard the facts, she'd see just how it was."

"You're trying to blackmail me, eh? Threatening to tell Mrs. Albany—?"

"I haven't made any threats," said Nolan, "and I haven't asked for any money."

"But you intend to later. That's obvious."

"To tell you the truth," said Nolan, "I'd never thought about blackmail until you brought it up. I thought the whole thing was rather funny."

"Funny?"

"Comic. So damn crude, telling me to stay there till you came, and them calling up to say you weren't coming. And then coming, late at night, with your witness. And finding the kid there. I thought it was funny. I still do."

"You're insolent!" cried Duff.

"Could be," said Nolan, easily.

Duff could think of no way to cope with this behavior. There were no demands made, no menaces to parry, nothing here to fight.

"I'll write your check," he said. "But remember, if I hear anything more of that lie of yours—"

Nolan said nothing. He didn't smile; there was nothing to be read in his alert face. He took the check Duff held out to him.

"Thanks," he said, and turned away.

And where was he going? What did he intend to do?

If he does go to Aunt Lou with that tale, Duff told himself, she'll make short work of him. I don't see *her* listening to servants' gossip.

No . . . he said to himself, with a dreadful sinking of the heart. *She'd believe it.*

He was sure of that. She was completely loyal to him, she was fond of him, but, better than anyone else, she knew his weaknesses, his potentialities. If she heard this story, plainly told, all the facts provable, she would believe it, and she would forever despise him.

He could imagine no greater misfortune than to lose her approval. She was his conscience. Whatever she said was right was right; what she condemned was wrong. Since his childhood, her opinion had been the important one. His parents had left little impression upon him. He had respected them, he had been grief-stricken at their funerals, but he had almost completely forgotten them. It was his

Aunt Lou who had completely captured his imagination, that spare, energetic woman, back from jungles and veldts. The presents she gave for birthdays or Christmas had an almost mystic value. Above everything else on earth he was proudest of being her heir.

He knew nothing about poverty, in any degree; he had always had enough money, and he had now. He was not extravagant, nor ambitious. But the money Mrs. Albany was going to leave him represented The Future for him. It was the fortune he was going to leave his son; it was the thing that was going to make him a man of importance. Mrs. Albany's lawyer had pointed that out to him on his twenty-first birthday. You'll want to understand something about the science of investment, he had said. You are going to have considerable responsibility one of these days.

If Nolan goes to her . . . he thought. It's the sort of thing she'd never forgive. Never. To set a trap for my wife; to bring Vermilyea along . . .

But is Nolan going to her? I don't *know*. I can't make the fellow out at all. He's got something up his sleeve, that's certain. But what? I didn't handle him properly.

He went up to his bedroom and, locking the door, got the bottle of rye out of the bag. I shouldn't have fired him, he thought. That was a great mistake. No . . . I should have taken the whole thing lightly, laughed at him. I should have made him see that I had perfect confidence in Reggie.

His brain began to work well now; now he could see what he ought to have said, the turn he ought to have taken. I acted like a fool, he thought. Gave myself away completely. I can't let that fellow loose in the world with *that* idea in his head. No . . . I'll tell him I've thought things over, and I've decided to let him stay.

56

Then I'll go to Aunt Lou myself, and tell her about Nolan's idea. Tell her I thought it best to keep him on. Tell her I talked it over with Reggie.

He locked up the bottle and went downstairs. He rang for the housemaid.

"Tell Nolan I'd like to see him after dinner, please," he said. "Half-past eight."

Then he went into the sitting-room, where Miss Castle was drinking tea. She made a charming picture, with the late afternoon sun shining upon her smooth hair.

"May I join you?" he asked.

"Oh, do!" she said. "I'll ring for another cup. It's nice to see you home so early. Mrs. Duff's quite worried about your overworking. She's so anxious for you to see a doctor."

"I have seen one," said Duff, pleased by her interest. "I'm a little run down, that's all."

"You've no appetite," said Miss Castle.

"No, I haven't," he admitted. "But I've got a tonic for that."

How much he liked this! Her pleasant well-bred voice, the little ritual of pouring tea, the calm assurance of her manner were balm to him.

The room was growing shadowy; the air that came in at the open window was cooler.

"The nicest hour of the day, don't you think?" said Miss Castle.

"I do" said Duff. "Are you going, Miss Castle?"

"It's time for Jay's supper," she said, "and I've promised to read to him. That quiets him before bedtime."

She made everything so peaceable and decent. He lit a cigarette and leaned back in his chair, thinking wearily of all the trouble before him, the talk with Nolan, with Mrs.

Albany. All this damn fuss and bother—and all on account of Reggie.

"Hello, Jake!" she said. "Don't you want a light on? It's so dark."

"Not for me, thanks."

"I've been addressing envelopes for old Mrs. Vermilyea—"

"Very nice," he said.

"It's that appeal I told you about. For the fresh-air children."

"Oh, yes. That's very nice."

Everything she said bored him and irritated him. We have absolutely nothing in common, he thought.

"Old Mrs. Vermilyea is just darling, don't you think, Jake?"

Old Mrs. Vermilyea was Mrs. Charles Vermilyea, and that was enough.

"Yes," he said, raising. "I'll go up and get ready for dinner now."

He was resolved to be very courteous and kind to Reggie, always, but he could not stand much of her company. At dinner he made an effort, a great effort, to talk to her, and with Miss Castle's help it went well enough. But after dinner he wanted time to prepare for his talk with Nolan. When they went into the sitting-room for coffee, he excused himself.

"Doctor advises me to cut it out for a while," he explained, and went upstairs.

Ridiculous to go upstairs every time I want a drink, he thought. It looks queer, too. I ought to keep something in the study. But the problem was, how to get it there unnoticed. He could not walk along carrying a bottle. He sighed, exasperated by these incessant petty annoyances.

He took a small drink of gin; then he put the bottle into a little suitcase, and the bottle of rye into a dresser drawer.

It was necessary, of course, to explain the suitcase, and he stopped in the doorway of the sitting-room.

"I'm moving some papers," he said. "I thought I'd do it all in one trip."

"That's a good idea," said Reggie. "Would you like to play gin rummy, Jake?"

"If I finish in time," he said. "But there's quite a bit of work to plow through."

He went off with the suitcase to his study; only ten minutes. Nolan, he would say, I've been thinking this thing over, and it's a tempest in a teacup. You're a good chauffeur; we've been perfectly satisfied with you. I've talked it over with Mrs. Duff, and she agrees . . . Or maybe I'd better leave her out.

Nolan was taking his time; it was well after half-past eight. At quarter to nine, he rang for the housemaid.

"You gave Nolan my message, Mary?"

"Yes, sir, I did."

"You told him half-past eight?"

"Yes, sir."

"Thank you," he said, after a moment, dismissing the idea of sending her after Nolan.

But at nine o'clock a sudden fury rose in him, and he rang again.

"Just run out to the garage, will you," he said, "and tell Nolan I want to see him *at once*."

He put a little gin and water into a tumbler, and sat waiting. Damn that fellow! He's doing this on purpose. But I've got to keep my temper. I've got to handle him. It's important.

"Nolan's gone, sir," said Mary with an air of surprise.

59

"Gone? Gone where?"

"I don't know, sir. I called and called, and then I went up in his apartment and all his clothes were gone and he wasn't there."

"Thanks," said Duff.

He was in a panic. I'll call up Aunt Lou, he thought. I'll warn her that this fellow's coming to see her with some cock-and-bull story. No, I can't. Because maybe he isn't. I don't *know* . . . I can't see my way . . . I can't stop him, if he wants to tell her. And she'll believe him. I couldn't fool *her*.

I don't give a *damn* how much I drink now, he thought. I'm sick of the whole thing.

Chapter Eight

This time I've gone too far, he thought. Oh, my God! This must be it. I've got DT's. Oh, God . . .

He was trembling all over, his hands, his legs, his mouth. A deadly nausea swept over him in waves. This is it . . . I don't dare to take a drink now. Not in this state. I might start yelling . . .

What am I going to do? How am I going to face anyone? He remembered that last night he had stumbled on the stairs and Reggie had run out. She had tried to take his arm, to help him. Maybe I was rude to her, he thought. I don't remember. I need a doctor. But I can't let anyone see me. I wish I could die. Now. Let me die.

He was losing all control of himself, he was going to pieces. Aspirin . . . he thought, and staggered into the bathroom. But the aspirin made him sick. He went back to the bedroom and took the bottle of rye out of the drawer; he took a drink out of the bottle and it strangled him. Oh, God, he groaned, and poured a drink into a glass, with his shaking hand. He added some water and sat down to drink it. It's too late. I've gone too far. This won't help me now.

No, he thought. A lot of this is psychological. I feel guilty because Reggie saw me last night when I was pretty tight.

All right, I'll admit I'm ashamed of that. It's the sort of thing a gentleman doesn't do. Sit drinking all alone at home. I'll admit I'm ashamed of it, and it won't happen again, and that's the end of it. I've got a whale of a hangover this morning, but it's not as serious as all that.

His hands were fairly steady now, his lips no longer trembled. He took a cold shower and dressed, and by that time he felt fairly good. He went to knock at Reggie's door.

"Who is it?" she asked.

"Me."

"Oh, come in," she answered.

She was barefoot, in a pale-blue satin slip, her dark hair loose about her shoulders; she looked beautiful and delicate as an angel.

"Reggie," he said, "I'm very sorry about last night."

"Oh, that's all right," she said, "I just was worried about your health."

"That's nothing, compared with the question of morale. I want to tell you I'm sorry, Reggie, and it won't happen again."

"Jake," she said, "please don't mind about me knowing. I know how little you drink. And if it's just once, when you were extra tired, or worried, if you took a little too much— I mean—" She sought for a word. "Please don't feel sheepish or anything."

'Sheepish,' he said to himself. What a word to use! Typical of her.

He patted her bare shoulder.

"You're very kind and patient, Reggie," he said.

"I'll be right down to breakfast," she called, as he went out of the room.

He nearly ran down the stairs, with a desperate hope

that he might be finished and out of the house before she came. Miss Castle and Jay were at the table. Jay rose.

"Good-morning, Daddy."

"Good-morning. Good-morning, Miss Castle."

The ritual did not please him this morning. I want to think, he said to himself. I've got to think. I've got to find out where that fellow Nolan's gone. I can't go on like this. Suppose he's already seen Aunt Lou? Well, if he has, I'll hear from her, all right. But why should he do that? He'd have nothing to gain by it. Unless it's sheer malice. Class hatred.

Reggie came into the room, and he had to pay some attention to her. He had to talk, at least a little, when he wanted time to think.

The taxi Mary had ordered came, and at last Duff could get away. I'm going to act, he thought. I don't intend to wait in this misery, to see what that fellow feels like doing.

When he reached Grand Central, he telephoned to Mrs. Albany.

"I'm going to be uptown today," he said. "How about your having lunch with me?"

"I'd like to, Jacob, but I'm taking a Citizenship Class to the Museum. If you're free at five or so, come in for a cup of tea."

"I'll certainly try, Aunt Lou," he said.

He was sure she had heard nothing from Nolan, for not only was she incapable of any pretense, but she was incapable of wanting to pretend anything. Yet this gave him little relief. At any moment Nolan might approach her.

He called up his office and said he would be delayed. He went into the bar of a big hotel and ordered a double rye, while he looked through his newspaper for something he

63

vaguely remembered. Information. Private inquiries. Dependable Agency.

The address was on Forty-Second Street. When he had finished his drink, he set out resolutely. I am going to find out what that fellow's up to, he told himself. Very fishy, the whole thing. First he makes this preposterous accusation, practically threatening blackmail, and then he simply disappears.

Walking along the busy street, in the clear spring sun, he was assailed by a sudden and dreadful loneliness. He had no confidant in this wretched affair, no friend to stand beside him. He was going, alone, on this fantastic errand, to a private detective agency. Jacob Duff.

They'll be pretty tough, I suppose, he thought. They might even be blackmailers themselves. I'm taking a big chance, to go to these people I don't know anything about. I should have asked someone to recommend a good firm. Ask who? No. I've got to take the chance, that's all.

But suppose they find out too *much*? He began to sweat, his lips began to tremble; he stopped and looked in a shop window. Suppose they find Nolan and he tells *them*? No . . . Better drop this, here and now.

But in a moment he rebelled against this. Good God! he told himself. I haven't committed any crime. There's nothing anyone *could* blackmail me for, if they wanted. It's simply that I want to know where that fellow Nolan is. I may want to see him, give him a final warning, or I may not. Simply, it makes me uneasy not to know where he is.

On the directory board in the small old-fashioned building he found The Dependable Agency, fourth floor, and he got into the elevator. There was a mirror there, and his own image reassured him, his ruddy face, his impeccable grey felt hat, his well-cut light overcoat, his excellent tie.

He looked prosperous, dignified and confident, and so he was, so he was. He was Jacob Duff, wishing to make inquiries about a discharged servant. Why? Nobody's business why.

The anteroom was perfectly ordinary; a nice-looking girl sat at a desk.

"I'd like to see the—manager," said Duff.

"Yes, sir," said the girl, and spoke into the telephone fitted with a device which made her words unintelligible and turned her voice into a peculiar quacking. Quack, quack, quack, she said, and waited. Quack, quack, she said, and hung up the instrument.

"Mr. Fearns will see you, sir," she said. "This way, please."

He followed her down a short corridor, and he was pleased that she had not asked his name. Very discreet, that was. She opened a door and he entered an office a little shabby but in no way sinister. The man sitting at the desk rose, a stocky, square-shouldered man, with a pale face, pale eyes, and yellow hair parted on the side.

"What can we do for you, sir?" he asked.

"I'd like somebody found—traced," said Duff. "A chauffeur I discharged."

"Sit down, sir," said Fearns. "Now, if you'll give me the details . . . Your name?"

"Duff. Jacob Duff. This fellow was very insolent, threatening, in fact. I discharged him, but I told him I wanted to see him before he left. He didn't come, though; he simply disappeared."

"Take anything?"

"His own clothes. Nothing else, as far as I know now."

"Collect his pay?"

"Yes. Yes, he did that."

"Cash?"

"No. I gave him a check."

"D'you want him followed, Mr. Duff, or just located?"

This gave Duff a new idea.

"I'd like to know exactly what he's done since he left my place, if it's possible."

"Yes. After he's located, d'you want him followed?"

"Yes," said Duff, after a moment.

"I'll tell you our rates," said Fearns, and they seemed to Duff very high.

Fearns then started questions about Nolan: age, height, weight, color of eyes and hair; any special gestures, way of walking? Duff's answers were not good and he knew it. He could not describe Nolan, yet in his mind he could see him with unpleasant clarity.

"Okay," said Fearns. "Want us to notify you by phone, or not?"

"You mean instead of by mail?"

"By mail, yes, or we can send a man along, soon as we get anything."

"That would be better," said Duff. "At my office."

The whole thing had been very much easier than he had expected. He had not had to give any reason for wanting Nolan found; it had all been entirely business-like and matter-of-fact. And this idea of having the fellow followed, he thought, that's excellent. Now I'll know.

He went out to lunch at a quarter to twelve. And I'm going to have a drink, he thought. I want it, and there's no reason on earth why I shouldn't have it. He had a double Martini and then a single, and then he tried to eat. But he had no appetite and he felt tired and depressed. If I could take a nap, he thought, even fifteen minutes . . .

He lit a cigarette and leaned back, looking away from

the untouched food before him. It's a damn queer thing, he thought, the sort of civilization we've built up. Absolutely no place where you could take a nap for fifteen or twenty minutes. That's all I need. I had a very poor night. I don't know what time I got to bed.

His drowsiness had become a misery. But he couldn't close his eyes here, in the restaurant; he had to go back to the office. And why the hell shouldn't I go to sleep there, if I want? he asked himself, angrily. I've got to do it, that's all. I can't keep my eyes open.

He went into his own office and spoke quietly to Miss Fuller.

"I don't know what's wrong with me," he said. "I can't keep my eyes open."

"Spring fever," she said. "I get that way myself."

"I suppose that's it," said Duff, pleased with the girl. "If you'll just see that I get fifteen or twenty minutes without being disturbed—?"

"I will, Mr. Duff!" she said, heartily.

He put his feet up on the desk and made himself as comfortable as he could. He closed his heavy eyes.

"Mr. Duff! Mr. Duff!"

"Oh, what *is* it?" he cried. "I told you I didn't want to be disturbed for fifteen minutes."

"But it's over half an hour, Mr. Duff, and there's a man here to see you. He says it's personal. Here's his card."

The card was in a sealed envelope. Mr. Martin McGinnis. The Dependable Agency.

"Oh . . . Show him in, please," said Duff, with that feeling, now growing familiar, of dread and confusion.

McGinnis was a lean and wiry young man with thick black brows and black hair that grew low on his forehead.

"Well, sir," he said. "I've located your man for you."

"Pretty quick work," said Duff.

"Yes. I didn't waste no time," said McGinnis. "I located this here Nolan for you."

"Where is he?"

"Why, he's just about next door to you, out in Vandenbrinck."

"What do you mean? I know the neighbors—"

"You know that road that runs back of your place? Well, there's a little house there, and that's where he is. You could even see the house from your windows."

"What's he doing?" Duff asked.

"Drinking is one thing he's doing," said McGinnis. "He's sent out three times already to the liquor store. He hasn't left the house since he got there."

Duff was silent for a moment.

"I'm going away for a day or two," he said. "Doctor's orders. Here's the telephone number where you can reach me. Keep an eye on Nolan and let me know when he makes any move."

Chapter Nine

"It's out of the question, Jacob," said Mrs. Albany. "I'd like very much to pay you and Reggie a little visit, but there are any number of things . . ."

She leaned across the tea-table and put her hand on his arm.

"But it's a nice idea, Jacob," she said. "I'm glad you're going down to the shore alone with Reggie. I hope it means you're going to lead a proper married life again."

Her light-grey eyes, clear as water, were fixed upon his face, and he flushed with irritation.

"Oh, yes . . ." he said. "But the thing is, I'm not feeling any too well."

"You drink too much," said Mrs. Albany.

"You're mistaken," he said, curtly.

"No, I'm not," said Mrs. Albany. "There was liquor on your breath when you came in this afternoon, Jacob, and you're overweight and puffy."

"I'm not *well!*"

"You're the type that could very well take to drinking," Mrs. Albany went on. "Like your Uncle Eugene. You're like him, in a good many ways. So easily bored."

"That's hardly a crime," said Duff.

"Yes, it is," said Mrs. Albany. "The Church used to call

69

it so, in the middle ages. Nobody has any right to be bored, and if you don't watch out, Jacob, if you don't take more exercise, if you don't lead a fuller, more active life, you'll take to drinking alone at home. And that's the beginning of the end."

"Very well!" he said, rising. "If that's your opinion of me—"

She rose too. "There!" she said. "I was only warning you, Jacob. You're much more sensible than your Uncle Eugene. He never married, you know. If he'd had a sweet, pretty young wife, as you have, I dare say he'd never have got into such a state. I'll tell you what I'll do, Jacob. I'll come out to the shack tomorrow as early as I can and stop for lunch."

"It's a tiresome trip, just for a few hours' visit."

"Nothing is tiresome to me," said Mrs. Albany. "That's what I'll do, Jacob. I'll take a train around nine, and I'll get a taxi from the station."

"It's very good of you, Aunt Lou," he said.

But it was not what he had wanted. He had wanted both his aunt and his wife down there in the shack for a few days, where Nolan could not reach them. Just until I get this settled, he thought.

For the thought of Nolan, in some little house just outside his gates, Nolan drinking, was unbearable. As soon as McGinnis had gone, he had called up Reggie.

"Look here, Reggie!" he had said. "I've been able to fix things up in the office so that I can take a few days off. Suppose we go down to the shack tonight?"

"Oh, tonight, Jake?"

"Why not?"

"Well, I mean, we only just got back, didn't we? Jake, we haven't got enough gas to drive—"

70

"I know that. We'll go by train. If you'll be good enough to pack a bag for me and bring it along, I'll meet you in Grand Central. We can have an early dinner and then go along. And don't bring Jay, please."

He had thought that he could persuade Mrs. Albany to come with them, and he was bleakly disappointed by his failure. Nothing to stop Nolan from getting at Mrs. Albany now. And if the fellow's drinking, Duff thought, he'll be absolutely reckless. God knows what he'll do.

He had almost forgotten what it was that Nolan might do; his dread of the man was formless, but far more acute now. I've got to think things out, he told himself. Got to find some way to dispose of that fellow, once and for all. I can't go on like this.

He could scarcely stand the sight of Reggie, looking so happy.

"This is fun, Jake!" she said, when he met her.

Fun, was it?

"Jake, what's that funny little bag?"

"I bought it this afternoon. I'm taking some papers with me."

"Oh, I hoped you wouldn't work, Jake! I thought we might make it sort of like a picnic. I'll cook nice little meals for us, and we can sit out on the beach, and take walks, and all."

I couldn't dream up anything worse, thought Duff. I don't know how I'm going to stand being shut up down there with her, anyhow.

"Aunt Lou's coming out for lunch tomorrow," he said.

"Oh, *that's* nice!" said Reggie. "She's the grandest person, isn't she?"

He didn't have to answer her idiot remarks; she didn't even notice. He took her to a restaurant, and she liked it;

71

she liked her dinner, she liked every damn thing. Absolutely no critical sense whatever, he thought.

"Sort of like another honeymoon, isn't it, Jake?" she said, when they were on the train. "I mean, just you and me—"

"Unfortunately, no," he said. "I'm taking this time off from the office because I'm not well. It's not a pleasure trip, for me. I'm doing this because I can't afford to break down."

"I'm terribly sorry, Jake, dear," she said.

He regretted this trip bitterly. Without Mrs. Albany it was pointless. Nolan could still strike. All he had done was to make for himself a nightmare of boredom. Nightmare was the right word. The train was curiously dreamlike, dimly-lit, filled with a strange dank smell; the other passengers looked pale and hopeless. He closed his eyes, so that Reggie should not talk to him, but it seemed to him that he felt a radiation of life and energy from her; she sat quietly enough, but she was too alive.

The little station was deserted; one taxi stood there, and he thought it was lopsided, like a crazy painting.

"Oh, you can smell the sea, can't you?" said Reggie.

"Yes," he said, with a sigh.

The main street of the little village was forlorn; only one or two shops lighted.

"They go to bed early here, don't they?" said Reggie. "It's only about nine o'clock, and look at it!"

"I'm going to bed early myself," said Duff.

"Yes. We've got enough left in the icebox from Saturday for our breakfast, anyhow, and tomorrow I can go to market. I brought our ration books."

The shack itself was unbelievable. It was horrible, with a bone-like whiteness under the starry sky; the sound of

the sea was like a beast panting faintly. Duff unlocked the door and turned on the switch, and the taxi driver set down the bags.

"Thank you, sir," he said, pleased with his tip.

The door closed after him.

"I have about half an hour's work to do," said Duff, instantly. "I'd rather do it now, and get it over with."

"Would you like to work in the dining-room, Jake? There's the table and a good light—"

"I'll work in the guest room, thanks," he said.

He locked the door and opened the new little bag, which snugly held the three bottles he had bought that afternoon. He poured a drink and then unlocked the door. Because if Reggie did come to bother him, it would look queer to be locked in. He spread out the papers, which he had taken at random from the office; he picked up the drink, and set it down again, overcome with nausea. I hate the stuff! he thought.

Puffy, he thought. Well, it's possible. I was pretty high last night. But after a good night's sleep. . . . There won't be any more of that. Now, about Nolan.

Nolan bored him, and that wouldn't do. He began to sip the gin, to start his brain working. Oh, the hell with Nolan! he thought. These agency fellows will tell me if he makes a move to see Aunt Lou, and then I can act. Do what I planned to do. Well, what was that? The hell with it. Nothing's going to happen tonight. What I need is sleep, and plenty of it.

He had a magazine with him; he began to read it and he felt a great deal better. In the morning, he thought, after I've slept off last night's jag, I'll be able to cope with anything that comes up.

There was a knock at the door.

"What *is* it?" he called, hiding the magazine under the papers.

"It's me, Jake."

"I told you I had work to do."

"But you said half an hour, Jake, and it's much more. I just feel worried about you getting enough sleep."

"I'll look after myself, thanks."

"Would you like a cup of cocoa, Jake?"

"I would not, thanks."

She came into the room, to his side.

"I'll get you some fresh water," she said, taking up the glass.

"Put that down, please!" he said. "I don't like to be waited on."

She raised the glass to her nose.

"Jake!" she cried.

"Put that down!" he shouted. "Now will you mind your own business, please, and let me *alone*?"

"Jake . . ." she said, very unsteadily. "Jake . . . Couldn't I help you?"

"I don't want any help," he said. "I want to be let alone."

He glanced up at her, and their eyes met, in a long look; then she turned away and went out of the room. He sprang up and locked the door; he got the bottle out of the bag. I'll drink when I please and as much as I damn please, he told himself. I can't stand her. She'd drive anyone to drink.

I hate her, he thought.

He had been bored by her, exasperated, utterly tired of her. But this was hatred. All right! he thought. Maybe she'll realize that now, and get out. He took another drink and lay down on the bed, frantic to go to sleep, and stop thinking. But his heart was pounding; he began to cough,

so violently that he had to sit up. I've got to get some sleep, if I have to drink the whole bottle, he thought.

There was something the matter with him, something frightful. A heart attack? Something frightful . . . He finished the drink in the glass, but it did him no good. And if this did not help him, where could he turn?

The doorbell rang.

"Good God!" he cried, aloud.

This was urgent. He unlocked the door and went lurching down the hall. Reggie was standing in her doorway, in that blue satin negligée; he went past her, and tried to slide the chain off the door. The bell rang again, and it vibrated in his head. This was urgent. Something had happened. He got the chain off and opened the door.

"Mr. Duff?" said a voice. "I want to speak with you."

The light from the hall showed Duff a spare elderly man with close-cropped white hair, very neatly dressed in a dark suit.

"What d'you want?" Duff asked. His heart was still pounding; his anger still shook him. "What d'you mean by coming here at this hour?"

"I want to speak with you about Gerald," said the other.

"Who the hell is Gerald?"

"Gerald Nolan," said the other.

Duff stepped out on the porch and closed the door behind him. That name meant danger to him.

"Mr. Duff!" said the stranger, sternly. "You have set police after Gerald."

"Nothing of the sort!"

"It is very surely you. You have kicked Gerald from your house—and I know why."

"Shut up!" said Duff. "Get out!"

"I shall not shut up. You shall put in writing to take off this police, or I shall beat you."

The light from the window showed him with a riding-crop in his lifted hand.

"You damned old fool . . . !" said Duff, astounded. "Get out!"

"No! Gerald is telling me you have already made him a frame-up. Now comes this police, asking questions of me and of others. You shall put in writing what I say, or I shall beat you."

Duff gave a short laugh.

"Oh, the hell with you!" he said. "I can't be bothered with a maniac like you. I'm going to bed."

He turned to open the door when the crop struck him on the temple, a stinging blow. He spun round, and struck at the man; the flailing blow caught him on the chest and sent him falling back down the steps to the ground.

"Now maybe you'll get out!" said Duff.

The other was struggling up on one knee. Duff went down the steps after him. His slippered foot felt the riding-crop, and he picked it up.

"You're not going to hit me in the face and get away with it," he said. "Stand up!"

More light came streaming out; Reggie had opened the door.

"Get up!" said Duff. "Stand up—like a man!"

He took the man's arm and pulled him to his feet. He held him by the collar with his left hand, and struck him with the crop, somehow, anyhow.

"Now get out!" he said, and turned away.

"Jake!" cried Reggie.

"Get back in the house."

"Jake, he's fallen down!"

76

"Let him stay down. Damn maniac!"

"Jake, it's Mr. Paul—"

He pushed her aside and entered the house.

"I don't care who he is. He came here—he hit me in the face—here. D'you see?"

"Jake, I've got to go out—"

"You're not going out," he said, standing against the closed door.

"Jake, please . . . I've got to see—"

"You can see this," he said, touching the cut on his temple. "That's enough."

She started down the hall, but he caught her arm.

"You're not going out of the back door, either," he said. "You're not going out of the house, d'you understand?"

"Jake, I've got to see if he's hurt. Jake, please—!"

I mustn't hit her, he told himself. You must never hit a woman. No matter how you hate her.

"Jake," she said, "I beg you please to let me go and see if Mr. Paul's badly hurt."

Her tone was different, steadier; she had got hold of herself, and she was very much more dangerous to him now. He must be steadier, too, quieter.

"Reggie," he said. "I can't let you go out. The man's drunk."

"No," she said.

"I tell you he is. Come in here and sit down."

"I can't. Please let me go."

He pushed her, as gently as he could manage, into the sitting-room; he pushed her into a chair.

"Don't be so—silly," he said. "The man's gone, by this time."

"Let me look—"

"No!" he shouted. "I will not! Good God! This man—

77

this drunken maniac comes here and hits your husband in the face—and all you can think about is whether *he's* all right."

"Let me look . . ." she said again.

Anger so shook him that his lips and his chin were trembling. This won't do, he told himself.

"I'll go and look," he said. She rose. "Sit down again," he said. "Stay where you are, or I won't look, and I won't let you look."

When she had sat down again, he went to open the door, he looked out, he closed the door and put on the chain.

"Of course he's gone," he said, scornfully.

"Let me see . . ."

"You think I'm lying?"

She looked up at him and then lowered her black lashes; her face was white as paper.

"I'll get you a drink," he said.

"I don't want a drink. I never—"

"You need one," he said. "After all this hysterical nonsense . . ."

The bottle of rye he had opened for Vermilyea was in the dining-room. He poured half a tumblerful and filled the glass with water and brought it to her.

"I can't, Jake. I—"

"Drink it!" he said. "I've had enough of this."

"Is it—strong?"

"Naturally not. I know what I'm doing."

She took a swallow and choked on it.

"No more, please—"

"Finish it!" he said. "And then for God's sake go to bed and let me have some peace and quiet."

She sat for a time with the glass in her hand; then she began to sip the drink, slowly and steadily. She looked,

78

he thought, as if she were drinking poison and knew it and did not care. Well, it isn't poison, he thought. It won't hurt her. It'll do her good.

"Now get to bed," he said.

"I can't," she said.

He lit a cigarette and sat down opposite her. He took out his handkerchief and touched the cut on his temple; it was still bleeding. She saw that, but she said nothing. Because she doesn't care, he thought. She wouldn't have cared if that damn maniac had killed me.

She just sat there, in that tawdry blue satin thing, pale and still. She pretended she had never had a drink in her life, yet she could put down half a tumblerful and never turn a hair. The room was cold, very cold, and he was ill, but he had to stay. He couldn't leave her here, to open the door and look out. He lit another cigarette. How long . . . ?

"I'll—go to bed . . ." she said, thickly.

She could scarcely walk; he put his arm around her and helped her to her bed. She lay back on the pillows and looked up at him with glazed eyes. In a moment she was asleep.

He went back to his own room and took a drink; he got a flashlight out of a drawer, and went quietly along the hall. He did not fumble with the chain now; there was no tremor in his hands, no haze in his mind.

The man still lay there on his back on the sand. Standing at the top of the steps, Duff turned the flashlight on him. His hair glittered like silver, his eyes were closed, his mouth a little open. Dead? Duff thought.

He had to go down the steps and look. He knelt beside the man, opened his coat to listen for a heartbeat, and heard none. He lifted the man's hand, and it was chilly and

damp. Well, I've done it, he thought. This means the police.

It was in self-defence, he thought. There's no doubt about *that*. I've got Reggie for a witness, and I've got this cut on my face.

But I don't want the police here. This fellow had something to do with Nolan. I don't want that story to come out. He turned off the torch and rose, he stood still in the dark, trying to remember what the Nolan story was. But he could not. He could remember only that Nolan had threatened him with something horrible, ruinous.

No, he thought. I'll go back to the house and leave the fellow here. Somebody else will find him. I'll say I didn't know he was here. I'll say he threatened me, hit me, and then he went away. I'll say he must have come back. I don't want to get mixed up in this. I couldn't face—

Face things, Jacob. That was what Aunt Lou was always saying. Face things, Jacob. Whether it's a rhino or a lion, or a visit to the dentist, face it. If you face things, you have a chance. All you can ask or expect in life is a chance, Jacob.

All right, he thought. I've got a chance. If I take it. But not if I sit down in the house and simply let things happen. Let the police get into it. Let Nolan talk.

I'm cold sober, he thought, and thank God for that. It's the shock, I suppose. Whatever it was, he felt a vigor, a quick-wittedness, a feeling of power such as he had not known for a long time. We'll take Mister Paul for a little ride, he said to himself. Nobody asked him here, and nobody wants him here. I'm damned if I'll get into a nasty scandal for that maniac.

He took hold of the man's ankles and began to drag him down the beach. He was light; he came along fairly easily; the chief trouble was, having to bend over so far. The

80

tide must be out, Duff thought, it was such a long way to the water's edge. But he got to it.

It was not until the water reached halfway up his shins that the cold of it struck him, the bitter cold. But he went on, walking backward, dragging Mr. Paul along. If he wasn't very, very dead, thought Duff, this would rouse him, all right. His face and his white head were under the icy water. Only I want him to float, Duff thought. I want him to float the hell away from here.

He was crying now, waist-deep in the icy black water, and Mr. Paul just lay there on the bottom, not floating. How does it go? They float after three days? Or it's unconscious people that float? Or dead people? How does it go . . . ? O God! If I can get him into some current that will carry him away . . .

He dropped the man's ankles; he waded back, behind him. He stooped and lifted him under the shoulders and dragged him farther out. But there was no current; only the gentle wash of the tide. He was growing numb with cold; the water was up to his chest. Get out! he cried, and gave Mr. Paul a shove. But Mr. Paul sank like a stone.

He had to get him up. He wasn't going to have Mr. Paul drifting up in front of his house, when the tide turned. He kicked off his slippers, and plunged down into the bitter water, and pulled the man up by one arm. He looked around him in despair; only one little light in his own house and the stars in the sky and the illimitable black water. What'll I *do* with him? What'll I *do* with him?

I can't swim with my clothes on, he thought. But he could if he had to. He began to swim, pulling Mr. Paul by the arm. Until he was gasping, freezing, perishing, in the middle of the ocean. He gave the man a push, and turned back toward the shore. But his strength was gone; his arms

81

and legs moved feebly. This is it . . . he thought. He sank under the water, and then he began to fight. He kicked out wildly, and his foot touched bottom. In all this nightmare stretch of time, with all this monstrous effort, he had not got out into six feet of water.

He waded out, panting, his teeth chattering, and he became aware that he was making some kind of noise, groaning, sobbing, something of the sort. That had to be stopped. He came out of the water, and the wind froze him to the marrow. The light in his own house was a dull, hazy orange, incredibly distant, incredibly lonely. Freezing and shivering, he toiled up the beach, so exhausted that he walked like an ape, and sometimes stumbled, his palms flat on the ground.

If *she* hears me . . . he thought, in terror. He got up the porch steps, bent nearly double, but without stumbling. He opened the door. Suppose *her* door opened, and she stood there, pale and still? Don't let her come now! he cried in his heart. Because I couldn't stand it.

Water was dripping from him all along the hall. Never mind. Only let him get into his own room and lock the door, without seeing *her*. Just keep *her* away.

He got in there; he locked the door. Now let her come. Let her knock at the door, let her bang. Let her call, let her yell. I'm safe now.

Chapter Ten

She was knocking; she was calling.

"Jake . . . !"

He was sure, from her voice, that something had happened. He sat up in bed.

"What is it?" he shouted.

"It's after nine," she said. "What train is Aunt Lou coming on?"

The sun was streaming into the room; it caught the bottle of gin and made it glitter like a diamond. He looked at it for a moment, breathing fast. Damn bad thing to be waked up this way out of a sound sleep . . .

"She'll be here around nine-fifty," he said. "If you'll be good enough to make some coffee—"

"It's all ready," she said.

Duff got out of bed and poured himself a drink. I opened the other bottle last night, he thought. Well, God knows I needed it. He stood drinking, leaning one hand on the dresser, and remembering last night very well. He had taken off his wet clothes and thrown them into the closet; he had locked them in and taken out the key. There were damp patches on the floor, but that was nothing; that could be a spilled glass of water. He put the newly-opened bottle and the empty bottle back into that bag he had bought

yesterday, and began to dress. I've got to pull myself together for Aunt Lou, he thought, and he did.

When they find that old maniac washed up on the beach, he thought, very well. Nothing to do with me. If I'm asked any questions, I'll simply tell the truth. He came here, drunk. Or maybe they'll find out that he wasn't drunk. Simply crazy. He demanded money. He attacked me, and I knocked him down, and went into the house. *I* don't know what he did, where he went, after that. Don't know who he is, or anything about him.

He examined his face critically as he made ready to shave. Puffy? he thought. A little, maybe. But the welt on his temple was healing very nicely. I must be in pretty good shape, he said to himself, when you think what I went through last night . . .

He had clean underwear with him, he had a second suit of clothes hanging in the closet; he was able to make himself very neat and presentable. He locked the closet door again upon the heap of sodden clothes. I'll have to do something about them, later on, he thought. Otherwise, there's absolutely nothing to prove, or even suggest that I put that old maniac into the water. If I'd been able to get him far enough out, it would have been a very sensible move. Now, of course, he'll be washed up on the beach when the tide comes in. But even at that, it's better than having him found just outside the house.

Only, he wished that Mrs. Albany were not coming out today, the day on which the old maniac would be found and the questions asked. It would have been easier without her. Moreover, she was going to complicate his routine, seriously. She would notice it, if he locked himself into his room every now and then; she would want to know what sort of 'work' he was doing. And he could not have

his little drink of gin and water out in the open any more. Not after last night.

If Reggie would mind her own damn business, he thought, with a surge of anger. She had no right to come in here and pick up that glass. If she'd let me alone, I wouldn't want so many drinks.

He put the key to the closet into his pocket and looked around the room. The wet clothes were locked up, the bottles were locked up; let her snoop as much as she pleased. He went out of the room, leaving the door wide open, and went along the hall to the kitchen, where he heard Reggie moving about.

"Good-morning," he said.

"Good-morning," she answered. Not hello.

She turned toward him, away from the sink, and he was startled to see her so pale, with dark circles under her eyes, no smile.

"Don't you feel well?" he asked.

"Not very," she answered.

"Why? What's wrong?"

"Nothing much, I guess," she said. "Shall I make you some toast?"

"No, thanks," he said.

She would have to stop looking like this and acting like this before Aunt Lou came.

"After all, I should like some toast, if it's not too much trouble, Reggie," he said. "I'll just get my watch . . ."

He had to hurry, to get in another little drink before Aunt Lou came. He didn't want it; it made him feel sick, but he had to have it, if Reggie was going to behave like this. What's the matter with her? he thought, angry and alarmed. He rinsed his mouth with peroxide and returned to the kitchen.

85

"Oh, thanks, Reggie!" he said. "That looks good. Aren't you eating anything?"

"I've had my breakfast, thank you, Jake."

"Well, sit down with me while I eat," he said.

She sat down at the end of the dining-room table.

"Tell you what," he said. "I'll get a taxi later on, and we'll all drive over to the Yacht Club for lunch. You look tired. You want to take it easy. Not do any cooking, and so on."

"Thank you, Jake, but I like to cook."

"You ought to get out in the fresh air, Reggie. The sunshine. You're pale. See here, Reggie! Why don't you put on a little rouge?"

"I haven't got any rouge, Jake. I've never used it."

You mean you've never been pale, like that. Well, what the hell's the matter with you?

He reached across the table and patted her hand.

"I dare say we both need a little rest and change," he said. "I'll try not to be irritable, Reggie. I'll try to make things pleasanter for you."

"Thank you, Jake," she said, passive, utterly unresponsive. He had never seen her like this. She would have to stop being like this, before Aunt Lou came.

"Reggie—" he began, but it was too late; the taxi had come.

Mrs. Albany was dressed for travelling; she wore a grey suit with a shoulder cape and a small black hat tilted forward in a point on her forehead; with her high-bridged nose and her heavy-lidded eyes she looked, thought Duff, rather like Sherlock Holmes. Reggie took her into the bedroom, already made neat for her reception, and presently she joined her nephew in the sitting-room.

"No, thanks," she said, when he offered her a cigarette. "I always use my own, these days."

He lit it for her and she leaned back a little, crossing her bony knees.

"What's the matter with you two?" she asked, briefly.

"Why, nothing. What makes you think—?"

"You both look—" She paused, seeking a word. "Ghastly," she said. "What's that on your temple, Jacob?"

"I slipped."

"Drinking?" she demanded.

"No!" he said, resentfully. "Good Lord, Aunt Lou, you're getting obsessed with the idea that I'm a drunkard."

"I didn't mean it that way, Jacob. Only I do worry about your taking more than is good for you. I hope you're not taking up this habit that seems to be growing on people, this taking a cocktail before lunch. Your Uncle Fred always said—no drink before sundown."

Now how am I going to manage? thought Duff. If we go to the Yacht Club to lunch, how can I get into the bar without her noticing?

"And if you've quarrelled with Reggie," she went on, "it might very well be from one drink too many. It makes you irritable, Jacob. I've noticed that."

"But I haven't quarrelled with Reggie."

"Then what's wrong with the poor child?" she asked. "She looks wretched."

"I don't know what's wrong with her," he said. "And I don't see why you take it for granted it's my fault."

"She has a very happy nature," said Mrs. Albany.

He had known that he would have to explain Reggie's queerness; he ought to have had something prepared.

"Suppose we take a little walk?" he suggested.

87

"I'd like that," said Mrs. Albany. "But get a hat, Jacob. The sun's quite strong now."

"I very seldom wear a hat down here."

"Well, you ought to," said Mrs. Albany. "You're a heavy man, and full-blooded, and you shouldn't go out in the sun without a hat."

He went to his room to get a hat, and Reggie was there, making the bed. He could not unlock the closet while she was here.

"Reggie," he said, "would you mind looking in the dining-room for my wallet? I think I must have dropped it."

She went without a word, and he unlocked the closet and got a hat. He was relocking the door when she returned.

"I didn't see it, Jake," she said.

"Never mind. It can't be far. I'm just going to take a walk with Aunt Lou. You'll join us in a few moments, won't you, Reggie? We'll be on the upper road."

"All right, Jake," she said.

"I wish you'd smile, Reggie," he said, anxiously. "It—it upsets me to see you like this."

"I'm sorry," she said. "Only I can't."

Better not ask her any questions now. He found Mrs. Albany in the sitting-room, with her hat on.

"We'll walk along by the sea," she said.

"Oh, no!" said Duff. "The upper road is much better. Trees, and so on."

"I'd rather walk by the sea," said Mrs. Albany.

All right! All right! he thought, in a rage. Walk along by the sea, then, and you'll be the one to find that old maniac. You asked for it. Then I'll say—Good God! Why, that's the old fellow who came bothering me last night!

Drunk, or crazy. As a matter of fact, that's how I got this welt on the forehead. He hit at me with the riding-crop he was carrying.

Where is that crop? Still lying in the sand outside the house? I forgot it. That's a definite clue.

Here, here! Take it easy. Clue to what? There's been no crime committed, and anyhow, I never intended to deny that the fellow had come to the house. If the subject ever came up. There's nothing to worry about, absolutely nothing. Only I've got to have a drink before lunch. After all I went through last night.

"Now tell me," said Mrs. Albany.

"Tell you what?" he asked, startled.

"Tell me what's wrong with Reggie."

He lit a cigarette, and his mind began to work on that; it had to.

"You won't like it, Aunt Lou."

"Let's hear it, Jacob."

"Very well. I fired that fellow Nolan, and she's been like this ever since."

"Nonsense, Jacob!"

"I knew you'd say that."

"Jacob," she said, after a moment, "I dare say you've made yourself believe that. But it's not true. It's simply an excuse for your own unfaithfulness to Reggie."

"I've never been unfaithful to Reggie," he said, curtly.

"The worst sort of unfaithfulness there is," said Mrs. Albany, "is to get tired of people, as you do. You're fickle, Jacob. Where are the friends you had in prep school and in college?"

"I used to see them, when we lived in New York."

"You used to go to your clubs," she said, "and you'd talk

89

to anyone who happened to be there. But you didn't care who it was. No. You haven't kept up any faithful friendships, Jacob."

"You can't say I've been fickle toward you," he said.

She put her hand through his arm.

"No, you haven't," she said. "You haven't, Jacob. But I'm getting old. I shan't be here—"

"Don't talk like that!" he cried.

"There's no use blinking facts," she said. "There's—"

He did not hear what else she said, for he had caught sight of one of his red leather slippers lying in the sand, not red any more, but black and sodden with water. Where the slipper had come, the old maniac would also come, he thought, borne by the same currents. He looked along the beach, but as far as he could see there was nothing like— that. But it might be floating.

"Let's sit down and wait for Reggie," he said.

They sat down side by side on a great log half-buried in the sand. If we go to the Yacht Club, he thought, I don't see how the hell I can get a drink. I can't get away from them . . .

"There she is!" said Mrs. Albany.

In dark-blue slacks, she looked taller; the light wind blew her hair back from her pale face; she came on steadily, inexorable, and, watching her, he felt a stir of fear. What did he know about that girl, anyhow, about her thoughts, her feelings?

He saw her stop, and look down at something in the sand. He knew what it was. It was his slipper.

Chapter Eleven

"I'll make Scotch scones for tea," said Mrs. Albany. "I make them with soda."

"Oh, I'd like to watch you!" said Reggie.

"Have I got time for a snooze?" asked Duff. "Fifteen minutes? The sea air always makes me sleepy."

"Yes," said Mrs. Albany.

He locked the door very quietly, and got a bottle out of the bag. But he had an angry suspicion that they both knew what he was doing. Probably they were going to talk about him, in low, grave voices, making plans for his welfare. He had had a horrible day, boring beyond endurance. Mrs. Albany and Reggie had preferred home cooking to the Yacht Club; they had got a taxi to take them into the village, and Mrs. Albany had asked him to come, too. To help. They had come back with huge bags; they had talked about prices, about ration-points.

Mrs. Albany had lived in hotels since her husband's death, over ten years ago, and during his lifetime they had spent most of their time travelling. But she believed herself to be an experienced and excellent housekeeper and cook. I could get up a nice little meal anywhere, she liked to say. In a ship's galley—on the veldt—in a jungle.

I don't believe she ever did anything of the sort, Duff thought, for the first time with irritation. Uncle Fred's

expeditions were always done in style. But if she likes to think so . . .

He swallowed his drink quickly, put the bottle back into the bag, unlocked his door, and lay down on the bed. They say it's a bad thing to drink so quickly, he thought. Well, I wouldn't, if I could help it. If I could have had a couple of cocktails this afternoon, in a decent, civilized way, without being called a drunkard . . .

He was not in the least sleepy; he lay on the bed with his eyes closed, and examined the situation. That slipper . . . he thought. Reggie couldn't possibly *know* it was mine. Nobody could identify it, in that condition. Unless she came snooping in here, to see if my slippers are missing. And that wouldn't do her any good, either, because the closet's locked.

When they find that old maniac . . . he thought. I wish to God they would find him, and get it over with. Makes you nervous, waiting like this. Coming out here was a mistake, in every way. I can't stand being shut up here with Reggie.

He frowned, trying to get it clear in his mind why he had come here. It was on account of Nolan, he thought. Yes . . . I got those agency people to keep an eye on Nolan. That old maniac said he knew why I'd fired Nolan. That means that Nolan's already started to talk. All right! Let him talk. I'm getting sick of all this. What was it he was going to talk about? Oh, yes. That preposterous story about my trying to frame Reggie.

Anger made his face burn, gave him an odd and very unpleasant feeling of fullness in his head. It's disgusting, to be involved in a lot of petty chicanery of this sort, he thought. Not like me. All these details . . . My slippers, and those wet clothes in the closet . . . I'll pack them in

the big bag and take them home. But *then* what'll I do with them? Good God! I have to behave like a criminal, plotting and planning—simply because I can't trust my own wife.

The riding-crop. I'll have to get that, after dark. There's no end to this thing.

"Jacob!" called Mrs. Albany. "Five minutes till tea!"

He got up at once and washed in cold water, but his face was still darkly flushed; he still had that feeling of pressure in his head; he loathed the thought of sitting there and drinking tea, and talking. If I could be let *alone,* he thought, I'd quit drinking. It's affecting my health.

He accepted one of Mrs. Albany's scones, and when he began to eat it, he was surprised to find it like a stone.

"Very nice, Aunt Lou," he said.

"No," she said, with a sigh. "They didn't turn out right."

A silence came down upon them. He resented that. He was not much of a talker himself, and all his life he had taken it for granted that women would keep a conversation going. It was their business to do so; they *never* sat like Reggie, not even making an effort.

"My taxi will be here in half an hour," said Mrs. Albany.

"I wish you were going to stay longer," said Duff.

But still Reggie said nothing. What's the *matter* with her? Duff thought. I tried to be friendly and nice with her this morning. I told her I was sorry if I'd been irritable. But there she sits . . .

The telephone rang, and Reggie went to answer it, an old-fashioned wall telephone in the hall.

"It's for you, Jake," she said.

"Who is it?"

"He just said it was personal."

"Mr. Duff?" said a man's voice. "McGinnis speaking.

93

Your party hasn't made any move. Still in the house, and still seems to be drinking. But there's one thing might be of interest. The party that rents the house where your party is seems to have disappeared."

"What's his name?"

"He's got one of those big long Russian names, but he don't use it. Paul, he calls himself, Mr. Paul. Now, what occurred to me is, it might be of interest to find out is there any tie-up between Nolan living there in that house and this here Mr. Paul being missing. I could start—"

"No," said Duff. "Just drop it."

"You mean just keep an eye on Nolan?"

"Not that, either. Just drop the whole thing. You'll hear from me tomorrow. Don't do anything more."

"Well . . ." said McGinnis. "Okay!"

Duff hung up the receiver and went back to the sitting-room.

"Business thing," he said. "I'll have to go back to New York tomorrow."

The taxi came for Mrs. Albany, and Duff helped her into it; then he strolled off along the beach. He might find that slipper and bury it; he might even come across the old maniac. But his chief object was to keep away from that house and from Reggie.

We'll be there all alone now, he thought, in dismay. It was as if that had never happened before, and he did not know how to deal with it. The sun was low; after a while it would be dark, and they would be shut up together in there. By heaven, I feel like simply walking away and never coming back, he thought. My lawyer could arrange for her to get an adequate income. That's probably all she wants, anyhow; all she married me for. She hasn't the

sense to care for social position, or anything of that sort. Just money. Very well; she can have money.

If I could only get rid of her, he thought, I'd move back to New York, get away from this damn suburban life. Then if I wanted a cocktail before my dinner, I'd have one, without all this locking doors and hiding bottles. It's degrading. And it makes me take more drinks than I normally would.

He reached the log where he had sat with Mrs. Albany, without having seen the slipper, or anything else to worry him. He sat down there, looking out over the pallid water, with a great sense of loss in his heart. I used to be happy, he thought. But now I never am. I used to feel well and happy. Used to like to go fishing, used to enjoy swimming. But now I don't enjoy anything. Not with Reggie around.

He was physically tired; it was a wretched effort to get up, to plod through the sand, back to the house he hated and the woman he dreaded. It was dusk now, and there was only one light in the house, in the kitchen. He went round the side and looked in at the window, saw Reggie at the stove, an apron around her waist. She had a submissive and humble look that disgusted him. You'd never have caught Helen alone in a kitchen with an apron on, he thought.

He watched her go into the dining-room and turn on the light there; she was beginning to set the table. We'll be eating there alone, he thought. Nothing to say to each other. And all evening—and tomorrow. And after tomorrow, how long?

I want to go home! he cried to himself. He had a vision of Miss Castle pouring tea, so beautifully easy to talk to,

composed, cheerful, adult. A real woman, he thought. I want to go home.

Even with Nolan just outside his gate? It came into his mind that Nolan must almost surely have known that the old man was coming out here; perhaps Nolan had sent him. I shouldn't have called off the agency, he thought, in a panic. Now, if Nolan starts to come out here, I shan't know anything about it. He may be on his way here now. He might—I don't know what he might do. He might accuse me of killing that fellow.

And I did kill him, he thought, in great wonder. Of course, it was entirely an accident, but I did kill him.

He straightened his shoulders. And all through the whole thing, I never turned a hair, he thought. This fellow suddenly appearing in the middle of the night, threatening me, attacking me—and I was perfectly cool. I made up my mind what was the best thing to do, to avoid a lot of gossip and trouble, and I did it. Entirely alone. When the emergency arose, I met it. I don't see why I should be afraid of Nolan.

He stood in the twilight, thinking. You must face things, Jacob . . . Why not face Nolan, instead of running away from him? All right, he thought. If Nolan comes tonight, I will face him, just as I did that Paul.

Very suddenly, he remembered the riding-crop, and he went to the front of the house and found it lying in the sand. He picked it up, stuck it through his waistband and buttoned his coat over it. I shouldn't mind using it on Nolan, if he tries to make trouble, he thought. That's the way to handle a fellow like that. A discharged servant. A blackmailer.

As he opened the door, Reggie called out to him.

"Dinner's ready, Jake."

"Ten minutes," he said. "I want to wash up."

He locked his door, he unlocked the closet and got out the bag and put the riding-crop in there. Good God! he thought, taking out a bottle, what a way to live! Skulking around, keeping everything under lock and key . . .

It was Reggie's fault, all of it. He had to take his drink far too quickly, dreading a knock at the door. He had to lock up the bag again, unlock his door; no end to all this locking and unlocking. He went into the dining-room and Reggie came in from the kitchen.

What's the *matter* with her? he thought. Why doesn't she smile?

"I hope you'll like this," she said. "I couldn't get anything but some breast of lamb, so I made a little sort of stew."

"Very nice," he said. "The trouble is, I haven't got my appetite back yet. The tonic's supposed to look after that but it hasn't done much good so far."

"I'm sorry," she said, and fell silent.

She is thinking about that slipper, he told himself. Very well; why doesn't she say so? Why doesn't she say—that looked like one of your red slippers, down on the beach. My dear girl, I didn't bring any slippers. No. She packed my suitcase herself. My dear girl, those slippers are in my closet at this moment.

He was ready and eager to face things now, but what could he do when she sat there in silence? He ate a few mouthfuls of food, and his mind was working fast.

"Did that damn dog wake you up last night?" he asked.

"No, I didn't hear anything," she answered.

"Waked *me*," he said. "Howling, just outside the window. I got up and heaved one of my slippers at it and it ran away. But it came back, and I let it have the other one."

97

"Did you?" she said.

"The funny part of it is," he went on, "that both the slippers are gone." He glanced at her, and her black lashes were down, her face unreadable. "Dog must have carried them away," he said.

He waited.

"You're not very talkative," he said. "Not very civil."

"I'm sorry. Only—"

"Only what?"

"Jake," she said, "I could send Ellen out here to cook for you, and all."

"What are you talking about?"

"I'd—like to go back to Jay," she said. "I'd like to go to-morrow."

He could not understand this, and he must. It was dangerous.

"Why?" he asked, after a moment.

"Well, I miss Jay—"

"No. Why do you want to go?"

"I—just do, Jake."

"By all means!" he said, pushing back his chair. "By all means. Go to hell, if you like."

Locked in his room, he lay down on the bed and fell asleep at once. He waked with a start, in a flame of anger against Reggie. She wants to leave me here, does she? All right. Let her go. Let her go to hell.

He could hear faint sounds from the kitchen, the clink of china, the rattle of a drawer closing. She was still working in there, toiling, in an apron, like a maid-of-all-work. Let her. It was what she liked. Mrs. Jacob Duff.

He heard the switch click off in the kitchen, and Reggie's footsteps, light and slow, coming along the hall to the

room next to his. The door closed, and he heard a key turn in the lock; he heard that plainly. He sat up straight in the dark.

Why was *she* locking her door? She never did that. What was *she* afraid of? It made him shiver.

Chapter Twelve

He could not forgive Reggie.

"There's a train at nine-forty," he said, as they sat at breakfast. "I'll telephone for a taxi to get us there in time for that."

"I'm afraid I couldn't get ready by then, Jake."

"I'll pack my own things. You can certainly pack your own bag in an hour, can't you?"

"Yes, but there's the dishes and—"

"My dear girl," he interrupted, "I'd appreciate it if you'd stop this talk about your dishes and your kitchen and so on. You're not a laborer's wife."

"All right, Jake," she said.

He telephoned for a taxi and then he locked himself into his room, and unlocked the closet where the wet clothes lay on the floor of the closet. They had to go into the big suitcase, and it was an infuriating job. He was not used to packing. He had long ago lost the key, so he put a leather strap around it. What's more, he thought, I've got to lug that empty bottle all the way back to New York. I can't so much as throw away an empty bottle in my own house without all this criticism.

When his bags were closed, he took them into the sitting-room, and there he found Reggie, in her hat and coat, her bag beside her. Through the open doorway he could

100

see the breakfast dishes still on the table. What's wrong with her? he thought.

He was no longer worried about Nolan, nor about the old maniac. All that was past. He was going back to the house in Vandenbrinck, to a normal life, under the roof with normal Miss Castle. I'll simply ignore Reggie, he thought. Anyhow, until she's got over this fit of sulks, whatever it is.

They spoke scarcely a word on the way in to New York. Then he took her to the Grand Central and to the gate of the train.

"I'll be home to dinner," he said, briefly.

He had a minor but annoying problem before him. In the small new bag he had an empty bottle, one that was quarter full, and a full one. He wanted to buy two bottles to take home with him, but the bag would hold no more than three, and he could think of no way for disposing of empty bottles.

Preposterous! he thought. Here I am, in a city like New York, and there's absolutely no place where I can leave an empty bottle. He sat down in the waiting-room, frowning in bitter resentment.

By God, I'm going to leave them here, in the men's room! he decided, and rose. He locked himself in; he got the empty and the almost empty bottle out of the little bag and set them on the floor in a corner. But then panic overwhelmed him. When he opened the door, he might come face to face with someone he knew. Or, far worse, he might meet someone unknown to him who would recognize Jacob Duff, who would go around telling people how Jacob Duff left empty bottles in the men's room in Grand Central. Like an old souse.

He put the bottles back into the bag and returned to the

101

waiting-room. He sat down, and glanced at his watch, and he saw that it was nearly twelve. I'm wasting my whole *day* over this damn nonsense! he cried to himself. I'd better get some lunch, and then I'll see . . .

He checked both the bags and crossed the street to a hotel bar. It was jammed; he had to stand and wait to get near the bar, and he was beginning to feel sick; his hands were shaking again. When he at last found a place, he ordered a double rye, straight, with water on the side; he drank it, but it didn't help him. The drinks here, he thought, were extremely small.

"Make it another double," he said to the bartender.

"Hel-*lo*, Duff!" said a voice beside him.

It was Vermilyea.

"Martini," he said to the bartender and then turned his ruddy, serious face toward Duff. "Bad business about old Mr. Paul, isn't it?"

"What is it? I haven't heard," said Duff.

He felt remarkably cool and alert now.

"Why, the poor old fellow's disappeared," Vermilyea told him. "Left his house a couple of nights ago, took a train to New York, and he's never been seen since."

"I don't think I know him," said Duff, frowning thoughtfully. "Paul . . . ? Paul?"

"Riding-master," Vermilyea explained. "Your wife took lessons from him. Very decent old boy. Personally, I think it's one of these cases of amnesia. *You* know. Forget your name, and so on."

"Yes, I'd think that was very likely," said Duff.

"My mother's very much upset," Vermilyea went on. "Paul was a sort of protégé of hers, y'know. She met him two or three years ago in New York; he was giving Russian

102

lessons, hardly making both ends meet. In fact, she was the one who got him out to Vandenbrinck, found pupils for him, got him on his feet. Have another drink, Duff?"

"No, thanks," said Duff. "To tell you the truth, I don't go in much for drinks in the middle of the day."

"You're right!" said Vermilyea. "I don't either. Not once in two or three months. But today I happened to find myself in this neighborhood, with time on my hands . . . Y'see, I told my secretary I shouldn't be back until two-thirty or so. I thought this thing would take more time. But the people seemed very efficient. My mother's idea, this was. She doesn't think the police are taking enough interest in poor old Paul, so she found this agency."

"What agency?" asked Duff.

"Forgotten the name. She saw it advertised in the newspaper. Wait . . . Here's the card. Dependable Agency—right here on Forty-Second Street."

"Vermilyea," said Duff, "I happen to know something about those people, and I advise you to have nothing to do with them. They're very good people to keep away from."

"How's that, Duff?"

"It was told me in confidence, by a friend," said Duff. "Those people make a business of blackmailing their clients."

"Whew!" said Vermilyea, whistling. "However, they certainly couldn't find any possible excuse for blackmailing my mother. At the worst, it'll simply be a waste of money, and at the best, they might find the poor old boy." He finished his drink. "Had your lunch, Duff?"

"Yes," Duff answered, looking at his watch. "I'll have to get going now. See you soon!"

He went back to the Grand Central and stood in the

103

rotunda, smoking. This is too much, he thought. What am I to do? If that McGinnis comes out to Vandenbrinck again . . .

Take it easy. Take it easy. What if he does come? I hired him to watch Nolan, and Nolan happened to be living in this Paul's house. That doesn't incriminate me. Involve me, I mean. I mean, why should I care?

For a paralyzing moment, he was aware of the frantic confusion in his own mind. He felt himself threatened on every side, and knew himself to be helpless. Nolan, Mc-Ginnis, Paul, even Vermilyea, all dangerous to him, and he could not think why.

I need food, he told himself.

When he moved, his knees were weak. I can't get across the street, he thought. There's a place here . . . Food, that's the thing. I've *got* to quit this drinking, or it'll get me down. Got to keep my wits about me.

He went into a restaurant, and looked and looked at the menu.

"Scrambled eggs and sausages," he said to the waitress. "Toast and coffee. And oatmeal," he added.

"Oatmeal?" she said. "We don't have oatmeal for lunch."

"This happens to be breakfast, for me," said Duff, with an amused smile.

He forced himself to eat as much as he could stand; then he lit a cigarette. I'll go home, he thought. I'll get a nap on the train and that'll help. I'm absolutely cutting out the drink. But I'm not going to be stuck out there without a couple of bottles in case I want a shot. I may find it's better to taper off, instead of quitting cold.

There was a liquor store opposite the restaurant; he bought two bottles of gin there and carried them away

104

in a paper bag. He got his two bags from the checkroom, and thus loaded down, he went back to the men's room. He put the empty bottles into the paper bag and replaced them with the full ones. He left the paper bag in a corner. I don't give a damn if anyone does notice, he thought. I'll say it isn't mine, I don't know anything about it.

Boarding the train early, he got a seat by a window, and at once closed his eyes. If anyone who knew him came along, they could damn well let him alone. It was hot in here; no air, and he felt miserable. He grew drowsy, and then came awake with a start, thinking that his big suitcase was toppling over on him. But it was quite safe, up in the rack. With those wet clothes in it.

Another problem, another worry. He could not dry them anywhere without being noticed. He could not take them to a cleaner's without causing talk. Absolutely Reggie's fault, he thought. She's made it impossible for me to confide in her. I can't simply go to her and ask her to look after these clothes. It's her fault about these bottles. All of it.

He slept for a time, and waked, greatly refreshed. There were windows open now, and cool air blew in; he sighed and looked out at the river. And he felt in some way purged of error, he felt tranquil and innocent. At the Vandenbrinck station he was lucky enough to get a taxi to himself, and he looked with a certain indulgence at the green Spring world. It may be better for Jay, out of the city, he thought.

He thought of Jay with somber affection. A handsome child, very intelligent, too. It was his irrevocable misfortune to have lost his mother so early in life. But if he goes to a good school, Duff thought, if he makes the right friends . . . If he marries the right sort of girl . . .

That's of paramount importance. A girl with breeding, loyalty, poise . . .

He went into the house and, to his delight, he found Miss Castle alone in the sitting-room.

"How are *you*?" he said. "I'll be down in a moment."

He hurried up to his room, locked the two bags in the closet, and descended again.

"Is Jay around?" he asked.

"Mrs. Duff took him for a walk," said Miss Castle.

"It seems to me he's rather old to be 'taken' for walks," said Duff.

"Oh, he likes it," said Miss Castle. "He's a very companionable child. Will you have tea, Mr. Duff?"

"Thanks, yes. My aunt's as fond of her tea in the afternoon as you are, Miss Castle."

"Oh, I'm a creature of habit," she said.

And all her habits, he thought, were well-bred, quiet, civilized. She was wearing a grey wool dress and a small string of pearls, and with her neat shining hair and the pretty color in her cheeks she looked, Duff thought, like some healthy and happy royal person.

"It's a shocking thing about poor old Mr. Paul, isn't it?" she said.

"Oh, yes!" said Duff. "But as I never set eyes on him—"

"He was a very fine old man," she said. "I do hope they'll find him."

Find him? thought Duff. Where *is* he, anyhow? Why doesn't he get washed ashore somewhere, and be done with it?

"It's too bad you couldn't have had a longer time at the seaside," said Miss Castle.

"It's rather a cheerless place, that shack," said Duff.

"Oh, is it? I've heard such glowing accounts of it from Jay."

"Well, he used to go down there with his mother," said Duff. "Very different, of course."

"Poor little boy!" said Miss Castle.

She understands, thought Duff. She can see what the child's lost—and what we've got here, in Helen's place. If I could talk to her frankly, some time—

"Mr. Duff," she said, "if you wouldn't mind my suggesting it—?"

"No! Certainly not! Please go ahead!"

"I know you have Doctor Staples and, of course, he's excellent. He was so good when Jay had the measles, wasn't he? But sometimes another opinion, don't you think . . . ? This doctor in the village, Doctor Hearty— Mrs. Vermilyea recommended him to me, and I liked him very much. He's rather old-fashioned, but he is so sensible."

"Doctor Hearty, eh?" said Duff.

He liked this conversation, yet the gravity of her tone made him a little uneasy.

"It seems to me I'm improving," he said.

"Oh, yes!" said Miss Castle, but not convincingly. "It's simply that I thought Doctor Hearty might have some quite simple, old-fashioned tonic . . . It's only a suggestion."

At that, thought Duff, he might be a damn sight better than Staples. I can't see that Staples has done me much good, with *his* pills and so on—

But I haven't consulted Staples, he thought, with a faint shock. I never got that medicine I talked about. It's all very well if I want to tell Reggie things like that, to stop

107

her from nagging, but I've *got* to keep things straight in my own mind. I haven't seen a doctor for the last two or three years.

Mary came into the room.

"Nolan's here, sir," she said. "He says could he see you a few minutes, please?"

"Yes," said Duff. "Take him in to the study."

He rose; for a moment he hesitated, not sure whether or not he should make Miss Castle some sort of explanation. But, after all, he didn't know what she had heard about Nolan.

"If you'll excuse me, please . . ." he said. "I'll just see what he wants."

I'll go upstairs and have a drink first, he thought. But at the foot of the stairs he stopped. No, I won't, he thought. I need a clear head, to deal with that fellow.

Only the worst of it was, that a few drinks gave him a clearer head, made his hands stop shaking, made him steadier in every way. That's bad, he thought. This can't go on. It's dangerous.

He had his drink; he went through all the irritating locking and unlocking process, and then he went down to the study. Nolan was standing by the window, very straight and still, with the stillness of a strong, wary animal. His handsome face in profile had an almost brutal vitality, with the dark hair springing up from his temples, his blunt nose, the sharp angle of his jaw.

"Well?" Duff asked, curtly.

"I just wanted to ask if you'd seen old Paul," said Nolan, speaking just as he always had spoken. You could not call it an impudent tone, although it was certainly not respectful.

108

"Paul . . . ?" said Duff. "Oh, the man who's disappeared? No, I never set eyes on him in my life."

He turned, to close the door upon this interview, and, in the short passage outside stood Reggie, hand in hand with Jay.

Duff slammed the door with a crash that shook the walls. But it was too late. He was sure Reggie had heard what he had said.

Chapter Thirteen

"Why should I have seen this man?" Duff asked.

"Well, to tell you the truth," said Nolan, "I don't remember what I told Paul about you."

"About me? And what do you think you've got to tell about me?"

"If I'd told him the whole tale," said Nolan, "he'd have been plenty mad. And he was absolutely fearless, poor old boy. Nothing he wouldn't do for a friend. But I can't remember what I told him."

"Why can't you remember?"

"I was drunk," Nolan explained. "Blind. Sometimes, when I'm not working, I feel like drinking for a couple of days."

"You'll get yourself in trouble that way," said Duff.

"Could be," said Nolan.

Suppose Reggie were to walk in now, still holding Jay by the hand? Suppose she were to point at her husband, accuse him—?

Of what? Duff thought. The man attacked me. He hit me, and I struck back. Reggie knows that; she saw that. The man was crazy, anyway, and it's very probable that he has got amnesia.

Stop this. You know where he is. Don't try to fool yourself, ever. He's in the sea.

But suppose he isn't? Suppose he wasn't dead? Suppose he got out—and now he's coming home? Suppose he's here *now*? Outside the window—dripping water—white hair—white face . . .

I'm going crazy, Duff thought. Like that fellow who wrote the stories about people being buried alive and coming out of their tombs. Poe, that's the one. Edgar Allan Poe. *He* drank. Maybe drinking . . .

He had to have a drink.

"Have a drink, Nolan?" he asked.

"Thanks," said Nolan.

Duff got the bottle of gin out of his desk drawer.

"Oh, gin?" he said, with a look of surprise. "That's not so good, without the fixings."

"It suits me all right," said Nolan.

Duff poured out two moderate drinks, one into a clean glass and one into a dirty one.

"Water?" he asked, and poured it from the carafe, water full of bubbles and coated with dust.

"The great thing," Duff said, "is, never to take a drink before five o'clock."

"I don't think it matters what time you take a drink," said Nolan.

"It does matter," said Duff. "Anyone who starts drinking in the morning has got the skids under him."

"Could be," said Nolan, without interest.

"Personally," said Duff, "I don't think that anyone who really starts drinking is ever cured."

"I've known plenty that were," said Nolan.

"Actually known them?"

"Sure. My father was one. He drank like a fish, and then

111

one day—I don't know why—he quit cold. Never touched another drop."

"Maybe he never drank very much."

"Quart a day," said Nolan.

"He must have gone through hell when he quit," said Duff, after a moment.

"If he did, he never said anything about it. And, drinking or not drinking, he never fell down on his job."

"What job was it?"

"Captain of a cargo steamer."

"Even when he was drinking a quart a day?"

"Even then," said Nolan.

"It's a curious thing . . ." said Duff. "What makes a man drink?"

"Makes you feel good," said Nolan.

Feel good? thought Duff. You fool.

"It's a great problem, for many people," he said.

"Not for me," said Nolan. "If I feel like going on a binge, I do. But I never drink when I don't want to, or when it's going to do me any harm."

There was, thought Duff, something rather likeable about Nolan. It was hard to give it a name, to define it. Normal, Duff thought, very normal. When you came to think of it, it was hard to place Nolan in any category. He had no sort of accent; in fact, he spoke very well. His grey suit was well-cut; his tie in good taste. You wouldn't take him for a chauffeur; he might have been anybody.

"You've had a good education . . ." said Duff.

"Two years at Yale," said Nolan.

"Didn't care about finishing?"

"Uncle Sam wanted me," said Nolan. "I was drafted."

"I see!" said Duff. "You could certainly get something better than a chauffeur's job, Nolan."

112

"I like being a chauffeur," said Nolan.

"Would you like to come back and work for me again, Nolan?"

"Why not?" said Nolan.

"Another drink?"

"Why not?" said Nolan.

Duff felt a great relief; he was almost happy at getting Nolan back. He knew about the frame-up, and still he was willing to come back. He couldn't be dangerous.

"I'd certainly like to know what's happened to Paul," said Nolan, thoughtfully.

"Mr. Vermilyea thinks it's a case of amnesia."

"I think a lot of the old boy," said Nolan. "I could always go to his place and stay as long as I wanted, do whatever I pleased. Once he liked you, everything you did was okay."

"The police are sure to find him before long," said Duff.

"A good many missing people are never found," said Nolan.

How about drowned people? Duff thought. But Paul wasn't drowned. He was dead before he went into the water. In that case, do they float, or not? Do they *always* come ashore somewhere?

He thought they did. Always. Very well. Very well. There was nothing to connect him with Paul. Nobody would suspect anything—except Reggie. God! She looked —horrible, standing out there in the hall. What was she doing, anyhow? Eavesdropping?

"You could call off your sleuth now," said Nolan.

"My 'sleuth'?" said Duff, as if bewildered.

"He's still around," said Nolan. "Still snooping. I don't like it. I'm trying to hide."

"To hide?"

"I've got a mother and father and two sisters and a fiancée up in New Haven," said Nolan. "I don't want them to find me."

"Oh," Duff said.

"When I got back from overseas," said Nolan, "I was in a hospital for a while, and they all came to see me. As soon as I got out of the hospital, I disappeared. I wrote them some nice letters. I said I'd have to have time to work things out before I came home to settle down."

"I see!" said Duff, a little confused.

"What I hope to do," said Nolan, "is, never to set eyes on them again."

"Oh . . . I see!"

"It's a new neurosis," said Nolan. "Home-fatigue. I don't want any part of home, sweet home any more. I don't want anyone helping me, or looking after me, or checking up on me." He picked up his hat. "You might tell your bloodhound he's barking up the wrong tree. I'm not the man."

"What d'you mean?" cried Duff. "You mean you know of someone . . . ? Nolan, see here! If you have any information, I'll—make it *well* worth your while—"

"Not for sale," said Nolan, rising.

Duff rose, too. He could not be quite sure what Nolan meant, and he was afraid to commit himself. But 'I'm not the man . . . '? Did he mean that there was another man in Reggie's life?

"Nolan," he said, "give me just a hint . . . ?"

"All right!" said Nolan. "Try looking at check-books."

Chapter Fourteen

"Beyond good and evil," Duff said to himself.

That was how Nolan impressed him; a man, he thought, without conventional scruples, a man who did what he felt like doing. A genuinely free man.

If I could be free, he thought, sitting at the table with Reggie and Miss Castle, if I could get out of this situation and start over again, I'd do very differently. None of this damn suburban life. None of this—this slavery. I can't do anything I want.

He thought of the wet clothes and the empty bottles, locked in his closet, and it made him sick with rage and frustration. How could he get rid of those clothes? Simply walk off with them in a bag, walk off somewhere, into the country, until he found a place to bury them. That's fine, in a book. But, in real life, somebody asks you where you are going with a bag. Somebody asks you, whatever has become of that blue suit, Jake? And, in real life, where do you find a place lonely enough, and how do you dig without a spade?

All right! All right! he thought. It must have been Reggie's check-book that Nolan meant. I may find something there that will settle this whole business. *I'm not the*

man, Nolan said. He must have meant there was another man.

He glanced at Reggie, saw her still with that mask-like blankness, that pallor. If Aunt Lou could see her now, he thought, she might change her mind. She might believe now that Reggie isn't quite the naive, sweet girl she's built up in her own imagination. If only I can find something in her check-book, something I can show Aunt Lou . . .

"I'll have to work this evening," he said, when they were drinking their coffee.

"Oh, that's too bad!" said Miss Castle.

"Well, in war times . . ." said Duff, rising. "I'll say good-night now, ladies. Don't wait up for me, Reggie."

He went along to the study and locked himself in, but no sooner had he lit a cigarette and settled himself with a book than there was a knock at the door.

"Who is it?" he called, sharply.

"It's me," Reggie answered.

He unlocked the door and she came in, like a ghost in her black dress.

"Jake," she began at once, "Jake, I want to go away."

"What are you talking about?"

"I want to go. I've got to go."

"D'you mean leave me?"

"Yes," she said.

"You mean permanently?" he asked. "You mean, break up our marriage?"

"Yes.

He was stunned.

"You mean you want to walk out of my house? Desert me?"

"Yes," she said.

The shock made him cold sober. This was dangerous.

116

"May I ask what's your reason for this sudden decision?" he asked.

She did not answer.

"What reason are you going to give other people? Aunt Lou, for instance?"

"None," she said. "I'm never going to tell anyone."

His heart was beating too fast.

"Tell—what?" he asked.

She had lowered her lashes making her face into that mask again, and it was beyond bearing. He rose.

"I will not—" he began, when she looked up at him, and in her eyes he saw something incredible. He saw a fear, a horror of him.

It took him a moment to quiet his breathing.

"Very well," he said. "We'll discuss it tomorrow."

"I'd like to go now. Tonight," she said.

She heard me tell Nolan I'd never set eyes on that old Paul, he thought. She can't go away, run around telling people . . .

"If you'll have the goodness to wait, at least until to-morrow . . ." he said. "After all, I'm a man with a certain standing in the community. I don't think it's too much to ask you to manage this thing with a little decency, a little dignity. Unless you enjoy humiliating me."

"No. I don't," she said.

She was stupid beyond belief. Nothing to say for her-self. He had, at one time, thought it a virtue in her that she never fidgeted, but now, seeing her there, straight, her hands hanging easily at her sides, her head a little bent, this quietness seemed to him moronic. She was a fool, and a very dangerous one.

"We can talk this over in the morning," he said. "Have you told Miss Castle yet?"

"I haven't told anyone anything," she said.

"What *is* there to tell?" he shouted, and when she did not answer, he caught her by the wrist. "I'm sick of these veiled hints—threats—whatever they are. If you've got anything to say, say it!"

"I won't say it," she said, and she did not flinch from his shouting, his furious face; her voice was entirely steady. "I won't say it to you, or even to myself. I took a vow to stand by you."

"And you're running away from me. You call that standing by me?"

"It's the only way I can," she said. "I've got to go."

"Good God!" he said, and dropped her wrist. "You're crazy."

He turned away toward the window, and in a moment he heard the door close after her.

He locked the door and poured himself a drink. He had intended not to take any drinks this evening, but after a scene like this . . . You read all these Cinderella stories, he thought, the prince marrying the kitchenmaid, King—what was his name—Cophetua, and the beggar-girl. But you never hear the truth about it. The beggarly kitchen wench doesn't change. Doesn't appreciate anything, never understands . . .

Now, on top of everything else, she wants to make a fool of me, publicly. Probably it'll get in the tabloids. Certainly it'll be common gossip in the locker-rooms. Poor old Duff! That common little nobody he married has walked out on him. Twenty years younger than he. Maybe he wasn't so good. He-he.

And there was more to it than that. He remembered her standing out there in the passage, eavesdropping . . .

She threatened him with something more than humiliation. She was the only one who *knew*.

He opened his door and looked out, and the sitting-room lights were still on. He looked out, at intervals, for nearly two hours, sweating with furious impatience. Once he went along the passage for a few steps, and saw Reggie and Miss Castle in there, talking.

But at last the lights went out. He waited for half an hour by his watch before he went in there, and turned on a lamp. He knew where Reggie kept her check-book; it was in an unlocked drawer, because, until she had married him, she had never had anything worth locking up. He got it out and took it into the study.

It was a big check-book, three checks to a page. He had shown her how to keep it, and it was neatly and carefully done. He had given her three thousand dollars for a wedding present, and for a while he had given her an allowance. But she didn't seem to care about it, and it had long ago become a matter of a check every now and then. He had never asked her what she did with the money.

This book began two months ago; the stubs were painstakingly filled out. Drug-store for cosmetics and first-aid. Red Cross Fund. Weber for shoes. And then came Captain Wilfred Ferris $250.00. Duff lit another cigarette, and went on. Weber for scarf and gloves. Advance to Mary for family illness. Watch repaired. Captain Ferris $500.00. In two months Captain Ferris had got a thousand dollars.

Now I've got her! Duff thought. Now she's not going to walk out on me, make a fool of me. Now she's going to be turned out, disgraced.

119

Chapter Fifteen

I drank very little last night, Duff thought. But I feel as godawful as if I'd had a quart. I wonder if it isn't something else, after all? Liver? Heart?

A formless dread possessed him. There's something *wrong* with me, he thought. Maybe I'm going to have a stroke . . . I don't drink enough to account for feeling like this. No appetite. No *strength*. I'm as weak as a kitten. No . . . Something's wrong. I've got to check on this Captain Ferris thing, and I haven't the physical strength. My *mind's* all right—which it wouldn't be if this was all—drinking.

Puffy, he thought, and, lying in bed, he held out his shaking hands. They were puffy. "That's physical!" he cried to himself. Kidneys—or heart. I've got to get some sort of medical advice, because I have a lot to do today. When you come to think of it, I *never* feel well any more. That's why I take more drinks than I need.

A doctor, he thought. Doctor Hearty. Sensible, Miss Castle had said, and a little old-fashioned. All right! That's just what I want. I need help.

As soon as he got up, nausea swept over him; he staggered into the bathroom to be very sick, and even then, in his extremity of misery, he had to make desperate efforts to be quiet. Nobody must hear him being sick, above all,

not Miss Castle. When he went back to his room, he was trembling from head to foot; he had every symptom of a violent head-cold. I can't go on . . .

But I've got to check this Captain Ferris affair, he thought. I've got to go on. That means I'll have to take a drink—and I don't *want* it.

He took it. Then he bathed and dressed; he even managed to shave. He went downstairs, and there at the table sat Reggie and Miss Castle and Jay. He gave them all a brief good-morning and sat down; it was impossible for him to talk, and he was not going to try.

"The car's here, sir," said Mary, and he pushed back his chair. He did not want even a cup of coffee this morning.

There was Nolan, the same as ever, the man beyond good or evil.

"Nolan," said Duff, "ever hear of a Doctor Hearty?"

"Oh, yes!" said Nolan. "Maple Avenue."

"Well, I think I'll stop by there. I think I've got a throat infection," said Duff.

"All right," said Nolan.

Duff got into the back of the car and lit a cigarette. And he had to begin, no matter how he felt.

"D'you know anything of a Captain Ferris, Nolan?"

"Yes," Nolan answered.

"Well . . . ? What about him?"

"I hate his guts," said Nolan, with simplicity.

"Well, why?"

"I hate all captains," said Nolan. "All officers. All Englishmen."

"Oh . . . Ferris is an Englishman?"

"Couldn't be more so," said Nolan.

"Where did you meet him?"

121

"Taking him to and from your house."

"How many times?"

"Five or six."

Duff was silent for a time.

"What made you think about—checks?" he asked, at last.

"I heard Mrs. Duff say to him once—'I'll send the check tonight, Wilfred.' He said—'Two-fifty?', and she said—'No; it's five hundred this time, Wilfred.'"

"D'you happen to know where he lives?"

"A little hotel in New York."

"How do you know?"

"I saw the address on a letter Mrs. Duff gave me to post."

I've got to be careful, Duff thought. I mustn't give myself away. Must not let Nolan see how eager he was.

"You did right to warn me about this, Nolan," he said.

"The idea was, to get Ferris in trouble, if I could," said Nolan. "I'd thought of writing to his wife, but she's away somewhere, and I couldn't get hold of her address."

"He's a married man?"

"Oh, yes."

It seemed to Duff prudent to remain silent for a time. As if stricken.

"This—" he said. "Naturally, this is very disturbing to me. But there's no reason to think there's anything—wrong, really wrong about it, Nolan."

"Well," said Nolan. "She gives him money. And she went to his hotel to see him."

"How do you know?"

"I went there. I made friends with the desk clerk, and I asked questions."

"Why didn't you tell me all this before?"

"We never used to be so pally," said Nolan. "I didn't use to understand you. Didn't know how you'd take it."

Duff was startled and alarmed.

"I take it the way any decent man would take it," he said.

"But after that frame-up—" said Nolan.

"There *was* no frame-up."

"Have it your own way," said Nolan. "After what I *thought* was a frame-up, I began to change my mind about you."

I've got to be careful, Duff thought, extremely careful with this fellow. I must not let him go too far. He's—I don't know what to call him.

"So," said Nolan, "after the episode that I thought was a frame-up, I got the idea you might be interested in fixing a genuine frame-up."

"I certainly should not!" said Duff.

"Well, here we are," said Nolan.

He stopped the car before a big, old-fashioned frame house on a tree-lined side street; in a front window was a sign. Alexander L. Hearty. M.D.

"I don't know . . ." Duff said. "I don't know if I'll bother . . ."

But he wanted, he needed to feel better than this. There was thinking to be done, action to be taken; he needed to be at his best. If this doctor was one of the kindly, old-fashioned sort, he might help him. He got out of the car and went up the steps to the veranda. He rang the bell and presently the door was opened by a stout grey-haired woman in a green print dress.

"Is Doctor Hearty in?" asked Duff.

123

"Well, his office hours don't begin till eleven."

"My name is Duff," said Duff, and his tone impressed her. "I'm on my way to my office in New York, and I'd hoped I could see the doctor for a few minutes."

"Well, I'll see . . ." she said, and went off, leaving him in the hall.

She returned promptly.

"The doctor'll see you, Mr. Duff," she said. "Step right in."

This is a mistake, Duff thought, looking around him with distaste at the ugly, shabby waiting-room. A doctor with a place like this couldn't possibly be successful.

"Come in, sir! Come in!" said Doctor Hearty from the doorway of his office.

He looked, Duff thought, like a country doctor on a calendar, lean and grizzled, with spectacles before his deep-set grey eyes, and thin lips rather oddly pursed.

"Sit down! Sit down!" he said. "Now, then, sir, what do you complain of?"

Queer way to put it, Duff thought.

"It's nothing very definite," he said. "It's what you might call a general malaise."

"Let's see your tongue," said the doctor.

A mistake, ever to have wasted time over this preposterous old hick, thought Duff. He felt like a fool, sitting there and sticking out his tongue.

"How's your appetite, sir?"

"That's one of the things that bothers me," said Duff. "I have practically no appetite."

"Sleep well?"

"No. Poorly."

"Now take off your coat, sir, and open your shirt," said the doctor.

He did the usual things with a stethoscope; he took Duff's blood pressure.

"Hold out your hands, sir," he said.

Duff did not move.

"Hold out your hands, sir. Arms' length."

"Well, they won't be very good," said Duff, with a laugh. "I took two or three drinks last night, to get some sleep."

"Hold 'em out, sir," said the doctor, patient and inexorable.

Hot with resentment, Duff did so.

"All right," said the doctor. "You can put your coat on, sir. What's your age?"

"Forty-four," said Duff, curtly.

The doctor leaned back in his chair behind the desk.

"How much d'you drink, Mr.—?"

"Duff is my name. I've been taking a few drinks lately at bedtime, to get some sleep."

"How many?"

"I don't know. Three, perhaps four."

"It hasn't done you any good," said the doctor.

Damn fool! thought Duff. He hasn't even written down my history. Doesn't make any attempt to understand my psychology.

"Are you under any particular strain just now, Mr.—?"

"DUFF. Yes, I am. War contracts. Surgical and dental instruments."

"Not Hanbury, Mardin and Duff?" cried the doctor.

"Yes," said Duff.

"Upon—my—word . . . !" said the doctor.

Wonderful, isn't it? thought Duff.

"Well . . ." said the doctor, coming out of a trance, "I'll tell you what I'm going to do for you, Mr. Duff. I'm going

125

to prescribe a sedative, for a short period. One capsule at bedtime. But no liquor. I want you to remember that, Mr. Duff. If you take any liquor at all, along with this sedative, you'll be worse off than ever."

"What's wrong with me?" asked Duff.

"Nothing to worry about, if you'll follow my directions. I want you to eat six light meals a day.—Married man?"

"Yes," said Duff.

"Well, you give your wife this list," said the doctor, taking a mimeographed paper out of a drawer. "Get all the exercise, all the fresh air and sunshine you can. Take one of these capsules at bedtime. And no alcohol."

Damn horse-doctor, thought Duff. Absolutely no understanding of anyone who isn't a phlegmatic yokel.

"I want to see you in three days, Mr. Duff," said the doctor. "After you've had three good nights' sleep—and no alcohol."

They both rose, and the doctor put his hand on Duff's shoulder.

"Carry on!" he said. "You're doing a fine job in this war, Mr. Duff."

Like a Boy Scout leader, thought Duff. Use your will-power and eat six meals a day. Be good and you will be happy. It was a relief to see Nolan, standing beside the car and smoking a cigarette. At least Nolan was not a Boy Scout. He drinks, Duff thought. He said so. He'd have some idea . . . Not like that blasted horse-doctor.

"How did you like old Doc Hearty?" asked Nolan.

"Not at all," said Duff. "Still, I might as well try his damn pills. Take this to the Modern, will you?"

He watched Nolan, straight, strong and alive, going into the Modern Pharmacy on Main Street. Remarkable fellow, in many ways, he thought. You can't exactly call him

impertinent. He's—natural, that's all. He's free. No inhibitions.

It was fifteen minutes before Nolan returned.

"We've missed a couple of trains," he said. "They could have given me this stuff at once. Standard brand. But they like their hocus-pocus. I see you've got some knock-out drops."

"What d'you mean?"

Nolan mentioned a brand name. "They gave me that in the hospital," he said. "I liked it. Put me to sleep in half an hour. Now, whenever I go on a binge, I take that stuff for a couple of nights, and it straightens me out."

"You can't get it without a prescription," said Duff.

"I can," said Nolan.

"Well . . ." said Duff. "When is the next train?"

"Thirty-five minutes."

"I suppose we haven't enough gas to drive down the line to the next station?"

"I can get gas," said Nolan.

"You mean, black market?"

"I mean I can get gas, if I pay for it."

"You haven't any too many scruples, have you?" said Duff.

"Oh, plenty," said Nolan.

He stood there, still smoking, and he plainly didn't care whether he got black market gas or didn't get it.

"I'd never patronize a black market, in any circumstances," said Duff.

Nolan didn't care about that, either. Duff leaned forward in the car, miserably irresolute. He did not want to go to the railroad station and sit there waiting, alone. He wanted to bring the conversation back to Captain Ferris, yet, in a way, he dreaded the idea. He could not quite

127

remember what Nolan had said, but he knew it was dangerous, all of it. He had to remember; he could not tolerate this haziness in his mind.

"Look here!" he said, suddenly. "D'you know any place around here where I can get a glass of beer? A—quiet place. These damn doctors upset you."

"Sure," said Nolan, and got in behind the wheel.

He drove for fifteen minutes or so, through the village, and out on to a highway unfamiliar to Duff, a flat and desolate road. He stopped the car before a one-storied wooden building with a broken windmill thrashing slowly about on the roof. Olde Dutch, the sign said.

"Come in and have a drink, Nolan," said Duff.

It was a bleak place; nobody in it, nothing but chairs and tables around the four walls, leaving the center empty. A thin, insolent dark girl with a Dutch cap on the back of her head came in through a door at the back.

"*Yes?*" she demanded, fiercely.

"I think I'll have a straight rye," said Duff, frowning and thoughtful. "Better make it a double, and water on the side. What's yours, Nolan?"

"Coke, thanks," said Nolan.

This distressed Duff.

"I suppose you think it's a pretty bad idea, to take a drink at half-past nine in the morning," he said.

"If I wanted it, I'd take it," said Nolan.

The insolent girl brought the drinks and went away again; they were alone in this barnlike place with all the empty chairs and tables. The sun shone in at one end, and the dust seemed to rise there like a fog.

"What you told me about this Ferris . . ." said Duff. "It's upset me very much, Nolan."

"That's too bad," said Nolan.

128

"I'd like to hear anything more you've got to say about the man."

"I haven't got anything more that you could use," said Nolan.

"What d'you mean 'use'?"

Nolan gazed down into his little glass and said nothing. He looked young, healthy, and happy, nothing more.

"You said you'd like to see this man in trouble," said Duff. "Well, did you have any ideas about how that could be done?"

"Yes, I had ideas," said Nolan. "But I couldn't work them out, alone."

"Well, what ideas?"

"You'd be surprised," said Nolan.

"I can't quite see why you've got it in for Ferris, this way," said Duff.

"I'll tell you," said Nolan. "The last time I saw him, this was. I was talking to Mrs. Duff in the driveway; we didn't notice Ferris come out of the house until he stood behind me. 'Nolan!' he said, in that damn parade-ground voice of his. He told me he didn't like my 'tone'; he said I needed a 'sharp lesson'. He went on like that."

"What did you do?"

"Nothing," said Nolan. "That's what three years in the Army did to me. I'd got so damn well trained in taking that sort of talk that I took it that time, too. If I'd knocked him down, I'd have forgotten the whole thing in a couple of hours. But I didn't. And I haven't forgotten it."

"I have no use for violence, in any form," said Duff.

"Then you're lucky you weren't drafted," said Nolan. "There was quite a lot of violence around, in those Pacific islands."

We're getting nowhere, thought Duff, and a great im-

patience came over him, almost desperation. It was as if this were his last chance, and he could not seize it. He could not even seize upon the idea that had been forming in his mind before he had gone into the doctor's office.

"Think you could get hold of that girl, Nolan?" he asked. "I'd like another drink. A double. They're very small here."

Nolan rose promptly and went off to the door through which the girl had come. He stood there, speaking to someone invisible to Duff, and presently he came back to the table, with two little glasses of whiskey.

"Thanks," said Duff. "Sorry you won't take anything."

He took a few sips of neat whiskey, and he was beginning to feel better; his head was clearer. No more after today, he thought. I'll start on those pills tonight. Knockout drops . . . Of course, that's just a figure of speech. But there is something they call knockout drops. They put it into drinks, for sailors, and people like that.

"A man like Ferris . . ." he said. "Skulking into another man's house, behind his back. Hanging's too good for a fellow like that."

"I'd settle for hanging," said Nolan.

"I'd like to see him *disgraced!*" said Duff, hotly. "Publicly disgraced. Ruined. I'd like to see him caught in some compromising situation. Trapped."

Now it was said. His hand was shaking, and he started on the other little glass.

"That wouldn't be so easy," said Nolan.

"Why not? In his hotel, for instance . . ."

"I don't like the hotel," said Nolan. "Too many chances for a slip-up. And they might meet downstairs in the lounge. That happened before."

Duff finished the drink.

"There's the shack," he said.

A great relief came flooding through him, as if at last, after a long and desperate effort, he had remembered a forgotten and vitally necessary fact.

"That would be better," said Nolan. "Only that has drawbacks, too. We'd have to get *both* of them out there."

"Yes," said Duff. "That's almost impossible."

"Not impossible. Just hard."

"How could it be done?"

"Letters, maybe."

Duff's mind was cool and alert now.

"No," he said. "That means making two perfect forgeries."

"Forgeries don't have to be perfect," said Nolan. "It's not so hard to imitate anyone's handwriting, and you can count on the fact that it's not going to be studied. People don't notice much. Didn't you ever forge an excuse for absence or tardiness, when you were in school?"

"Never!" said Duff. "Never thought of such a thing."

"Plenty of kids get away with it," said Nolan. "Or there could be one letter and one telephone call."

"Disguised voice? No. That wouldn't work."

"Could work," said Nolan.

The dust looked golden in the shaft of sunlight; it was very pretty, Duff thought. He felt quiet, strong, relaxed, here with Nolan.

"Who'd get the note?" he asked.

"Ferris."

Gazing intently at the shimmering dust, Duff had something like a vision. He could see the shack, in the setting sun; a taxi drew up, and Reggie came out on the porch, not pale and strange, but happy, with her wide smile.

"It wouldn't be too hard to get them there," said Nolan, thoughtfully. "The trouble is, to keep them there."

131

"What?"

"As soon as they start talking, they'll know it's a frame-up."

"Of course," said Duff, stricken.

"But it could be worked," said Nolan. "Those pills of yours—"

"No!" said Duff, mechanically.

"If there was some whiskey left out . . ." said Nolan, as if talking to himself. "If it was well loaded . . . The Captain would never pass it up. He could be sound asleep when she got there."

"Then she'd leave, at once."

"Maybe she couldn't."

"What would stop her?"

"If the telephone didn't work, and she couldn't get a taxi—?"

"She'd walk. She'd see that something was wrong with the man, and she'd walk, to get help."

"Why wouldn't she just think he was drunk?"

"She wouldn't stay there with a drunken man. She feels very strongly about things like that."

He remembered that scene in the shack, when she had come into his room and picked up the glass of gin. Oh, Jake! she had cried. Anger rose and rose in him. Absolutely inexcusable meddling, he thought. She's *always* interfering, always knocking at the door . . . Now she wants to leave me, desert me, make a fool of me. Absolutely unwarranted. She's been giving *my* money to this man. She went to his hotel. And now she thinks she can walk out and leave me, for everyone to laugh at.

Well, she won't. She's not going to walk off, like a blameless victim. Only, my God, how complicated this is!

"It won't work," he said, bitterly.

"Oh, I think so," said Nolan. "It takes about two hours to drive out to the beach. If she took a little dose before she left the house, she'd be too sleepy when she got to the shack to go right out again."

"But don't you *see*—?" said Duff, angrily. "If they're to be found there together, they can't be drugged. How d'you think *that* would look? No. It's no good."

"I could turn on the gas," said Nolan.

"Good God!" cried Duff. "What are you saying?"

Their eyes met for a moment.

"I could turn on the gas," said Nolan, "and ten minutes later—before any harm was done—you could come along and find them, and turn it off. Suicide pact."

"They'd deny it."

"Who'd believe them?" asked Nolan.

"No," said Duff. "I couldn't do a thing like that."

"All right," said Nolan. "Look here! You've missed your train. The next one's at ten-twenty."

I can't go to the office, Duff thought. I'm sick. I've had too many drinks. I'll go—

"Where? Home!" he said to himself. I'll say I was taken ill, and I'll go to bed. I'll *make* her let me alone. I have every right in the world to go home, to my own house, whenever I feel like it.

But that white-faced, secret girl would not let him alone; he was sure of that. She wouldn't believe in his illness. She would come knocking at the door. She might even send for a doctor, without consulting him. Doctor Hearty, even.

And what if he was really ill? He would be helpless then, and she would find the empty bottles; she would find the wet clothes. She would disgrace him, ruin him. She would tell everyone that he had killed the old maniac and dragged him into the sea.

"I'd like to drive out into the country somewhere," he said. "Stop somewhere for lunch, and take it a little easy. If you've got enough gas—"

"I can get it," said Nolan.

Duff took up a paper napkin from the table and wiped his face.

"All right," he said, coldly.

Chapter Sixteen

At five o'clock he had a few more drinks. He had them, sitting at a little iron table, on the lawn outside a roadhouse fronting the Sound. Nolan sat with him, drinking another coke.

"No whiskey, thanks," Nolan said. "After a binge, it takes me two or three days to dry out, and then I'm all right."

"Two or three days?" Duff repeated. "I suppose they're pretty unpleasant . . . ?"

"Well, no," said Nolan. "But then I'm in pretty good shape."

"I'm not," said Duff. "Not at all. Along with this new diet I've got, I've been thinking of cutting out drinks. Or anyhow cutting down. One cocktail a day, maybe, before dinner."

Nolan said nothing. Duff glanced at him, to see if he was disapproving, but he looked as he always looked, vigorous, handsome and lively. No . . . Duff said to himself. I'll try that. I'll 'dry out,' as he calls it for three or at least two days, and just see . . .

"We'd better be going," he said.

"All right," said Nolan. "D'you want me to go ahead with the plan?"

"Well . . . I suppose so," said Duff.

"I've got to have the green light," said Nolan. "I couldn't be left holding the bag."

"Very well," said Duff. "Mind you, I don't think it will work. I don't think either of them will go to the shack."

"We'll see," said Nolan.

They drove home, through the fresh Spring country-side, and Duff went to sleep in the back of the car. He waked, with the sweet cool air in his face and he felt sad, very sad, but resigned.

When he entered the house, Reggie and Jay were coming down the stairs, hand in hand. There's entirely too damn much of that, he thought. Why doesn't she let the child alone?

"Jay, go and kiss your daddy," said Reggie.

"I think we'll shake hands, Jay," said Duff. "You're getting a bit old for this kissing and holding hands and so on."

He held out his hand, but before Jay took it, he glanced over his shoulder at Reggie, as if seeking her approval. She's got the child entirely away from me, he thought. We never have any good times together any more, no little jokes, nothing of that sort.

"You run along and see if your nice supper's ready, honey," said Reggie.

With all his heart Duff resented her air of authority, and his son's ready acceptance of it. Still in his hat and light overcoat, he stood looking at Reggie, the woman he had put in Helen's place. She was wearing a sheer black blouse with long sleeves and a design of gold leaves round the collar.

"Why are you wearing so much black lately?" he asked. "It doesn't suit you."

136

"Aunt Lou picked this out," she said.

"I've got to call Aunt Lou at once," he said, and went in to the telephone.

Mrs. Albany was at home.

"Aunt Lou," he said, "can I see you tomorrow afternoon?"

"Yes, yes," she said. "I'll be here from four o'clock on. Is it anything special, Jacob? You sound—upset."

"Yes," he answered. "It is something special, Aunt Lou."

He hoped that Reggie was still in the hall and could hear him; he hoped that his portentous tone would worry her. When he hung up the telephone, he saw her out there. It seemed to him that he was always seeing her like that, standing in a hall, waiting, pale and secret.

"Jake," she said, "can we talk about my going away?"

"Now?" he demanded, outraged. "The moment I set foot in the house?"

"I know. But there never seems to be a time—"

"I've been trying to make certain arrangements today," he said. "If you can endure your sufferings a day or two longer—"

"Couldn't I go and stay in a hotel while you're fixing things up?"

"Regina," he said, "I happen to be rather ill. I saw the doctor today—again. I'd intended to go to bed at once and have a tray sent up. Unless you insist upon it, I'd like to postpone this discussion."

"All right," she said. "I'm sorry you don't feel well."

But there was a look, an air of indifference about her he had never seen before. She doesn't care whether I live or die, he thought, and it frightened him.

"Is there anything for me to read?" he asked, briefly.

That was another thing Helen had done; she had got

137

him books out of the lending-library; she had taken the trouble to learn what he liked.

"Well, I got two books out yesterday," Reggie said. "One's about the Japanese, and one's about famous operas."

"Scarcely what I want at the moment," he said, with a faint smile, and went up the stairs.

Damned hypocrisy, for her to get books like that, he thought. I doubt if she even tries to read them, but if she does, she couldn't understand them. She'll never improve in any way. She'll never learn how to behave, how to speak, how to dress.

He locked his door and stood near it, frowning, wondering if he should take a drink. He felt depressed beyond measure, sick with weariness and sadness. A drink *might* help me, he thought, but it doesn't always. Not by any means. You—can't count on it.

That was a bad thing, a serious thing. He had used to be able to count on three or four drinks making him feel good, but now—

There was a knock at the door.

Damn it! he cried to himself. There she is again!

"What *is* it?" he shouted.

"I've brought you some books," said Miss Castle's voice, and he unlocked the door.

"Mrs. Duff told me you were looking for something light to read," she said, with a nice air of concern. "I'd just bought some paper books to send to my nephews overseas. Perhaps there'd be something here to amuse you."

She had six little books with her; she *wanted* him to be amused; she was concerned about him. She looked charming, he thought, in her grey dress, with her shining hair, her fresh color; there was a hint of some clean, artless perfume about her.

138

"This is very kind of you," he said. "Very!"

"I hope you'll have a good night's rest, Mr. Duff," she said.

She left him with a feeling of great solace, of being cherished and valued. He did not want a drink now; he took a shower and got into bed; he felt like a convalescent in his clean blue pajamas. It gave him a sense of blamelessness to leave the door unlocked.

Mary brought him a tray. Helen would have brought it herself, he thought. So would Miss Castle. But not Reggie. Reggie doesn't care whether I live or die.

One of the little books was an anthology of short stories such as he had never read, stories about men getting to other planets by rocket, stories of strange new races with new powers, stories of people projected into other eras, other dimensions. He was enthralled. Leisurely, and reading all the while, he ate a better meal than he had for weeks and weeks.

And no drinks, he thought. This is what I need. Peace and quiet. He got out the bottle of yellow capsules the doctor had prescribed. One at bedtime. Repeat in one hour if needed. He had never taken anything of this sort in his life, and it interested him profoundly. I mean to say, he thought, what will the symptoms be? He had read about people taking opium and floating into blissful dreams. It might be like that, he thought. But, on the other hand, it might be unpleasant. Dizziness? Or they might not work at all, for him.

I'll wait until ten o'clock, he told himself. Mary came to fetch the tray, and he went on reading those curious stories. This was, in its way, the most curious evening in his life. Nobody came near him; he heard no voices, no footsteps. There he lay, clean, innocent, not drinking, not

wanting to drink, waiting to take the strange yellow capsule.

At ten o'clock he got a glass of water and swallowed the thing. I'll go quietly on reading, he thought, until something happens . . . He went quietly on reading, and nothing happened. He was growing drowsy, but not in any unusual way. At eleven o'clock he took a second capsule, and within ten minutes he.was yawning until tears ran down his face.

It certainly works, he said to himself, laughing, and turned out the light.

It was eight o'clock when he woke. Good God! he said to himself. Nine hours' sleep. I haven't had that much for years. I feel—wonderful. Never felt better in my life.

It was the beginning of a new era for him; he knew that. Now that I've cut out drinking, he thought, everything will be very different. Two or three days to 'dry out' . . . Four o'clock today will be twenty-four hours. Four o'clock? What's about four o'clock? Oh, yes. Aunt Lou.

The burden descended upon him again, all the complexities, the menaces. It was even worse now, when he felt so well and clear-headed. If Reggie chose to tell about the old maniac, it would mean very serious trouble. Why didn't I call the police myself? he thought, appalled. I couldn't have done a worse thing than—what I did. Now, if the body's found and if Reggie talks, it will look—

It would look like murder. What he had actually done was perfectly simple, justifiable, and right. The man had attacked him, and he had defended himself. I think I hit him twice, but that doesn't matter. What does matter is, that I—disposed of him in that way. I acted like a guilty man. Like a murderer.

There were still the wet clothes in the bag, and the rid-

140

ing-crop, and this morning he could see clearly the danger they were to him. Someone else might turn up, he thought. Somebody might have turned up already, somebody who knew Paul had been going to the shack. Then the police would come, to ask him if the old man had ever got there. And if he said no, there would be Reggie to say yes. They would search the house, and they would find the wet clothes and the crop.

How can I explain? he thought, in growing panic. Good God! Everything I've done is what a murderer would have done. Good God! *That's* what drink does for you . . . I've got to handle this properly, or it means—absolute ruin.

If it wasn't for Reggie, he thought, I could manage. I'd get rid of the clothes and the crop, and then I'd deny everything. Say I'd never set eyes on the man. After all, I'm not simply a nobody. I have a certain standing in the community. My word would mean something. But if my own wife goes back on me . . .

That's what she intends to do. And she knows I know that. That's why she's afraid of me. Locks her door. Wants to go away to a hotel. And then tell the police. She's afraid of me, because she knows I know she's going to betray me. Well, how can I stop her?

His hands were shaking, sweat broke out on his forehead, back came the nausea, all the old cycle, all over again. Just when the new, bright, hopeful life was about to begin.

If I could have this one day free and clear, he thought, I could manage. Nolan will have to arrange that thing for tonight. Then by tomorrow she'll be so thoroughly discredited that nothing she says will matter.

If she tries to betray me then, everyone will think it's sheer spite and malice. Which it is. But I haven't *got* today

141

free and clear. Suppose the police come today—before I've got rid of that bag? Oh, God! I didn't want to take any more drinks. I was feeling so well . . . But I've got to.

He took only two jiggers, and it helped him. I'll take that bag to the office, he thought. And if I can get Reggie out of the house . . . But she's got to get the telephone message. All right. She'll get the message early; that can be fixed. Then I'll get her away from the house, so that if the police come, she won't be here, and the bag won't be here.

His brain was working well. He brought out the direful bag, he locked the closet door on all the bottles, full and empty, and went downstairs. There was the usual group at the table: Miss Castle and Reggie and Jay.

"I hope you had a good night's rest, Mr. Duff," Miss Castle said.

A damn fine woman. A real woman.

"Thanks, yes," he said, smiling at her. "And it's such a fine day . . . Reggie, how would you like to make a little excursion to Rio Park? There's some sort of circus there, I understand. Nolan could drive you down; he says he has enough gas. You could have your lunch at the Casino and then he'd pick you up, you and Miss Castle and Jay."

"Quite a treat!" said Miss Castle.

"Thank you, Jake," said Reggie. "Only it's my day at the hospital."

"Can't you postpone it?"

"Reggie, pos'pone it!" cried Jay. "Reggie, please! I *want* to go to the circus!"

"You can go with Miss Castle, honey."

"I want you," said Jay. "Pos'pone it, can't you, for goodness *sakes*?" He jumped up from his chair, with that

feverish excitement so distasteful to Duff. "Reggie, *please!*"

"Well, all right, honey," she said, reluctantly. "I guess I can go to the hospital tomorrow."

Oh, no, you won't, thought Duff. I know you're an angel of mercy, and a saint. But you won't be, tomorrow.

"Good!" he said. "Then Nolan will come back for you in—say an hour?"

"Quite a treat!" said Miss Castle, again.

She was pleased; she appreciated it when he planned a little outing for his household. He gave her another smile as he rose, but the smile stiffened on his lips at the thought that came to him. If she ever knew . . . he thought. In the hall he picked up that bag, and it seemed to him that forever and ever he had been carrying a bag filled with something shameful and dangerous. Forever and ever he had been going from one place to another, in search of rest, of peace.

Nolan was waiting for him in the driveway.

"Can you see to it that she gets the telephone message before ten?" he asked.

"Why not?" said Nolan.

"But suppose you can't get hold of Ferris, to give him the note?"

"I'll find him. You want it fixed for tomorrow?"

"Tonight."

"Tomorrow would be better. Give us more time."

"It has to be tonight," said Duff, curtly.

"Why?" Nolan asked.

Even Nolan would turn against him, Duff thought, if he knew what was in that bag.

"I might have to go to Washington tomorrow, on business," he said.

143

"Well, I guess we can manage," said Nolan. "Got the pills?"

"I forgot them," said Duff. "I'll have to go back."

"You can leave your bag here," said Nolan.

Duff pretended not to hear him. He dared not leave that bag with Nolan, with anyone. He went back into the house, past the dining-room where those three still sat at the table, up the stairs to his own room. Everything he had to do was laborious and painful; his body felt heavy as lead.

He got into the car again and Nolan drove off.

"I said you'd come back in an hour and drive them to Rio Park," Duff said.

"What did you do that for? I've got to get that note to Ferris, and all the rest of it."

"I didn't realize . . ." said Duff. "Jay was very anxious to see the circus they've got there."

It seemed to him the final misfortune that he could no longer be easy and safe with Nolan. When they had been talking yesterday, he had never once thought of old Paul, but now, with the bag at his feet, he realized that Nolan too could be a menace.

"Well, I dare say I can manage," said Nolan. "But I'll have to have more money for gas."

Duff handed him three ten dollar bills and the bottle of capsules.

"Take what you want and give me back the bottle," he said.

"I will," said Nolan, and put the bottle into his pocket.

"You might as well give me the bottle now."

"I can't carry the things loose in my pocket. I'll give you the bottle later."

He drove on for a time.

144

"I'll leave them at the Park," he said, "and then I'll call at your office for the note."

"What note?"

"The note you're going to write to Captain Ferris."

"*I* can't do that!" said Duff. "You'll have to do it, Nolan."

"I've got an envelope here that she addressed to Ferris and threw away, and here's part of a letter she started. It's an easy hand to imitate."

"I tell you I can't do it! You'd make an infinitely better job of it."

"Well, no," said Nolan. "I don't want to."

"Why? I thought it was understood that you'd do it."

"I'll tell you why," said Nolan. "I don't want to be the guy who does it all, the fake telephone call, the note, the pills, all of it. We've got to be in this together."

"I can't do it."

"All right. We'll call it off."

I can't call it off, Duff thought. I've got to see that Reggie's thoroughly discredited, before the police come. It doesn't matter how much I don't like this, how tired I am, how damn sick I am. I've got to go through with this.

"Nolan," he said, in a sort of heavy desperation, "I'm simply not able to do this. I'm—not very well. My hand isn't steady."

"Then we can wait."

"All right," said Duff, after a time. "Give me the envelope and go on. I'll try."

Nolan reached the papers back to him.

"You're going to put a couple of those pills in a whiskey bottle out at the shack . . ." Duff said. "But how are you going to manage with the—other?"

"You'll telephone and say you won't be home tonight. She'll have got Captain Ferris's telephone message, and

145

she'll jump at the chance. She'll get me to drive her to the station for the seven-forty, and on the way I'll stop and get a couple of cokes."

"Suppose she doesn't want one?"

"She'll drink it anyhow, out of politeness, if I bring it to her."

"Have you ever done that before?"

"Plenty of times," Nolan answered.

That's my wife, Duff thought. He could picture her, at some roadside stand, drinking out of a bottle through a straw. With his chauffeur.

"Suppose she goes to sleep before she gets to the shack? On the train?" he asked.

"Someone will wake her up. She's only going to get one pill. That won't knock her out. Only make her drowsy, too drowsy to go out of the place, once she gets there."

"Are you sure?"

"Sure enough."

"If anything goes wrong . . ." said Duff.

"Then they can talk about a big plot against them," said Nolan. "But nobody's going to believe them. And even if you admitted it was a frame-up, it wouldn't be too bad for you. You wanted to be sure they were meeting each other, that's all. The injured husband always gets sympathy."

Only Nolan doesn't know about old Paul, Duff thought. He doesn't know what Reggie could do to me, if she wanted.

Chapter Seventeen

He bought a pint of rye and put it into his overcoat pocket; he went to a hotel near the Grand Central and got a room for twenty-four hours. He registered as Harold Carlton, from Buffalo, without thinking at all about it. He tipped the bellboy and locked himself in, to write that note.

But he could not use the hotel letterhead; he had to go out again at once, to buy some plain paper. Every detail was so laborious, so painful. He bought a box in a drugstore and, coming back, he laid out the envelope and the letter Nolan had given him.

Dear Wilfred
    I am so sorry about

"I cannot do this!" he cried to himself. "I don't know what to say. I can't do it!"

All initiative, all power, mental and physical, had drained away from him. He could not think. He could scarcely move his heavy limbs. He put his head down on his folded arms and cried.

But if this thing did not happen tonight, the other thing would happen. The police would come, or Reggie would go to them. I've got to get *rid* of this damn bag! he told

himself, with a sob. I've got to get *out* of this. I've got to be done with this.

He hated and dreaded the thought of a drink, but he had to try one, to see if it would give him a little strength and clarity. It nearly made him sick, but he got it down, and in a few moments he felt surprisingly better. I'll have to have courage, he thought. And it would have to be quick courage. He could not count on it; it might go, as fast as it had come.

He made a draft first.

Dear Wilfred:
  Something has happened that I have got to talk to you about. I have fixed things so that I will be alone in the shack at Driftwood Beach tonight. Please come by nine o'clock. It is honestly terribly important.
  In haste,
  Reggie

That'll do, he thought. That sounds like her. 'Honestly terribly important.' He was pleased with himself. Then he tried to copy it, in writing like hers, even a little like hers. He could not. His unsteady hand made an almost illegible scrawl.

He tried again and again, but he could not.

She knows how to type, he thought, suddenly. I'll take it to the office and type it.

He got into a taxi, with that damn bag. Every detail so laborious, so painful.

"Going away?" Hanbury asked him.

"Oh, no!" he said. "Just some things my wife wanted me to get. Easiest way to carry them."

He went into his office, where Miss Fuller sat typing.

"I'd like to use your machine for a few minutes, Miss Fuller," he said.

"Can't I do it for you?" she asked.

"No, thanks, just a little personal note," he answered.

He had to do this, with Miss Fuller in the room. He didn't know how to type. He made mistakes. And when he pulled a sheet out of the machine, he dared not throw it away; he had to put it into his pocket. He sat there, sweating, pecking at the keys, horribly aware of his queerness in the eyes of Miss Fuller.

"Your chauffeur is here, Mr. Duff," she said.

"Tell him to wait," said Duff.

He got the thing done. He addressed an envelope, and spoiled it, a second, a third; his pockets were stuffed with crumpled paper.

"Send Nolan in, will you, please, Miss Fuller?" he said.

There was something unhuman, he thought, about Nolan's alert vitality.

"Oh, you typed it?" Nolan said.

"I couldn't manage the other way."

"Let's have a look," said Nolan, and took it out of the envelope. "Well, you signed it, anyhow," he said. "Now then. He'll be there by nine, and she'll get there around ten. That gives him time to take his little drink. A little after ten, I'll turn on the gas. Ten minutes later, you'll come by, and you'll look in the window. Then you'll drive somewhere, fast, and call the police. Say there are two people in there, apparently unconscious."

"How will you turn on the gas?"

"I'll just reach in the kitchen window. The stove's right there."

"Nolan . . . The gas might—"

"Not in that short time. And they'll probably have some windows open."

"But if they're not asleep?"

149

"They will be."

"You're damn sure of yourself," said Duff, angrily.

"I have a right to be," said Nolan. "I haven't had many failures in my life."

"It's a dangerous thing, to be so cocksure."

"Could be," said Nolan. "Now there's this. Are you able to drive yourself for a few miles?"

"What d'you mean 'able to'?" Duff demanded.

"No offence," said Nolan. "You could rent a car at the filling-station at the beach and you could park outside the railroad station, until you see me go by, in your car. I'll give you a signal." He made a V with two fingers. "You give it back to me. Then you'll know I'm on my way, to turn on the gas. Give me ten minutes' start, and then you drive along to the shack. Right?"

"But if they're not asleep, and you don't turn on the gas?"

"Then you'll meet me coming back and I'll tell you."

"I ought to meet you anyhow."

"No. Because when I've turned on the gas, I'll go on past the shack and back to Vandenbrinck by the new highway. I don't want to be noticed."

"When I telephone the police, I suppose I'll have to say that something had made me suspicious . . . ?"

"God, no!" said Nolan. "Don't say who you are. You're just someone passing by. You've lost your way, and you saw a light in the shack, and you stopped, to ask for directions. When you look in the window, and smell the gas, you're worried, so, like a good citizen, you call up the police."

"Where can I telephone from?"

"Filling-station, drug-store, anywhere."

150

It was disgusting, to be obliged to turn to Nolan for advice all the time.

"You're sure there's no danger from the gas?"

"Not if you come along, ten minutes after me."

Miss Fuller came in and out, but that did not trouble Nolan. Nothing troubled him. All the monstrous burden lay upon Duff, with his damn bag, his shaking hands, his misery and fear.

"Would you like to clear up this WMC thing, Mr. Duff?" asked Miss Fuller.

"Not now," said Duff. "I'm going out to lunch now."

"You're early today," she said.

He looked at his watch and it was only quarter past eleven. Everything he did was queer. He knew that . . . And his worst ordeal still lay before him—his visit to Mrs. Albany. I've got to pull myself together for that, he thought. Only, could he pull himself together better by taking more drinks, or by not taking any? I don't know . . . he thought. I don't know.

He was sure enough that he could not eat any lunch. He did not know where to go, or what to do with himself, until four o'clock. Back to the hotel room, which was still his? No, he thought. I couldn't stand it. Couldn't sit there alone. I want to be where there are people around.

The only places where there were people around, yet where you were not bothered and questioned, were bars. I could have a beer, he thought. That's nourishing.

He had to take the damn bag with him and, to his dismay, tears came into his eyes while he was riding down in the elevator. This won't do! he thought. I'm in a bad state. This whole thing is a strain. He put his hand into his pocket, for a handkerchief, and there was all that

crumpled paper. It's—just too damn much! he thought, compressing his quivering lips.

He walked, carrying the bag, downtown, at random, until he came to a bar he had never seen before. He had two double whiskies there, and then he took a taxi uptown to the hotel. When he got out of the cab, he was very unsteady on his feet. He knew that, for the first time in many years, he must appear obviously, grossly drunk. And yet—I'm not! he thought. I can take twice—three times that much, and not show it. It's—this other thing . . .

When he got into the bleak, neat hotel room, he lay down on the bed, still in his hat and light overcoat; he buried his face in the pillow and cried for a time, and then he went to sleep.

When he waked, the magic refreshment had taken place again. He turned over on his side, and felt for cigarettes in one pocket after another, and met with all that crumpled paper. That could be coped with here, in peace and quiet. He lit a cigarette and looked at his watch, and he was shocked to find that it was after four.

He got up; he tore the papers into small scraps and flushed them away. He washed in cold water, combed his hair; he looked narrowly in the mirror at his tired, ruddy face; then he picked up the damn bag and went downstairs.

A thin rain was falling as he came out into the street. "Taxi," he said to the doorman.

"I'll do the best I can, mister," said the doorman.

Duff did not like to be called mister; he felt a strong dislike for this man. There was something impudent in his swarthy face; in his light-blue overcoat, much too big for him, he had the look of a swaggering old soldier from a

Napoleonic campaign. A stream of traffic was rushing past, one taxi after another, dozens and dozens of taxis. But none of them stopped and all that fellow did was to blow his silly whistle.

"Go up to the corner," said Duff, frowning. "Then you can get them coming two ways."

"It isn't no better at the corner," said the doorman.

"Of course it is!" said Duff. "When the cabs come past here, they're running on a light. Go up to the corner. I'm in a hurry."

"Well, you're not the only one," said the swarthy door-man.

"*What!*" said Duff. "Don't talk to me like that."

The man shrugged his shoulders inside his big coat, and blew his silly whistle. Duff stood rigid, struggling against the fury that shook him. He wanted to knock that fellow down, to kick him, to yell at him. No! he told himself. No! You can't do that. It's—not a good thing, to feel like this. Upsets you. Take it easy.

A taxi drew up before the hotel and two women got out. As the doorman came toward them with his big umbrella, Duff got into the cab and slammed the door. He gave the driver the address of Mrs. Albany's hotel. If only she'll understand . . . he thought. If only she'll take my side, wholeheartedly.

A black anxiety filled him. Her approval was vital to him, indispensable. And she's so damn stubborn, he thought. She's got it into her head that Reggie's an angel, and facts won't bother her. Just now, when I need her, she's as likely as not to be pig-headed and critical and utterly unsympathetic.

She opened the door of the suite herself.

"Well?" she said, looking at him with bright sharp eyes.

"Well . . ." he echoed, with a sigh, and set down the bag.

"Are you going away, Jacob?" she asked.

"No," he answered. "I had a lot of papers and so on to carry, and this seemed the handiest way. I'm sorry I'm late, Aunt Lou."

"You didn't mention any special time, Jacob. Sit down and light a cigarette. There'll be tea in a few moments. You look tired."

"I've had a shock," he said.

"Some friend overseas, Jacob?"

"No," he said. "No. It's Reggie."

Glancing at her, he could see her inward resistance expressed in the set of her thin lips, and a sort of desperation came over him.

"It's no use!" he cried. "I wanted to tell you . . . I'm so damn miserable, I don't know which way to turn. I've been through . . . I couldn't tell you. It's no use, anyhow. You've made up your mind already not to believe anything against Reggie."

"No . . ." she said. "It's simply that you're not just and fair toward her, Jacob. You've got tired of her—and when you're tired of people, you're inclined to be ruthless, Jacob."

"'Ruthless' . . . That's a nice word," he said, somberly. "I can't recall that I've ever injured anyone in my life."

"You've hurt a great many people, Jacob."

"All right!" he said. "It's no use. I'm 'ruthless'. Anything you like. No good."

"I never said that, Jacob."

"You think it. You don't believe I'm capable of any

154

feeling. You don't believe I could be hurt—miserable—just about at the end of my tether."

"Tell me about it, Jacob."

"It's no use!"

"Come now!" she said, with a sort of kindly severity. "The only thing I *don't* like and *don't* believe is the nasty, spiteful gossip you listen to about the poor girl. If there were anything serious—"

"Probably you won't think it's serious. It's simply that she's been seeing this man under my roof while I'm in the office. And she's given him a thousand dollars—of my money."

"Jacob! Are you sure?"

"I'm so sure that I looked at her check-book stubs. I suppose I shouldn't have done that. I should have had 'faith' in her."

"Who is the man?"

"Some Englishman. Ferris."

"Oh . . . Captain Ferris?"

"Why? D'you know the name?"

"I've heard Jay speak of him. An Army officer, isn't he?"

"So I've been told. I haven't had the pleasure of meeting Captain Ferris. He doesn't call when I'm at home."

"Have you spoken to Reggie about this, Jacob?"

"I have not. She'd deny everything. There'd be a scene."

"She must have a chance to defend herself, Jacob."

"I'm going to give her a chance," he said.

Rose came in, with the tea.

"Muffins," said Mrs. Albany. "With real butter. You like muffins, Jacob."

"Thank you," he said.

Mrs. Albany and Rose exchanged a glance of infinite

155

complicity; they looked, Duff thought, like two under-ground workers communicating, and he did not believe in the real butter.

"How are you giving Reggie a chance, Jacob?" she asked, when Rose had gone.

"In a way you won't like," he said. "You won't think it's gentlemanly."

"Tell me, Jacob."

"I'm telephoning her that I won't be home tonight. But I am going home, later, and I hope to meet Captain Ferris."

"Oh, Jacob! Jacob! In your own home, with your son there? An open scandal, Jacob?"

"That's what I want," he said. "I've gone through such hell . . . You wouldn't believe it. No one would. But *I've* known, for a long time what she is. She's a cheap, slovenly, lying little bitch."

"Jacob!"

"That stands," he said.

"Eat a muffin, Jacob, with real butter."

"Sorry, but I can't. I haven't been able to eat anything for days. I saw another doctor this morning—but doctors can't help me, in a thing like this. Don't tell me it's all my own fault. I know it. I know I shouldn't have married a little tramp I picked up in a cheap restaurant. But she looked like a saint, and I believed she was one. So did you."

"Jacob, try not to be so bitter."

"What else could I be? I suppose the whole neighbor-hood's known about this Ferris for weeks, months. They've been laughing at me."

"But don't do it this way, Jacob. Get a lawyer. Get

156

Harold Mallinger. He'll advise you. But don't have a scandal in your own house."

"It'll be a lesson for Jay. When he's old enough to marry, he'll think twice before he picks out a girl like that."

"Jacob, stay away from home. I'll go out there, and I'll talk to Miss Castle—"

"No," he said. "I'll handle this myself, my own way."

She was greatly distressed, and that was balm to him. That made him feel strong, quiet, confident.

"I don't like it, Jacob," she said. "Setting a trap—"

"Don't you think I have a right to set a trap for the man who's stolen my wife—and my money?"

"Well . . ." she said, and was silent for a time, her thin hands clasped in her lap. And she's not blaming me, he thought. She can see for herself it's the right course for me to take.

"Of course," she said, presently, "in a way, you've brought it on yourself, Jacob. You've neglected Reggie—"

"And that justifies her for *this*?" he cried.

"No . . ." said Mrs. Albany. "No. But give her the benefit of the doubt, Jacob. If you don't find this Captain Ferris in the house—"

"Then I'll see a lawyer. All I want is to feel that you're standing by me."

"I wish you'd do this another way," she said. "Especially on Jay's account. But—yes, I'm standing by you, Jacob."

"That's all I want," he said, with a deep sigh.

He rose, and she rose, too; he kissed her on the temple. She was his conscience, and when she gave her approval, the whole weight of dread and wretchedness was lifted from his spirit.

"You won't use violence toward this Ferris, Jacob?"

"I don't promise not to kick him out of my house."

"Whatever you do, Jacob, think of Jay."

"I will."

"You're forgetting your bag, Jacob."

Suddenly he thought of the solution.

"May I leave it here for a while?" he asked. "There are some rather confidential papers in it, and so on."

"I'll look after it," said Mrs. Albany.

So that burden, too, was gone. It was the one right thing to do; she was the one person to be trusted without reservations. If he had left it half open, she would never even have glanced into it.

I've got the green light now, he thought, as he left her. I'm all right now.

Chapter Eighteen

He bought newspapers and magazines and took them to the hotel room; he ordered his dinner from room service. He ate fairly well, and he took no drinks and wanted none.

When he had finished eating, he sat in an easychair under a lamp by the open window and read. He felt quietly composed and resolute. I've got the green light, he told himself. Aunt Lou saw that. I'm doing the right thing. The only thing.

He had left behind him all that wretched life of empty bottles, of fearsome bags, all that confusion and suffering. He was free now, a man of dignity and independence. It's possible, he thought, in fact, it's very likely that I'll never see Reggie again after tonight. I certainly shan't allow her to come back to the house where my son is.

He was not nervous, not impatient. He kept track of the time, and when the moment came to go, he rose. The pint bottle of whiskey was half-empty, and he decided to leave it, and buy a new one. It was a splendid symbol of his new freedom that he could do this, simply walk off and leave a bottle here; no more of that hiding, locking bags and doors.

He got into the train for Driftwood Beach. It was almost empty at this hour and this time of the year, but it was

possible that the conductor or some of the passengers might recognize him. Let them. Let them observe how very grave he was, a man upon a stern errand.

I had received information, from a source I don't care to divulge, that my wife had arranged to meet her lover in my house at the beach. I went there, with the intention of either proving or disproving the rumors I had heard. But no, he thought. No. A gentleman wouldn't admit that.

He envisaged himself standing before a judge and jury, and speaking, gravely and sternly. Mr. Duff, said the judge, or a lawyer, or someone: up to this time, had your marriage been a happy one?

A. My marriage was at no time a happy one.

Q. You mean that there were frequent quarrels?

A. There were no quarrels.

Q. In what way was your marriage unhappy, Mr. Duff?

A. I prefer not to answer that question.

Q. Were your marital relations with your wife normal and satisfactory?

A. (reluctantly) We had not lived together as man and wife for some months.

Driftwood Beach! Driftwood Beach! called the conductor, and Duff opened his eyes. Automatically he looked up at the rack for that bag, and again sighed with relief to realize it was gone.

When he got out at the dim and quiet little station there was a wind blowing from the sea, cool and salt, a tonic for the spirits. He walked leisurely across the road to the filling-station and into the brightly-lit room with a lunch counter. A man in shirtsleeves sat there, reading a newspaper.

"Yes?" he said, looking up.

"I'd like to rent a car for a couple of hours," said Duff.

160

"Couldn't do it," said the man, a young man with a broad, turned-up nose.

"My name is Duff," said Duff.

"Well, I can't help what your name is," said the other. "We don't rent cars no more."

"Where's the owner of this place?"

"Home."

"Get him on the telephone. He knows me."

"Hasn't got a telephone."

"See here!" said Duff. "I own a cottage here, and I want to drive out there to see about something."

"You could get a taxi."

"I want a car to drive myself."

"We don't rent them out no more. Don't you know there's a war on?"

"Look here! I told you my name was Duff. Jacob Duff. I'm a property owner here. Everyone knows me."

"Well, I don't," said the young man. "You could get a taxi."

"Look here! I want to hire a car for a couple of hours. I've got the money to pay a proper deposit and I've got gas coupons. I'm a responsible person; anyone here will vouch for me—"

"Well, I don't see why you'd want a car," said the young man. "A taxi—"

"I'm not accustomed to being questioned," said Duff.

"Ain't that a shame?" said the young man, tilting back in his chair.

Damn scum! thought Duff, struggling with his rising fury. But he could not afford to be angry; the time was getting short.

"Look here!" he said. "I'll *buy* one of your damn cars, and sell it back to you in a couple of hours."

"Couldn't do it. You got no priority."

"If you know anyone who'll rent me a car for two hours," said Duff, "I'll pay you a commission. Twenty-five dollars." He saw no interest in the other's face. "Fifty dollars," he said.

"You must want it bad," said the other.

"Oh, go to hell!" cried Duff. "I'll borrow a car—from the druggist—the grocer, someone."

"You go to hell yourself," said the other. But he was wavering. "You got the cash to pay?"

"I'll give you a check. That's good enough."

"Says you."

The effort to control his rage had given Duff a sharp headache. His hands were beginning to tremble, all that precious composure was going, all of it. The details were so laborious and painful. Better to give it up . . . ?

"If Mr. Hilley will okay your check," said the other, "I'll leave you take my own car."

"All right. Get Mr. Hilley."

"I can't leave here. You go see him."

"Who is he?"

"Thought you knew everybody here."

"I don't remember the names of the local people."

"Well, he's the druggist, on the opposite corner. You go see him, and he could give me a ring."

The whole thing had started again, the shaking, the nausea, the intolerable tension. Duff walked round to the side of the filling-station, and, in a dark spot, took the new pint bottle he had bought out of his pocket.

But he put it back again. If I smell of whiskey, he thought, maybe that fellow won't let me take his car. I've got to *truckle* to him. But this Summer, when we come

162

down here to stay, I'll see that he gets what's coming to him. And a little over.

There was small comfort in that. He wanted direct action now. I want to knock him out of that chair, he thought. I want to teach him a lesson. But he had to forego that; he had to fight down his fury, and sickness, and walk quietly across the road.

Mr. Hilley, the druggist, was soothing. His pleasant, sheeplike face was not familiar to Duff, who was not in the habit of observing people carefully, but he knew Mr. Duff, and greatly admired him. He telephoned at once to the man in the filling-station.

"So you're worrying about *Mr. Duff's* check?" he said. "That's a good one! Why, Elmer, Mr. Duff's check's as good as United States greenbacks. Mr. Duff's been coming down here Summers for five, six years and he's—What say? Certainly! Any amount."

Duff had to go back to that Elmer, had to pay him, had to take his car. It made him sick. God! What a world we live in! he said to himself. When a reputable citizen like myself has to truckle to a fellow like that . . .

It was a cheap, shabby little sedan, a make he had never driven before. And now he was nervous about his driving. He had not driven himself for a long time, and it seemed to him that his eyesight was not what it had been. The wheel was stiff, and his hands seemed curiously weak. He wanted a drink.

He drove the car across the road and parked in the circular drive outside the railroad station. The wind blew steadily, and the village had a queer look, too empty. The thing is, he thought, would a drink make me better—or worse? He did not know the answer. It might make him

better, it might make him sleepy, it might make him sick. He didn't *know*. I'll wait, he thought. Later on, if it gets too bad . . .

And then Nolan went by, slowing up a little under the arc light; his arm came out, he raised two fingers in a V-sign, and Duff returned the signal.

This is it, Duff said to himself. He looked at his watch, kept his eyes on it. Give Nolan ten minutes' start. No more. Then I'll follow. I'll look in the window and see them lying there, and I'll telephone the police. Then it will be over.

The ten minutes went by, and he started the car. It's a straight road all the way, he told himself, and very little traffic. Nothing to be nervous about. Except that it's a stinking little car . . . But just drive straight ahead, and in a few moments it will all be over.

It would not be over. Reggie could talk. She could tell about the old maniac. Let her. He would deny that he had ever set eyes on him, and there would be nothing against him but the word of a guilty, discredited wife.

And if she told about the bogus telephone call? If Ferris produced the bogus letter? All right! Let them! *Let them.* If I'm forced to, I'll admit I set a trap for them. When a man has good reason to believe that his wife is deceiving him, he's completely justified—

It was as if a light came on in his mind, a cold white glare. He did not believe that Reggie was deceiving him. If she was in that house with Ferris, it was only through a cruel trick. She had only to speak and everyone would believe her. Everyone.

He could see her, standing before Aunt Lou.

"I saw him kill that poor old man. He struck him down,

164

and then, when he was struggling to get up, he held him and struck him again.

"He hated me, but he would not let me go free. He forged my name to a letter. He gave Nolan a drug to make me helpless. He wanted to destroy me. He wanted to kill me."

The car swerved wildly, and nearly smashed into a tree. Duff shut off the engine and leaned forward, coughing. He was choking; he could not draw any air into his lungs. His neck swelled; there was a frightful pressure in the back of his head. O God . . . This is it . . .

This is dying, he said. He tried to get the bottle out of his overcoat pocket, coughing, choking, shaking from head to foot. He got it out, and he could not unscrew the top. With those horrible, uncontrollable hands, he knocked the neck of the bottle against the window-frame, but too feebly. He tried again, and broke it; he took a swallow and coughed and threw it up. He took another swallow and he kept that down. He was still coughing, but between the spasms he could swallow.

He leaned back, gasping, taking a sip from time to time. I've got to hurry, he thought. Got to get over this. Got to hurry.

But he could not move, just yet. The budding trees rustled overhead, and he could hear the sea running up on the sands and draining back, with the labored sound of his own breathing.

He drank, and waited; he drank, and waited. Then at last the thing that had seized him let go. With a great, loud sigh, he threw the broken bottle out of the window and started the car.

How long had that thing, that attack lasted? Never

165

mind. Go ahead, do the best you can. Heart attack? I don't know. I feel very weak, very cold . . . It was a dreadful thing, whatever it was.

He did not dare to drive fast, with his hands so weak and unsteady. But he got there. He stopped the car and got out; he started down the wooden steps to the beach. He could not hurry here; he had to go carefully, holding tight to the rail.

When he got down to the beach, he was shocked to see no light anywhere. He had expected to look in at a lighted window. Why was the house dark? What were they doing in there?

He took out his flashlight and turned it upon the sitting-room window. It was empty, the breakfast dishes still on the table. He moved on, close to the house, and turned the beam into the kitchen. There he was, face down on the floor, a fair-haired man with a white muffler round his neck. He was there, all right. The smell of gas came leaking out through the walls, strong and sickening, making Duff cough again.

He smashed the window with the flashlight, and turned away. He ran to the steps and clattered up them, pulling himself along by the railing. He got back into the car and drove, steadily and fast, back to the village. He was sorry to see Mr. Hilley's drug-store closed and dark. The one bright spot . . . he said to himself. The one bright spot.

Elmer was still sitting reading in the filling-station. He looked up.

"For Crissake, what you done to yourself?" he cried.

"What d'you mean?" Duff asked.

"Your mouth's all blood."

"That's nothing," said Duff. "I've got to telephone—quick—to the police."

"What's the matter?"

"Get me the police," said Duff.

"Here you are," said Elmer presently, and Duff took up the receiver.

"Police?" he said. "There's been an accident in one of the houses on the beach. There's a man lying on the kitchen floor unconscious. There's a very strong smell of gas. I broke a window. I understand it's Mr. Duff's house."

"Where are you at now?"

"That doesn't matter," said Duff.

"What's your name and address?"

"I prefer not to give them," said Duff, with simple dignity.

Chapter Nineteen

The trip home was effort-less. He got a train almost at once from the Vandenbrinck station; he had only a few minutes to wait in the Grand Central. An immeasurable stretch of time was going by, but he did not mind that. He was not exactly tired; he felt quiet, his thoughts were quiet.

It's out of my hands now, he thought, over and over. I've done all I can, and now it's out of my hands.

He got a taxi to himself at the Vandenbrinck station and lit a cigarette, leaning back in a corner. It's out of my hands now. It's unfortunate, more than unfortunate that I had that attack to delay me, but there's nothing I can do about that now.

The police would certainly get in touch with him, sooner or later. Someone would identify Reggie. Then he would simply tell the truth. I was the one who reported the ac-cident, but naturally, I was most reluctant to tell anyone . . . Naturally, the shock . . .

It was queer, he thought, that he did not feel any shock. Even the sight of the fair-haired man on the kitchen floor had been no shock. He had felt only a sense of recognition. Captain Ferris was there, all right.

The lighted windows of his house looked beautiful to him, tranquil and welcoming. Home . . . he thought,

with a sigh. I must remember to get those pills from **Nolan.**
I need a good night's sleep.

He paid the driver, and as he mounted the steps, **Miss**
Castle opened the door.

"Oh . . . ! Mr. Duff!" she cried.

"Good-evening!" he said, entering the hall.

"Mr. Duff . . ." she said. "What's happened?"

He was terrified. Was there something in his face, **his**
eyes . . . ?

"Your mouth, Mr. Duff . . ."

"Oh, that? I cut myself. In the taxi. Driver swung around
a curve and threw me against the window."

"Let me dress it for you, Mr. Duff."

"No, thanks, don't bother."

"Please!" she said. "It looks—"

"No, thanks," he said. "I have other things to think
about. I'm going to have a drink, Miss Castle. Will you
join me?"

"Thank you, yes. I'll fetch it, Mr. Duff."

"No," he said. "No. Sit down, Miss Castle."

He wanted to pour out his own drink. He went into the
dining-room where, in a locked partition of the sideboard,
the public supply of liquor stood. He seldom touched those
bottles, which could be checked on, even measured, by
anyone. He poured himself a drink of gin, a large drink,
and colored it with whiskey; he poured a small whiskey
for Miss Castle and filled the glass from the carafe.

My God, it's good to be able to sit down and have a
drink in my own house, openly and decently, he thought.
No locked doors, and all that nightmare nonsense. Miss
Castle is a woman of the world. She doesn't see **anything**
criminal in a man's taking a drink in his own **home.**

"Mr. Duff, your mouth is bleeding."

He patted his mouth with a handkerchief, and he was a little surprised to see the crimson stains. He was pleased by his own fortitude.

"Mr. Duff, you don't look at all well," she said.

For a long time, he thought, nobody had cared how he looked, how he felt; nobody had noticed. The whole story would be out tomorrow, about Reggie being found there dead, with Ferris. There was no risk in talking, a little, to this sympathetic and sophisticated woman.

"I've had a shock," he said, sipping his drink. "Miss Castle, do you know anything about a Captain Ferris?"

"Well, yes . . ." she said.

She was alarmed, poor girl. Always loyal to Reggie.

"I have good reason to believe that my wife was—is carrying on a love affair with him," he said.

"Oh, no, Mr. Duff!" she cried. "You're *quite* wrong."

"I happen to know that she's given the fellow money."

"But that was sheer kindness, Mr. Duff."

"Odd sort of kindness."

"Really, it wasn't. Really, she did it on my account."

"What?" he said. "You mean—*you* were interested in this fellow?"

"He's my half-brother," she said. "I'm quite fond of him, but I'm afraid he's—a bit of a rolling stone."

"What?" said Duff.

"He'd got himself into debt," said Miss Castle. "It *did* worry me. Mrs. Duff noticed that, and when I told her, she insisted upon helping Wilfred to get on his feet."

Duff slouched down in his chair and stretched out his legs. He felt tired, crushed by fatigue. It was a blow, to hear this about Ferris. But I—am—not—going—to—worry, he told himself. What's done is done. And if it's true that Reggie was simply playing Lady Bountiful—with my

170

money—it's certainly going to look like something else. Nobody on God's earth could blame me for being suspicious.

And anyhow, he thought, Miss Castle is too honest and upright herself to be suspicious of anyone else. Too loyal. Reggie could have been carrying on an affair with this fellow under her nose, and she wouldn't have seen it, wouldn't have admitted it, even to herself. No. What she's told me hasn't made any real difference.

"Mr. Duff . . . ?"

"Yes, Miss Castle?"

"I'm very sorry to trouble you when you're so tired . . ."

"Why? Is there anything wrong?"

"I'm afraid there is, Mr. Duff. Mr. Duff, Jay—isn't here."

"What d'you mean?" he asked, carefully.

"Jay has gone, Mr. Duff. He went out with Mrs. Duff after lunch."

"Stop!" said Duff. "Stop! I don't understand you!"

"Mrs. Duff and Jay went out after lunch—"

"You had lunch at Rio Park."

"No, Mr. Duff, we didn't. When we got there, we found the circus had closed, and everything seemed quite dreary. We took the first train home. We had lunch here, and after we'd finished, Mrs. Duff and Jay went out. They didn't take the car. Mrs. Duff didn't leave any message. I saw them strolling across the lawn, hand in hand. And that's all."

"I don't understand you," said Duff, flatly.

"I called the Vermilyeas, and they weren't home. I called your office, Mr. Duff, and they said you'd left early. Then I called Mrs. Albany. She's on her way out now."

"I don't know what you're talking about," said Duff.

"Please, Mr. Duff!" she said, in dismay. "I think that perhaps we ought to get the police."

171

"And why? Because my wife chooses to desert me?"

"She wouldn't do that, Mr. Duff."

"As a matter of fact, she told me she was going to."

"But she wouldn't take your child, Mr. Duff."

She took my child with her before, Duff thought. And now she's taken him again. And now my child is dead. My son is dead.

Chapter Twenty

"It's after midnight, Mr. Duff. Don't you think the police should be notified?"

"No," he said.

"Mr. Duff, I realize it's a shock to you, but—would you rather leave it to me?"

"No," he said, with an effort. "We'll wait."

He was waiting to *feel* this. He was waiting for something to stir his dreadful apathy, for his numb spirit to wake to pain. The shack was dark, he thought. Jay was asleep before the gas came on. No suffering.

Miss Castle struck a match, and he glanced up, to see her lighting another cigarette. She too was waiting, only she didn't know. They'll bring Jay back here, he thought. Any moment now. Everyone at Driftwood Beach knows him. He's been going there since he was a baby.

He was a fine baby. I was very proud of him. He was my son. Dimly, and with astonishment, he remembered days at the beach with his son. They had used to go in a sort of royal progress from the house, first the chauffeur, carrying a beach umbrella, a steamer rug, a folding canvas chair for the nurse, who did not care to sit on the sand. Then the nurse, carrying the baby, and then Mr. and Mrs. Duff, in bathing suits and terry robes.

He remembered how well and alive he had been then;

173

two or three swims a day, sometimes one before breakfast, always a dip in the late afternoon. Youth . . . he thought. But he had still felt like that four even three years ago. Youth did not vanish so quickly, did it?

Drinking? he thought. No! I used to drink in those days, whenever I felt like it. We always had cocktails before dinner, and I used to drink at the club. Plenty, too. And when there was any special occasion, I certainly could hold my own. Only never a drink in the morning. Never *this* . . .

A car was coming up the drive.

"That's probably the police," he said.

"But we didn't notify the police, Mr. Duff," said Miss Castle.

He rose as the doorbell rang.

"I'll go," he said.

There would be endless formalities to go through, but he didn't care. He didn't care about anything, or feel anything, only a vague worry about what sort of face he ought to have when they told him about his son. As he stepped into the hall, he raised his eyebrows very high. *What? What are you telling me* . . . ?

He opened the door, and it was Mrs. Albany, in a sealskin jacket and a small white flower hat.

"Any news yet?" she asked.

"Not yet," he answered.

"I brought that bag of yours," she said, setting it down on the floor. "I didn't like to leave it in the hotel when I was away. Oh, Mary? Good-evening. You'd better take Mr. Duff's bag up to his room."

She went into the sitting-room where Miss Castle stood waiting; she held out her hand.

174

"Mrs. Albany," said Miss Castle, "don't you think we'd better notify the police?"

"Let's talk it over first," said Mrs. Albany. She sat down and began to peel off her gloves; she blew into them and rolled them into a ball. "You're sure there isn't a note or a telephone message that's been overlooked?"

"I'm very sure, Mrs. Albany. I've asked the cook and Mary, and we all looked everywhere."

"What about Nolan?"

"He's gone."

"Gone?" said Duff.

"Yes. He drove the car back here, and then he said goodbye. He was very much upset about poor old Mr. Paul. He'd had to go this morning to identify him."

"What about old Mr. Paul?" asked Mrs. Albany.

"He was found this morning, you know. The police told Nolan he'd been caught under a pier, a few miles from Driftwood Beach."

"Fell in?" said Mrs. Albany.

"I'm afraid not," said Miss Castle. "Nolan said the police told him the poor old man had been hit on the head and was unconscious before he fell into the water. They think he may have been thrown off the pier."

Duff sat motionless, leaning a little forward, his hands on his knees. The numbness had left him utterly; his stillness was a fearful animal wariness. That damn bag is back in the house, he thought. I've got to get rid of that—quick.

"Gangsters," said Mrs. Albany. "Or possibly foreign agents, in *his* case. Well, the police will find out."

She was done with old Mr. Paul now, a stranger whom she had never seen.

"Now, tell me, Miss Castle, about Reggie's leaving the house," she said.

There's nothing now but the bag, thought Duff. That's the only danger now. But, after all, there's no reason to think the police are going to search the house. No reason on God's earth why they should ever think of me in connection with—that case.

Unless Nolan told them something. But he doesn't know anything. Nobody did, but Reggie. If I keep my head, don't say anything, don't do anything, don't make any mistakes. . . . This will blow over. The whole thing was nothing but a most unfortunate accident. I took every reasonable precaution to make sure the man was dead. I'm extremely sorry. Extremely.

"Jacob!" said Mrs. Albany. "You look worn out. D'you think you could get a little sleep?"

"No, thanks," he said. Then he thought of the bag. "I might lie down for a few minutes," he said. "Until the police come."

"I've just been saying to Miss Castle that I can't see any point in sending for the police, Jacob. They always cause a certain amount of unpleasantness. If there'd been an accident, you'd certainly have been notified by this time. And if there hasn't been an accident, it's better to wait."

"I don't like to suggest such a dreadful thing . . ." said Miss Castle. "But—kidnaping . . . ?"

"Two of them?" said Mrs. Albany. "I've never heard of *that* being done. But if they were kidnaped, there'd be a note, or a telephone call. Ransom, y'know."

"But where *could* they be? Where *could* they have gone?"

"Reggie is careless sometimes," said Mrs. Albany. "Young."

"She wouldn't be careless about letting people worry so," said Miss Castle.

"No," said Mrs. Albany. "No, I agree with you. But she might have sent a message by some unreliable person. Have you got in touch with her family, Jacob?"

"She hasn't any family. Only a brother overseas."

"She has a father in Alaska," said Miss Castle. "She's shown me letters from him."

"We must *think*," said Mrs. Albany. "Did she ever speak to you, Miss Castle, about any particular friends in New York or nearby?"

"She hasn't been in New York very long, you know," said Miss Castle. "I do remember her speaking of a Mrs. Williger, who has a lingerie shop in Brooklyn."

"We'll get in touch with Mrs. Williger, first thing tomorrow morning," said Mrs. Albany. "And if she doesn't know anything herself, she can tell us the names of other people Reggie knows. I feel sure the whole thing will turn out to have been a mistake of some sort."

"I think I will lie down for a few moments," said Duff, rising.

"That's the best thing you can do, Jacob. Have you had any dinner? Eaten anything?"

"I—think so," he said.

"I'll make you a cup of cocoa, Mr. Duff," said Miss Castle.

"No, thanks," he said.

They were very sympathetic. As soon as he had got rid of that bag, he would be able to rest here, in the house with these two kindly and understanding women. He smiled at them both, and moved toward the door, when the bell rang again.

Mrs. Albany moved with surprising quickness, past him,

177

and out into the hall. It's Jay, he thought. They've brought Jay back.

"Jacob," said Mrs. Albany, returning, "it's a policeman."

"What does he want?"

"He says he wants to ask you some questions."

"What *about*?"

"He didn't tell me. Jacob, this is a great strain, and I'm very sorry for you. But you must face things, Jacob. Come, my dear boy, pull yourself together."

"I think I'll have a drink," he said.

"Well . . ." said Mrs. Albany. "Perhaps, in the circumstances . . ."

He went into the dining-room and poured out a drink of gin; plenty. He drank some of it, and refilled the glass, and put in enough whiskey to give it the look of a very mild highball. He carried this back to the sitting-room.

"Jacob," said Mrs. Albany, "this is Lieutenant Levy."

Lieutenant Levy was a tall young man, with big hands and feet and big ears that stood out a little, and fine dark eyes, grave, even a little sad.

"I'm from the Horton County police, sir," he said.

"Horton County?" Duff repeated.

"That includes Driftwood Beach, sir."

"Oh, I see!" said Duff. "Sit down, Lieutenant. Will you have a drink?"

"No, thank you, sir. Not on duty. If there's some other room . . . ?"

"We'll leave you," said Mrs. Albany. "If it's necessary."

"I thought Mr. Duff would prefer to see me alone."

"No," said Duff. "Let them stay."

He wanted them here; he needed them. Is this about old Paul? he thought. Or about Jay? If I only knew that . . . He swirled his drink round and round in the

178

glass, and he wondered why it looked so oily. Fusel oil . . . ? he thought. Very bad for you.

Lieutenant Levy sat down opposite him, in a somewhat hierarchal attitude, in a high-backed chair, his big feet planted side by side, his big hands flat on the arms of the chair. He looked, Duff thought, like a young Egyptian king, sitting in judgment. He looked sad. Maybe he was stupid.

"Mr. Duff," he said, "I was given your name and address as that of the party who notified the Horton County police of an accident at Driftwood Beach tonight."

"Yes," said Duff, with an inward sigh of relief.

This was not about old Paul. These questions were going to be the ones for which he was prepared. He lit a cigarette. I know all the answers, he thought.

"After you notified us, Mr. Duff, you came directly back here?"

"Yes."

"Will you describe this accident, as you saw it, Mr. Duff?"

"Yes. When I reached the shack—the house—it was dark. I turned my flashlight on the kitchen window, and I saw a man in there, lying on the floor. There was a very strong smell of gas escaping, so I broke the window with my flashlight, and went at once to report the matter to you."

"You believed that this man was overcome by gas, Mr. Duff?"

"Naturally. Anyone would."

"You made no attempt to rescue this man?"

"I told you I smashed the window."

"You own that house, don't you, sir?"

"I do."

"But you didn't attempt to enter it and turn off the gas?"

179

"I did not," said Duff.

This was going exactly as he had pictured it. He was answering the questions quietly, and with dignity.

"When you reached the Driftwood Beach station, Mr. Duff, I understand that you went to a good deal of trouble and expense to rent a car for two hours."

"I did."

"I understand that you were advised to take a taxi. Will you explain why you didn't care to take a taxi, Mr. Duff?"

Here it was. The big moment. It was unexpected good fortune that he should have Mrs. Albany and Miss Castle for audience.

"I preferred to be alone," he said.

"Did you expect to find something wrong at your house, Mr. Duff?"

"I'm sorry," said Duff. "I can't answer that question."

"You're not obliged to answer it, sir, but I'd advise you to do so. For your own sake."

Very civil, this fellow was; almost gentle.

"No," said Duff, quietly. "It's a personal matter."

"Are you willing to make a statement and later to sign it, to the effect that when you reached your house, you noticed a strong smell of gas, that you saw a man lying on the kitchen floor, that you then broke the window and telephoned the police a report?"

"Yes," said Duff.

"Do you wish to reconsider that, Mr. Duff?"

"I do not," said Duff.

He noticed then that, if Lieutenant Levy's dark eyes were sad, and even gentle, his mouth was like a steel trap.

"The man on the kitchen floor was dead, Mr. Duff," he said.

Chapter Twenty-One

Duff took a sip of his drink. "I had no means of knowing that," he said, still quietly.

"You have keys to that house, Mr. Duff?"

"Naturally."

"It didn't occur to you to enter the house and turn off the gas?"

"I thought it was better not to disturb anything until the police came."

"What was your reason for that, sir? Did you think a crime had been committed?"

"No. I thought this man, whoever he was, had tried to commit suicide."

"Why did you think that, Mr. Duff?"

"Anybody would, seeing a body—a person lying on the floor of a room filled with gas."

"Why did you go to the house, sir?"

"That's a personal matter."

"Why did you refuse to take a taxi, sir?"

"I told you before. I wanted to be alone."

"Mr. Duff, I understand that you left the filling-station in the car you had rented at approximately five minutes to nine. Is that correct?"

"I dare say. About then."

"The drive to your house from the filling-station takes approximately fifteen to twenty minutes?"

"About that."

"Mr. Duff, I understand that you returned to the filling-station at approximately ten minutes after ten. Is that correct?"

"I don't know. I wasn't watching the time."

"We have witnesses to that, Mr. Duff. Are you prepared to admit that you returned to the filling-station approximately an hour and twenty minutes after you left it?"

"It's possible. I don't know."

"Can you account for the interval of at least fifty minutes not occupied by driving to and from your house?"

"I can. On the way there, I had an attack. Heart attack. I tried to take my medicine, but I broke the bottle. That's how I cut my mouth. Then I blacked out."

"Are you subject to these attacks, sir?"

"Recently, yes."

"What is the name of the doctor who prescribed this medicine, sir?"

"Doctor Parrot," said Duff.

He was surprised by his own readiness, his instant invention of this odd name, his lack of any alarm or dismay. When Aunt Lou learns the truth, later on, he thought, when she realizes that I went through this ordeal, knowing I'd lost my son, she may be a little less critical in the future.

Miss Castle, too. When this ordeal was over, when she knew what Reggie had done to him . . .

"What is Doctor Parrot's address, Mr. Duff?"

"I couldn't tell you offhand. Somewhere in New York. I'd have to look it up in my office."

"Mr. Duff, what was your reason for leaving the scene of this accident without waiting for the police?"

"Why should I have waited? I reported it."

"Has the man been identified?" asked Mrs. Albany.

"Yes, ma'am. He's a Captain Ferris."

"Oh . . . !" cried Miss Castle. "Oh . . . !"

"Do you know him, ma'am?"

"He's my half-brother. Oh . . . He's dead?"

"I'm very sorry, madam. If I'd known, I wouldn't have been so—abrupt."

"He's dead?" she said. "He killed himself?"

"I'm very sorry, madam. I'm afraid this will be a shock to you . . ."

" 'Will' be?"

"He didn't kill himself, madam."

She looked like someone in a play, her eyes dilated, her hand against her heart.

"Then—what?"

Levy was watching her carefully.

"I'm very sorry, madam. He was strangled."

She said 'Oh!' again; her hand went to her throat, her eyes were blank. Mrs. Albany rose and went to her side.

"Do you mean—murdered?" she asked, after a moment.

"There's no doubt about it, madam," said Levy, grave and gentle.

There was a startling silence.

"Then what about the gas?" Duff asked.

"There was no gas turned on in the house, sir."

"There was when *I* got there. I smelled it, very strongly."

"We were there within eleven minutes of your report, sir, and there was no gas turned on then."

"Then someone had turned it off."

183

"There was no odor of gas whatever, Mr. Duff."

"That's because I broke the window. Let the air in."

"The smell would still have been perceptible, sir."

Confusion was beginning in Duff's mind, like a little puff of fog in one corner. It must not spread. This was dangerous.

"I think I'll have another drink," he said, rising.

"No," said Mrs. Albany. "Better not, Jacob."

"Sit down, please, sir," said Levy. "Perhaps one of the ladies would be kind enough to get you a drink."

But neither of the ladies responded.

"I'm afraid I'll have to see Mrs. Duff for a few moments, please," said Levy.

"What?" Duff asked, frowning.

"I realize it's very late," said Levy, "but I'll have to see Mrs. Duff for a few moments."

"But—didn't you see her?" asked Duff.

The fog was rushing out, blanketing everything. He was stupefied.

"You mean she's here, downstairs?" Levy asked.

"No," Duff said. "Get me a drink, Miss Castle. Bring the bottle."

"May I ask one of you ladies to get Mrs. Duff?" asked Levy.

"She's not at home," said Mrs. Albany.

"Where is she, ma'am?"

"We don't know," said Mrs. Albany. "We're very much worried."

"I want a drink," said Duff.

"Mr. Duff," said Levy, "I'm afraid you don't realize the situation."

"Pull yourself together, Jacob!" said Mrs. Albany.

"Your account of this evening's actions is not satisfactory, Mr. Duff."

"Just how isn't it?" Duff demanded.

"We'll want a better explanation as to why you went to that house at just that time, sir."

"I told you it was a personal matter."

"And why you reported a smell of gas."

"I told you I thought I did smell gas."

"And why you made no attempt to rescue this man you state you believed to be overcome by gas."

"I *told* you. I thought it was suicide, and I thought you people liked things to be left undisturbed."

"And why you went to a lot of trouble to rent a car."

"Good God! I've *told* you all this!"

"Your account is not satisfactory, Mr. Duff."

"Why the hell isn't it?"

"I'll have to ask you to come to the Horton County Station with me, sir."

"What d'you *mean*? D'you mean you think *I* did that? Walked into the house and strangled that fellow? You're accusing *me*?"

"I'm not accusing you of anything, Mr. Duff. It's simply that we want a better account of your movements this evening."

"You'll never get it. I've told you everything, exactly as it happened."

"I'm afraid it isn't good enough, Mr. Duff. I'll have to ask you to come with me now—"

"All right! All right!" shouted Duff. "I don't care where I go. But I want a drink first."

"No, sir."

"You can't tell me that, in my own house. I'm *going*—"

185

"Jacob!" said Mrs. Albany.

Nobody was showing him the least consideration or sympathy, nobody. He was sick; his hands were beginning to shake; the fog had come into his eyes. If I go with this fellow, he thought, they may lock me up overnight, even longer. And I won't be able to get a drink. I feel—so damn queer . . .

"We'll get going now, Mr. Duff."

"No . . ." he said. "No. I'll tell you who killed Ferris."

"Do you want to make a statement, sir?"

"Yes. But I want a drink first."

Levy turned to Miss Castle.

"You might get him one," he said, in a low voice.

"Bring the bottle," said Duff.

The doorbell rang, and they all turned their heads like a herd of deer.

"I'll go," said Levy. "Don't leave the room, please."

The moment he had gone, Duff moved toward the dining-room.

"Jacob!" said Mrs. Albany. "Don't—"

He went on. He poured himself a drink and swallowed it, and refilled the glass with gin.

"Jacob," said Mrs. Albany, "you must keep a clear head. This is serious."

"No, it isn't," he said. "I had no more to do with that man's death than you had."

He lit a cigarette, and then Levy came back, with a grey-haired policeman in uniform.

"Sergeant Mack will take down your statement, Mr. Duff," he said. "You wish to state that you know who killed Captain Ferris?"

"I do," said Duff. "It was my chauffeur, Nolan."

"Why do you think that, sir?"

186

"I don't think it. I know it. I saw him on his way out to my house."

"Where were you when you saw him, sir?"

"Parked outside the station."

"Why were you there?"

"Because I wanted to be."

"Why do you think he was on the way to your house, Mr. Duff?"

Duff took a swallow of gin.

"Because we'd arranged it," he said.

"What was this arrangement, Mr. Duff?"

"I prefer not to go into that."

"I'm afraid it's necessary, Mr. Duff."

It is necessary, Duff thought. I have no intention of being locked up in a cell.

"I had reason to think that Captain Ferris was going to use my house for—a rendezvous," he said.

"A rendezvous with whom, Mr. Duff?"

"I'm not going to answer that."

"What was your arrangement with Nolan?"

I wish I could get drunk, thought Duff. So that I couldn't speak at all.

"Nolan was to go there first," he said, "and see if what I thought was correct. If it was not, he was to drive back and meet me on the road. If I didn't meet him, I was going on to the house myself."

"What did you expect to find when you reached the house, Mr. Duff?"

"Nothing. I simply wanted to see—what was going on there."

"Mr. Duff," said Levy, "had you arranged with Nolan that he was to turn on the gas?"

Duff glared at him.

187

"Damn it, no!" he cried.

"How did Captain Ferris enter your house, Mr. Duff?"

"*I* don't know. It wouldn't be hard."

"You went to the house, expecting to find Captain Ferris. What reason do you suggest for his going there?"

Duff turned his head from one side to the other, as if looking for a way out. These questions goaded him intolerably, and they were beginning to frighten him now.

"Mr. Duff, have you any evidence that Nolan actually went to your house?"

"I *told* you I saw him on his way there."

"You stated that you saw him drive past you. Have you any evidence that he actually went to your house?"

"Damn it, he must have! Somebody certainly went there. What's the sense of all this quibbling? You're not a lawyer."

"Well, yes, I am a lawyer," said Levy.

"Mean to say you're not a policeman?"

"I'm a member of the police force, yes, sir. You state that you had reason to believe Captain Ferris had a rendezvous in your house. With a woman, Mr. Duff?"

This was getting bad, very bad.

"I simply wanted to—make sure," said Duff. "I'd heard rumors . . ."

"What woman did you expect to find there, sir?"

"I refuse to answer," said Duff.

There was a moment's silence; then Levy went to the open doorway.

"Mrs. Duff," he said, "will you step in, please?"

So she was here. And how long had she been here, and how much had she heard? How much had he said? He could not remember. She came in from the hall, shocking

188

to Duff as a ghost. She was pale, her black hair a little untidy; she was wearing a black cardigan much too large for her; she looked like a waif. She kept her brilliant dark-blue eyes fixed upon Levy's face, and looked at no one else.

He took a paper out of his pocket.

"Mrs. Duff," he said, "this letter was found on Captain Ferris. Will you look at it, please?"

She took it from him and glanced at it and then raised her eyes to his face again.

"Have you ever seen that letter before, Mrs. Duff?" he asked.

"Yes," she said. "I wrote it."

"You wrote this letter asking Captain Ferris to meet you at that house?"

"Yes," she said, again.

I wish to God I could get drunk, Duff thought.

"Did you go to the house to meet Captain Ferris, Mrs. Duff?" Levy asked.

"Well, no . . ." she said, "I didn't."

Nolan never called her, Duff thought. Never meant to.

"Why didn't you go, Mrs. Duff?" asked Levy.

"I couldn't."

"Why not?"

"We've been stranded on a little island, ever since three o'clock this afternoon."

"Who was with you, Mrs. Duff?"

"My husband's little boy, and Mr. Vermilyea and his mother and father."

"Quite a family party," said Duff, loudly.

He did not quite know why he said that, or what bitter resentment and envy stirred in his mind.

"Had you intended to meet Captain Ferris, Mrs. Duff?"

189

"Yes," she said. "I wrote him that letter."

"Mrs. Duff, have you ever had reason to believe that your husband was jealous of Captain Ferris?"

"No," she said. "I'm sure he wasn't."

Her voice was low and pretty, but with little inflection; not in her tone or in her face was she ever able to express whatever emotion she might be feeling. And heaven knew she was not eloquent. Yet Duff understood her now.

"You didn't want your husband to know of this proposed meeting with Captain Ferris, Mrs. Duff?"

"He wouldn't have minded," she said. "It was just a sort of business thing."

"Mrs. Duff, have you any information about Captain Ferris's death?"

She was silent for a moment.

"I hate to say it . . ." she began. "But I guess I have to. Nolan just hated him."

"Why?"

"He knocked Nolan down once, in front of me. Could I say what I think happened?"

"I'd be very glad to hear it."

"Nolan had a terribly mean streak in him," she said, in her always inadequate words. "I think he told my husband there was something wrong going on in the shack. I think he went there and killed Captain Ferris, and I think he fixed it so that my husband would come along later, and get all the blame."

"Is this the case, Mr. Duff?"

Very well! Duff said to himself. She's got me out of this very neatly. By lying about the letter. Very well, I didn't ask her to lie for me. And I don't *want* her to.

"Is this the case, Mr. Duff?"

"Yes," he said. "More or less."

"What did Nolan tell you to expect to find in the house?"

"Ferris and a woman. Some woman."

"Was there any arrangement for Nolan to turn on the gas?"

"No! I told you before. No!"

"If you had found Captain Ferris there with a woman, what did you intend to do?"

"Nothing. I didn't have any plans. I simply wanted to see . . ."

"When you saw Captain Ferris on the floor, what did you think had happened?"

"I didn't know. I didn't care."

"Did it occur to you at that time that Nolan might have killed him?"

"No, it didn't," said Duff. "For one thing, I didn't know he was dead."

And for another thing, it had never once come into his head that Nolan might double-cross him. Never. He could see now how smoothly Nolan had arranged matters, with everything devised to point straight at Duff, the jealous husband. The tale about turning on the gas, about giving the capsules . . . All he had wanted was, to get Ferris there alone, and he had made Duff do that for him.

I believed everything, Duff thought. I did everything—to ruin myself. That letter . . . The police would have traced it to me, with no trouble at all. Written on my typewriter. I was a cat'spaw. A dupe. Such a fool . . .

"The point I don't understand, Mr. Duff," said Levy, "is your reporting this strong smell of gas."

Duff was as quick as any goaded animal to notice the change in his tormentor. Levy was different. Not ominous now. I'm out of it, he thought.

He had gone willingly, even eagerly, into a situation

that might well have been fatal to him. If he was out of it now, it was only by Reggie's suffrance. If she had not acknowledged that letter, if she had not spoken of Nolan's hatred for Ferris . . . She must know the truth, know what he had meant and had tried to do to her, and still she had saved him. And that made his freedom almost worthless to him.

"About the gas, Mr. Duff?"

"I'm afraid I can't explain that," Duff said. "Unless it was some sort of hallucination. I'd had that attack—heart-attack, y'know. I wasn't feeling at all well."

Somewhere in the house somebody screamed, or squealed, like a terrified horse.

"Oh . . . !" cried Miss Castle, with her hand at her heart again.

Chapter Twenty-Two

"**B**ut who was it?" asked Mrs. Albany. "There's no one *here* . . ."

She got no answer. Levy had left the room; they sat there, Mrs. Albany and Miss Castle and Duff and the grey-haired Sergeant Mack; only Reggie in the big black cardigan, was standing. There were no more screams, no sounds at all.

"Where's Jay?" asked Duff, looking straight at the wall before him.

"Mrs. Vermilyea put him to bed at their house," Reggie answered. "He was sort of overtired. He just loved the whole thing. I mean, we made a sort of adventure out of it."

There were footsteps coming down the stairs now; again like a herd of deer they all turned their heads toward the door. Mary came in, and after her came Lieutenant Levy. With that bag.

"I'm sorry, ma'am," said Mary, weeping.

"Wait!" said Levy.

He opened the bag and brought out the jacket, sodden and crumpled.

"Is this yours, Mr. Duff?" he asked.

"No," said Duff, mechanically. It was no use; he knew that.

"Mrs. Duff, do you recognize this garment?"

"No," Reggie said. "Oh, well, yes. I guess I do. It's an old coat of my husband's I threw away months ago."

"Mrs. Albany . . . ?"

"I don't care to examine it," she said, her head averted.

"I'm sorry, ma'am," said Mary, tears raining down her face. "I couldn't sleep till we heard about Master Jay, and I thought I'd unpack for Mr. Duff. And when I opened the bag, a kind of a lizard or a little snake thing run out, and I let out a yell. I didn't mean—"

"Wait!" said Levy.

He brought out the riding-crop.

"Whose property is this?" he asked.

"It's mine," said Reggie.

"Mrs. Duff, there's a small metal plate in the handle, with initials other than yours."

"Someone gave it to me," said Reggie.

"The initials are P.I.K., the initials of the man whose body we found under the pier this morning. Why were you carrying this in your bag, Mr. Duff, with an outfit of clothes, all of them wet?"

Duff did not answer.

"Mr. Duff, when did you last see Paul?"

"I never saw him."

"Mrs. Duff," said Levy, "did you see Paul while you were at Driftwood Beach?"

"No, I didn't," Reggie answered.

"I'll have to have an explanation for the contents of this bag, Mr. Duff."

I knew that bag would finish me, Duff thought. I've known a lot of things—for a long time. Maybe he had not known them in his mind, but he had felt them. He had been walking through a thick fog along a strange road,

but he had known, or felt, where it would end. This was that end.

"Duff," said Levy, "Paul was stunned by blows on the head with some instrument and thrown into the water unconscious."

Duff, he said. Not sir. Not Mister Duff. Never Mister Duff, never again.

"He wasn't thrown in," said Duff. "I dragged him in. I thought he was dead."

Miss Castle made some choked little sound, but he did not look at her.

"Mr. Paul fell down," said Reggie. "Jake thought—we thought he was dead. We thought—"

"No," said Duff. "I did it. I hit him, twice, I think. Later on, I dragged him into the sea. I wanted to get rid of him."

"*Jacob!*" said Mrs. Albany.

That was a direful voice, the voice of his conscience, rejecting him, abandoning him.

"Mr. Duff," said Levy, "it's my duty to tell you—"

"*I* know! *I* know!" said Duff, impatiently. "I'll finish my drink and then I'll come along."

He drained the glass and set it down; he rose, and confronting him was his image in a long mirror. This was Jacob Duff, with a cut and bleeding mouth, dark stains under his eyes, a sagging weariness in his face.

"Jake . . ." said Reggie. She touched his hand, but he drew away. "Jake, I can swear—I can go in court and swear you had too much to drink that night. You weren't responsible."

"No, thanks," he said. "I was responsible. Thank you, Reggie, for all you've done. You've been very kind."

He looked down at her, and their eyes met. He was sure

195

that what he saw in her pale desperate face was love, but not the kind of love he had ever wanted. Her love was almost illimitable, almost impersonal; it embraced God knew how many people. He didn't want that.

He turned to look at Miss Castle, and she was nothing to him now. His last look was for Mrs. Albany, the most important figure in his life, and she was an old woman now. There was nothing left at all. He never wanted to see Jay again. Mister Jacob Duff had gone, forever.

"Jake," said Reggie, "we'll do everything—"

"Please don't," he said, with a quick frown. "It doesn't matter."

And really there's nothing to wait for. Really, he thought, I'm sick and tired of everything.

"I'd like to go up to my room," he said.

"Sergeant Mack will go with you," said Levy.

Then I'll have to make another plan, Duff thought. I'll have to be quick about it, too. I've had too much to drink tonight, and pretty soon it will begin.

He knew all about that. Pretty soon, very soon, he would begin to grow sleepy. They would ask him questions at the police station, and he would not be able to answer; he would not be able to keep awake. Then they would put him into a cell, to sleep it off. That's what they called it.

But it was not like that. You slept yourself *into* something. Into that nausea, that shaking, that unnameable dread and wretchedness. The horrors, they called *that*.

"You'll have to leave the bathroom door open, sir," said Mack.

"All right," said Duff. "I suppose I can take a toothbrush along?"

"Yes, sir," said Mack.

Duff dropped the toothbrush behind the washbasin.

"Look here, Sergeant," he said. "Would you be good enough to pick that up for me? My knees aren't so good."

"Okay," said the sergeant.

While he stooped, Duff took a razor blade from a package on the shelf and put it into his pocket. Really, there's nothing left, he thought. After this, everyone will know about . . . About everything.

Of course, it's nothing but manslaughter, he thought. Aunt Lou will get in touch with Harold Mallinger at once, and maybe they'll arrange bail. But I don't want that. I mean, where could I go? Not back here, with Miss Castle, and Reggie—and my son. Not where I'd ever see Aunt Lou again.

He went down the stairs with Mack, and Lieutenant Levy was waiting in the hall. They went out of the house, to the car that was standing in the drive.

"I hope you'll catch Nolan," said Duff.

"We'll do our best," said Levy.

Mack got in behind the wheel and Duff and Levy sat in the back together. It seemed to be very dark.

Manslaughter isn't so serious, Duff thought. After it's all over, I could go away. Rio, or some other pretty place. I've got enough money to live on. I could go off by myself, and start all over again.

Only, there's tomorrow morning, he thought. I'll wake up, and I'll have it. The horrors. And they won't let me have a drink, that's sure. I can't stand that.

They might get me out on bail very soon, he thought. Even tomorrow. But not early in the morning. Not soon enough. He could not wake up to that tomorrow morning. And other mornings. Anyhow, there was nothing left. He was sick and tired of everything.

Not my wrists, he thought. That takes too long. Petro-

nius—who was the fellow we had in prep school? Hours
. . . It has to be my throat. The double-edged blade cut
his fingers, but he did not feel it at all. Alcohol is an anaes-
thetic, he thought. He flinched from the idea of a cut
straight across his neck. Under each ear, he thought.
There's something there. Some vein.

It was not hard, not painful. Glad to be finished, he
thought. After all, I did kill that old maniac. And Jay, and
Reggie. And somebody else . . . Who else?

"What?" asked Levy. "Did you say something?"

There was no answer, and he turned his head in the
dark to see Duff lolling back in the corner, his chin on his
chest. I heard something, Levy thought. Snoring, maybe.
The man's half drunk.

It's not going to do much good to question him now, in
the state he's in, Levy thought. Unless he's frightened
enough to sober up all at once. They do that, sometimes. I
don't think we'll charge him. Not tonight. Maybe never.
He *knows* something, that's sure, but it doesn't seem likely
that he actually—

The car swung round a curve, and Duff lurched forward, on to the floor.

"Stop a moment, Mack!" called Levy, and turned on
the light.

He took Duff under the shoulders and lifted him back
on the seat. Then he saw what Duff had done.

"Mack," he said, "drive to the hospital—as quick as you
can. Use the siren."

They went along the dark country roads as if floating on
the wailing stream of sound. Duff, supported by Levy,
leaned back in the corner, his eyes opened to slits, his
breath bubbling softly.

In the hospital they gave him blood from some unknown

198

fellow-creature, but it was too late. He lay in a glaringly-lit white-walled room, and fainted into death.

But why? Levy thought, in great wonder. Things didn't look too bad for him. He certainly had a fighting chance. He had everything to live for, money, good name, beautiful young wife.

He must have been guilty as hell, thought Levy.